The Final Transmission

By
Brian F.H. Clement

To Karch

Watch for
tentacled monsters
at the con!

Damnation Books, LLC.
P.O. Box 3931
Santa Rosa, CA 95402-9998
www.damnationbooks.com

The Final Transmission
by Brian F.H. Clement

Digital ISBN: 978-1-62929-109-3
Print ISBN: 978-1-62929-110-9

Cover art by: Ash Arceneaux
Edited by: Avril Dannenbaum

Printed in the United States of America
Worldwide Electronic & Digital Rights
Worldwide English Language Print Rights

Thanks to Beth Mally for editing the first draft.

Thanks to Special Agent K for Inspiration.

Chapter One

Toronto, 1956

Mary felt warm.

Her hands were tucked into the ends of her wrap. Her red up-do and soft green outfit perfected an idealized picture of beauty. She sat in the passenger side seat of a rumbling Packard as it bounced through a tiny pothole on the residential street in Toronto's West End. The bump in the road had made her crinoline peek out from under her dress. She casually tucked it away before Dean, oblivious to her while driving, could notice.

She looked at him sideways without moving her head. He had perfectly cut features. Hair that looked to have been trimmed that day or the night before. *He must be trying to impress me. No wonder he wore his varsity jacket out.* It was chilly outside, but probably not so cold that he couldn't have worn only his sweater vest. The vehicle hit another bump, parting the light fog that hung seemingly frozen above the street, a silver veil over the oncoming darkness.

The soft song whispering from the radio faded away. The announcer's voice came through, sounding like someone speaking through a tiny tin can.

"Our favorite hit from last year, that one was for all the young people in love. But enough from 1955, here's something new and fresh from this year, and just as romantic. Hoping you're having a good autumn evening, and keep listening..."

A new song began, the voice of some far-off crooner pining for a lost love. Mary smiled shyly at Dean. He glanced in her direction, a smile crossing his lips as well. She looked away, her heart racing. Her eyes wandered back to him. He looked back at the road, the smile lingering on one side of his mouth. Mary took her hands from her wrap, and held them together. She opened her mouth, a tiny hesitant "ah" emerging, followed by moments of silence, until she was finally able to speak.

"I had a really nice time tonight," she said, her fingers intertwining nervously.

"Good. Me too." Dean's wry smile was audible in his voice. "Thanks for picking me up."

"Oh yeah, of course."

Mary looked down, as if focused on some tiny, imaginary knitting her fingers wanted to be working on, instead being forced to work on each other. Again she opened her mouth to speak, but again only silence. Her eyes tried to look toward Dean, but were held down by her shyness. To her, the rumbling of the car's engine was drowned out slowly by the seemingly increasing volume of her own heartbeat. Dean's voice broke the tension Mary felt as he spoke up, his eyes fixed on the road.

"I really like you, Mary."

Mary blushed, and swallowed anxiously before speaking.

"I...like you too," she managed to say.

Dean slowed the car, the brakes emitting a soft squeak as he stopped and shut off the engine. Out of the corner of her eye she saw him turn to look at her. Mary's face stayed downcast, eyes on her hands, unable to return Dean's look. His arm had moved across the back of the seat, and his hand was near her neck. Her ears warmed. Dean's charm was almost hypnotic. She felt his deep soulful eyes fixed on her, neither urging her to look back at him nor wanting her to stay turned away. Would he kiss her? She was excited, frightened. Mary spoke quietly, still looking down.

"Well I...guess I'd better go then."

She looked up, and the nervousness was replaced by confusion.

"Oh...this isn't my house," she said, frowning.

The neighborhood wasn't hers. She hadn't noticed with her eyes fixed permanently downward which way they had gone, but this street was bordering an industrial area, and she didn't recognize it. Beyond the row of identical brick houses was a wide, empty field of dead grass, strewn with trash and broken furniture. Smoke plumes could be seen coming from distant factories beyond, outlined in moonlight. She turned to Dean. He pulled back, his smoky charm withdrawn as well.

"Yeah...sorry. This is a friend's place. I have to pick something up."

Dean stepped out of the car, then turned, looking back in at Mary.

"Why don't you come in? I'll be a minute or two. Wouldn't want you to freeze out here."

"Well, I..."

Dean's door shut and in a second he was already around the car, opening Mary's.

"Come on inside where it's warm. We'll just be a second."

Mary frowned, confused.

"Okay, I guess so..."

She reluctantly stepped from the vehicle, Dean's hand guiding her out. He shut the door for her and took her hand. He moved across the street and his fingers slipped away from hers as his speed increased. She stopped in the middle of the road. The cold night air chilled her, and she shivered. She drew the wrap closer around her shoulders. *I don't think I care about his jacket. Or his charm.* She watched his form move toward the house, growing darker and becoming little more than a shadowy silhouette under the trees. She could make out his smile as he turned back to her.

"Come on! It's cold out here!" he said.

No lights were on inside the house Dean now stood by. No activity on the street, no sound of automobile engines, no human voices, no dogs barking, only the wind rustling the branches of the nearly bare trees. A few dry leaves blew by her feet.

Dean continued walking to the house. Instead of heading for the front porch, he moved into the alley to the right of it. A tiny space walled in by the brick of the houses on either side. The next house over was boarded up, slats of wood criss-crossing the doors and windows. The building Dean aimed for could just as well have been shuttered, sitting silent and dark. It loomed over Mary. Her enthusiasm for Dean's charm waned. She looked around into the alley beside the house. The silhouette of Dean waited at the end of it, a dark form blocking the way into the backyard. Mary looked at him, hesitating.

Dean's quiet voice came from the silhouette, echoing along the walls of the alley.

"What are you waiting for? Don't be scared."

Mary started backing away, her fear overtaking her. How well did she really know him? They had met in the college library over similar reading material he used to strike up a conversation. Then he had asked her out to dinner, and they went. He asked her on a second date, and here she was. But all she really knew about him—or what he told her—was that he had moved to town for school. His parents lived on a farm in Saskatchewan, and his grandparents had emigrated from Russia. He seemed nice enough, he was handsome, charming, gentlemanly, but it could easily have all been an act. Panic welled up within her.

"I...I'm just going to wait in the car. I'll be in the car," she said, half-stuttering, pointing over her shoulder.

Her feet moved back, increasing in speed until she turned, and walked straight into a massive figure. It felt as though she had turned and walked into one of the trees in the yard, but this was a man. A man in a leather jacket whose arms might as well have been tree trunks as they pinned hers back, one of his enormous dry hands over her mouth. His face was severe, stony, nearly expressionless with the slightest hint of disgust turning his upper lip. A second man, as large as the first, leaned in, leering in her face as he held his index finger to his cracked lips.

"Shhh..."

Mary struggled, trying to break the grip of the first man's fists that felt like metal shackles around her body. The second man seemed to be enjoying his work, his sallow features betraying a repulsive smile. All Mary could do was squirm, her pleas for help muffled by the rough hand over her face. The two thugs carried her down the alley toward Dean, now smoking a cigarette as he watched his associates work. His demeanor had changed, his smile gone, replaced by a blank expression of threatening purposefulness. Instead of charm, all he radiated was sinister intent, the meaning of which Mary was too terrified to guess at, her eyes darting back and forth. Dean took a drag from his cigarette as the two men waited.

"Get her inside."

They carried her down the soot-encrusted steps toward the cellar, one of them pulling the door open with a loud creak. Dean followed them down, crushing the cigarette under foot.

* * * *

The flickering of hundreds of candles placed on every available surface in the basement illuminated the gruesome scene before Mary's eyes. Incomprehensible symbols, runes, mathematical equations of an alien design, interspersed with Latin phrases covered the walls on three sides. All painted with blood, which ran thickly down and pooled on the floor.

Someone unseen beat regularly on a large drum, a single menacing thud every few seconds.

Mary heard whispers from three voices around her, not in conversation but in incantation of something that sounded ancient, almost unearthly. Dull moonlight penetrated the heavily smeared windows near the ceiling, the alley above cast in a cold blue glow. Mary lay on the floor, her arms tied behind her back, her legs bound at the ankles, and a gag covering her mouth. Her makeup ran down the side of her face, and she blinked tears from her eyes.

The first of the two men who had grabbed her had removed his leather jacket and instead wore a long black hooded robe. His features hidden in shadow, he continued painting symbols across the walls from a bowl of blood in one hand, a brush made from the dried paw of a dog or cat in the other. She saw his lips moving as he whispered to himself, the only part of his face visible from beneath his hood. The incessant scratching of the limb's claws along the wall made Mary grit her teeth under her gag, more tears welling up in her eyes.

Next to her sat a large animal skull, long enough to be a horse or cow, with a distorted rune painted in blood across its forehead. The runes looked drawn by someone blindfolded and half-crazed. As if someone had taken the writing on the chalkboard in the physics lab at the college, wrapped it in on itself, tied it in knots, and thrown the warped symbols up at random, upside-down and backwards. She struggled to turn her head, desperate for any avenue out of the hellish chamber, but all she could do was squirm uselessly. The floor around her had lines of powder, black, white, connected, in some shape she couldn't make out. Candles encircled her at points in the ring of powders. It seemed almost incoherent, but with some purpose beyond comprehension.

Mary looked down toward her feet. She was barely able to see Dean and the second man, also in black robes, shrouded in darkness, working around a huge wooden bowl. Dean dropped in ingredients—shreds of dried plants, unidentifiable rust-colored powders, and a wriggling mass of tentacled flesh glinting in the candlelight that Mary guessed must have been a live octopus. She could see the drum they had, perched atop a high stool. The second man stirred with one hand, his other hand beating the drum that reverberated through her body. Was it an octopus? It looked...something...like one, but mottled purple and black, and its tentacles—too many of them—reached up and over the edges of the bowl. Both men chanted in whispers, not in unison, but somehow rhythmically entwined. Thick vapors swirled up and around them.

They seemed to finish their concoction. Each of them gripped one side of the bowl and hauled it toward Mary. They stood at a point of the powdered circle around her, whispering, with a single drumbeat, then moved to another point. Mary counted to herself. Nine times. *What did it mean?* The bowl thudded bluntly onto the floor, vibrating through Mary's chest. The first man ceased his transcribing on the wall and approached. She could see Dean and another, the third behind her judging by the sound of chanting. They seemed to form a triangle around the powdered circle, facing inward. Their whispering was flat. None of their voices individually increased in volume, but the effect of their unified chanting seemed to overwhelm the room, reverberating and battering Mary. Her eyes widened, staring helplessly, too terrified to cry out, silence gripping her. The second man produced a large machete, dipping it into the wooden bowl, withdrawing it coated in a thick, mud-like mixture.

Behind them, a fourth figure moved silently forward from the shadows—not cloaked like Dean and his two associates, but dressed in a black suit and overcoat, bowler hat, leather gloves, and on his face what looked like a First World War-style gas mask with a long hose attached to a filter—or something similar—on his hip. In one hand he carried an antique doctor's bag, and in the other a strange, elaborately designed brass-plated lantern-shaped device, looking almost Victorian in origin. The man, whoever he was, looked as though sent forth from an earlier age and into the presence of this bizarre ritual.

Mary looked on, baffled. Her fright dispelled as this strange masked person approached behind the first ritualist, who was still holding his animal-limb brush and bowl of blood. The man in the hat raised his lantern-device and touched something on the back of it. A bright green-yellow beam of light leaped forward and gripped the other man from behind. The black cloak and clothes were almost immediately blown into ash. His head melted, skin running away like liquid, a sickening gurgle from his throat becoming a rasping of dust as his blackened bones fell clattering to the floor, denuded of flesh.

The animal limb brush and bowl fell and bounced, flinging blood across the room haphazardly.

Mary let out a choked cry of terror at this new, more horrifying event. Dean and his other companion turned. As the third burned away, they immediately moved to attack the invader. The masked man's speed was inhuman. He pivoted and without hesitation turned the energy beam toward the machete-wielding man. The blade clanged to the stone floor, bouncing and splashing liquid. The formerly cloaked figure was rapidly reduced to a column of smoke and ash. Dean came at the attacker from the side, but it was futile. The doctor's bag dropped to the floor and the arm that had held it shot forward and gripped Dean's throat, lifting him slightly. The beam from the lantern-device continued working, dissolving the other man completely while Dean struggled against his assailant's iron grip. Dean's fists beat against the motionless arm as he gasped for breath. The masked face turned toward Dean, looking him up and down. He seemed to study Dean a moment before tossing him against the wall, the blood-written runes smearing as Dean's back slid down. The lantern-device turned toward Dean, who only raised his arms pitifully to shield his face, before being burned into a distorted skeleton.

The masked man seemed to watch his work unfold dispassionately. The mask moved little and betrayed no reaction. Mary struggled onto her knees, her legs and arms still tied, tears running down her face. The man turned to her. He approached and with his free hand removed Mary's gag. She coughed it away from her mouth and gasped for air as though rescued from drowning. Her voice warbled, her lower lip trembling.

"Thank you...thank you! They...I thought they were going to kill me...they..."

Her expression changed from one of sobbing gratitude to fear, then terror as she spoke, her words trailing off. He simply stared at her, no expression discernible from behind the cold black facade of the mask. There was no movement, no sound of muffled breathing. Mary tried to shuffle backwards, squirming feebly. The man again raised the lantern-device and switched it on. Mary barely had time to scream as the toxic green-yellow light engulfed her.

Chapter Two

Toronto, Present Day

Detective Benoit Michaud sat slumped in the driver's seat of his compact hybrid, away from any streetlights outside the Regent Park housing development. He didn't stick out and that's how he wanted it. His dark, Haitian-Canadian features caught only a hint of light from the nearby sports field, brightly illuminated for night use. Waiting for a murder suspect who might never show up wasn't exactly engaging, but he had to stay focused, and he was fighting sleep.

A few years ago, he might have lit a cigarette to occupy himself, then would've realized the light would give him away. He'd stub it out in the car's ashtray, then pull out his hip flask and take a sip. Then a drink. Then a couple more. Then he'd lose the fight with sleep. He'd wake up as day was breaking, and he'd try to reassure himself that the suspect didn't come by anyways.

Michaud shook off the fantasy-memory. Those days were over. Doctor's orders. He was tired of being a cartoon stereotype of the hard-drinking, chain-smoking detective. The doctor told him his bad habits with stress piled on top would catch up to him and kill him faster than any goon's bullet. No more junk food, no more treating his body like a trash bin. Reluctant at first, he started to feel better, look better. The smoker's cough was gone now, but the insomnia remained. That wasn't going anywhere, not with his heavy case load.

Sleeplessness still dogged him when he was working an annoyingly vexing case. He'd keep a note pad beside the bed to hurriedly jot down ideas and insights that often came quite frustratingly in the middle of the night. Thankfully, he no longer woke up feeling like the human equivalent of a well-trodden alley behind a bar. He managed to keep jogging like the doctor suggested. He'd been at it this morning, up and down the trails in the Don Valley, even got a flirtatious smile from a passing female jogger. He had to remind himself she was probably ten or fifteen years younger than he was, so he had to be doing something right. *Am I really thirty-seven already? Where did the years go?*

An abrupt thump against the passenger side door snapped him out of the contemplation. His hand shot into his jacket, reaching for his holstered sidearm. An Asian kid of about thirteen years in shorts and a T-shirt came running toward the car, bent down, picked up a soccer ball. The boy looked warily at Michaud. Michaud knew what he must have looked like—a strange, half-asleep man sitting alone in his car, leather jacket with collar upturned. The kid turned and ran back to his game on the field.

Michaud scratched at his goatee thoughtfully. *I used to play soccer. Played as a kid in Jane and Finch, played in university. Why'd I stop?* Because your parents died and you turned into a teenaged hermit. Then after you picked it up again in university you started smoking and could barely run. Then you started drinking and stopped caring, dumb-ass. Now you're too busy.

His police radio, sitting on the passenger seat, chirped awake, pulling him back to the present. A garbled voice spoke matter-of-factly. "All units, possible ten-forty-four, Flag Alpha, intersection of Blackthorn and Rockwell. Emergency Task Force en route five minutes, support requested."

Possible murder, suspect probably armed. The Emergency Task Force is nearly there. It'd take at least twenty-five minutes to drive over, even this late with no traffic. *They don't need me.*

Michaud's phone, beside the radio, buzzed for an incoming call. He leaned over, looked at it. Matthew Simons according to the call display. The young Detective Constable was a rookie at the job, but Michaud identified with him. They'd joke in the lunchroom about the "hard knock life," with Michaud the orphaned son of Haitian immigrants escaping a dictatorship, and Simons the child of four generations of Haligonian fishermen. Simons had studied at McGill in Montreal, Michaud here in Toronto, both of them saving every penny (when pennies still existed) for their educations.

Despite the cordial understanding between the two of them, Michaud hesitated. *He doesn't really need me. We're not friends. Never let them get too close.* He moved his hand toward the phone, pulled it back, watched the phone buzz again. He looked at it, reached. The phone stopped buzzing, and he stared at it for a moment. It buzzed again, this time a text message. Michaud sighed, picking it up.

"Might be in over my head, potential case Blackthorn/Rockwell. Could use assist. Please advise."

He imagined Simons running a hand through his short red hair, his pale skin flushing, trying to coordinate whatever crime scene he was at. Michaud took a deep breath, let out a loud sigh, and turned the ignition. Twenty-five minutes. No traffic. *Okay, stupid suspect, you get a breather tonight.*

* * * *

In a basement suite, a gas-masked figure heard the repeating drumbeat of military boots echoing and growing louder. The boots' black outlines created a staccato strobe outside the high windows. The door burst inward with the crash of a handheld police entry tool, really a glorified miniature battering ram, and a shower of splintered wood flying off the doorframe. The end of the man's black overcoat followed as he slipped out of a small window.

* * * *

"Police. Search warrant!" a male voice barked, as the gloved hands holding the battering ram moved out and away. A group of hunched, stocky silhouettes entered, submachine guns tucked up against their shoulders. The police Emergency Task Force, in dark grey coveralls, suited up in body armor and tactical gear, swept the room with their weapon-mounted flashlights. The walls were covered in symbols and formulas drawn in red, looking to the officers like the mad ramblings of a drug-addled fanatic. One of the flashlight beams settled on the floor, onto something twisted, caked in a blackened roughness. As the officer moved closer, he could see that it was the remains of a human ribcage, the flesh burned away. The flashlight continued scanning, illuminating further skeletal remains, all wrapped in wafts of smoke, as if recently immolated. They were contorted, arms and legs bent into horrible poses of agony. The officer's eyes widened, his weapon slowly lowering as he realized the number of bodies strewn across the tiled floor. Even through his balaclava, the smell was nearly overpowering. All he could think of was a foul combination of burned plastic and hair, with a metallic undercurrent to it. The officer coughed, involuntarily raising an arm and covering his mouth with the back of his hand.

The rest of the Emergency Task Force moved further back in the opposite direction, toward a shut door. An officer's gloved hand shot out to the knob, the other hand holding the lowered weapon, while three other officers covered the door, their weapons raised. The officer with his hand on the knob turned it with a sharp jerk and pushed inwards, backing away while the others moved in, before he could follow. Their flashlight beams swept the room rapidly, methodically. Overturned furniture and garbage were scattered about, a dumping ground of unsorted waste. The flashlight beams converged in the middle of the space and onto the shivering form of a woman in her thirties, sitting and rocking slightly back-and-forth, cross-legged on a plain mattress devoid of covers. A black cloak covered the woman's head and flowed down her back, spilling onto the mattress and the floor. Her cloak was spattered lightly with a muddy substance, still wet and glistening.

"Freeze! Hands in the air!" one of the men shouted.

The young woman shivered uncontrollably. One of the officers held his flashlight on her face while another knelt down close to her, looking in her eyes, searching for a sign of recognition. He looked back at the other team members and motioned for them to search the rest of the room with a terse set of efficient sweeping and pointing motions. He turned back to the woman, slowly pulling his goggles up onto the top of his Kevlar helmet, and pulling the front of his balaclava down, revealing his face. He had a stern look across his face, softening as he spoke.

"Ma'am, are you all right? Do you need medical attention?"

Sweat ran down her pallid features, her glassy eyes fixed and staring into nothing, as if unaware of the heavily armed men aiming their weapons at her. Her lips barely quivered as she inaudibly mumbled obscure, arcane phrases.

"Ma'am, my name's Weltner. What's yours? Can you give me your name?"

She continued mumbling, her eyes locked ahead, as though in a trance. Welter kept his eyes on her but turned his head to the shoulder mic attached to his tactical vest and activated it with a squeeze.

"We're going to need paramedics in here. Young woman, totally unresponsive. Possible drug overdose."

He looked back at the others across the room. His fellow team members moved toward a shut closet, hints of movement visible through its slats. Weltner could see something moving inside as they shone their flashlight beams over it. They yanked the door open with a sudden movement, weapons covering the inside. The source of the movement was revealed, and they lowered their submachine guns, fingers out and away from their triggers and around the trigger-guards. It was a small boy in his pajamas, his face streaked with tears, clutching a stuffed dinosaur. The team let out a collective sigh, drawing goggles up onto their helmets, pulling their masks down to reveal their faces. The boy looked up at them, brushing aside his mussed bowl cut, gulping air between sniffles.

"Is...is my mom okay?"

* * * *

There was commotion in the street as bodies pushed up against the hastily placed wooden police barricades. Uniformed officers tried to manage the scene, reassuring without explaining. The early autumn evening air was warm, the last remnants of the waning summer, and most people gathered around were in T-shirts. The crowd murmured in a mixture of Italian, Portuguese and English, characteristic of the neighborhood just north of Saint Clair in the west end of town.

Flashing blue and red lights strobed from nearby parked police cars, the Emergency Task Force van, and an ambulance, illuminating the scene in a repeating pattern of colored light. The vehicles were parked haphazardly at opposing angles over the sidewalks and into the street, some with doors open, one with a uniformed officer speaking into the car's dash radio. One of the police cars slowly pulled away. The siren came on and the vehicle picked up speed down the block. The young boy in the back seat sat beside a female officer who tried to reassure him as they jostled back and forth. He hugged a plush triceratops to his chest with one hand and with the other held a bag of books he had been allowed to bring along.

Emergency Task Force members (ETF)—masks, helmets and goggles in their hands now—stood in small groups exchanging hushed mutterings and head-shaking expressions as they discussed the bizarre horror of the basement. Some of them smoked, hands jittering slightly. They were Toronto's equivalent of a Special Weapons and Tactics team, but this situation was more than they could have expected. Team leader Weltner walked slowly through them, patting them on the shoulders reassuringly. He looked each of them in the eye, nodding, few words exchanged. Weltner turned and walked back to the basement.

Beyond the crowd, others from up and down the street gathered, bobbing their heads or standing on tip-toes to see what was happening. The warm summer evening humidity had everyone out in sleeveless shirts, shorts, sandals. Within the barricaded yard of the simple brick house, a bewildered neighbor from the next house over stood in pajamas, having a statement taken by a uniformed officer. The neighbor ran a hand through his bed-head of hair, scratched behind his ear, eyebrows high, eyes wide, nonplused, unable to provide any useful information beyond the time he heard the screaming and when he had called 911.

From the basement, a pair of paramedics trotted out, heading to their ambulance, carrying back the portable stretcher that had been deemed unnecessary. Their expressions were of blank shock. While used to the sight of blood or the aftermath of violence, a room filled with a half-dozen skeletons burned beyond recognition had broken their usual stoic cynicism. Behind them emerged Weltner and a uniformed officer, escorting the young woman out. She still seemed oblivious to her surroundings, and her face remained a mask of cold dampness. The uniformed officer opened the back door of a patrol car while Weltner pushed the woman's head down and guided her into the back seat. He followed behind and shut the door. A pair of brightly colored news vans pulled up just as the patrol car switched on its siren and drove out, uniformed officers parting the crowd and pushing them back with the barricades to clear a path. The news vans had to be content with parking across the street as the officers pulled back in, the crowd following and resealing the opening.

* * * *

Behind the crowd, past the news vans with their hastily

working crews, the shadowy outline of a man stood partially obscured beneath the trees and behind a hedge in a neighboring yard. He stood in his bowler hat and overcoat, no one in the crowd noticing that he was standing there, or that he carried at his side what looked like a gas mask. The man watched carefully as the patrol car containing the young woman glided past. His specialized vision was easily able to hone in on her pale features, studying her at an accelerated rate, combing through tiny details. He could see that her eyes seemed to be glazed over with a slightly translucent film, a second eyelid within the first. He raised his wrist, speaking into a radio attached to it like a watch. His voice, hushed but audible, had a gravelly, hollow sound, more mechanical than human.

"We have a problem," he intoned, then lowered his arm.

* * * *

Another car pulled up, rolling silently to the curb and parking. The single flashing police light affixed to the dashboard shut off and the driver's side door opened. Out stepped Michaud, in his three-quarter length brown leather jacket. The flashing police lights from nearby cars exaggerated his angular facial features, and he scratched at his light goatee while surveying the crowd. He ran his hand over the back of his head, feeling his close-cropped hair and rubbing his neck.

Michaud pulled his badge from his belt as he walked. Brushing off reporters and camera crews, he held up an empty hand up to ward them off while nonchalantly saying he would speak to them later. Michaud held up his other hand with the badge in it to a uniformed officer at the barricade. The officer let him pass, leaving behind the curious neighbors and eager news crews. He clipped his badge onto his belt and held his jacket back as he walked, ensuring that it was visible to the other officers on the scene.

As Michaud stepped across the well-trampled front yard, Matthew Simons approached. Michaud's earlier mental picture of him was accurate. He looked bedraggled, his tie pulled out slightly and collar button undone. The rookie detective was trying to handle a situation too frenetic for his level of experience.

"Detective Michaud!" he said, relieved.

"Simons. Are you supervising the scene?" Michaud asked,

the slightest hint of a Haitian-French accent audible, a remnant of his early childhood.

"I'm ceding authority to you. This is beyond me. I know I've been on homicide a couple months, but..."

Simons' voice shook, his words stuttering. Michaud could hear the mixture of excitement and fear.

"What's the rundown?" asked Michaud.

Detective Simons walked toward the back of the house, Michaud following. Simons spoke, as they moved through the narrow alley between houses. A stray grey-clad officer moved out of their way and into the front yard.

"ETF were mobilized for an armed and dangerous call about two hours ago," Simons said, pointing at the bewildered neighbor. "Said he saw a guy with a gun, heard screaming. No idea if that's true or if he just wanted a quick response. Anyways, they breached the door, found three dead, two survivors. Paramedics checked out the survivors, one's a kid, he's all right, the other one's a woman, late twenties maybe, almost catatonic. Boy says she's his mother." Simons caught his breath. "We have them both in custody, for their own protection. Not really sure what else to do with them at the moment."

"You interview the ETF on the scene?"

"Took statements. They're all filling out their own reports too, once they get over what they saw."

"What's the condition of the bodies? Is the coroner here?" Michaud asked.

"Well, uh...I can't really describe it. You just need to see them."

"Why does everyone always say that?" Michaud asked.

Simons led the way down the back steps and under a strip of yellow police tape across the entrance. A uniformed officer chatted with a pair of the remaining ETF members in hushed tones next to the door, stopping as they saw Michaud enter.

"I mean, how bad could it—holy shit." Michaud stopped mid-sentence as Simons stepped aside, revealing the carnage. He was speechless as he looked over the room, trying to discern what could possibly have happened.

"Make sure this stays sealed off. Has anyone else been in here besides you and the ETF?" Michaud asked.

Simons slowly shook his head "no."

"How many dead you say?" Michaud asked.

"Uh, three, so far. It's a real mess down here though. The bodies...well, take a look."

Michaud stared in, shaking his head. *What could possibly have done this?* The bodies looked like someone had gone over them with a flamethrower, but there was little—if any—damage surrounding them in the room.

Simons looked up at the contorted runes scrawled across the walls, symbols and shapes that defied any human language. "What is this, detective? *Voodoo*?" he asked.

Michaud was slipping on a pair of light blue nitrile gloves, his attention focused on the bodies strewn about, and the massive nine-pointed symbol in the middle of the room drawn in black and white powders. He hunched slightly as he stepped into the doorframe—the ceiling in this basement apartment was barely tall enough for most people to remain standing. It was an unfortunately common practice in Toronto for a homeowner to badly refurbish his or her basement with cheap amenities and rent it out for an exorbitant rate, despite it being barely fit for human habitation.

Michaud returned his attention to Simons.

"No, voodoo doesn't involve human sacrifice."

"What about the blood? Is that what that...writing on the walls is painted with?"

Michaud squatted down, trying to stay near the door and as far back from the bodies as possible. He wanted to examine them closely, but knew he could risk contaminating the crime scene further.

"There are dozens of religions that use blood in rituals."

"Like what, Satanism?"

One of the uniformed officers on the other side of the yellow crime scene tape chuckled. Michaud looked back at him and the officer cleared his throat and looked away, wiping a hand down off his mustache. Michaud turned back to the bodies.

"Or the Blood of Christ, and these guys just took that literally."

"Are you joking?" Simons seemed genuinely confused.

Michaud looked back at him. "Maybe," Michaud said, his attention on the symbols around the nine-pointed shape. "Satanic sacrifices are an urban myth. No. This...this is something else."

Simons looked at him. "You're into this sort of thing, aren't you? I mean, I heard that around the station."

"I know a little bit..." Michaud's sentence trailed off, and he turned to look back at Simons. "Were these bodies on fire when the ETF arrived?"

One of the ETF members at the door piped up, "No sir. They were smoking, like the flames had just been doused."

Michaud stood, scanning over the symbols on the walls and floor. "Floor's not burned...no burn marks on the walls, no drag marks...hmm." He examined the positioning of the bodies, the way they lay, might have fallen, their hands, where they must have been around the room. He looked carefully at the three bodies. Two on either side of a third in the middle, the middle body laying in a fetal position, crumbling remnants of rope on its wrists and ankles. The bodies on the side were up against the walls, as if pushed back by a hard tackle, no rope, no bonds of any kind.

"It's my guess they were standing around the room in a specific pattern. Someone...a fourth person came in, burned them all, somehow. Could have been the survivor, but...we should clear out of here. Let the lab do its work. Make sure every one of these symbols and every piece of writing is photographed. Meticulously." Michaud carefully stepped back and out of the room. Simons held up the yellow crime scene tape at the door as Michaud ducked under.

"What do we tell the media?" Simons asked.

"Don't tell them anything." Michaud stopped, then turned at the door to Simons. "No, wait. I'll clear it with headquarters and make a statement. The last thing we want is a rumor spreading about voodoo sacrifices. Don't let anybody from the press down here at all. And don't let any of them near the boy or his mother."

Chapter Three

Karen Wendleton, Michaud's civilian researcher assistant, trotted down the station hallway. In one hand a bike helmet swung from three fingers, in the other hand a bag of fast food. A small blue knapsack hung over one shoulder, and under her arm was tucked a manila folder full of papers and reports. *Late again. Hopefully the boss isn't in yet.* She increased her pace, her ponytail of dark hair bobbing as she tried to keep a hold of everything. A filing clerk in a shirt and tie walked towards her, frowning. She smiled back, despite not recognizing him.

He passed, and stopped. "Are you lost, Miss?"

Karen turned, realizing how she must have looked. Sweat marks on her sleeveless shirt from just biking in, tattoos visible on her well-toned arms. She might have just run from an interrogation room for all anyone knew. "Yes, I work here." Not technically a police officer, she wasn't armed, and often didn't look as though she belonged.

The clerk looked her over. "Can I see some identification please?"

Karen was used to it and simply smirked her amusement. She juggled everything in her arms until the file was in her mouth and everything else was in one hand, using the other to pull out her red lanyard and photo badge. She held it up for him.

"Sorry. Never can be too sure," he said, then left.

Guess I do look pretty young, too. Twenty-eight? Nah. Blame the Japanese genes. Thanks Mom. The tan she had acquired from her daily bicycle commute kept anyone from guessing her family heritage, Japanese and English. She'd been mistaken for Hawaiian, Spanish, a dozen different ethnicities. She rather enjoyed the confusion it caused.

Karen stopped at the frosted glass door of the office with Michaud's name on it. They shared the space, one he was lucky enough to score during a departmental restructuring. Most detectives weren't lucky enough to get one of their own, but his work in bizarre cases tended to put others off and left him to his own corner. The door was ajar, and she poked her head inside. No movement, but there was sound. A tiny television sitting on her desk—really a fold-up table, fastidiously clean—pushed against the wall with a window overlooking the street

Michaud's voice emanated from the battered set, a decades-old cube that caused his video image to be slightly warped and badly color-distorted into a set of purples and greens. Camera flashes sparked around him, microphones jutted into the frame from all directions and reporters crowded around him in the front yard of the house, peppering him with questions. "...the incident appears to have involved a murder-suicide in which the perpetrators committed self-immolation. There were two survivors, but I'm afraid we can't release any personal details on them in order to ensure their safety..." Michaud's statement was carefully measured to give the minimum amount of information while still directly addressing what had happened.

Karen stood leaning against the doorframe to the office, watching the television, still catching her breath. Sunlight filtering through the half-shut venetian blinds created a zebra pattern of shadow across her as she turned to the rest of the room.

In contrast to her tidy table, Michaud's desk was cluttered, with several stacks of books about occult rituals and fringe cults piled haphazardly. Behind the desk was a large corkboard with a corner devoted to tattered wanted posters, and the rest covered in obscure newspaper clippings and photos concerning the occult. Beside the corkboard was a scattering of framed photos. Family portraits, graduation day standing beside his uncle Felix, Michaud with other police officers, and the day he had saved a famous local hip-hop artist from a crazed stalker. A pair of degrees and an assortment of certificates completed the wall display.

In the corner of the room a tall hat-rack held his leather jacket and shoulder holster. Stacks of files sat on top of a metal filing cabinet, not yet compartmentalized. *Time to enter the twenty-first century, Boss. Could put all that on a hard drive the size of my fingernail.* The seemingly disorganized state of the room suggested someone scatterbrained, if mildly obsessive, but Karen knew it was more the result of diligence and

Michaud burying himself in his work. His mind was perfectly organized; his surroundings were not. *Guess you don't need a computer if your brain practically already is one.* She had admired him as a coworker and as a man and lightly flirted with him on occasion.

Only once had they nearly broken the office romance rule after several drinks the year previous, their shared reward for her help in cracking a particularly vexing home invasion and murder with (what turned out to be faked) occult overtones. Michaud rarely drank and she was almost able to take advantage of him, until he passed out on the couch. "Never get too close. Never get too close," he had mumbled before falling asleep.

Karen spied movement behind the stacks of books on the desk—Michaud had been here the entire time, but either hadn't noticed her entrance, or ignored her. She stepped closer and peered over...he was nose-deep in a massive musty leather-bound tome, decades old, his finger scanning the text. The only light on him, other than the sunlight filtering through the blinds, was his green-shaded desk lamp. He hated using the overhead fluorescents, the incessant hum of which bothered him, not to mention the drab dullness they instilled in the room.

Karen spoke up, referring back to his televised statement, trying to get Michaud's attention. "Self-immolation? Is that for real?"

"Doesn't matter if it's real or not, it matters what people believe," he responded, not looking up.

"At least you look good on the news," she said, putting everything down on her desk.

"Where were you last night?"

"I told you, I had the night off," she said over her shoulder. She placed her knapsack down on her desk chair, and pulled out a collared shirt.

"Date?"

"None of your business," she said, her voice rising slightly in mock irritation as she slipped her arms into the sleeves of the shirt. "Anyway, I brought you the lab report for the burned bodies."

Michaud continued reading, speaking into the book. "What's it say?"

Karen pulled the folder out from under the bike helmet

and bag of food on her desk and opened it. She read aloud, her diction taking on the stilted, rhythm-less quality of unrehearsed cue-card dialogue. "No evidence of any fuels, solvents, or other flammable liquids. Combustion of bodies not by any known type of fire and cause is currently under further investigation."

Michaud looked up and spoke, half-laughing. "What?"

Karen simply shrugged, as if in apology.

Michaud frowned, looking back down at the book. "Tell them to double-check it."

"They already checked three times."

Michaud shook his head, perplexed.

"So what do you think it was?" Karen asked, challenging him.

"Spontaneous human combustion."

"You're joking."

Michaud looked silently at Karen with his eyebrows raised, a smirk on his face, as if thinking "of course."

Karen shuffled through the file some more. "Oh, looks like what you suggested was correct. Despite all the ETF boots in there, lab techs found another set of footprints, slipped out a back window. So there was someone else in that room, and he was standing in front of those people against the walls when they were burned."

"I'd think he was using a flamethrower if there were any burn marks around the bodies, but that part has me stumped."

"Are you on the crime scene photos?" she asked, looking around his desk.

"Mmm."

"Anything?" Karen sorted a mess of large, glossy photo prints from the crime scene. The symbols adorning the walls and floor and the badly burned skeletons were illuminated by the forensic photographers' camera flashes, in some cases with rulers or measuring tape beside them for scale. Michaud did not respond other than to make a slight grunting-humming noise. Karen leaned in slightly, her head turned halfway back, her eyes widening.

Michaud looked up, sighing, admitting defeat. "Ritual magic, of some kind, but these symbols and Latin incantations aren't anything I've seen before. There's some superficial similarities to *Voodoo, Hoodoo, Santeria, Brujeria, Macumba, Umbanda, Candomble*...but none of those involve anything like human sacrifice."

"Is it..."

"It's not Satanism, so don't say it."

"I wasn't going to!" Karen protested. She imitated Michaud's voice, reciting his words. "'Satanic ritual sacrifice is an urban myth, a load of BS, the result of badly written books from Victoria, paranoia about Dungeons & Dragons, the 80's Satanic Panic and false memory syndrome'...that's one of the first things you said to me."

"...and if there were any truth to it, you'd think the kid who survived would have been one of the first sacrifices." Michaud sighed again. "I mean, there are *Muti* killings, but this doesn't look like killing someone for imagined demon possession. *Conjuring* a demon, maybe. Police in India've been chasing fringe worshippers of *Kali* engaged in human sacrifice, but our case has no indication of *Shaktism*. Hell, ancient Druids maybe, I don't know...

"The one thing I'd guess about this crime scene, is that, based on the arrangement of the bodies, and the way one of them was prone in the middle of the others, with remnants of rope around its arms and legs, indicate that it was a first victim, of the others. They were taking part in a ritual, and this was the subject. The others, and maybe the survivors were all a part of it, and someone else, a third party attacked them, but I have no idea how he would have..."

The end of his sentence trailed off as he sniffed the air, smelling Karen's bag of food. He noticed the gaudy logo featuring a sumo wrestler fighting an enormous hamburger and the dual Japanese and English lettering indicating *Matsubuchi Burger.*

"What is that?" Michaud asked aloud.

Karen grabbed the bag and held it up. "Lunch."

Michaud took the bag, opening it with a rustle and looking inside. He chuckled. "Wendleton, you know I don't eat this stuff."

She acted incensed. "I bought you the veggie burger!"

Michaud, smirking at her, shook his head slowly back and forth as he withdrew his paper-wrapped package. He cleared a space amongst the clutter and splayed the paper out to eat.

* * * *

Michaud realized he hadn't actually had breakfast, and

the dull dryness in his head started to clear up as the food refueled him. He nodded rapidly, his eyes shut, trying to get down his mouthful before he spoke again.

He tried to think of parallel crimes in his experience. *Like that basement "suite" near Ossington and Dupont.* The crime scene he remembered had resembled a bizarre funhouse attraction or forced-perspective movie set that grew progressively smaller the further anyone moved into it, until they reached the last "room," a dirt-floor crawlspace barely a meter in height. He and his team had found multiple bodies buried in the soft earthen floor, covered over with tarps, over which furniture had been placed at comical angles. They had discovered that the occupant of the suite had killed three people and disappeared. The attempt to conceal them however was done by the owners of the building, fearing for depression of their property's value. *A third party after the fact.*

"The third party, the extra set of footprints."

"Who do you think it could have been? Any theories?" Karen asked.

Michaud shook his head. He shot out half-sentences, speculating. "Disgruntled cult member, got fed up, went crazy maybe. Intended victim who escaped, but that doesn't seem likely given the extent of the damage, whatever weapon was used. It all seemed very deliberate. Whoever was doing it had a plan, I think."

Karen's eyes roamed around, then refocused on Michaud. "Maybe it was part of the ritual. Maybe they intended for things to happen that way. The guy was supposed to kill everyone, burn them, as part of it, then leave."

"Hmm, possible, but not probable. It just doesn't fit with the strict geometric placement of the symbols, the placement of the others in the room. The foot patterns would indicate they struggled, didn't want it to happen. But maybe...I won't dismiss it outright. Then there's the other possibility I thought of, what I think is most likely..."

"What? Is it crazy?" Karen said, smiling.

"What if it's a vigilante? Some nut in a costume. Black mask, cape maybe, I don't know. Guy in a ski mask. Someone unhinged, hunting down cultists, even more dangerous than they are. Or worse, a serial murderer with a fixation on this kind of thing. Some wild-eyed inventor who's come up with this funky new weapon that can burn people up."

"Maybe it's just a coincidence. Maybe it's a killing that has nothing to do with the ritual and it's unconnected. The guy was just some lunatic who happened to chance upon these people, and he would have killed them if they were a family watching television," Karen suggested.

"It just seems to me that the guy who did it was...exacting. The lack of any other damage around the room. The precision kills," Michaud said, his eyes narrowing as he thought.

"But that could be because the ETFs got there before he could finish. Maybe he was going to burn the place to the ground, but they scared him off."

Michaud nodded. "I think they did scare him off, but I don't think he was going to be that chaotic. There was no damage to the room outside the bodies...I think if he was a firebug he would have trapped them inside, lit the place up from outside, then watched them, and it, burn. Plus," he said, slapping another photo down in front of Karen, "he wouldn't have wasted his time burning this."

"What is it?" she asked, leaning over and looking into the shot.

"Looks like a big bowl, some ash, residue inside, not much of anything left though. Hoping to get it analyzed, but I'm not holding out much hope. I'm guessing it was part of the ritual. And he burned it." Michaud shook his head. "Too much purpose. The guy had a plan. Or thought he did, if he was a psycho."

"How do we know it was just one guy?" Karen said.

Michaud pondered. "You're right. I guess we don't. Could've been someone else outside the building, no one was looking for that. The guy who did it might be part of a group who does this, or is just starting to do this. But still, from the available evidence, I'm going to go with one person. Until we have more to work on."

"A serial killer who goes after cultists engaging in human sacrifice. That's new."

"And here's the worst part—what if this guy thinks he's doing something good? I mean, if it is a vigilante thing, maybe he thinks he's a hero, saving us from these cultists, or whatever it is they were trying to do." Michaud swallowed his bite of burger. "But that's all speculation. There's not a whole lot of evidence in any of these directions. Just a lack of evidence that doesn't particularly lead away from any of them. I guess you could say the lone vigilante theory is the one that seems... the least implausible to me at the moment." Michaud took another bite from his burger.

"That sounds convoluted," Karen remarked dryly.

"Right. I don't want to work backwards. When I think too far into the maybes, I get sidetracked off what we know happened, and I feel like I'm starting from a conclusion and working backwards."

Karen comically widened her eyes. "Gee detective, maybe we should hire a psychic," Karen smirked. "Get a crystal ball, some tarot cards, an astrology chart..."

He looked at her, almost glaring. "You know Wendleton, if you ever get hungry, you can just take your stand-up act on the road. They'd throw so much fruit at you, you could make a salad out of it every night." He smiled. He knew she was teasing him, being well aware of his disdain for police use of psychics. Michaud considered it an insult to the profession.

"So, fine. Real research. We look for more information on the ritual. And here you are."

"Exactly. If there's more than one crime at the crime scene, we start with the one we can see for sure, and work from there. So..." he gestured, displaying some of the research items he had collected. "One thing I did find was some information on this nine-pointed symbol, the *nonagon*, with the irregular interior connecting lines," he said, chewing and swallowing. He used his free hand to turn a large photo of the symbol around for Karen's viewing. "It was painted up on the east wall. It's mentioned in the *Occulta Philosophia de Libri Tres* from the Fifteenth century as being a potent symbol of evil for use in summoning demons. See if you can dig up anything more on it. I have to question the woman we took into custody last night."

Karen looked up quickly from the photo. "You didn't question her right away?"

Michaud stood, finishing the last bite of his burger, his other hand grabbing his jacket off the rack and slipping into one of the sleeves. "She was too out of it. Totally non-responsive. She's been in a holding cell for twelve hours now. We don't even have her full name, no identification on her, and nothing to tell us who she is from the crime scene, other than her son, who says her name is Rachel."

"Was she actually arrested?"

"Detained. Sort of a grey area. Not sure if she was in-volved in the crime, or a victim of it. Paramedics on site said she appeared physically okay, other than being out to lunch. Psychiatric assessment is today though, bringing in a doctor to look at her. Her son might be more helpful, hopefully. He was uninjured, seemed all right, other than the obvious shock of being there. Still not sure what he saw, if anything."

"Where is he now?" she asked.

"Protective custody. If he was part of the ritual, and there's more of these people out there, or if someone got away, they might come after him. Or worse, the extra set of footprints, whoever that was." Michaud pulled a handheld digital audio recorder out of his desk, hoping to record the interview with Rachel. He slipped the recorder into his pocket.

Karen put the file with the coroner's report on the bodies on top of Michaud's closest stack of books, and replaced it in her hand with the photos of the *nonagon* symbol. "All right, I'll do some nosing around."

Michaud stood, folding down the collar of his jacket, and retrieved his empty water bottle, intending to fill it at the kitchen water cooler. He followed after Karen out the door, and they parted ways, heading in opposite directions along the hall.

* * * *

Michaud walked toward the office of Inspector Terrence Friesen, thinking over the report he had handed in. The Inspector was Michaud's superior, the equivalent to an American police forces' Lieutenant. Far from the movie ste-reotype of a bellowing petty dictator who daily chewed out the officers under his command for cowboy-like misconduct, he came across as even-tempered, even cold. Sometimes too even-tempered, many thought, due to his habit of simply looking at people with a flat stare during disagreements or disciplinary actions. His emotions were often unreadable be-low the surface of an outwardly calm demeanor, earning him nicknames like "Freezin' Friesen," "Mister Freeze" and to the younger officers, "Scary Terry."

Michaud suspected that Friesen deep down, was some-thing of an ideologue, not a very creative thinker, somewhat rigid, and would probably have preferred being a police officer in world where he could wear a Sam Browne belt to go with knee high boots and a truncheon for battering jaywalkers. Keeping his emotions in check was more of an occupational requirement, so to keep from brutalizing suspects he had always adopted the opposite tact and simply suppressed his passions.

The door was open, and Michaud looked in. Friesen sat at his desk, reading glasses perched on his nose as he flipped through reports from different officers on the disturbing set of events from the night previous. The cuffs of his pinstripe shirt were rolled back, and his dark navy suit jacket was hung up on the back of his chair. The large windows in his office looked out on the street several stories below, and unlike Michaud, Friesen had his blinds drawn entirely up, making the room bright and open. Bookshelves and filing cabinets lined the walls. Plants hung from the corners of the ceiling, sat along the window ledges, and lined the tops of the shelves. Along with the plants, the Inspector kept in his office multiple awards, including those he was most proud of, his bowling trophies.

As he read, he absentmindedly twisted the end of his thick grey mustache, then raised his lower lip to chew on it slightly, a habit no doubt he had picked up over years of stultifying investigative work. Michaud knew that as a youth, the Inspector had been a strapping man, but now in his early fifties, while still barrel-chested, wasn't as fit as he would have liked. His pale skin had become redder with age and stress, and his formerly dark brown hair had gone salt-and-pepper grey, which he combed back.

Michaud's hand twisted around the inside of the doorframe, his knuckles rapping a greeting as he stepped into view. Friesen looked up, then pulled his glasses off and put them on top of the report, both on the desk in front of him. "Michaud. Come in, sit down."

Michaud entered, and pulled out the chair at the desk facing the Inspector and sat in it. "Inspector. Did you read over—"

"Your preliminary report about the burned bodies last night, I did," Friesen said, cutting him off. "It's uh...strange, to say the least."

"It doesn't even seem real. But I have a few things I want to look into."

"No suspects at the moment though," Friesen said, half-questioning.

"Not really. Rachel, the woman taken into custody, doesn't seem like a suspect. Although, it looks like more than one crime was committed at the scene, and she might be part of the first, then someone else at large was part of the second. It's kind of a mess. I'm going to question her, and then talk to the boy as well. They're mother and son."

"Right," Friesen said, picking up and flipping through Michaud's report, sitting aside on the desk. "So you think there were, what, three to five people who had another tied up, they were doing something, and an unknown outsider attacked all of them?"

"My guess," Michaud said. "Fits the available facts. Just some weird inconsistencies. The burned bodies, with no damage surrounding them. Hoping to get something out of that. Have a few theories at the moment, nothing too solid."

"Such as?"

"Doesn't look like the bodies were moved into the basement after being burned, but it's certainly plausible. And the, uh, attacker...a few ideas there. Could be a member of their group who went crazy, or a vigilante, or maybe the most out-there idea we had, that he's part of a rival group, or a group of vigilantes."

The Inspector furrowed his brow, contemplating. "All right...I'd concentrate on the first part of this at the moment. Who the group had...kidnapped, whatever. Who these people were. The third party attacker, that's still just a theory, yes?"

"Well, it is, in a way, but..."

"So, I'd suggest sticking to the facts. These people were probably crazy, they might as well have just burned themselves up."

Michaud looked at Friesen, not wanting to argue, trying to think of something placating to say. A few seconds of silence passed as Michaud twisted the corner of his mouth, thinking. "I'll do my best."

Friesen nodded. "The kidnapping victim. Any chance that's..."

"I had thought of it. The Smalls girl," Michaud said. Teresa Smalls was a fifteen-year old girl from Etobicoke, a western suburb of the city. She had disappeared two weeks earlier after her evening ballet class, while waiting for her parents to pick her up. Their usual meeting place was in front of the building where her class was. Left at the scene were Teresa's cell phone and purse, raising the disturbing specter of abduction for reasons other than monetary gain. No ransom had been asked for, and the only lead they had, and most probable one, was the man she had been seeing, Patrick Garneau—fifteen years her senior—had become unreachable. The man's address had been searched, but turned up nothing, and he had seemingly vacated weeks previous. "The body at the scene, the one that looked like it had been tied up...it was about the right size. Won't know until we get dental records back. It was pretty badly burned."

Friesen sighed. "Monsters. I have no idea how we stay sane when we deal with this. People out there have no idea."

"No sir, they don't," Michaud said, going through the motions. Friesen was an adherent of the "thin blue line" idea that civilization needed a strictly authoritarian force to keep it in check. Without it, only the tiniest push would cause everyone to go berserk and engage in a rapacious spree of wanton slaughter. Michaud maintained his cool rationalism and detachment by reminding himself that as police officers, being daily exposed to the worst of the worst could easily warp one's perspective. Michaud tried not to judge—people were good, people were bad, sometimes people were really bad. His job was to observe, to analyze, to apply his investigative skills. He only sought the truth, wherever that led. He sometimes thought he'd make a better scientist than detective.

"You don't need any greater allocation of resources for this, do you? It seems like it could require more manpower. That, uh, whatsername..."

"Karen. Wendleton."

"Yeah. How's she working out?"

"Great. Better than a real cop. Just wish she could go out armed."

"She enough for this?"

"For now. Simons has been helping. We could definitely use him for checking some of our leads."

"You got him. But until this thing gets any wider, try to work with what you've got. You've been working under me for what..."

"Seven years."

"Seven years. You know me by now. More guys means more paperwork for me to read, fill out and file, and you know I hate paperwork. Just keep it simple."

"Understood."

"All right, I'll look forward to your full report. And keep me updated. I'm curious where this goes."

"Of course," Michaud said, getting up. "I'm heading to speak with Rachel, the survivor, shortly."

"Oh, Michaud," Friesen said. Michaud turned, stopping by the door. "Good work with the media. Stay on that. Say what you want, tell them only what they need."

"I will," Michaud said, before disappearing.

Chapter Four

A tiny figure—the man who wore the bowler hat and overcoat—stood illuminated in a spotlight in an immense dark chamber. His mask off, he looked up at a row of men in suits seated along a long desk on a raised platform. They were also cast in spots of light, their faces partially obscured, the entire room cloaked in shadow and its details darkened. The space had the aspect of a courtroom, with judges lined up, presiding over the accused. This was the Ruling Council chamber of the *Ordo Sanctus*, affording security and anonymity to its members, who operated in secrecy behind the facade of the modern worlds of commerce and governance. Some, due to the flexibility afforded them by their wealth or station, were able to attend every regional meeting. Others, in government, law enforcement, business, were sporadic attendants, but maintained allegiance nonetheless. The prevalence of dark expensive suits along the chamber table made the situation seem almost funereal.

The council chamber was resplendent in enormous red curtains, hand-crafted wood council desk and platform, and extensive lighting arrangements—all designed to impress upon anyone that they were the subject of a greater authority, instill a sense of fear, and make identification of the actual geographic location of the facility impossible. From the outside, the building would never be recognized, and the area it was located in was somewhere no one would have thought to look at or notice.

The council leader was a man in his late fifties, grey-haired, still in athletic shape despite his advancing years. His bearing and voice projected power as it echoed forth in the darkness, addressing the figure before them. "Cleaner, what is your report?"

The figure's hollow voice echoed in response. "They succeeded in completing the ritual this time. Before I arrived on the scene." The members of the council murmured anxiously, exchanging words with one another, before the Cleaner continued. "One of them escaped. She is in police custody. And the *Encyclopedia Nefastus* was in their possession."

Another council member, a slight man in his seventies, spoke anxiously. "Where is it now?"

"I am...uncertain. It was recovered neither by the police nor myself. I was forced to flee when they arrived. My...photograph may have been taken. There were reporters."

The second council member spoke, the volume and tension in his voice rising. "This is unacceptable! How could we have let one of them escape with it? We keep the book so well-guarded..."

"It does not matter now," the council leader said.

"How can you say that?" the second council member pleaded.

The council leader gestured outwards with his hands to the other council members for calm, as if parting an invisible sea, palms down. "All that matters is retrieving it before they can enact their plan. We have our own, and ours will be the one that succeeds." He turned his attention back to the Cleaner. "What of our people within the police?"

The Cleaner spoke matter-of-factly, without a hint of emotion. "I will have access to the survivor."

* * * *

Michaud entered the holding cell area of the station, a loud buzz accompanying the unlocking of a door for him by the guard officer. The guard sat in a Plexiglas enclosed booth with an opening similar to a ticket window, situated beside the larger door that led to the holding cells. A single fluorescent light tube illuminated the booth, casting the man in a dull green hue. Michaud approached the desk and read the officer's name tag aloud into the intercom.

"...Wellburn."

"Morning, Detective." Wellburn's voice replied, sounding like a staticky radio broadcast. The intercom microphone had been positioned next to his face so that he barely had to move when speaking. Michaud knew of Pete Wellburn, but tried not to associate with him, which thankfully was easily accomplished due to Wellburn's banishment to baby-sitting duty over the holding cells. Wellburn was a thoroughly dislikable person who had been the subject of several disciplinary incidences for mild sexual harassment of female officers and support staff. If his extreme social awkwardness weren't enough, he clearly spent considerable time at the gym and tanning on the beach in a bizarre attempt to make up for his goblin-like countenance and diminutive stature. His pointed nose and small chin, combined with a terribly maintained brush cut, were off-putting as it was, but the excessive weight-lifting made his head appear cartoonishly tiny. Michaud shuddered, this man was in his early forties and wore *rollerblades* to commute to work.

Wellburn put down his copy of the city's trashy tabloid, *The Sun*, which blared out the lurid (and unsurprisingly inaccurate) headline "Satanic Cult Murder-Suicides Shock City" accompanied by a blurry photo of some of the wall-scrawlings and symbols. Michaud looked at this with distaste and frustration. He knew the full details of the case might eventually escape to such publications, but he hadn't anticipated that it would be this quickly. Beneath the larger, page-filling headline was another smaller story asking "Where Are You Teresa?" regarding the disappearance and possible abduction of fifteen-year-old Teresa Smalls.

Wellburn pushed a clipboard through the small opening at the bottom of the window, pen attached by a small length of beaded chain. Michaud scanned down the list of names and found the first empty space, signing himself in. He turned the clipboard around and pushed it back through the opening. "You should read a real newspaper, you know."

"Reading this thing's better than reading the reports from upstairs," Wellburn replied, defensively.

Michaud tried to swallow his contempt, and changed the subject. "She say anything?"

"The one they brought in last night? No. Something might be wrong with her though. She's curled up in the back of the cell. Acting kinda weird."

Michaud nodded to Wellburn in thanks and turned to the large door leading to the cells. *Yeah, she's probably acting weird because you were staring at her and acting like a creep.*

Wellburn's tin-cup voice spoke up from the intercom speaker. "Number seven." Another buzz, another automatic unlocking, and Michaud pushed the door open and moved through. He entered a long hall, lined on either side with traditional metal-barred cells. Several of the overhead lights flickered on and off—prisoner creature comforts were not a high priority in the departmental budget. One light held steady in front of Rachel's cell as Michaud approached, bathing him in its dull glow. He turned and looked inside, drawing the digital recorder out of his pocket. He could hear Rachel's labored breathing, and could see that she was curled up against the bunk at the back of the cell, her knees against her chest as she sat, her face downcast. A thin shaft of light penetrated from the small exterior window, lighting her hands and feet, keeping her head obscured in shadow.

"Rachel?" Michaud offered as he activated the recorder. She made no response. Her breathing sounded as though she suffered from a terribly severe chest cold. Michaud could hear the phlegm rattling around in her throat. "The little boy in the house last night...he was your son, wasn't he? He's all right, and he'll be safe."

Rachel was either ignoring him or was oblivious. The only sound coming from the cell was more foul breathing.

"I'd like to ask you some questions about what happened last night. We need to know if you were involved, or if you were a victim."

"Wa...water..." Rachel's voice managed to push out quietly between breaths.

"What was that?" Michaud asked, leaning in slightly.

"I need water..." she said, louder. Her voice gurgled, as though made in simulation of human vocal cords, making her speech stunted and difficult to understand.

Michaud looked at the water bottle in his hand, then back to Rachel. He noticed that half in shadow on the floor were small piles of her hair. Her hands, still wrapped around her knees, were peeling as if from a bad sunburn, but were a pallid grey, rather than red. Michaud's eyes squeezed into slits as he squinted at her. "Are you all right?"

Rachel lunged out and into the light. "I need water!"

Michaud was shocked back a step at what he saw. Her skin was falling away, molting like a snake's, revealing another layer underneath that appeared a sickly, mottled grey. Her hair had fallen out in clumps, leaving only a few stray strands hanging from her head. Her nose and ears had flattened into tiny holes, and her mouth was wide, with small pointed protuberances around it, giving her the appearance of a catfish.

Her eyes were completely black, with no visible irises or pupils. Rachel stepped quickly to the bars and reached for the water bottle in Michaud's hand, but he stepped back, keeping it away from her. He stared in horror, unable to guess at what had happened to her.

"I'm...I'm calling a doctor," he stuttered, jaw agape, as he reached for the cellphone in his pocket.

Rachel yelled now, her voice becoming guttural with the sound of the gurgling in her throat. "Give me the water!"

Michaud swallowed nervously. He realized he had completely forgotten the recorder in his hand, stunned as he was by Rachel's appearance. "I'll give you this if you tell me what you were doing last night." Rachel reached pitifully through the bars toward the water bottle, revealing webbing between her fingers as her hand stretched out. Michaud grew uncomfortable, hoping she would answer. He looked back toward the entrance door and the guard station, then back to Rachel.

"What were you doing last night?"

Rachel's phlegmy breathing slowed, and she looked up, finally making eye contact with Michaud. "The Ninth Darkness...we invoked the Ninth Darkness."

"Who killed everyone? Was it you? Why were they burned?"

"The man...the man with the hat, and the bag, and the mask...he'll come for me."

Michaud, sickened by her pitiable condition, relented and gave Rachel the water. She grabbed it like a desperate alcoholic reaching for liquor, practically throwing the contents in her mouth and dousing herself with it as well. She bounced the bottle with a clang through the bars back at Michaud, and as he reached for it she wriggled backwards into the corner, in a way that seemed less human than it should have.

Michaud drew a breath, wanting to ask more questions, but he stopped himself, knowing he had to call for paramedics or a doctor. He switched off the recorder and replaced it in his pocket. Michaud looked back and forth in a moment of uncharacteristic uncertainty, the surreal situation almost overwhelming him. *Paramedics, a doctor.* He needed Karen down here. *A photo camera, a video camera, something, anything.* He looked at the entrance door, back to Rachel, the door...then began walking quickly toward it. He pounded on it loudly, and the buzz came, the mechanical unlocking sound seeming agonizingly slow. Michaud impatiently yanked the door open. He stepped through and moved immediately to the booth, still occupied by Wellburn.

Michaud spoke forcefully, "We need paramedics down here now."

Wellburn looked up from his tabloid sleepily. "Hmm?"

Michaud raised his voice but remained calm and kept his words even, making stern eye contact with Wellburn. "Get on the phone, call the switchboard, tell them we need paramedics immediately. Do you understand?"

Wellburn seemed to realize the seriousness of the situation. His eyes widened and he fumbled away the newspaper, then reached for the phone, dropping it.

"I need you to let me out. I have to get upstairs," Michaud requested, his voice still calm. Wellburn slapped his free hand down on the door control panel, releasing the outer door. Michaud moved quickly, and Wellburn watched him leave, one hand now gripping the phone. He kept his view on the door, slowly putting the phone back down on the receiver as Michaud disappeared from view. Just before the exterior door closed, a black leather-gloved hand snaked around it and pulled it open. In stepped a figure clad in overcoat and black bowler cap, carrying a doctor bag.

Wellburn looked up, no expression crossing his face. The man approached the window, putting on a gas mask. He replaced his bowler cap, regarding Wellburn, then nodded. Wellburn nodded back and hit the interior door release button, the buzz again signaling the door open. The Cleaner moved through, his shoes making deliberate, slow clip-clops on the tiled floor. Wellburn hit a group of buttons on his control panel, then stood and walked out of his booth, pulling his attached keychain out to unlock the exterior door, and headed out, not looking back.

* * * *

Michaud took two steps at a time as he bounded up the stairs to the next floor, standing by a large window between floor landings. Wellburn was a nitwit, he couldn't be counted on. Michaud pulled his cell phone out and dialed rapidly, a short set of three numbers that would take him directly to the police phone system.

"Switchboard..." a bored-sounding female operator said.

"This is Detective Michaud. Has anyone called in for medical personnel to the holding cells?"

"Nothing sir. Would you like me to..."

Michaud cut her off. "I need a doctor and paramedics to the holding cells immediately."

* * * *

The Cleaner stepped slowly down the row of holding cells. Entering and infiltrating the police station had been simple, given the detailed instructions he had been provided with. He appreciated that the other cells along the row were vacant—less work for him to deal with. The mask he wore was a modern model, no longer tethered to a hip unit, a copper-colored add-on piece attached to the mouth filter, etched with tiny designs. The lack of any tell-tale breathing sounds revealed that it was not in fact a gas mask, and the effect of the silence would have been unnerving if anyone were there to see him.

He moved in front of Rachel's cell. The fluorescent light glinted off the metal attached to the front of the mask as he positioned himself carefully at a set distance from the bars. Rachel looked up from her shadowy corner, silent.

The Cleaner's voice came through the mask, even more mechanical, filtered by the copper-colored mechanism. "Where is the book?"

Rachel lunged, her graying, webbed fingers grasping toward him.

The Cleaner's placid, monotone voice repeated, "Where?"

Rachel gurgled out her words contemptuously. "You can't... you can't stop us..."

The Cleaner ignored her, pulling out his lantern device, unchanged in over fifty years. He adjusted dials on the side and turned toward Rachel.

Her voice raised as half-drowned words barked out. "The Ninth Darkness will come and consume you all! *Olgog'lahai'kuhul nos vestri valde vinculo totus!*" She blurted broken Latin, as the Cleaner calmly aimed his lantern device toward her. The beam of energy burst forth and Rachel's voice became a rasping yowl, the green-yellow glow illuminating the Cleaner and reflected in the eyepieces of his mask as he worked.

* * * *

Michaud's voice sputtered from the phone, trying to repeat the word Karen had just spoken to him. "Olog'la-what?"

Karen sat in the reference library in front of a huge floor-to-ceiling window, gray sky behind her, surrounded by stacks of books, carefully framed scrolls and research papers. She wore nitrile gloves, required by the library for handling rare and obscure material. "*Olog'lahai'kuhul*," she read aloud from a dusty, yellowing volume. "This was the name of that which was summoned by the combination of the *Terlian Incantations* and the *Hectus Exsemmet Nonagon*—the nine-sided symbol in the photograph."

"Is there any mention of a 'Ninth Darkness?'" Michaud asked.

Karen flipped back and forth, scanning down the page. "... yes." She continued reading from the book. "The Ninth Darkness was the final great shadow that would befall the Earth after the coming of *Olog'lahai'kuhul*, that which consumes all life and light."

"Where'd you find all this?" Michaud asked, somewhat surprised.

"Book on occult lore, it references something called the *Encyclopedia Nefastus*, supposedly one of the first grimoires written in the thirteenth century by a group called the *Ordo Sanctus*."

"Good work. Dig around a little more for anything on the cult, and that Encyclopedia, but get back here soon. I want you to see what's happened to the suspect from last night. I gotta go. Oh, wait! Bring your camera. Don't forget."

"All right, I'm on it." Karen replied, then shut off her phone.

* * * *

Michaud hung up. He had hoped she'd be able to make it down sooner, but as long as she arrived with the camera he'd be satisfied. As he was shoving his phone back into his pocket and turning to descend the stairs again, it immediately buzzed. He raised it back up and answered, "Michaud."

"Is this the detective who asked for medical assistance at the holding cell area?" a voice asked.

Michaud frowned. "Yes..."

"I think your suspect is beyond my help."

* * * *

Michaud approached the outer door to the holding cell area. A new officer buzzed him in. He stopped momentarily at the booth. "Where's the other guy? Shift change?"

The new guard was younger, a second year uniformed officer grabbed in haste to fill the post. He had a look of concern on his face as he leaned into the intercom microphone. "No sir, not that I know of. The paramedics had to call the switchboard for someone to let them in. Not sure where Wellburn went." Michaud twisted his mouth up in a look of annoyance, and moved toward the interior door to the cells. The young officer hit the door release, buzzing him through. As Michaud raised his arm to push the door, the officer spoke through the intercom. "You...you'll want to be warned about the smell." Michaud looked over his shoulder, slightly confused, but pushed on into the holding cell area.

The familiar smell hit him immediately—a metallic odor of burnt hair. He looked down the corridor toward Rachel's cell—in front of it were two paramedics and two uniformed officers, the paramedics wearing filter masks, the officers holding cloths over their mouths and noses. One of the uniformed officers, a stocky, goateed Indian man, winced strongly as he coughed. Thin wisps of smoke crept from Rachel's cell. Michaud increased his walking speed and trotted to where they stood, looking in. They looked at him, their faces all clenched in looks that mingled dumbfounded with disgust. He peered into the cell—Rachel had been reduced to a charred skeleton, knotted up into a fetal position, on the floor of the cell.

Michaud turned to one of the paramedics, a bespectacled, redheaded woman in her late twenties. Michaud read the name tag on her shirt. "Derocher. When did you get here? Was she still burning?"

The paramedic spoke in a voice slightly muffled by the turquoise filter mask. "She was like this. We got here about three minutes ago, right before we called you." The other paramedic, a tall, thin man in his early twenties who looked like he might as well have just finished his emergency medical training, shrugged feebly, his eyes wide.

Michaud rubbed two fingers up against his temple, pulling one eyebrow up into a false expression of surprise, before wiping his hand down over his mouth, while his eyes stayed on the charred remains of Rachel in the cell. "I was only gone for five minutes. Somebody got in here and fried our suspect in that time? Where the hell is the guard who was on duty?" he said to no one in particular, his voice rising.

One of the uniformed officers, a broad man with grey dappling the sides of his head of dark hair spoke, lowering the cloth he held over his mouth. "There's no sign of him. He's not answering his phone or radio either."

Michaud's frustration boiled over. "Well, fucking find him! He can't be far!" he spat out. Both the uniformed officers turned to leave, one of them coughing and clearing his throat. Michaud closed his eyes deliberately and exhaled through his nose, checking himself. *That's the hotheaded chain-smoking rookie kid. Be cool.* He stopped the grey-dappled officer by the shoulder, and both turned back to him. Michaud read their name tags aloud. "Hey...Kehoe, Sidhu, sorry. This is crazy. He's got to be around. Send a unit to check his house. And we need a forensics team down here to go over this cell millimeter by millimeter. I want an autopsy on this body."

He looked up at the security camera that sat observing the scene, silently. "And somebody get me surveillance videos!" he said. The two officers nodded, both in understanding of Michaud's apology and acknowledgement of the importance of his order. The two men trotted out, the door buzz signaling their exit. Michaud turned, looking at the remains of Rachel. It was the same as the scene at the house—no burn marks on the floor. Nothing in the cell damaged, and the bars untouched.

The anger was subsiding, and Michaud's mind raced. Someone was either sent in to kill one of the only witnesses, or else it was a very resourceful individual trying to clean up anyone who could identify him. Somehow, gotten inside the police station, into the holding cells, and set fire to someone without setting off any alarms. *How was that even possible?* It could have been Wellburn himself, but that would be too easy, and it was never easy.

At least they probably knew Rachel wasn't a suspect now. Hell, for all he knew she somehow burned herself. That wasn't terribly likely...and best not to get too far outside plausibility. Since she was in police custody, the vigilante angle didn't seem too likely, and if it was a pattern killer it was doubtful he'd risk coming into a police station, unless he was terribly obsessive. *Doubtful? It had happened.* Someone got in here

and repeated what he did the night before, and escaped.
Michaud sighed through his nose, frustrated.

Chapter Five

Michaud moved up the stairs two at a time. He had met with three forensics examiners and a photographer, giving them what little information he had on the scene when he arrived. Knowing he could contribute little to their work, and would only suffer impatience if he stayed to observe them, he had decided to head back to the video room to look at the security videos that had been recorded in and around the holding cells. As he rounded the corner of the flight of stairs between the third and fourth floors, his phone buzzed insistently in his pocket, nagging at him like a tiny mechanical baby. He pulled it out and answered tersely, "Michaud."

"Detective, I have information you're going to need concerning your current case," a stony male voice said.

"Who is this?" Michaud replied.

"Someone you need to meet with. I can't discuss it over an open line."

"How did you get this number? This is my personal phone. If you want to call my office line, you can.—"

The voice cut him off. "I'm not in a position to talk about it now."

Michaud flared his nostrils and pursed his lips, annoyed. This game was tiresome. "Okay, I'm hanging up then. Bye-bye..."

"It's about the *Ordo Sanctus,* detective. I will contact you within the hour to arrange a meeting." The phone gave a tiny electronic gurgle as the call was ended. Michaud looked at the phone—not surprisingly, the number was blocked. He looked around, thinking. There was nothing he could do about this call, and at the moment it was an inconsequential nuisance that might only burden him with further mysteries. He concentrated on the problem at hand, that of the missing guard and the death of Rachel, and continued upstairs, heading for the video room.

* * * *

Karen walked out of the library through a maze of hallways and corridors carrying a file folder stuffed with photocopied pages and headed for the washroom. She had spent just over five hours poring through antiquarian books in a sealed room, with a dust mask and nitrile gloves on to protect the frail and brittle paper. Despite washing her hands, they still smelled of the gloves, but she needed to get back to the office. Michaud had sent her a text message saying that she was urgently needed back, with no explanation. Even without the message, she would have been in a hurry. The information she had gathered was startling, and had given her anxious, excited chills.

* * * *

As she exited the women's restroom, a silver-haired man in his late fifties walked out of the men's room opposite and went directly to the hand sanitizer pump on the wall. He depressed it with his sleeve and carefully rubbed the translucent gel first into his palms and then all over his hands. He walked, still rubbing his hands as he headed toward his wing of the biology department. He always used his sleeve to push open doors, or preferred an automatic push-button door, as was the case upon entering the building containing his office. It was a shining glass and concrete structure, provided for by a generous grant from the Perpendex Corporation three years earlier. He walked by the reception area, and the plump brunette behind the desk, today wearing an up-do, spoke up in a chipper voice, "Good morning Doctor Horatio!" He nodded in acknowledgement and continued on to his office. His name was engraved into a plate on his door, above his title, "Head of Viral Research."

The phone on his desk was ringing as he stepped inside the stark, fluorescent-lit office, large windows providing less light than expected. He walked to the desk and picked up the receiver. "Yes? Thank you, that is excellent news. Do we have the book yet? I see. Continue attempting to locate it and take steps to retrieve it." He slowly hung up, and moved around the desk, sitting in his chair. Horatio frowned, clasping his hands together and forming an upside-down "V" with his index fingers, pressing them to his lips as he thought. He closed his eyes, thanking God for all he had, silently praying, deep in pensive reflection.

Horatio opened his eyes. He rested his elbows on his enormous polished mahogany desk. He looked around his office, over the dry white walls. It was spotless, sterile, perfectly organized, nothing out of place. *The infected woman had to be eliminated.* She was a danger. She could spread the contagion. Even if she didn't, her very presence was a problem. If she had transformed, and others had seen—The Cleaner was doing his work admirably, if belatedly in this case. Samples would be needed, of course, of other specimens, but Rachel was a hazard that had to be liquidated. Unfortunate that we need any of these disgusting samples, but the research is moving too quickly. We need live subjects for tests and further experimentation. The computer models can no longer suffice.

He swiveled the chair around, looking into the distance, over the university campus. The bulletproof glass allowed him the luxury of such an impressive view. Grey clouds were gathering on the horizon, moving rapidly into the city. He did not relish the thought of a rainy commute to the *Ordo Sanctus* chamber where he would sit as its head that night.

Chapter Six

Michaud sat, hunched slightly, one fist against his chin, staring into the grainy glare of the video monitor, using an editing suite to go over the security video recording from the holding cells. He shuttled back and forth over the black and white footage, focusing in on Wellburn, the guard, watching his actions.

The video and sound analysis room was reasonably advanced, giving Michaud or any of the officers the ability to analyze clips digitally, filter out distortion, background noise, or static when necessary. The files Michaud was working from, thankfully, were almost completely clean, and despite the graininess of the footage, the images were clear enough for him to discern details. Around him, two other officers worked, one in a suit and tie, holding on enormous headphones as he squinted and listened intently, the other a chubby uniformed officer carrying away a set of printouts, heading to another office.

Michaud fast-forwarded through the clips, seeing himself entering and leaving, then speeding past the entrance of someone else...a man in a hat? Michaud spun the jog shuttle of the editing deck backwards and rewound the footage, then paused it. He expanded the image, making it grainier, zooming in on the blurry shape, but the angle only showed the back of the man's head. Michaud tried to shuttle forward, but the clip ended suddenly, cutting to black. He frowned, confused.

He switched to another angle, the camera that looked down the row of holding cells. As soon as the hat-wearing man came into view, the file ended, again cutting to black. Michaud frowned, frustrated.

Who the hell are you? Wellburn, if you could only come in for questioning, you disgusting little bridge-troll.

Michaud leaned in, his fist digging into his chin, then moving up to cover his mouth with his knuckles. He switched to the angle that looked down over Wellburn from inside the booth. Michaud could see himself entering, being buzzed in, leaving...Michaud fast-forwarded. The strange figure appeared again. As he entered, Michaud could almost see the features of the man's face...still, partially obscured by the hat's brim. Was he wearing a mask? Or was it just an optical illusion caused by the light bouncing off the inside of the booth? If only he had a magical "enhance" button like in the movies! Michaud went forward a frame, then another...then the clip cut to black. Michaud sighed, rewound, went back a few seconds in the clip. He watched the whole shot, not just the stranger. Wellburn reached down to his panel...and deactivated the security camera, just as the mysterious man approached. The light from the video screen flickered against his face as Michaud squinted.

Wellburn was in on it, whatever was going on, now Michaud was sure of it. Even if he didn't burn Rachel, he seemed to have an accomplice who did. Michaud backed the clip up, finding the best, clearest frame of the man in the hat. Staring into a video monitor this closely and for this long, he almost felt like the cliché his parents would admonish him with, that his eyes would turn square. After a while, the images stopped looking like what they were a recording of and started to become just a conglomeration of millions upon millions of tiny multi-colored blocks. He just needed to find the best collection of blocks that he could use to identify this man in a hat, and send it to a printer.

* * * *

Karen dashed up the stairs and down the hall, her lanyard and identification badge flapping against her chest, and a large folder tucked under her arm. She passed a middle-aged, portly uniformed officer, clearly someone who had eased into a life of desk-work, and thought of how he'd fare running up several flights of stairs. *I might be a researcher but at least I can run this building top to bottom without losing my breath.* Her cycling did come in handy on occasion, although her current level of excitement had probably boosted her adrenalin and fuelled her ascent somewhat. Possibly her smugness toward the out-of-shape desk jockey, too.

Karen breezed in to the office holding her folder full of photocopied pages. Michaud stood, slipping his arms through the loops of his shoulder holster, attaching the clips to his belt. He loaded and checked the chamber on his sidearm, clicking it to "safety", and holstered it with a tiny whoosh. Karen looked from Michaud to the weapon.

"What's going on?" she asked.

"Someone got inside the holding cells and killed the survivor from the crime scene last night. Burned, just like at the house." Michaud explained. He pushed forward the grainy printout of the Cleaner, taken from the holding cell security camera. "Might have been this guy."

"He killed the woman?"

"Yeah, the guard who was on duty's gone. The unit that went by said there's no answer at his house, so I'm heading over to check him out. Definitely a suspect at this point."

"Was that what you needed me back here so fast for?"

"I can't really explain it. There was something happening to her. She was changing...she didn't look human."

Karen swallowed nervously. "Then this won't surprise you too much. The ritual, the one they were trying to enact last night, it's called "*ritus mutatio*." It means "Rite of Transformation." It was designed to create the Army of the Ninth Darkness, the ones who would spread the Shadow over the Earth. The Army would be composed of humans, altered humans, that had been...changed, mutated, into warped and distorted forms of life that represented different classifications and species. Insects, mollusks, fungi, everything that lives or dwells in darkness."

Michaud listened intently. Karen opened the file folder and they both cleared a space amongst the books and papers on the desk. Karen spread her findings out, including photocopied newspaper articles, diagrams from ancient texts and copies of photographs. She pointed to a photo of the *nonagon* emblem, painted on a wall in blood. "Look at this," she said.

"So? It's a photo from the crime scene last night."

Karen was visibly excited, the way an anxious gift-giver was impatient with someone too slowly opening a present. "Wrong." She held up the photo in front of her face, image toward Michaud, as she tapped the bottom right corner of it to indicate the typed date and location. "This photo was taken in 1956 at a crime scene, right here in Toronto. Guess what happened."

Michaud's interest built. He looked at Karen with energetic, apprehensive eyes. "Bodies burned to skeletons, nothing left of anyone, including their victims," he said, half-questioningly.

"Exactly. The Children of *Olog'lahai'kuhul* were thought wiped out until the turn of the twentieth century, when word of their existence began circulating again."

Karen looked to her file folder. Michaud looked at her admiringly, a smile spreading across his face. Karen shuffled through the clippings and photos to illustrate to Michaud as she spoke. She looked back up at him and he cleared his throat, assuming his usual stoicism.

"They resurfaced in 1947 when they killed nine burlesque dancers, but they couldn't finish the ritual. Something about destroying beauty. Anyways, in 1956, this happened," she said, pointing at the older crime scene photo.

Michaud held the photo into the light, staring into it. He put it on his desk, and swung over the magnifying lamp he used to examine photographs. "The burn patterns look almost identical."

"I know," Karen said. "Look." She pointed into the corner of the frame.

Michaud moved the photo over. "A bowl. Another bowl, just like at our crime scene. God, it's like the same thing. The same ritual, and..." he looked up at her, frowning.

"The same guy burning them?" she asked.

Michaud shook his head in disbelief. "He'd have to be in his seventies, or older. I can't imagine...unless this is a family thing. Guy passes it on to his son, and so on...or a group of people, like we thought. Like a competing cult. Or it really is part of the ritual." He stared blankly, frowning harder, thinking. He shook his head, dispelling his frown. "Going to have to look into that further. Weird. What else did you find?"

"Well...after that incident in '56 there was no activity from them again until a few years ago when some writer got a hold of the *Encyclopedia Nefastus*, you remember, the book I mentioned from the thirteenth century. The cult was after him, and he managed to destroy the book, but not before it drove him crazy. That was one of four known copies. That copy was the same one that was found in a town in the south of Italy by Canadian soldiers in World War II, who attacked and killed German soldiers looting the subterranean chamber beneath an old monastery. One of the Canadians smuggled the book back to Canada and either already was, or became one of the cult members involved in the murder of the burlesque dancers in 1947."

"Another copy was in the possession of a family group in a hamlet in the Ural Mountains, but their entire town was razed and burned to the ground, the book with it, during a purge by Stalin in the 1930s. A sect in rural Japan held onto the third copy. They attempted to release a biological agent at a train station in Sendai in the early 90's. They all died in a shoot out with police at their hideout on Mount Iwate. The leader of the sect died by blowing himself and the book up with dynamite. The fourth copy—the original—was in the hands of the *Ordo Sanctus*, the ones who created the book in the first place. Now, it looks like someone else has that copy, or stole it, and they're using it...to build their army."

Michaud clenched a fist against the desk. He frowned , mumbling arithmetic to himself. "...plus nine equals...holy shit. This year. '47, '56...and this year. I think...this year is one in a sequence of nines. They must believe it has some significance, they're trying to make something happen, now. Soon."

"Their ritual. Part of a larger plan, maybe," Karen said.

"Ugh, numerology," Michaud grumbled, shaking his head. Karen knew what Michaud was thinking, having heard his harangues before. It was all too common in their line of work to encounter people who either hated and feared things they didn't understand or chose to make them objects of cult-like worship. So easy to do with nearly any scientific discipline— math, astronomy, medicine, to name a few. Michaud cursed under his breath. As an investigator he needed to try to understand things that were obscure, but the attitude of coming up with a phony science in place of the hard work of real science frustrated him.

Karen smirked. "Gosh, maybe we should call in that psychic, eh, Detective? Give us some unseen insights." She giggled.

Michaud sighed, smiling back. "Why must you torment me, Wendleton?"

Karen rolled her eyes. "Okay, Mister Grumpy-pants. They think it has importance, and they might act on it. We have to assume and act as though it has real significance because to them, it does."

"Of course," he sighed. "That writer you mentioned, is he still around?"

She slumped in her chair, holding a hand to her forehead. "I feel faint..."

"Are you all right?" Michaud asked, concerned.

"I see...I see a vision," Karen said melodramatically. "The writer...he wants you to...go away...and give Karen the day off..."

Michaud relaxed, chuckled, and looked at his assistant with one eyebrow raised. "Seriously though."

She returned to her normal sitting pose, dropping the comedy act. "I'll have to do some digging. You want to talk to him?"

"Might help. Doubt I'll be able to speak to him in person though." His phone buzzed in his pocket. He huffed and pulled it out. A text message from an unknown blocked number, simply saying "Grenadier Pond East, thirty minutes."

He put his phone away, took a deep breath, and turned to Karen.

"I've got a meeting. I know I told you that I'd go with Simons to Wellburn's house, but this is more important. You can go instead of me. Simons should have a warrant in order. Take a pair of uniforms just to be safe. They'll go in with Simons and secure the place. If Wellburn's not there, look through everything. Find out who he's with, and what the hell is going on. If you can get me any bio information on Rachel Atwater that'd be great too, school records, renter info, bills, where she grew up, whatever." Michaud slipped on his jacket. "If you get a minute, try to find businesses, clubs, whatever, in town that use the number nine a lot, in names, addresses, phone numbers."

He moved toward the door, slipping the printout of the Cleaner into his inside pocket. "I want something to piece this whole mess together," he said as he walked out.

Chapter Seven

Michaud stood looking at the reflection of sunlight cast in the water's surface. The parting clouds had slowly revealed the sun as Michaud drove to High Park, the rain easing off until it had stopped. Grenadier Pond was far enough from the road that it felt isolated, but not so far that the noise of speeding vehicles wasn't audible, especially with the rain-slicked roads. The tires racing by sounded like breath blown through teeth in imitation of a snake's hiss.

Michaud took a deep breath, trying to take in fresher air than he was afforded downtown. Just for a moment he could picture himself in Haiti standing on a beach during the trip he took after his parents died. He grasped at the memory of the smell of ocean air. *Hard to believe that was more than twenty years ago now.*

High Park took up a large area, but there were so many amenities in it—playgrounds, a restaurant, a pool, tennis courts, little league fields, a zoo—that it didn't really feel like getting away from the city. Michaud had gone hiking on the west coast of Canada multiple times, and remembered the feeling of standing on top of a mountain. The silence, save for the wind, a bird, and insects buzzing. *Now that was nature.* In the city he preferred the Toronto Islands. Once an escape from the crowds of families and summer tourists could be effected, it was much more relaxing. *High Park's all right. More for city people though.*

A pair of college-age cyclists, smiling to one another and pointing at birds chirping in the trees above, awkwardly and narrowly missed a young woman walking her tiny fluff ball dog. They blurted curses to no one in particular then offered mild apologies to the woman before moving on. A group of women in painted-on yoga pants strutted by, speed-walking. Michaud caught himself staring and averted his eyes, then chuckled to himself.

He took off his sunglasses and looked at his watch. This could be little more than a prank. A waste of his time when he could be out furthering his investigation. He probably should have gone with Simons to Wellburn's place. Still, the caller knew his personal number. If it was the same man who had called him in the stairwell, he knew more than he should have about what was going on. He might even be a suspect.

"I'm sorry if I kept you waiting, Detective. Traffic was terrible," a voice from behind him said. Michaud turned, keeping a hand on his holster, to see a man of about fifty, wearing a nondescript charcoal-grey suit and plain brown tie. He held a black umbrella in one hand against the ground like a cane.

The gravelly voice was immediately recognizable as the same that had called him and not given a name. The man stood at a respectful distance of a few meters, far enough that a weapon could be drawn if danger were imminent. He was wearing sunglasses, his hair neck-length but combed back, like a 1980's businessman. Wrinkles creased his face around the eyes and mouth, with slight jowls hanging down and a blandly average middle-aged body type. His posture was stern, almost statuesque, as he drew himself up.

Michaud said nothing, skeptical of the stranger, who returned the look of wariness.

"You *are* detective Benoit Michaud. I recognize you from your departmental profile."

"Who are you?" Michaud asked, looking at him, squinting slightly.

The man hesitated. His calm professional exterior betrayed a hint of worry, but seemed to have assessed Michaud and was no longer on the defensive. "I can't tell you that. I'm risking my life just coming here, but it's important that I speak to you without the possibility of being monitored."

"What can I call you then? Bob?"

The man began walking slowly along the edge of the pond, and Michaud followed beside him. "I'm just someone with information. An informant."

Michaud's skepticism grew, bordering on hostility. The man sounded like a conspiracy theorist. "You said you had information on the *Ordo Sanctus*. I'd like to know how you think this will help my case."

"They've gone by many names—The Holy Order of the Soldiers of Christendom, the Keepers of the Forbidden Knowledge, and now it's just *Ordo Sanctus*—'The Sacred Order.'"

"What do you mean, 'now?'"

The Informant stopped walking and turned to Michaud. He looked around, regarding for a moment a passing young mother pushing her baby in a stroller, dachshund attached by a leash to one of the handles, and a bright orange balloon tied to the other. The Informant waited for them to pass, then spoke softly, "The cult is just a sideshow. They're small potatoes compared to what you're on to. The *Ordo Sanctus* is a vast network of men at the highest levels of government, business and the military who've been at war with the Children of *Olog'lahai'kuhul*—among others—for centuries. They have a secret, private mercenary force in the tens of thousands on call, ready to be mobilized at the first order. They've kept the cult from completing the final rituals for decades, but they haven't succeeded in wiping them out completely." He leaned in closer. "The *Ordo Sanctus* is trying to enact something—something horrible. I don't know exactly what yet. But it's big. Huge."

"How big? Are we talking bombings? Terrorist actions?"

"You're not thinking big enough. This isn't limited to this city. It's global. They have members and bases in Washington, Moscow, London, Rome, among others. Tactical and training facilities from North Carolina to Eastern Washington on this continent to bases in the Philippines, Portugal, everywhere. But it's here, now, that they believe their final battle will occur. The people they have in this city are enacting the plan."

Michaud was incredulous. "What people? Who? Who's a part of this organization?"

"People you probably know. Men in your own department."

"Can you give me a name?"

Michaud thought of Wellburn. *Were there more? Who in the command structure might be tied into this? If any of this was even legitimate information.*

"I can't give you anything that will lead directly back to me. But you're on the right track. Just keep looking where you're looking and you'll get there." He pulled out a pack of "Good Catch" brand "therapeutic" cigarettes and held them out for Michaud.

"I don't smoke anymore."

"Take them, you'll need them." The Informant pushed his hand out again.

Michaud looked at the pack, which featured a smiling man

festooned in fishing gear hauling in a huge fish off the shore of a lake. He reluctantly took them and stuffed the package in his inner jacket pocket. "The *Ordo Sanctus*...are they the ones burning the bodies?"

The Informant looked at Michaud a moment. His thoughts were well-guarded. Michaud could usually appraise a person's mood easily, not just because he was a detective, but because it also came very naturally to him. This man seemed to have considerable experience giving nothing away and knowing how to avoid being "read" by an outsider.

"I can't tell you anything more. I have to go or I'll be missed soon," he said.

Michaud pulled the folded printout from his jacket and held it out. "Is it this guy? Who is he?" The Informant looked at it, looked back at Michaud. His lower eyelid twitched, almost imperceptibly. Michaud knew he had something. "That's it, isn't it? What are they using? How are they doing it? I'm sitting on four bodies right now, and for all I know there could be more. If you have any information, I need it."

"There'll be more. A lot more."

"What's that supposed to mean?"

The Informant started walking away, but turned to walk backwards. "Just one piece of advice, take a Geiger counter with you." He turned back and walked briskly toward the nearest path, and was gone within seconds.

Michaud watched him leave, feeling now more confused than ever. All the answers he heard from this man only left bigger questions. Michaud stood contemplating, then walked back to the parking lot he had left his car in, thinking as he went.

His phone buzzed, signaling a call. He pulled it out and answered, "Michaud."

"Hey boss, it's Karen. I'm at the guard's house with Simons."

"And?"

"There's nothing here."

"You didn't find anything?"

* * * *

Karen stood in an empty room devoid of decoration or furnishing, the sun streaming in through the large bay windows, casting bright squares on the hardwood floors. "No, I mean there's nothing here. No furniture, nothing. The place is cleaned out. We just found some mail in the mailbox that came today. Looks like a pay stub from a company called Perpendex Pharmaceuticals." Simons and the uniformed officers opened and closed closet doors, peered in cupboards that were entirely bare. It was a well-renovated early-20th century apartment, the style graciously maintained rather than obliterated by an overzealous landlord, and looked for all purposes ready to be moved into. A few torn scraps of packing paper littered the floor.

"All right, see if you can figure out what the hell he was doing for them. It might just be a night job, moonlighting to pay off debt, but it's all we've got on him right now, other than his departmental profile, which isn't a lot to go on. Any more information on Rachel?"

"Um, yeah..." Karen looked at her phone and scrolled through her email messages, then returned it to her ear to speak. "According to everything I could dig up on her she's originally from Brampton, her parents both died when she was six in an auto accident. Grew up in a foster home, ran away, had some mild run-ins with the law..."

"Mild?" Michaud asked.

"Yeah, the usual: vandalism, shoplifting, pot possession, nothing huge."

"All right, what else?"

"Well, after she got her head straightened out, she finished high school, went to university in Guelph for biology. Wasn't really involved in much outside of schoolwork, no big social activities. Oh, she was a teenage mother. Had her kid, Thomas, just six years ago when she was seventeen. I guess that coincides with right after her running away."

"We'll want to look more into what she was doing and who she was with. Hopefully the kid can give us something, knows his father if we're lucky. How about Rachel's address? Anything?" Michaud asked.

"It's a place in the Junction. Near Dundas and Keele. The lab pieced together her driver's license, looks like it was chewed up at the crime scene."

"In a paper shredder? Was it in little pieces?"

"No, literally chewed up. As in, someone put it in their mouth, ground it up and spat it out. Anyways, her full name is

Rachel Atwater. I'll text you the street number now. Oh, and you'll love this. Dental records came in for one of the burned bodies at the crime scene—same address as Rachel."

"How about dental records for the tied-up body at the scene?"

"Yeah," Karen sighed. "I was hoping it wasn't her, but it looks like the last burned body was Teresa Smalls, the high school girl who went missing last week in Etobicoke. And the other male body...it was the guy she was seeing, Patrick Garneau. Guessing he and the others grabbed her once she trusted him."

* * * *

"Ugh," Michaud shuddered. He sighed, standing at his car door, about to get in. "Okay. We'll check out the Atwater place later on. I want you to meet me back at the station so we can interview the Atwater kid. What was his name?"

"Thomas."

"Great. Meet me there soon. Bye." Michaud deactivated the phone and slipped it in his pocket as he sat. He looked out his window, thinking a moment, taking in the silence afforded by both the park and the interior of his vehicle. The Atwater boy. Kid lost his mom and he might not even know it yet. *Do I have to be the one to tell him?* Michaud remembered what it was like when a police officer told him his own parents had been killed. *Kid's younger than I was when it happened. A lot younger.* He sighed. After a few seconds, he reached over and clipped on his seatbelt, then drove out.

* * * *

Thomas sat in the sixth floor day-care room revving a wooden truck back and forth across the carpeted floor. Out the window, the city was visible, and the room was filled with daylight. He had been given new clothes to wear, a set of simple corduroy overalls and a plain white T-shirt, since the ones he was found in were dirty. His plain brown bowl cut was tucked underneath a slightly ill-fitting purple Raptors cap, the logo of a basketball with a dinosaur footprint embroidered on the front. Thomas had made the seemingly odd choice to play with the toy truck rather than go for the multitude of available video game systems in the other corner of the room. His teeth were against his lower lip as he made vrooming engine noises, moving the toy along an imaginary street made out of blocks and cardboard boxes.

Michaud and Karen stood by the large windows to the hall-way, watching him from outside the room. Beside them was the departmental counselor who dealt with young children whose parents were injured or killed. She was short, plump, and had drab mousy-brown shoulder-length hair. She looked more like a schoolteacher than a police department associate, which seemed appropriate for her job.

"He hasn't shown any of the signs most kids show when they find out a parent has died. It's as if he already knew it would happen, or at least accepted it completely. I don't think he's in denial, or convincing himself that I'm lying either," she explained.

Michaud nodded and nervously rubbed the back of his neck. He felt guilt for his relief that he wouldn't have to tell the kid. He turned to Karen.

She looked back at him. "In here?" she asked.

"Definitely. Unless we want him to pee his pants in the in-terrogation room," Michaud replied.

"Would you like me to do most of the talking? I think I'm a bit less imposing than you," Karen asked.

"Sure. I think you know what we're looking for."

The counselor gestured toward the door. They walked in, Karen leading the way. Michaud pulled up a chair and Karen squatted next to Thomas while the counselor looked on. Michaud drew out his recorder and switched it on.

"Hi Thomas, my name's Karen. This is my friend Benoit. Do you go by Tommy, or Tom, or Thomas?"

"Thomas," he stated flatly, focused on his truck. His face was hidden beneath the purple brim of his cap, the basketball logo pointed up at them.

"Okay, we'd like to talk with you for a bit," Karen said.

"Sure." He continued to maneuver the truck back and forth.

"We were hoping you could tell us a bit about your mom..."

"She's dead," he said without looking up.

Karen looked back at Michaud, who raised his eyebrows in modest surprise. Michaud looked to Thomas. "Can you maybe tell us a bit about your dad? Or your mom's friends? We think she might have had some bad friends," he said.

Thomas stopped moving the truck. "Mom said one of the guys we lived with was my dad. I dunno. I didn't like that house. It was real dirty." He started moving the truck back and forth again, smashing it into the blocks. "Pow! Ksssh!"

"Is this the house on..." Karen unfolded a piece of paper and looked at it. "Pacific Avenue?"

"Mm-hmm," Thomas nodded.

"Was your dad with you the night we found you in that basement?" Karen asked.

Thomas sighed and stopped the truck. Karen looked at Michaud. Thomas stayed silent.

Michaud moved off his chair and sat cross-legged in front of the tiny toy street. "Thomas. It's okay. You can talk to us about it. We want to help you."

Thomas sat motionless, his eyes down. His hands fiddled with the truck.

"You know, I had a truck like that when I was your age. Before I lost my mom and dad," Michaud offered.

Thomas looked up, his eyes meeting Michaud's. He turned to look at Karen, who nodded.

Michaud continued, "I lost my mom and then my dad. It hurt. It hurt a lot. But my uncle took care of me. It'll be okay. It doesn't seem like it now, but it will be."

Thomas looked back at Michaud.

"Was your dad there that night?," Michaud asked.

Thomas sighed again. "Yeah...he was doing that thing with all the loud talking and painting and stuff."

Karen and Michaud looked at each other.

"Can you tell us his name?" Michaud said.

"I think my mom called him Pat. I guess his name was Pat. I never called him anything, he wasn't really like a dad. He was a jerk."

Michaud looked at Karen, then spoke softly. "Patrick Garneau?"

Karen studied Thomas. "Did anyone tell you..."

"Yeah, I know he's dead too. They told me it would happen."

"They? You mean your mom's friends?" Karen asked.

"Yeah, all the others in the house, and everybody who would come over, and at the clubhouse too. I never went there, but they talked about it a lot. All they did was practice their loud talking and reading old books and painting and waving their arms a bunch. And stuff in the basement, I never went down there, it stunk."

"What's the clubhouse?" Michaud asked.

"I don't know. They just said it a lot."

Karen looked at Michaud again, who shrugged. She turned back to Thomas. "Do you remember what they talked about? The things they wanted to do?"

"Sometimes. Sometimes they didn't talk English, I don't know what it was. Sometimes when they talked about the clubhouse and practicing and stuff they forgot I was there. I got really hungry a lot." He looked down again as he said this. "But they talked all the time about the new world and all the changes. Sometimes Mom would take me and try to make me feel better and said things would be better and we'd all have lots of food and have a porpoise."

Michaud smiled inadvertently at the mispronunciation.

"A...purpose?" Karen offered.

"Yeah, a purpose," Thomas enunciated.

Karen looked at Michaud, who nodded. "Thank you, Thomas. You've been very helpful," she said.

"Thanks Thomas," Michaud said with a broad smile as he switched off his digital recorder.

Thomas tried to force a smile, but it wouldn't come. He went back to revving the truck across the carpet as they walked out. The counselor stayed behind while Michaud and Karen chatted at the door.

"Ideal home environment," Michaud muttered sarcastically. He shook his head, his eyes focused on nothing in particular as he looked past Karen. *To lose parents, even useless ones like that...* "I told him it'll get better, but for him, I don't know." *They all eventually die. Never get too close.*

"Everything okay in there?" Karen asked, searching for his gaze.

Michaud met it. "Just brings back bad memories is all."

"Your parents? How old were you?"

"Fourteen. I guess it was a bit easier to deal with. I could explain it to myself, try to make sense of it. Store owner shot down for a few bucks. Tell myself that studying law and then becoming a cop would help. I don't know how Thomas'll work it out. Wouldn't really help if I just said, 'get used to it kid, everyone you know will be dead someday'."

"You don't want to warp him."

"Pretty sure we're too late for that."

"So what do you think about the mother?"

"My guess? The cult offered Rachel something she never had, a family and a place to belong to. She lost her parents when she was young. Gave her a sense of meaning that she lacked for her entire life. Maybe they wanted her because of Thomas too, I don't know. But getting young people who've had a rough life and need a place that accepts them completely is a pretty standard recruiting tool for cults, ideologies, you name it."

"What do you think about this clubhouse he mentioned?"

"Definitely going to want to find it. Speaking of, did you have a chance to dig up any places in town that use the 'nine' thing conspicuously?"

"Just cursory, you've kept me pretty busy. Uh..." She reached into her pocket. Pulling out a note pad, she flipped through it until she found her most recent page of scribbled information. "Lots of ninety-nine cent discount stores, but that's doubtful." She looked at him with a sarcastic smirk. "Nine Times Nine, the math-themed bar in the Distillery District. Dressed To The Nines Social Club over past Corso Italia. Um...Niners, bar down by Front Street. Club Sixty-Nine..." She smiled at Michaud with one corner of her mouth.

He chuckled in response. "All possibilities, except that last one. Hopefully there's something, an address, whatever, at Rachel's place."

"This afternoon?" Karen asked.

"Yeah, get Simons, head over there. Get any rental info on the place too, tenants, what have you."

"Don't need a warrant?"

"Well, Rachel's dead, two of the dead guys from the basement had the same address you said, which means they were probably roommates. If anyone else lives there they'll want to know their roommates are dead, or else they might be dead themselves, or the guy who killed the others might be after them, putting them in danger. I'd call all that reasonable grounds for entry."

"What about you?"

"I have someone else I need to talk to before I meet you there."

Chapter Eight

Michaud strode across a busy street as pedestrians and cyclists wove around each other in the chaotic milieu that was Kensington Market. Skateboarders rolled by in long shorts and ballcaps, hippies doused in patchouli oil and dreadlocked Rastafarians wandered in and out of the hemp café. Street kids and punks walked their mangy dogs—the underground exposed to the open air. Delivery trucks and vans sat, half up on curbs, as overall-clad workers hauled crates of fresh fish, or work boots, or sunglasses. People tended to wander through the streets pell-mell. Murals were spray-painted up on walls, and the mish-mashed spectrum of colors the shops represented made the area look as though a gigantic scrapbook had exploded in the air and spread designs at random.

Michaud walked past a health food store, then turned right down an alley. Hanging from an ornate metal bracket, a small wooden sign reading "Felix's Rare Books and Sundries" swayed slightly in a light post-rain breeze. The sign was at the end of the graffiti-laden alley sandwiched between a tattoo parlor and a used clothing shop.

Too long since I've been back here. His uncle's was a store that served a select clientele and most of them sought it out specifically, despite the obscure location.

Michaud quietly opened the front door, grabbing the door chime to prevent it from ringing. He slipped in, staying out of sight. He could hear a shuffling of paper, the clink of jars and bottles. Michaud looked up at the shelves of the shop. They were lined with dusty tomes and antique books of varying size, shape and vintage, with a smaller area dedicated to newer publications.

Hanging in one section were bundles of dried herbs with tiny paper labels. On another shelf behind the counter were large glass jars containing preserved specimens of what appeared to be marine life, unidentifiable invertebrates, and bloated, gigantic dragonflies. Lit from above, the orange of the liquid within glowed warmly. It was cozy, comforting.

Nostalgia for his younger years crept up on him, for the hours spent here with his uncle Felix.

Michaud looked around the corner of a shelf and saw him, a Haitian-Canadian man of about sixty-five with short grey hair who stood sorting through dozens of vials of oddly-colored liquids, powders and dried herbs. He had put aside the cardboard boxes his most recent shipment had come in, and was attempting to categorize and place on the shelves his newest acquisitions. He had everything lined up on his main glass counter organized by type and by name, alphabetically. *Runs in the family.*

The sleeves of his shirt were rolled up, and he had gold-rimmed spectacles sitting on the end of his nose. His breast pocket was full of tiny metal instruments, just visible over the edge of his black apron, giving him the aspect of a combination watchmaker and apothecary. Felix stopped, and looked at himself in the mirror hung behind the counter. A long scar running from his left temple to his chin was a permanent reminder of his past. Michaud realized he was also visible in the mirror over his uncle's shoulder. Felix turned.

I've been spotted! Michaud grinned.

"Benoit!" Felix nearly shouted as he moved around the counter. "You haven't been stopping by to visit much lately." Felix embraced and hugged Michaud heartily, then held him out at arm's length, holding Michaud's shoulders. "I never get to see you," he admonished, smiling. His French-Haitian accent was markedly more pronounced than Michaud's.

"I know, I'm sorry Uncle Felix. Work's been keeping me busy. That's actually why I've come. I was hoping you might know some things I'm trying to find out about an organization. Two organizations."

"Well, what are you looking for? I'll help you however I can," he replied, still smiling.

Michaud hesitated a moment.

"The...Children of *Olog'lahai'kuhul,* and the *Ordo Sanctus*...do you know anything about them?"

Felix's smile faded, his facial muscles going slack, then forming into a concerned frown. "What is this about, Benoit?"

"Last night, there were three murders. The bodies were burned, nothing left but skeletons. It looks like they enacted a ritual—they killed someone and then were killed themselves by someone else, we don't know who. The killer probably killed one of the two survivors this morning. The woman I'm working with thinks the ritual was the "*ritus mutatio*"."

Felix looked fearful, lost in thought. He seemed to turn inward, searching for information, going over deeply buried memories.

"What is it? Who are these people?" Michaud asked.

Felix held up a finger indicating "just a moment" before walking quickly to a set of shelves, scanning along until he found a massive volume as large as a pair of phone books, bound in exquisite leather, with hand carved metal titling, The *Compendium Pandaemonium*. He pulled it off, blew some dust from the top, and began flipping through it on his way to the counter. Felix laid the book down, open to a page on the *Ordo Sanctus*. The information was sparse, with only a few small illustrations of medieval weaponry and brutal torture devices. Felix adjusted his spectacles and turned to Michaud.

"The *Ordo Sanctus* has been hunting the Ninth Darkness for 800 years. They were created by a knight in the thirteenth century to crush the Children. They try to kill them all, but they can't. The Children want to build their army, making themselves into the life from another world, to change the Earth. Make everyone like them, killers and monsters, no conscience, no humanity. The *Ordo Sanctus* has grown tired of the holy war they wage...the *Ordo Sanctus* are madmen, who want to cleanse the world, wipe us all out and start over." He looked away, past Michaud, lost far off in memory of some horrible past event he was reminded of. His voice became wistful, and he nodded slightly as he spoke. "I know...I know..."

"Uncle?" Michaud ventured.

"We all lose people we love," Felix said. He seemed distant.

Michaud looked at his uncle. The scar, he knew, was from what "Papa Doc" Duvalier's *Tonton Macoutes* thugs had done to him for being suspected as a union organizer. Michaud had heard the stories in the shop during his teens, after his parents were killed. *Is that where you are now, Uncle? Haiti?*

Felix sighed, and refocused his eyes on Michaud. "I'm...I'm sorry Benoit. You should get back to work. I can't help you much. If any new books with more information come in, I'll contact you."

Michaud frowned, looking slightly sideways at his uncle,

clearly concerned. "All right Uncle, please give me a call and let me know if you think of anything that might help."

"I don't know if *I* can help. Maybe only God can help you now," Felix said somberly.

Michaud smiled limply, hugged Felix and turned to leave. As he opened the door, Felix called out to him.

"Stay out of trouble!"

Michaud left, wandering the maze-like streets of the market toward his car parked on Spadina, avoiding the path of a badly sunburned, wild-eyed man singing to himself on a bicycle that looked as though a birthday party had exploded all over it. Despite the aggressively cheerful display, Michaud dwelled on the deaths of his own parents. Felix's melancholy had again brought the old memories to the surface. How Michaud had been taken care of by his uncle after the robbery and murders.

This whole case is depressing.

Chapter Nine

Michaud pulled up and parked his car. Karen and Simons both stood wearing protective vests in front of Rachel Atwater's address, a large nineteenth century Victorian home. It was tucked away on a side street just north of Dundas West, in a part of town that had recently gentrified toward young middle-class family habitation. Further down the block, a playground had been constructed. A swath of train tracks cut the neighborhood off from the industrial area to the north just over the playground's fence, and attested to the area's original character. Some of the industrial buildings nearby had been converted to studios and lofts, and on this side of the train tracks, one lone warehouse remained. It looked like a 1930's movie studio office perfectly preserved, including the jailyard-style lunch area visible through barred gates.

The area north of High Park in general was very pleasant, tree-lined and almost picturesque, but none of these adjectives described the house the group stood in front of. While the rest of the neighborhood was relatively sunny in the late afternoon light, this house and its yard looked as though the color had been sapped out. The formerly white paint had peeled and cracked like the skin falling from a desiccated corpse, leaving the house grey and drab. The picket fence was rotting into softness, with slats hanging flaccidly from rusted nails.

Its overgrown yard was choked with diseased-looking weeds all swollen and bloated, growing at distorted asymmetrical angles that caused pangs of disturbance among observers. Everything looked as if it had been grimed with a foul slick of oil.

The windows of the building, already encrusted with years of accumulated soot and dust, appeared to be covered from the inside with makeshift shades made from a motley collection of soiled blankets and paint-spattered drop-cloths. Michaud felt a twinge in his stomach. He saw no activity or movement, but the very appearance of the place had unsettled him.

Michaud closed the door of his vehicle and caught Karen and Simons mid-conversation.

"I was in the department gym, I mean I have a membership. I was using one of the machines, and the guy tries to chat with me. Asks me about my tattoos, and when I said I was busy, he just stands there for two or three minutes not saying anything, creeping me out," Karen said.

"Seriously? What's wrong with this guy?" Simons asked, frowning.

Karen shook her head. "Not at *all* surprised if it turns out he was involved in whatever happened to that Rachel girl. Guy was a shitbag."

"Who are you two talking about?" Michaud asked.

"That weirdo Wellburn. Guy has a reputation. Beyond the, you know, skipping town and being wanted for questioning thing," Karen answered.

"Oh, I know," Michaud said. He walked toward the trunk and gestured to Karen and Simons, prompting them to follow. "How many tenants here?" he asked. He opened the trunk and pulled out a Kevlar vest, undoing the Velcro straps up the sides.

"As far as we can make out, she had three roommates, two of whom were the guys burned in that basement yesterday," Karen replied, her tone now serious, businesslike.

Michaud slipped the vest over his head, tightening and slapping the Velcro straps closed. "So, only one resident still alive that we know of, could be others though." He drew out two large metal police flashlights, one for himself and another which he handed to Karen. Simons checked his sidearm and holstered it. Michaud looked at both of them. "Simons, I want you at the back door. I'll take the front. Turn on your radio. Karen, you're with me."

Karen cleared her throat conspicuously. "You know I don't have a gun, right boss?"

He shook his head, tried to sound reassuring. "It's just a routine check. We just want to talk with these people, if there's even anyone here. If it gets hot, just get out as quickly as you can. You want to be police someday, Wendleton? Well, here you go."

"I guess this flashlight doubles as a club..."

"That's the spirit," Michaud said, smiling broadly. "Don't worry. If it looks bad, you can back right out."

"You'll come to my rescue, won't you, oh Knight in Kevlar body armor?" Karen said, fluttering her eyes and clasping her hands together. Simons stifled a chuckle.

Michaud sighed through his nose, looking at her with half-closed eyes. "There's just no hope for this one. Might need a doctor to issue a Form One," Michaud said, referring to a psychiatric assessment.

Karen scoffed and lightly tapped his arm with her flashlight. Michaud responded with a rattle of his handcuffs.

The attempts at levity didn't fully break the unease imparted by the building. "Christ, I hope this isn't like that fucking basement," Simons muttered.

"What, filled with dead bodies?" Karen asked, still smirking. "I'm sure it's much worse than that."

Michaud checked the chamber of his sidearm, made sure the safety was on, and slid it into his shoulder holster. He spoke as though giving an order. "Hope the worst thing we find is some moldy garbage."

Simons forced a smile, nodded and moved toward the back of the building. A sound of weed-stalks breaking and crushing under foot followed him as he waded through the tangled plants along the side of the house. Karen trailed behind as Michaud walked toward the front door.

"Find anything out about Wellburn and that company?" Michaud asked.

"Nothing new. Just that he worked for them as security." Karen was looking down at the front walk, or what remained of it. Vile weeds crept up through its broken remnants. Michaud moved carefully onto the porch, avoiding the crumbling steps. Weeks' worth of trash was littered about, shoved into the corners to clear a way in and out of the front door. Karen stood on her tiptoes, trying to peer through a space between sheets covering the inside of one of the front windows. She raised a hand and rubbed at the layers of dirt with her sleeve.

"See anything?" Michaud asked.

"Mmm...not really. Just looks like old furniture in there."

Michaud stood at the door and raised a fist to knock. With the first rap of his knuckles against the flaking paint the door pushed inwards—it was already ajar. Michaud and Karen looked at each other. Michaud drew his sidearm slowly, holding it down toward the ground with one hand as he used his other to speak into his radio. "Simons. The front door's open. We're moving in."

Michaud first peeked in, then pushed through with his shoulder. The hinges whined as the door opened. He held his flashlight up, piercing the musty darkness. The beam of light dueled with shafts of waning sunlight penetrating the spaces between the makeshift curtains taped up to and tacked hastily around the windows. The main entrance area was surprisingly large. The ceiling rose to nearly the height of the house itself, with stairs on the left leading to a visible upstairs landing. A dust-covered chandelier looked as though it hadn't been cleaned in decades. Opposite them and the front door was a short hall that appeared to lead to a kitchen, and beyond that, a back door. To their right was what must have been the living room Karen had peered into. Its few articles of furniture were filthy and mildewed. Foul black mold crept up the walls. Michaud's nostrils twitched as he sniffed the pungent reek of rot hanging overhead in the stuffy air. A fly's lazy buzzing swayed back and forth.

Karen used her flashlight to look up the staircase on the left. Michaud could see the beam shaking in the dusty air. He raised a reassuring hand to her shoulder and she jumped, then turned to him, exhaling. Michaud looked her in the eyes, nodding slightly. Her shaking ceased. They turned to the kitchen's back door. Simons had entered and stood silhouetted in the outside light, one hand raised to them. Michaud returned the wave, pointing Simons toward another side room directly to the right of the stairs.

Michaud and Karen began walking up the rickety staircase, each step creaking pitifully. Michaud looked back toward Simons, who scanned a bedroom with his flashlight, highlighting piles of mildew-covered, sweat-stained laundry. A tap on his shoulder brought Michaud's attention back, and he turned to look at Karen. She was looking at the floor, and he followed her gaze down. She had directed her flashlight beam onto the stairs. Evenly spaced shapes formed in a bright blue dust, as though asymmetrical footprints left by an inhuman set of feet, leading either up or down the stairs.

Karen frowned. "What is that stuff?"

Michaud shook his head slowly, baffled. They continued up the stairs, stepping around the shapes, Michaud leading the way. They moved past another small bedroom much like the one downstairs, grubby mildewed laundry scattered about. Amongst the refuse lay a cardboard box piled high with small arms and grenades. Michaud pointed it out to Karen. They kept moving, slowly walking along toward a door at the end of the landing. It was slightly ajar, pink light bleeding out, and the shapes of blue dust ended at it. Michaud stopped, smelling the air. He winced, the foulness of it catching him off guard. Karen wrinkled her nose in disgust. Behind the door, something dripped quietly into liquid.

Michaud reached the door and looked back at Karen. He touched the door lightly, pushing it open at arm's length, craning his neck around to look inside. It was a bathroom, and the dripping sound grew louder as the door opened. The walls were covered in thick deposits of black fungal growths spreading out cancerously across the tiles. Moisture had eroded the paint on the counter and cabinets, which bubbled with interior rot. The large exterior window opposite the door where Michaud stood was, like the others downstairs, covered over. Sunlight pierced through multiple holes and the spaces around the edges of a ratty red blanket. The red of the blanket, backlit by the setting sun, gave the room the sickly pink hue. The shapes of blue dust ended at the claw-foot tub, culminating in a larger circle half a meter across.

Michaud instinctively lifted his tie to cover his mouth at the overpowering stench. Karen followed suit with a handkerchief. Beside the circle of blue dust lay a pile of torn and shredded clothing. A shirt from a courier company and brown pants, both splattered with dried, crusty blood. Around the large tub was a stained and scum-covered shower curtain, torn in spots, with several of the rings that should have held it in place on the curtain rod instead pulled off and scattered about the room. The curtain had streaks of thick brown ooze along the inside, stretching chaotically across the length of it, five in a row...like marks from human fingers. The dripping was louder—something inside the tub.

Michaud pushed his flashlight forward and parted the curtain with it, peering in. To his revulsion, what lay before him was a partially dissolved skeleton, floating in a viscous, pinkish-brown slime that nearly filled the tub. Moisture within the room had condensed on the ceiling and was dripping into the muck, the sound they had heard earlier.

Michaud choked as he spoke, "What the hell?"

Karen coughed and turned away. "Oh my God..."

Michaud cleared his throat, daring to look more closely. The beam from his flashlight penetrated only a few centimeters into the thick liquid, showing only more bones and streams of melted flesh. He turned to Karen as he slipped on a pair of nitrile gloves. "You got a pen?"

Karen blinked hard and regained her composure. She drew out a ballpoint pen from her pocket and handed it to him, although her eyes were fixated on the horrific sight spread out before them. Michaud carefully bent toward the tub.

"What are you doing?" Karen asked. "You should wait until the forensic team is here and...hey!"

Michaud dipped the end of the pen in, then held it between his fingertips. He carefully slipped the glove off his hand, up and over the pen, and then did the same with the other glove, essentially double-bagging a sample of the material.

"Sure, just take my pen. I didn't need it anyways," Karen said, rolling her eyes. She stepped back out of the room, as did Michaud, who moved to the railing on the landing.

"Simons! We've got a body up here. Or what's left of one," Michaud shouted, reaching for his radio. He switched channels. "Dispatch, this is Detective Michaud at the Rachel Atwater residence. We've found a body on the premises, badly decomposed, we need Forensic Identification Services in here immediately, and there's evidence we need catalogued and bagged." The dispatcher answered with a garbled response of acknowledgment, and Michaud slipped the radio back on his belt.

Simons came bounding up the creaking staircase, holding a piece of paper in a gloved hand. "Downstairs, school notebook with Teresa Smalls' name on it. And Patrick Garneau's health card. They were here. And..." he held up the scrap of paper "found this in the bedroom."

Michaud donned another pair of gloves, and took the sheet.

Simons' words were scattered. "The date, with numbers from all...looks like a timetable, nothing but numbers, but I think that's yesterday's date in the middle there," he pointed at the middle of the sheet, then stopped, looking up. "Jesus, what is that smell?"

"Take a look if you want," Michaud said grimly. "But try not to throw up. Don't want to wreck the evidence." Simons stepped to the bathroom while Michaud looked over the cryptic paper. The letterhead immediately caught his attention: *Dressed To The Nines Social Club.* "Well, I'll be damned," he muttered.

"What is it?" Karen asked, looking at the sheet.

"Looks like the clubhouse Thomas told us about." Michaud pointed at the letterhead and symbol. "Number nine?"

"Quoting the *White Album*?"

"Very funny."

Simons stepped backwards out of the bathroom, holding his tie over his mouth as he coughed. "Holy fuck, that's nasty. Smells even worse than what's downstairs."

"You mean the rotting laundry?" Karen asked.

"No, something coming from the basement. I didn't want to go down there by myself."

"I'll head down with you," Michaud said, pulling out the glove-bagged pen. "Karen, can you get this analyzed? We should get it to the lab."

"Can I stay on site?" she replied. "This place is dead, pretty much literally. I'd rather stay behind with you and catalogue evidence."

Michaud contemplated. "Probably should've had you wait outside to begin with, Miss Unarmed Civilian."

"I don't think whatever's dead down in the cellar is going to make having a weapon worthwhile. You need me here Boss. I can take a first-hand account of what I've seen and figure out all the angles days before the forensics unit can get it to you."

Michaud frowned. "All right. Simons?"

Simons smiled, "You got it," he said, snatching up the gloves from Michaud. Michaud understood his eagerness to leave. The oppressive smells of the decaying structure weighed on him, as well.

Simons led the way down the staircase. He headed for the front door and shut it behind him as he went to his vehicle. Michaud and Karen moved to the kitchen, turning to the open basement door. The smell was indeed vile, but markedly different. Karen pointed to more of the blue dust shapes. Like footprints, they seemed to be entering and exiting from the basement door.

Michaud led the way, stepping cautiously down the stairs into the subterranean darkness. Light from the upstairs filtered around them, and they both held their flashlights out, casting bright beams into the room.

Karen grimaced, speaking quietly, "Smells like...smells like mold."

The walls of the room were brick and rock. Water dripped everywhere, the sound echoing, a soft pitter-patter that seemed to amplify the size of the space. Michaud set his foot down onto the floor from the last step, and it pushed in with a squish. The floor was bare earth, wet and soft, but not completely muddy. The air felt thick and murky, and Michaud let out a small cough. Only a few tiny beams of light filtered through a dirt-smeared window near the ceiling, blocked from the outside by a knot of oily weeds.

The room they stood in was covered in what looked like the same arcane symbols and scrawled Latin they saw in the first basement's crime scene. Drawn out on the floor in white powder, slowly oozing into the moist earthen floor, was another nine-pointed symbol, a *nonagon*, like the other. This one however had the blue dust shapes exiting the circle, leading up the stairs. Michaud and Karen followed them with their flashlight beams. The blue shapes came back down again, moving from the room through a poorly constructed doorway in the wall connecting it to another space. Michaud pointed at them, and they moved carefully around, leaving them undisturbed. From the connecting room emanated an unhealthy phosphorescent bluish glow. On the floor spreading from the doorway were blue-white tendrils, growing outward like a system of veins.

Avoiding the tendrils, Michaud and Karen stopped at the doorway, and stood shocked into silence. The small rock-walled room was filled with several dozen of a bizarre bioluminescent blue-white fungi. They were dotted with light purple mottling, and each stood about knee-high. They were like monstrously oversized mushrooms, bulging with an unearthly growth, their surfaces knobbed unevenly with bulbous pustules. Smaller specimens grew on the walls and the unnatural blue glow filled the space.

The beams of Karen's and Michaud's flashlights slowly lowered to the ground. They stared in disbelief. The air was heavier, dense with a foul vapor. The humidity was stifling. In the center of the room was a central fungal mass, from which the other growths sprouted, connected by the tendrils that reached out of the room.

The mass had a vaguely familiar shape, something

Michaud could not readily identify, creating a disturbing pang of recognition in him. Michaud turned his head slightly, aiming his flashlight beam at it. His eyes widened as he realized that it reminded him of a slumped over human figure with its "head" hanging down, "arms" and "legs" touching the ground and terminating in the root-tendrils reaching out into the wet earthen floor.

Karen also aimed her flashlight beam, focusing on the "head" of the growth. It seemed to tremble. Michaud stood staring, unsure of what they were witnessing. It moved again, shuddering. The large bulge at its top raised up, revealing the remnants of a human face, its eyes and mouth gone, with only slight indentations where they once were. Its "mouth" resembled the underside of a mushroom as it slowly opened, and it let out a dull, muffled groan. Michaud and Karen could only look on in horror, their eyes wide with astonishment.

With a loud croak, the vile fungal mound spit forth a sickeningly pinkish, lumpy pudding-like substance at Michaud, hitting him square in the chest. Michaud yelped in surprise, and stumbled back a few steps. He backed out of the room, Karen at his side.

Michaud looked down at the repugnant viscous glob on his protective vest. To his shock, it had started to dissolve the fabric. He fumbled with the side straps.

"Shit...shit!" Michaud muttered. The fungal mass groaned feebly at them from the room. Karen and Michaud tried to remove the vest as they backed away and up the stairs. The dissolving vest emitted a noxious fume, and they both started coughing. Michaud tore at the straps, his fingers moving frantically, with Karen helping him. As they fumbled, they tried to keep their faces away from the sickening stench of the fluid eating away at the Kevlar material.

Michaud grimaced, gritting his teeth, his hands shaking. Together they pulled the vest up and over Michaud's head. Once on the floor, light from up the stairs shone through the smoking hole now gnawed through the chest plate.

The two stumbled up into the kitchen, coughing and gasping for air. Karen seemed less affected and after a few moments breathed the fresher air calmly and slowly. Michaud doubled over while he hacked, coughed, spit, and gasped, drawing in long breaths before cycling back to hacking and coughing. He rested up against the doorframe of the kitchen that lead to the front hallway, his hands still on his knees, face bowed as he gathered himself. Karen stood, breathing deeply through her nose.

"Is that...is that what happened to the other... to Rachel in the holding cell?" she asked.

Michaud coughed, and answered in a strained, broken voice, "No...not like that...it was something else, more like..." Something in the periphery of his vision compelled him to look to the front door. Michaud's eyes widened with recognition. Standing there in the front hall, silhouetted by the outside sunset, was a dark figure. Clad in bowler hat, bizarre gas mask, suit, overcoat, carrying a doctor's bag and what looked like a lantern—the mysterious man from the security video! Karen looked to see the figure as well. Michaud blinked hard as he stood to his full height. He drew his weapon.

"Freeze!" Michaud managed to spit out in a raspy voice. "Don't move! Drop the...drop whatever the fuck that thing is! Do it!"

The masked man stood unmoving, as though thinking over his options...then bolted back outside. Michaud coughed and followed, keeping his weapon ready. "Karen! Get to the car and call for backup!" he blurted, stumbling for the door.

The brightness of the outside, even as the sun waned, caused Michaud to squint as his eyes readjusted from the oppressive gloom of the house. He looked right, then left, his eyes drawn to the motion of the man moving around the back of the house. "Damn it..." he muttered, holstering his sidearm. Michaud jumped off the patio and raced to the side of the house, his breath back to normal. He pushed himself over the dilapidated picket fence, one leg after the other, and then turned down the tiny alley separating Rachel's house from the next. The man darted left around the corner behind the house as Michaud deftly hopped over scattered and torn bags of trash, old boxes and broken bottles.

Michaud ran out from the alley and into the laneway behind the row of houses. He stopped, looking up and down for the strange masked figure. He drew his weapon again and held it out as he turned to his left and began cautiously moving further along the lane. Parked cars, garbage bins, a backyard garden, a cat chasing a squirrel up a telephone pole. No man in a hat, that Michaud could see. A noise—Michaud turned, aiming his weapon at the back of a house and scanning among the piles of trash for a sign of movement, but he saw nothing. *The balcony?* He looked up...and turned.

The masked man appeared behind him, stepping out from behind a dumpster. With a swish he sliced the air with a plank of wood aimed at Michaud, hitting him across the back of the head. Michaud's vision became flashes and blobs of white as he crumpled to the pavement. His handgun spun as it scraped away across the asphalt and out of reach.

The masked man discarded the board, which bounced before clattering to the other side of the lane. He calmly retrieved his bag and lantern-device from behind the dumpster and returned to Michaud, who was lying dazed, punch-drunkenly trying to move an arm and push himself up. The man with bag and lantern in one hand, reached for Michaud's pant-leg with the other. He yanked up Michaud's leg and dragged him out of the laneway and toward the dumpster, out of sight. Michaud blinked, his eyes wandering as he alternately frowned and widened his eyes, trying to regain his senses. The masked figure stood over him, holding the lantern-device, looking at Michaud curiously, as if deciding what to do...

"Hey!" Karen's growling voice rang out. The gas mask looked up to see her. Michaud's blurred vision caught Karen brandishing Michaud's weapon, standing down the laneway where the pistol landed. She sighted and fired three times, hitting the overcoat squarely in the chest, knocking him back and away from the dumpster. He stumbled, then regained his footing and turned to run, his bag and lantern still clutched in one hand.

Michaud's eyes rolled back in his head as he blacked out.

* * * *

Karen watched him go, weapon still sighted on him, then rushed to Michaud's aid, squatting down over him. "Are you all right? What did he do to you? Shit...shit!" She ran a hand through her hair. Remembering her emergency training, she collected herself and took a deep breath. Michaud was still bleary-eyed and could only gasp for air. Karen grabbed the radio off his belt. "This is Karen Wendleton assigned to Detective Michaud with Seventy-seven Division. I have a man down in a laneway north of Dundas West, between McMurray and Pacific." She looked around, keeping her cool. "We're uh...

just near the Vine Parkette. I need EMS here immediately. Suspect who assaulted officer fleeing on foot, uh, eastbound toward Pacific."

"Roger, units will be on the way shortly," the muffled radio voice responded.

Chapter Ten

The paramedics had already packed up their gear and one was climbing into the ambulance that sat in the laneway, lights flashing. A patrol car blocked the other end of the lane, also flashing its lights. Michaud sat on a concrete parking barrier, holding an ice pack over the bandage on the back of his head, wishing the cars would shut the lights off. In the dusk, they were particularly distracting and even more annoying with the back of his head throbbing in pain. Karen stood nearby, chatting with another detective, who jotted down notes on a pad.

"You'll be fine. No concussion, no stitches. Just take it easy until tomorrow, okay?" the female paramedic said, smiling and looking down at Michaud. Her hair was tied up into a bun and her curves were a bit too much for her slightly-too-small uniform to hold in. Michaud found himself noticing them more than he should in this situation, and attributed it to his current dazed state.

Michaud forced out a smile back as he stood. "Thanks." The paramedic joined her partner in the ambulance and drove out, past another patrol car that had blocked the closer end of the lane as well.

Karen approached, looking at him with a face that showed both concern and admonishment. "What happened?"

"I don't really..." Michaud wobbled on his feet.

"Whoa there champ," Karen said while steadying him. She eased him back into a sitting position on the parking barrier and sat beside him.

Michaud moved the ice away and rubbed the back of his head, feeling the large bandage that had been applied. "I guess he must have hit me. I mean, obviously. I don't remember though. I came out into the alley and...I don't remember anything else. Just flashes of light. You know when they see stars in the cartoons? It really is like that."

"I've been knocked out before. In a *Tae Kwon Do* tournament. From what everyone told me, after I came to, I won the next match but I can't remember it at all."

"Did you use my gun?"

"In the tournament?"

"What? No, on the street. Against the guy."

"I'm not going to face any charges am I?"

"What for? Improper discharge of a firearm? Not identifying yourself as a member of the police force?—which you're not."

Karen shrugged, rolling her eyes, an expression of guilt on her face. "I just did what I thought you'd do."

"I doubt anything will come of it. Sort of a life or death situation, at least that's how I'm going to write it up, and you should too. Pretty sure everyone will look the other way for you, Wendleton. Good thing you have firearms training."

"Figured it could come in handy if I was working with the police. I mean, I don't want to stay an assistant forever. It'd be nice if I could get into the actual investigating, but then I guess I'd have to become an actual cop."

He wanted to tell her she'd done well, but knew he shouldn't. He felt like squeezing her tightly. *Never get too close. They always leave.* "You *are* into the investigating, just try to stay away from the shooting and the guns and the bullets. You'll live longer."

Karen rolled her eyes. "Thanks, Boss."

"They didn't catch him, did they?" Michaud asked, already knowing the answer.

"Sorry. I called it in though," she said with a pleading expression on her face.

Michaud held the ice pack again to the back of his head, slowly closing his eyes.

"I'd offer you a cigarette but I know you don't smoke," Karen said.

Michaud pulled the package of Good Catch cigarettes from his jacket pocket and rattled them. "Thanks, I've got some."

"I thought you quit!"

"I did, these aren't mine."

"Yeah, sure. Why'd you quit anyways?"

"I figured if anything was going to kill me, it should be a bad guy that I take a bullet from while defending a partner, not my own bad habits. And being a walking stereotype of a chain-smoking detective with a minor alcohol problem isn't really anything to brag about."

"I think I need one of those," Karen said, pointing at the pack.

"Be my guest," Michaud said, holding them out further to her.

Karen puffed out a laugh through her nose, reaching for it. Michaud caught a glimpse of the bottom of the package as she took it, and he mumbled aloud what was stamped there, "Perpendex Pharmaceuticals..."

From the small alleyway between the houses that Michaud chased the masked man down came Simons. "Detective, the lab team is here. But something's happened."

The two reluctantly stood, Michaud still holding his ice pack to the back of his head, and Karen taking a puff from the "Good Catch" cigarette. The group headed to the back door of Rachel's house, and Michaud kept his head down as he walked. Something caught his eye and he paused momentarily to look at it: droplets of a blue fluid, scattered on the asphalt near where he was on the ground.

"Karen."

She turned, eyebrows raised as she blew out smoke. "Yeah?"

"You shoot that guy...right here?"

"Yeah, about there, why?"

"Was he carrying paint cans or something?"

"I...what?"

Michaud frowned. *Something in his bag, a bullet hit through it. It had to be paint*, he rationalized to himself...and right now he really wanted to get some rest. "Nothing. Just tell me about it later."

Inside the kitchen, several forensic technicians, outfitted head to toe in white coveralls, dust masks, goggles, and gloves, were carefully walking about while holding pieces of lab equipment, ultraviolet lights, evidence bags and cameras. Yellow crime scene tape had been placed up over the doors. Michaud, Simons and Karen stood outside looking in.

A haze of smoke hung in the air, seeping from the basement. Michaud knew exactly what had happened, and his fatigue left him. He tossed his ice pack to Simons, who caught it with a look of surprise. Michaud parted the yellow tape, ducked under it and dashed through the kitchen, ignoring the smoking basement and the forensics team.

"Hey! This area's sealed off!" One of them yelled through his dust mask.

"Doesn't matter!" Michaud yelled out over his shoulder as he raced up the stairs.

Simons turned to Karen. "What was downstairs?"

She raised her eyebrows. "You would *not* believe me."

Michaud slowly came back down the stairs, and moved back under the crime scene tape, his teeth clenched. "He was here."

"What?" Simons asked, befuddled.

Michaud spoke, eyes darting. "The one who knocked me out. He's the one burning all the bodies. He burned everything. Damn it!" He smacked the side of his fist against the door jam, causing Simons and Karen to jump. Did the same thing in the holding cells, got in and fried Rachel Atwater in just a few minutes. He doubled back here and cooked this place. How could he have been so fast? What is this guy on? *If it's even the same person...maybe there really is more than one.* He turned to Simons. "Did you get that sample to the lab?"

"Yeah, of course. They're analyzing it right now. Should know by tomorrow morning."

"Good. It's all we've got left from this place."

Karen looked at both of them, perking up. "Your vest." She signaled to one of the forensic techs who stood nearby carrying the vest in a sealed plastic bag. The hole was corroded through, and the vest hadn't been burned by the masked man. She took the bag from the investigator, who offered no resistance. The bag was sealed, and the evidence had been catalogued. They only needed to take it in to the lab now. "Everything down in the basement is gone. Nothing but ash. Even the markings on the floor and the walls, all gone. Except this." She held it up for them to see. "We can take it in and see if there's any residue left over."

"If you don't mind putting in the overtime," Michaud said.

Across the yard, a news van pulled up. A camera operator emerged with a reporter in tow, and the uniformed officer outside the yard held them back behind a line of crime scene tape. Michaud sighed, feeling exasperated. "Great. Just what I need," he breathed, straightening his tie and tucking in his shirt.

Simons scanned Michaud up and down, handing back the ice pack. "You look terrible, Detective. You should get home. I'll talk to them."

Michaud froze, looking at him.

"I know what to say, Detective," Simons muttered, while

smirking. He imitated Michaud's voice, "This appears to be a simple arson, unrelated to the recent deaths by self-immolation. The detective in charge of the case is unavailable for comment, but I can give you contact information if you'd like to follow up."

Michaud smiled. "Okay, I'll go."

"Are you all right to drive?" Karen asked, taking a last drag from the cigarette. She walked to the far end of the back yard, and flung the butt into the laneway, past the news van and away from the crime scene. "I have no idea why I smoked that thing," she grumbled.

Michaud held the ice to the back of his head again, wincing slightly. "I'm fine. I'll be fine."

Karen smiled. "Nice try. I'm driving you home."

* * * *

Karen drove while Michaud rode in the passenger seat, nursing the bump on the back of his head with the ice pack. He took it away, satisfied that the swelling had been reasonably taken care of, and rubbed at it absently with his other hand. They pulled up in front of Michaud's apartment.

"Thanks. Do me a big favor?" he asked. "Find out what you can on Perpendex Pharmaceuticals—who owns it, what they manufacture, anything."

"Sure. That cigarette they made was gross, by the way. Therapeutic my ass. Tasted like dirt."

"They're supposed to taste that way."

"Well, I'm not about to buy any more of them."

Michaud chuckled wearily. "Also, if you can, get them to put out a notice on the man in the gas mask. We have a description, at least of what he was wearing and carrying now, and the grainy shots from the security videos in the holding cells."

"Done, if they haven't already. Get some rest. Big day tomorrow," Karen said.

Michaud lurched out of the car and shut the door, then stopped before Karen could pull away. He leaned back to the window. "Wendleton. Thanks. You did all right today."

She smiled, hesitantly at first, then broadly. She didn't say anything back.

Michaud patted the car, turned, heading slowly up to his building.

Chapter Eleven

The cell phone buzzed with unusual aggressiveness, pushing itself across the surface of Michaud's side table. He had slept in his clothes after collapsing totally exhausted into bed. The phone continued to rattle along and Michaud groggily reached for it. After fumbling it to his ear, he was greeted by the voice of Karen.

"Good morning sleepyhead. Get downstairs, I'm waiting. We've got a meeting with Friesen in an hour."

"Shit," he mumbled. "Haven't even typed up my report..."

* * * *

Michaud pushed the front door of the building open. He looked somewhat disheveled in a rumpled but still clean suit he had hurriedly grabbed from the ever-growing "take to the cleaners" pile. He tucked in his shirt as he came down the front steps and tossed a banana peel into a green-bin. He continued to chew the last mouthful of fruit as he walked. Karen stood by Michaud's car, holding a file folder.

"You didn't sleep in your clothes, did you?" she asked.

"I did, but I changed. How'd you get here?"

"I drove your car home and then came back with it this morning. I can't believe you drive every day. Traffic is murderous out there."

"Not about to bike like you. Especially after that crazy mayor tried to tear out the bike lanes a few years back. You know, the one who had all those charges against him? What was his name..."

"You should at least walk, Mister Health-Conscious. You live so close to work..."

"No time. I'm a busy guy," he said, rubbing his eyes with one hand.

"You feel all right?"

"Great. Slept for twelve hours. Let's go." Michaud headed

to the driver's side. Michaud drove, weaving slowly through city traffic as Karen shuffled through her file.

"Pulled the background check on Patrick Garneau, out of curiosity, since the guys working the Teresa Smalls case already had it."

"You better not tell me he was into heavy metal and role-playing games," Michaud said.

"No. Well, maybe, but I doubt that has anything to do with it."

"I played some in university," Michaud said.

"Heavy metal?"

"No, gaming."

"Shut up. You did not."

Michaud realized he had opened a can of worms and rushed to clamp it closed. "Back to the guy. Have a record?"

"None. Guy was clean, cleaner than my mom. Sounded like a regular middle-class kid, graduated high school with honors, university grad, seemed very 'normal'," she turned to Michaud. "From Quebec, too."

"Hmm. Would've been nice to talk to him. Haven't interrogated a suspect *en Francais* for a while."

Karen smiled and turned back to the file. "Worked at a food processing plant, even though he had a degree. But he had a job, a house...maybe why he was so smooth and charming to Teresa and Rachel. Offered them stability, or something."

"Hmm. He went to school in..."

"Guelph, like Rachel. He met her years before she went there though. Don't know if it's related."

Michaud put a pair of fingers to his temple. "My powers of clairvoyance tell me you're about to reveal that he also studied biology."

"Good guess. Can I have the winning lotto numbers now?"

"I'm not a gambler, but I'd bet that it *is* related. More for us to dig into later. What else have you got for me?"

"The lab report came back about midnight last night. The stuff from the tub contained traces of human tissue, which is what you'd expect, probably from the skeleton it was covering...you have anything for breakfast?" Karen asked, changing subjects.

"Glass of juice and a banana."

Karen reached into the back seat and retrieved a crumpled paper bag. "Here, it's from the doughnut shop by my place."

Michaud took the bag with one hand, steering with the other, and glanced to the bag, then back to the road. "You're trying to turn me back into a stereotype."

"It's a muffin, don't worry."

Michaud used his free hand to open the bag and reluctantly broke off a piece of muffin, stuffing it in his mouth. "They make these with lard, you know," he said while chewing.

"That's the doughnuts. And I think it's vegetable shortening, so quit crying."

"Thanks Mom," Michaud said.

"You're welcome. Now eat up. You need your strength. Growing boy and all that."

Michaud shook his head and smiled, swallowing muffin. It was sweet and a bit dry, but without a proper breakfast he didn't dwell on it.

After a moment Karen spoke up again with a wrinkled brow. "Yesterday...with the gun..."

"What about it?" Michaud asked, taking another dry bite of muffin. He wished he had a glass of juice to wash it down.

"I was wondering...have you ever had to shoot, I mean, discharge your weapon like that at a suspect on the job?"

Michaud answered without hesitation, keeping his eyes on the road, "Drawn on suspects plenty of times, back when I was working a patrol car, rookie days. Fired at people. Never once had to put a bullet in anyone, though. Hope I never have to either." He turned to look at her. "I guess you have one up on me."

"That's the weird part...that guy. I'm sure I hit him right in the chest. Even if he had a vest on, should've broken ribs, been on the ground screaming, right?"

"Probably on something. But honestly, with what we've been seeing lately, I don't want to make any assumptions— The guy clearly wasn't normal."

"Understatement of the week."

Michaud swallowed muffin. "You were saying about the stuff on the skeleton?"

"Right." Karen found the page she was looking for and read from it, "The main component was the same as whatever hit your vest. Lab tech said it wasn't like anything he'd ever seen before—like a digestive enzyme with a potent mycotoxin."

"From our friend in the basement yesterday."

Karen looked at him. "If that stuff hit your skin, you would've been paralyzed for hours."

"Could've carried that guy upstairs after knocking him out. I mean, at this point I'm assuming what we saw in the basement used to be a person," said Michaud.

"The lab tech had to send his results to a biologist for another opinion." Karen raised an upturned palm, showing her astonishment. "The crime lab's used to human bodily fluids, looking at hair, skin samples, that sort of thing. Whatever it was, it wasn't very human any more."

"Yeah, I think we both saw that much." Michaud kept his eyes on the road as he switched lanes.

"The guy in the tub—delivery guy, from what we saw on the torn uniform—was probably consumed by the thing in the basement, my guess. Maybe before it took root in the soil. You remember those blue dust marks, like footprints. And the forensics team did what you asked." Karen flipped and found the page she was looking for. "They checked everything with a Geiger counter, and there were significant traces of radiation, like the burns were caused by high-powered, focused energy beams."

Michaud shook his head in amazement.

Karen continued, "Found out about Perpendex as well... not a lot but they do a lot of research and development with biotechnology. They primarily manufacture chemicals, including those 'therapeutic' cigarettes you gave me. The missing guard, Peter Wellburn, was a part-time employee. 'Independent Security Contractor' under the management of the Watershed Security Corporation, the private mercenary company. They're one of the companies that did a lot of work for the United States government in Central America, Iraq, Afghanistan—black ops, CIA type shit."

"A private military firm? I've heard of some ex-cops joining up with them because they pay so well. But never doing both at the same time."

"Yeah, governments employ them because they're essentially immune from prosecution. Useful for doing stuff like torture, assassination...they're not subject to military rules or international treaties, and they skirt around legality. Anyways, both companies under the same ownership group headed by Doctor Elgin Horatio. His father, Frederick Horatio was the owner of F-Central Atomic Energy Corporation, started in 1948, which formed Perpendex in 1966. Guess what Doctor Horatio does other than run Perpendex."

Michaud shrugged, lost in the labyrinth of new information, trying to keep his attention on the road as well.

"Head of viral research at the university," Karen stated flatly.

Good job, Wendleton. "Radiation, viruses, private militias, what the fuck is going on?"

"Beats me. It's too early in the morning to be thinking about this, and we've got that meeting with Friesen in an hour," Karen said, shutting the file folder. "And you've got muffin crumbs on your shirt."

Michaud looked down for an instant, taking his eyes off the road, then back as he brushed himself off. "I hope this day doesn't get any weirder..."

* * * *

"Holy crap, what a mess," Friesen said, shaking his head. "I just want to hear from you three that the evidence being burned up was in no way your fault."

Michaud and Simons sat across the desk closest to their Inspector, Karen behind them. "It's all in the preliminary report sir. I was attacked. The guy went back to the house, and burned the thing in the basement," Michaud said.

"The thing in the basement," Friesen repeated with a hint of contempt. He flipped through the report, and looked down his nose through his reading glasses. "A large, fungal growth with anthropomorphic qualities, that looked as though it may have been the result of the transformation ritual being enacted by the cult," he said, reading aloud. "Seriously?" Friesen's incredulity was a rare display of emotion.

"Yes sir. It's a...strange situation."

"I saw it too sir. I can verify everything," Karen said.

"You really shouldn't have even been in that basement if it was at all dangerous. You don't come through until after these two jokers have secured the premises."

Michaud looked at Karen apologetically. She returned it with a shrug.

Friesen sighed, and took a deep breath, trying to reassert his usual stoic demeanor. "All right, what about the dead people at the original crime scene? You figured out who they all were, right?"

"Teresa Smalls was confirmed as the victim of the crime,

she was bound, and most probably subjected to the ritual," Michaud said. "I have to finish my final report, but these are all tied together. She was seeing this creep Garneau, who was apparently the father of the Atwater boy. Patrick Garneau had met Rachel Atwater a few years ago and they joined this cult, or formed a cell, whatever, and were working on this ritual. Looks like the guy who burned all of them up somehow snuck into the holding cells and got Rachel, too. He's the one who came after me yesterday and then burned everything at the house, or so we think. I've received information that suggests the guy who burned everything is part of a larger group that's in conflict with the cult, and this thing is only going to get worse."

Friesen sat back, his hands clasped together over his stomach as if digesting this information.

Michaud continued, "There's someone else I want to talk to as well, a writer out on the West Coast. He had first-hand knowledge of the ancient text the cult used. He might be able to tell us about what they're doing, their behavior."

"No way you're getting a flight paid for," Friesen said.

"Don't want one. I can phone, or videoconference."

"All right."

"And this other guy, the attacker, the one who burned everything, I need to look further into him, too. The group he's a part of is just as dangerous as the cult, maybe more so."

"But you chased after him, it says that in your report," Friesen intoned.

"Well, yeah, but—" Michaud said, raising his hands in protest.

"So for all we know he thought you were one of the cult and that's why he hit you. He's not a priority, the cult is. These people are dangerous, we know for sure they're kidnapping kids, doing God knows what else..."

"The guy did sort of attack a police officer, sir," Simons said.

"I'm not talking to you," Friesen said without emotion. "I'm sorry he hit you, but other than that he's practically doing a public service. Someone else will be assigned to investigate him. If he drops into your lap, sure, bring him in, but I repeat, the guy is not your priority. The cult is."

"Well, that's part of what I was going to ask you about..." Michaud said.

"You need more people."

"I do, sir."

Friesen looked Michaud in the eye. "You're head of the task force."

Michaud jerked his head back, surprised. "That was easy."

"You're disappointed?" Friesen asked.

"Well, I thought there'd be some back and forth, discussion, haggling, pleading, then finally begging on my part for you to give me the go ahead to take a few people off other cases and put them on this."

"I wanted this to stay simple, not blow up, but it looks like the only way to keep any kind of a lid on it is to give you what you need. Take whatever personnel you require, get them together, and take these assholes down. Get started." Friesen took his files and held them upright in his hands, tapping the edge against the surface of his desk to straighten and organize the pile. He looked up at Michaud, Simons and Karen, in mock surprise. "Well go on, get out of here, you're dismissed."

The three of them stood up almost simultaneously. "Thank you sir," Michaud said, before they left.

* * * *

Karen and Simons sat on one side of Michaud's desk going through personnel files. Michaud had pulled two-dozen candidates, in order of his favorites, and handed them over to sort and vet.

Michaud had found the phone number for the Derek Barton Institute in Victoria, British Columbia, where Barry Frederick, the writer, was under care. Michaud was looking at the display on the desk phone, trying to think of what to say, and how best to ask. He dialed, putting the phone to his ear. A recorded woman's voice answered, sounding artificially cheerful.

"Welcome to the Derek Barton Institute. *Bienvenue a l'Institue Derek Barton*. For service in English, press one. *Pour la service en Francais, appuyez le deux.*"

Michaud pressed one, then navigated his way through the phone menu until he had been put on hold, waiting for an actual human recipient for his call. The bland elevator music caused him to sigh through his nose, annoyed. Karen and Simons continued quietly chatting back and forth as they flipped through the files.

"Derek Barton Institute, how may I help you?" a nasally female voice asked.

Thank you, a real person and not another recorded menu. "Hi, this is Detective Benoit Michaud with the Toronto police, I'm calling in regards to a patient you have there, who can I speak to about that?"

"You can speak with me, sir; and if I need to elevate the call, I can do that."

"Okay, thanks. I'm looking for a patient you have there by the name of Barry Frederick who was admitted some years ago, not sure exactly when. The information I had was that he was with your hospital, is that correct?"

"One moment sir, I'll locate that information and transfer you accordingly."

The drab elevator music returned and Michaud waited. He watched Karen and Simons working. As one of the files hit the desk in front of him, he pointed at it and silently gave Simons and Karen a thumbs-up. Karen took the file and placed it on the "yes" pile.

A male voice came through the phone. "Is this Detective Michaud?"

"It is. I'm looking for Barry Frederick, I was hoping to speak with him if possible."

"Right. I'm Doctor Christopher Dodds, I worked with Barry."

"Worked with? You don't any longer."

"I'm afraid not. Barry's no longer with us."

"He was discharged?"

"No, you misunderstand me. He's deceased."

Michaud paused, mouth agape. He searched for something to say. "I'm...I'm sorry to hear that. How..."

"He, uh...he took his own life. It was very recently."

"How recently?"

"Three days ago."

"Did he say anything to you leading up to it?"

"Barry didn't speak."

"He was quiet?"

"No, he didn't speak at all. Not a single word since his admittance."

"Can you give me any details of his death?"

"I...I'm sorry, without identification or further authorization I really can't divulge much more than I've already said.

You can go through the Victoria Police. They took his belongings since there was no family to contact, and they have all the relevant reports and interviews with staff."

"I'll do that. Sorry to have bothered you, thanks."

They both hung up. Michaud looked to Karen and Simons. "How's it going?"

"Seven definite good people so far who are available, a couple with heavy case loads already, a couple in the discard pile," Karen said.

Michaud sighed. "That writer in Victoria, he's dead."

Simon looked up from the files. "Ouch. That's no good. Was it related to..."

"Not sure," Michaud said. "I have to call the police there and get them to send over some documents. Just keep at it." He picked up the phone again and started dialing.

* * * *

Michaud went to the floor's printing room to retrieve a fat sheaf of documents faxed over from the Victoria police department. He returned to his empty office, Karen and Simons having left to speak to the officers they had chosen for their task force. He spread the various faxes out over his desk. Several photocopies of reports, interviews with Derek Barton Institute staff, and most interestingly, a set of photocopies that represented a journal Barry wrote while at the hospital.

The death had taken place within Barry's room, locked from the inside, and certainly appeared, as it was judged, to be a suicide. Barry had suffocated himself—rather horribly, by swallowing his own severed tongue. Three nights previous to his death he'd received a phone call. The Victoria police had traced the call log and found only a blocked number. Michaud could guess who it might have been. Barry Frederick was, as far as he knew, the only living survivor of an encounter with the cult and their deity, or whatever it truly was. Interviews with staff painted a picture of a quiet, withdrawn man, who spoke to no one, not even other patients, choosing instead to write or sit looking forlornly out the window of his room. Doctor Dodds had long given up any hope of genuine recovery for Barry. His patient was withdrawn and avoided any form of therapy, instead sitting in his room scribbling notes for hours.

The journal was the most interesting of all the documents.

Michaud realized it would offer no scientific or logical analysis of the cult, its operation or the nature of *Olog'lahai'kuhul* and the metamorphosis devotees would undergo. He was unprepared however for the depths of Barry's ramblings, or the fact that they were without a doubt the product of a man driven thoroughly insane.

Within the scribbled passages, Michaud was able to sift various scraps that seemed more or less coherent. There was no hint of the *Ordo Sanctus* or their conflict with the cult, only the intense sense of terror felt by Barry over what he had experienced, and the feelings of resignation to his eventual fate, one he believed would be shared by the world due to the cult's machinations. He wrote that some of what he saw was due to intense hallucinogenic drugs used to taint the water supply offered him by his publisher at a writer's retreat. He was also convinced that he had been worked into the cult's plans by an outside force, somehow empowered by the copy of the *Encyclopedia Nefastus* in his possession by writing scenarios in which the cult enacted its ritual. He believed that through him, the book was able to alter the fabric of the universe and open a gateway into another realm, from which the Ninth Darkness, *Olog'lahai'kuhul*, would enter our world.

Michaud wondered how much of this writer's experience was colored by his own perception. As Karen told him, and the diary appeared to corroborate, Barry had indeed destroyed the copy of the *Encyclopedia Nefastus* that held sway over him, and somehow put a temporary end to whatever the cult was doing.

Despite that, the diary indicated that he was pushed only further into a state of madness and incoherency. His world was warped and distorted into intense hallucinations to the point where he was unable to discern the difference between reality and the visions he had of writhing masses of protoplasmic organisms. To him, they were shifting and altering, swarming over the world, himself the lone human survivor battling in solitude, unable to either succeed or die in the attempt.

Maybe this guy was simply crazy to begin with? It was, after all, entirely possible that Barry had been an unstable man, and reading the Encyclopedia, or dealing with the cult, however much he actually did, pushed him over the edge. Discerning the fiction from the reality within Barry's writing was not in any way easy.

The second to last passage in the diary was composed of a single sentence: "It's been nine years." And after that...the number "nine" scribbled over and over. Michaud flipped to the next page. Dated four days ago, only the following. "They are coming." It seemed a rather ominous foretelling. Michaud wanted to look through more of the diary, but this was the final sheet sent by fax. He shut the file folder, closing his eyes. He cracked his neck and took a deep breath.

Simons entered. "Looks like everyone's on board."

Michaud opened his eyes and exhaled. "Good. Did you..."

"Got the floor plan. We're good to go."

* * * *

Michaud stood at the front of the fifth floor briefing room, his jacket draped over a nearby chair, and his sleeves rolled up to his elbows. Sunlight beamed through the floor-to-ceiling windows at an angle, and thankfully kept the overhead fluorescents unnecessary. Karen sat in a nearby chair jotting down notes, file folders stuffed with papers in her lap. Simons was seated next to her. Beside Michaud was a large whiteboard over which he and Karen had jotted down information regarding the labyrinthine case, accompanied by a diagram showing the various known members of the cult. Alongside these were circled question marks representing Wellburn and "the man in the gas mask", and their involvement in the deaths of the cult members. Michaud had felt the masked man to be an important element in the situation. Despite Friesen's insistence that they focus solely on the cult members, the masked figure was impossible to ignore. Next to all this was a simple sketch of the area they would be heading to, showing the layout of the building and the streets around it.

A few more police officers and detectives sat on the remaining chairs, including a recent addition to the detectives, a younger officer named Montrose. He had shot his way up through the ranks, and no one begrudged him his rapid ascendance, only his attitude that was one of borderline arrogance due to his seeming ease of ability. Michaud had requested him for the team, though. Montrose might have been a hotshot rookie kid, but he was good, and they needed good officers.

Michaud, holding a sheet of paper, looked back and forth around the room. "All right, everybody. What we've got so far is two murders of kidnapping victims. Very likely committed by this cult, and from what we can establish both in the past week. Now, one was definitely part of a ritual they're trying to complete, the other, we're not entirely sure about—"

A hand shot up, interrupting him. "Detective?"

"Montrose," Michaud said.

"Two kidnapping victims? One was dead at the scene of the first crime, who was the second victim?"

"Found him yesterday in a bathtub at the Atwater place. Was a delivery guy, looks like. Skin melted off. Digested."

The room seemed to ripple as the assembled officers shifted uncomfortably, looks of disgust and surprise crossing their faces.

"I'm sorry...you said digested?" Montrose asked, his face contorted into a grimace of revulsion.

"That's correct. He was nothing but a skeleton when we found him, floating in digestive fluid. It's all in the report we've handed to each of you. What we surmise is that the man was taken by one of the cult members who had undergone a...process...that caused him to, uh...radically alter his form and..."

"What?" Montrose said. He turned his hands up, waiting for the answer.

Michaud took a deep breath. "He ate the guy he abducted."

Looks of disgust around the room amplified, and shudders went through the officers.

"It was really gross," Karen said, trying to lighten the mood.

Simons chimed in, nodding. "I can back that up. I wanted to puke." Chuckles followed around the room.

"Thank you, Peanut Gallery." Michaud continued. "Now this cult has operated for years with different members, trying to finish this ritual, with varying degrees of success. Someone has been stalking the cult, burning their bodies, probably the guy who attacked me yesterday. He may be acting alone but probably in collusion with several others.

"Now here's the part you're going to love, the cult's ritual is one designed to alter physical structure and...transform a member into something else. What Wendleton and I both saw yesterday, and what happened to our suspect from Tuesday night indicates an alteration to their cells, or their genetic structure, or something, I'm not sure, I'm not a biologist. We're not entirely certain how it happens, but it does happen.

You're going to see things today you might not be ready for. I need everyone to keep an open mind...just not so open that your brains fall out."

Montrose frowned, looking up. "Is this for real, detective? Seems...seems kind of crazy."

"Unfortunately, it's very real."

"So, what, these people can do magic?" Montrose grinned. Nervous laughter from around the room followed.

Michaud smiled, refusing to be embarrassed. "A wise person once said that to a primitive culture any sufficiently advanced technology would appear as magic. If it looks like magic, it's only outside our current realm of understanding, and it seems like these people have tapped into something beyond what we understand. It's our job to try and understand it, because it looks like it's dangerous, and we can't stop it until we know what they're doing and how they're doing it."

Michaud looked around the room, making sure everyone was giving him their full attention. "Our objective today is the Dressed to the Nines Social Club, what we suspect is a front for the cult." He pointed at the simple diagram on the whiteboard. "The building is on the northwest corner of Saint Clair and Old Weston Road. Just east of Keele."

One of the uniformed officers, Kehoe, held his hand up. "Detective, isn't this just to the southwest of the first murder scene with the burned bodies? Am I reading that right?"

"You are correct," Michaud said. "It's not unlikely they had the house basement set up as a staging area that was nearby and accessible, but not tied directly to their clubhouse via ownership or rental. Probably a ten minute walk, five minutes by car tops."

"Doesn't exactly seem like a cultist or terrorist hotbed," Kehoe said, scratching his temple.

"These people won't fit into the standard playbook. Please go over the reports and you'll see what I mean." Michaud nodded toward Simons. "Detective Simons has pulled the blueprints for the building, so we have a floor plan, although they may have renovated or shifted things around inside.

"For all we know, there's just a bunch of people upstairs playing cards. That's what we'd like to hope, because we want to bring as many of these people in for questioning as possible. Quietly and without incident. We've had four of our likely cult members found dead in the past two days, though. Which means according to the ritual there could be five more who've been undergoing this transformation process. There could be any number of other members of the cult in support, potentially armed. There may be possible abduction victims being held here, because it looks like these guys were probably also responsible for the kidnapping of Teresa Smalls. So I need everyone alert...and ready for anything."

Chapter Twelve

The section of Saint Clair West Avenue which Michaud drove to had been borderline decrepit for some time. For several years it resembled a war zone due to the seemingly interminable construction of the dedicated-lane streetcar line that dominated the middle of the road, but had been revitalized considerably in the years after its completion. Michaud gripped the steering wheel tightly, going over the details of the building plans in his mind. *Single entrance staircase leading to second floor where the club is. Main room, probably their recreation room. Several adjoining rooms, toilet, one back entrance to fire escape.*

Michaud pulled up and hopped out of his car, accompanied by Kehoe and a uniformed officer. Three police cruisers pulled up slowly and parked on the street behind him, sirens and lights off. Out of them filed Simons, Montrose and multiple uniformed officers. All wore protective vests and carried their weapons ready, pointed at the ground as they trotted up to the door of the club. Uniformed officers took up positions on opposing ends of the building, warning bystanders off, many of whom were already dashing for the other side of the street at the sight of the police raiding party.

The structure on Saint Clair West near the intersection of Keele was nondescript, if somewhat squalid, being in a state of aged disrepair. Like the rest of the block around it, it looked like a holdover from the area's less pleasant years. Most of the *Corso Italia* neighborhood just to the east consisted of bridal shops, bakeries and sports bars, but this far western end of the street was the midway point to a grimy industrial zone. Despite the economic upswing, the intersection still maintained an embattled feel, no doubt contributed to by the enormous bingo parlor, flea market, and multiple mechanic shops patrolled by froth-mouthed dogs.

The door to the club was squeezed in between a pair of shops. One was a convenience store with a wooden board over one window and bars behind the other, sprayed liberally with graffiti, while the next business was a cheap furniture dealer with massive, tacky banners completely covering the storefront promising "Lowest Prices Across City." The door to the club itself was painted a brick red, recently so, and a small peeling decal displaying two playing cards, the nine of clubs and the nine of spades with the name "Dressed to the Nines" over a banner across them, was stuck squarely in the middle of the door.

Michaud stood to the right of the door, and the other officers and detectives were lined up behind him and along the wall on the left side. One of them worked the lock with an automatic lock-gun, until he was able to freely turn the knob. He held the doorknob, waiting for the signal to open. Michaud looked back and forth, took a deep breath and nodded. The officer to the door's left turned the knob with a jerk and shoved the door open. Michaud and the others moved in.

* * * *

Directly across the street and partway down a shadowed alleyway, the Cleaner stood partially hunched over, his mask off. He kept in shadow as he watched the police at work, then turned and began moving back and away, further down the alley. He gripped his side and spoke into his wrist radio as he lurched along.

"Our team has been compromised...they have new weapons...more powerful than expected. I've been wounded and require one half hour to recover. Was unable to locate the book. I'm coming in." Leaking from between his fingers was a bright, cobalt-blue liquid, running down and dripping onto the pavement. He walked, limping, bent over. Not from pain, but the damage was greater than it should have been, at least by his estimation. The small-caliber bullets he had been hit with the day previous were enough to damage him, but the recovery was swift. This was different. *How could they have accomplished so much with so little time?*

* * * *

Michaud led the way up the stairs. "Police! Search warrant!" he said, his weapon out and ready. As they ascended the steps, Michaud stopped near the top, his free hand grasping the carved wooden railing. The door at the top of the stairs was broken off its hinges. He smelled the air, noticing something was amiss, and signaled with his hand for the others to stop. He carefully peeked around the door frame into the large main room.

What he saw was a scene of total chaos, or rather the aftermath of it, frozen as if in a museum exhibit. Corpses littered the checkered linoleum floor. The air was thick with smoke, some of it still rising from the splayed bodies. Furniture overturned and smashed, upholstery on couches burned and melted, wooden chairs splintered and broken. Playing cards and potato chips lay everywhere, randomly scattered, some still clutched in the hands of the dead about the room. Disgusting globs of a viscous yellow substance were splattered across the walls. In any other situation, Michaud might have snickered at what looked like someone had fired an oversized paintball gun filled with mustard around the room. Any humor in the situation was quashed by the odor of death that hung still in the air like a fetid fog. The curtains hung undisturbed, and shafts of sun spilled through the spaces between them, infusing the room with spots of cold white light.

Michaud motioned for the other officers to move up into the space, and they did so, cautiously sweeping it with their weapons, but barely able to restrain their shock at what they were confronted with. Some checked bodies for vital signs, but it was clearly evident that there were no survivors. The bodies were burned, but unlike the others Michaud had seen in the past week, not so badly that they were beyond recognition.

Two officers who had covered the rear entrance stayed outside, squatting over a pair of bodies at the back door. The dead appeared to be average people, indistinguishable in any large crowd, mostly men, a few women, of various ethnicities, dressed in jeans and T-shirts. Most of them were in their twenties and older, but few were beyond middle age.

Michaud followed the other officers, and looked down at one of the corpses, noticing the pattern of the burns. It was as if a small beam had sliced across the bodies cutting clean lines fifteen centimeters wide back and forth. Clothes and flesh alike were cut through as if by an improbably fast welding torch. In the burned hand of one of the bodies was a vaguely gun-shaped object, fried into a blackened mess.

Michaud turned to look at another nearby corpse, this one

holding an intact weapon, or what Michaud assumed was a weapon, although it could have been an art piece put together by a deranged butcher. It appeared to be made of living tissue, with bones, tendons and muscle exposed, like a gun-shaped animal with the skin removed. He crouched down to examine it, frowning. Loaded into the presumed handle was a cluster of orange spheres the size of golf balls. Michaud leaned in closer, snapping on blue nitrile gloves from his pocket. Something was inside the spheres, like tiny juvenile fish or tadpoles.

He prodded the handle with an outstretched index finger. The "fish" reacted, all spasmodically twitching, causing Michaud to jerk back, startled. He blinked rapidly, attempting to process what he was looking at. He turned his head up, trying to trace the path of what this bizarre device was doing. Across the room, the mustard-yellow splatters were strafed along the wall in what could well have been a shooting aimed from the body's position. He stood up, his eyes wide, and looked at the other officers and detectives.

Simons had a look of combined surprise and concern on his face, not dissimilar to what Michaud was feeling, but something less than frightened and more than baffled. He and the officers at the rear door stood over two bodies. These were at the fire exit where they seemed to have entered. As Michaud had noticed, the burn marks radiated out from where they lay, while the splatters across the walls looked as though made by people shooting wildly as they were being hit by these two. Just an early assumption, not one Michaud would tie himself to if forensic examiners determined otherwise, but it fit the observable evidence and provided a working theory that might help them make sense of the seemingly nonsensical destruction.

Michaud approached. All Simons could do was point down silently. These bodies were unburned, very different from the others around the room. Both were clad in bulky overcoats. Michaud lifted one side of the coat with a gloved hand, and noted the material had a similar weight and density to the apron worn during an x-ray. Lead lined perhaps—or something even more advanced?

Gas masks, combat boots, helmets, bandoliers, and still clutched in their hands, massive rifles of a type unknown to Michaud. The rifles were 150 centimeters long, with barrels that were colored black and copper, lined with flexible piping, and containing large magazines—or something in place of where a traditional rifle's magazine would go—that resembled huge cylindrical batteries. On the shoulders of the men's coats were embroidered logos of a black cross against a red background. Both of the dead men had large, gaping wounds, one in his chest and the other in his neck. "Wound" was too small a word for what had happened to them. The wide holes looked as though eaten away by an animal. The one with the neck wound appeared to have died while pulling off his gas mask, leaving his face seized in a fit of horrible agony. Now Michaud saw what it was that had left Simons speechless.

"Wellburn," Michaud said out loud.

The guard from the holding cells was involved in "security contracting" of a most unique nature. Michaud squatted down, looking at the remains of Wellburn's neck and face. At the center of the opening was the same yellow muck splashed on the walls, and tiny fragments that looked not unlike the golf-ball sized objects from the organic "guns" on the other side of the room, shot at him and broken apart...

"Detective! Detective Michaud!" Kehoe blurted out from across the debris. Michaud approached the agitated officer, who was standing with his weapon aimed toward a pile of overturned card tables. Playing cards were scattered everywhere. "Something...I saw something crawl under there," Kehoe said anxiously.

Michaud looked at him. "What was it?"

"It was big. I don't know. I don't know what it was. But it wasn't a person."

The other officers began gathering around, some aiming their weapons at the pile of tables. Michaud noticed Montrose was absent, and turned around, eyes wide, to look for him. The young detective, lagging behind the group, had turned to look at a nearby door that was slightly ajar.

Montrose leaned in. Something was leaking from underneath the door—a vile purple growth that wriggled back underneath as he approached. Michaud stepped toward Montrose, not fast enough.

Montrose raised his sidearm with one hand, and reached for the closet door with the other to slowly pull it open.

Michaud could only watch in horror as Montrose stood frozen at the grotesque sight before him. Michaud's mind reeled, spinning back decades to his aquarium visits as a child. He had no time to react or shout a warning.

The massive purple-black maw of a slime-slicked anemone-like creature, fully three meters tall, its mouth ringed with hundreds of writhing tentacles the size of human forearms, bent forward and engulfed Montrose up to his waist. The creature straightened up, attempting to devour the detective completely. Michaud could barely hear muffled screams as Montrose's legs kicked futilely in the air.

The rest of the officers heard the commotion and turned to see the surreal scene. Michaud could only stare, trying to force himself to react. The girth of the monster, a meter in diameter, rippled as its prey struggled within. Some of the officers moved to rush over, but before they could so the anemone-creature erupted, its midsection exploding outward with gunfire and thick purple jelly as Montrose fired wildly. Michaud, Simons and the others ducked back, crouching or covering their faces. The creature groaned and collapsed, its grip loosened, and Montrose fell out of the mouth, rolling on the ground.

He gasped for air, wiping slime from his face, as another uniformed officer rushed to his aid, trying to clean the repulsive substance off with his sleeve. Montrose sputtered, spitting and coughing, trying to get the viscous substance out of his mouth. Michaud stood over the torn open monstrosity, as did others, baffled. The smell immediately brought to mind Michaud's memories of rotting seaweed left behind at low tide on his trips to the west coast. The creature looked like it had sprung from the Paleozoic oceans, a prehistoric terror somehow forced upon the modern world, inflated to even greater gargantuan proportions.

Distantly Michaud heard Simons call for a forensics team and an ambulance for Montrose.

Michaud turned his attention to the room it came from, which looked like a dark and neglected bathroom, overgrown with mildew and mold, the layer of condensation dripping from the ceiling onto the stained linoleum floor. He drew out his flashlight, switching it on and aiming it inside. Around the room in clusters were small, fist-sized polyps, growing amongst the fungus, protruding from corners. They glistened sickeningly, looking like lumps of burnt moss dipped in grease and given tiny mouths lined with feelers. As the beam from his flashlight hit the polyps, they withdrew perceptibly.

Michaud recalled his visits to the British Columbia coast

during his university years, peering down into tidal pools left behind on rocky beaches when the ocean tide was out. Crouching down, he would look in at the tiny fish, anemones, crabs and other inhabitants of the oceanic microcosm with fascination. This room was like some kind of perverse version of that, seen through a stained funhouse mirror.

Michaud shuddered, and moved the light to the other side of the room, revealing a shower stall. A trail of iridescent ooze led from the stall to the door. The creature itself must have had a need to be kept wet, and evidently well-fed. On the floor beside the shower stall was a pile of shredded clothes, over-grown with patches of mildew. Michaud wondered if it was a victim, or if the clothes had come from whomever the creature originated from.

Michaud turned from the room, wiping a sleeve over his nose and mouth, trying to rid himself of the mildew odor. Simons and a uniformed officer had moved behind him to see, and he pushed through them. Michaud wandered away from the group, who had turned their attention to the small room from which the creature emerged. Michaud sighed, then stopped cold as he heard something. Wood shifting and moving. *The pile of tables Kehoe had pointed at. What did he say he saw?*

From beneath the jumble of broken wood emerged a pair of dog-sized creatures resembling immense aquatic arthropods, but walking on land with long, thin legs like giant insects of millennia past. Their carapaced bodies were a mottled beige and pink, as though an exoskeleton covered in light-toned human skin, and their faces had a disturbingly child-like cast to them, yet dotted with a multitude of glassy black eyes like an arachnid. They chittered as they scuttled forward, emitting clicking sounds from their mouths as they went. One of the creatures hissed at Michaud, prompting a few of the officers to turn. Michaud tried to raise his sidearm, but too slowly.

One of the crustacean-creatures leapt forward with strik-ing speed, springing off its back legs directly at Michaud. It latched onto his chest and dug its forelimbs into his protective vest, while excitedly clicking and chittering. Michaud fired a round in reaction, hitting the pile of tables.

"Holy shit! Get this thing off me!" Michaud blurted.

The officers had all turned to Michaud. Some spread out with weapons up, unwilling to fire and accidentally hit the detective. Michaud spun around, moving like a drunken dancer, momentarily stumbling on an overturned card table, then righting himself. The second creature leapt out at the group, but Simons was quick on the draw and fired a burst from his weapon, cutting the exoskeleton in half, exploding outward in a splatter of mustard-yellow fluid.

Michaud let out a yell, wincing as the creature began chewing on his vest, its long antennae brushing across his face, while officers on either side desperately tried pulling it away. Michaud grimaced, raising his handgun and pivoting so that he faced away from the others in the room, pressing the barrel of the weapon to the crustacean maw chewing at his vest. He pursed his lips and let go a round, splattering him with thick yellow ichor. Headless, the animal fell away.

Silence descended on the room. Unable to speak or express themselves, there was only the faint gasping for breath from the officers.

"Hey…" Simons said, breaking the stillness. "Someone want to cover me?"

Before Michaud could react, Simons pushed open the door of another side room with a creak.

Three other officers, with Michaud behind them, converged around Simons, their weapons ready, aimed into the shadows. It was dark, and the light from outside filtered in only marginally, but it was clear something was inside, filling the room. Simons reached his hand around the corner of the doorframe and flicked on the light switch.

Nothing moved, thankfully, although movement wasn't necessary to surprise Michaud again. He was nonplused at what he saw. The light overhead flickered, but it was more than enough to see what had taken over the space. The room had been converted into a grow-op of sorts, though not like any that grew narcotics. Evidently excreted from something living, were large membranous sacks. They were an arm's length across, dull grey in color, partially translucent, and laced with red and blue veins, suspended along sinuous fibers crisscrossing the room.

"What the fuck…" Michaud mumbled. The others stood, frozen. Michaud stepped forward, looking into one of the sacks. He half-expected it to explode and shower him with slime, or move, or react in some way. It didn't. He leaned in closer, but still wasn't about to risk actual contact with it. He could see inside, floating in a sallow pinkish fluid, was a familiar shape identical to one of the weapons held by the dead cult members.

* * * *

Michaud leaned sitting against the hood of one of the patrol cars parked in front of the Dressed to the Nines Club, listening to his cell phone while a stout, middle-aged paramedic was dabbing at small cuts on the detective's neck with antiseptic. The soft orange dusk helped alleviate Michaud's previous anxiety about the situation and he felt considerably more relaxed.

"Thanks a lot sir. It'll be worth it. We're close. Today was... crazy. But we've almost got this one," he said, reassuring Friesen over the phone. The Inspector said thank you and goodbye, and Michaud shut his phone off, putting it back in his pocket.

Michaud winced at the antiseptic being daubed on a cut. He held his hand up to the paramedic. "Thanks, I think that'll be enough."

"No problem," the man replied, and handed Michaud some bandages before returning to his ambulance.

The street was now partially blocked off and a forensic team was picking over the remnants of the upstairs rooms. The bodies of the unidentifiable lifeforms had already been taken out in isolation tanks for study. Michaud had been too dazed to bother to ask by whom, since they didn't look like Forensic Identification team members, but he was certain the creatures would provide for very interesting specimens.

Despite his antagonistic encounter with one of the creatures (and that another of them had tried to devour his fellow officer) he was genuinely curious as to what they were, where they came from, and what part they played in the cult's plans. The organic weapon pods' purpose was more obvious, and they too had been removed in isolation tanks. The fact that they even existed was disturbing, but the technology and knowledge of genetics necessary to create them must have been extensive. That, or it was something gifted to the cult by the force they worshipped, and that thought caused Michaud even greater unease.

The large, oddly designed rifles found on Wellburn and his

companion would be seized as well, but Michaud had made clear to Simons that he specifically wanted one taken so that it wouldn't disappear in a bureaucratic mire. He wanted a good look at it himself. Unlike the organic weapon pods, or the life-form samples, the rifle didn't fill him with anxiety. He didn't find it likely that it might jump off the table and attack him of its own accord.

Michaud breathed deeply, looking around. He peeled back a bandage and put it over the spot the paramedic had been daubing.

Just what was this thing they worshipped?

Was it some earthly lifeform, ancient, powerful, hidden, previously unknown to the biological sciences? Or something not from here...another planet, another dimension, or something even more outlandish? Some crazy mental manifestation of the collective will of the cult?

Worse was the possibility that it was something that operated outside understood natural laws, something genuinely supernatural. *No way. It'd be fun to jump to that, as much as ten-year-old me wants to believe it. This isn't hocus-pocus, this is real.* He knew that if something alien were really to interact with Earth's environment, the gravity, radiation level, air pressure, atmospheric gases and bacteria, or a host of other factors, should be inhospitable if not entirely lethal. It seemed crazy, but after what he had seen in the past week, nothing would surprise him.

Michaud felt around for another cut, looking for a spot for the next bandage. *Need a mirror.*

He knew what it said in the bizarre literature they had researched, but what was genuine and what was myth was obscured in centuries-old prose, jargon, half-truths and drug-induced ramblings of mysticism and fantasy. This thing, whatever it was, might be powerful enough to warp lifeforms, alter DNA or genetic structure, but it couldn't be powerful enough to do what it was doing without human aid, or else it would have long since conquered the planet.

If its aim was to alter all Earthly life, to spread this shadow of the Ninth Darkness, apparently to take over, it hadn't done so yet. *It seemingly failed numerous times through history, so really just how tough was it?* Michaud recalled his thoughts on the writer Barry Frederick—*what did it really want?*

It might be that this idea of the Army, the writings of the

Encyclopedia Nefastus, was just a human interpretation, based on whatever civilization the writers had come from and their own prejudices and preconceived ideas. It might really have a will of its own, or it could be some mindless force of nature, distorted by ages of reinterpretation, not even genuinely destructive, but only made so by the coalescing of the wills of thousands of people, shifting and altering the aims of the cult over centuries. It might have been bastardized even further by the conflict with the *Ordo Sanctus—were they in fact more responsible for this than they realized?*

Unfortunately, the philosophizing would have to wait. The danger was present and clearly immediate. Understanding this force, this *Olog'lahai'kuhul*, was currently only necessary as a weapon to defeat it. People were dying, and the last thing Michaud could allow was for this bizarre, secret underground war to continue in his city.

Karen approached. She said nothing but her amusement showed. Michaud knew her smile was partially out of humor and partially due to her relief at him appearing unhurt. He only felt embarrassed at the increasingly common situation.

"I'm fine," Michaud said, not making eye contact.

"Glad to hear it. We found the membership roster of the club. Good news: the four dead people upstairs are on it, as well as the other four we already knew about, Rachel Atwater and her three roommates."

"Not Wellburn and the other guy, right?"

"With the weird rifles? No, my guess is *Ordo Sanctus*."

"How many on the list?"

"Not many more. One was on the driver's license found in the pile of clothes in that bathroom with the...the huge worm thing in it. There's just one name unaccounted for, guy named Aaron Dennis, at an address in the Annex. Do we have a Feeney?" Karen asked, referring to the type of warrant they would require.

"Being pushed through. These guys are armed and dangerous, possibly spreading toxic biological agents, and actively in the commission of terrorism. We'll have it first thing in the morning. Just got off the phone with Friesen, he went all the way to the top."

"Didn't need a warrant for Rachel's place but we do need one for this guy?" Karen asked.

"Yeah, that's different. This guy is just a name on a list, a 'person of interest'. For all we know he was just a donor to the club and had no knowledge of their criminal activity. But we'll find out. Not taking any chances, bringing out the ETF."

He sighed and looked up over Karen's shoulder. "How's Montrose?" Michaud eyed the man who had been engulfed by the anemone-creature. Montrose was sitting on the back steps of a nearby ambulance, shivering, wrapped in a blanket as a paramedic examined him. His pallor had diminished considerably, surprising for a man who had nearly been eaten.

"Shaken up, but they said he's all right."

"Tell him he should stay home tomorrow. Looks like he could use the rest."

"You too, Boss."

"No, not me. I'll sleep tonight, but I'm definitely coming in. You and I will be going along to check out the next name on the list. And do me a favor, if you can, try to track where they end up taking the organic samples they removed from this place."

Karen nodded. "Full plate," she said.

Michaud agreed. They would be busy, and their work was really just getting started.

Simons spoke into a walkie-talkie as he approached Karen and Michaud. "Roger that. Out." He looked up at Michaud, who returned the look with a slight nod of his head toward Simons' car. "You need a ride home?" Simons asked, frowning.

Michaud chuckled. "No, I meant, the...package, did you..."

Simons' frown was broken as his eyebrows lifted. The strange *Ordo Sanctus* rifle. "Oh! That. Yeah, it's in the trunk. You can take it and have it examined whenever."

Karen looked back and forth at the two detectives. "What are you guys talking about?"

"Something from inside, a weapon," Michaud replied. "Need to have it examined by a specialist. I'll explain later." It might not just be bureaucracy he'd be entangled by trying to get a look at the rifle. The Informant had mentioned "men in your own department." Michaud hated to think of that rifle "disappearing" before it could be examined.

"Your friend at the university?" Karen asked.

Michaud knew a researcher who had worked on weapons development before turning to physics and alternative energy research.

Michaud nodded, then turned to Simons. "And the ride, were you offering?"

"I was. You look dead on your feet."

Michaud looked at him, exhaustion in his eyes. "Thanks. Too common these days. I'll pick up some food on the way if you don't mind."

* * * *

Michaud had put down a payment on a property in an effort to help a beleaguered relative, a real estate agent direly in need of a sale. It had worked, but he now found himself living in an area that had as yet developed little real character. The oddly-named Liberty Village, a neighborhood manufactured by real estate companies if there ever was one, had at one time been an industrial zone. Like many such formerly manufacturing-based areas in Toronto, it had gradually gentrified as digitally-based businesses and startups had moved into loft spaces in search of inexpensive rent relatively close to the downtown core, and construction of condominiums boomed. Michaud's twelfth floor apartment was really a condo, or rather it had been built that way, but he hated the word and its associations. He tried as hard as possible to distance himself from the stereotype of condo dwellers as overprivileged yuppies with obnoxious attitudes and popped-collar polo shirts. While he knew it wasn't really accurate, the number of young business professionals was something he found mildly cringe-inducing, having spent much of his youth after moving to Canada in the more working-class Jane & Finch neighborhood. Proximity to work had also been a factor, plus the fact that he was rarely at home.

The floor-to-ceiling glass windows let in a considerable amount of light from the city, instilling the living room and kitchen with a soft orange-pink glow. There was very little furniture, no clutter, and the place barely even looked lived in. It could easily have been mistaken for a show-suite to tour prospective buyers through. Michaud only slept in his bed two or three times per week, usually collapsing on the couch, and more than occasionally in his office at the police station.

The door unlocked and Michaud stepped inside, carrying a bag of takeout food. He reached for the lightswitch as he slipped off one of his shoes, shutting the door by leaning back into it.

"Nice place you have here, Detective. Little bit Spartan, though," a voice said calmly from the shadows.

Michaud instinctively dropped his bag of food, drew his weapon and pointed, scanning the room, looking for where the intruder was.

"Who's there? Show yourself!" he commanded. He stepped forward, squinting in the darkness.

Silhouetted by the city light, a hand reached over from the couch and switched on a table lamp. Light spilled onto the side of the man's face. It was the Informant Michaud had met in the park. He sat, blank-faced in his suit and overcoat on the side of the couch, his back to the window. "You should shut your blinds. There's two cameras aimed at your place."

Michaud, perturbed at this invasion of his space, frowned. He kicked off his other shoe and went to the windows, holstering his weapon, and activated the automatic shutter controls, causing the opaque blinds to lower. "You could've done this yourself."

"I didn't know where the controls were. And I just got here before you arrived."

"Weirdo..." Michaud muttered, opening his fridge, reaching for his jug of water. He poured himself a cup and drank, then returned to the door and picked up his bag of takeout. He looked at the Informant. The corner of Michaud's mouth turned up as he frowned, annoyed.

"I'm sorry I had to surprise you like this, Detective, but it's about what you'll be doing tomorrow. The *Ordo Sanctus* team you saw today severely underestimated—"

"So, that *is* who they were?" Michaud interrupted.

"...they severely underestimated the cult's resources," the Informant continued. "The Cleaner was wounded, so you have a window of opportunity—"

"Cleaner? Is that the guy with the hat and the bag? You know he knocked me unconscious yesterday, right?"

The Informant went on, ignoring Michaud, "You have a brief period where you'll be able to get to one of the cult's operations before the Cleaner. This is a unique opportunity for you. You may even be able to get into one of their growing facilities..."

"What?"

"Where they grow those weapons you saw today. The ones used against the *Ordo Sanctus*."

"We already found it. It was in one of the rooms at the Dressed to the Nines Club."

The Informant paused, staring at Michaud. "I can't give you much more of our intel. I've probably already given you too much. But this is important. Both sides are getting too dangerous. I can only do so much from the inside. I'll just say there are more growing facilities."

Michaud stepped closer, raising an accusatory index finger as he looked down at the Informant. "Listen, I barely even know what it is we're up against. It's bad enough I have to try and sound like I know what I'm talking about to the other officers. All we have is historical background on these people, and most of that are fragments and ramblings written by lunatics in half-legible rotting books hundreds of years old. And this *Ordo Sanctus*, Perpendex Pharmaceuticals, whatever they're all wrapped up in together isn't making things any easier."

The Informant paused. "My sources say two rifles were left behind at the scene by the *Ordo Sanctus* security contractors today. But only one was recovered. You wouldn't happen to know where the other one is?"

Michaud felt the sudden urge to grab this guy and throw him in handcuffs, then take him downtown and put him in an interrogation room for a few hours. But that was the angry, chain-smoking rookie within him welling up, or possibly the smell of his takeout magnifying his gnawing hunger and making him cranky, he wasn't sure. "I might. But if I did, I wouldn't tell you," he said.

The Informant chuckled lightly, looking to his side. He turned back to Michaud. "You realize that we can't have that technology getting loose. It's very...contentious."

"Sure, but it's okay for a shadowy private military force to have them? Nice try. I want to know what it is we're dealing with, and if it means dismantling the weapons used against the cult to see what's being used and give us an advantage, so be it. I don't want any more officers or citizens of this city being put at risk."

"I'm sorry detective. You've been exposed to some of the worst. But tomorrow will be dangerous, if what I've seen is accurate. You'll need to enlist the Emergency Task Force. Don't make the same mistake the *Ordo Sanctus* did."

"Thanks, but they were coming anyways. Now I'd like to eat my dinner in peace, so if you don't mind..." Michaud said, leaning his head toward the front door.

"Of course," the Informant replied. "Just one more thing..."

He reached into his side pocket with a gloved hand and pulled out a small black box with a blinking red LED light that looked not unlike a garage-door opener, then set it on the table. He pointed at it. "That doesn't last long, so you'll want to go over your apartment."

Michaud frowned, looking at him.

The Informant backed toward the door. "You don't think I'd be here and talk to you without making sure they weren't listening, do you? Oh, and your phone. Wouldn't use it to discuss anything about this case or the *Ordo Sanctus* if I were you. You have a bug detector?"

"Yeah, my last two got worn out after spy school. I'll just run down to the corner store to buy a few more. Or to the spy shop up Yonge street," he said through gritted teeth. The Informant's words were barely registering with him. Hunger and impatience had taken over.

"Doesn't really matter. Wouldn't work with what the *Ordo Sanctus* uses."

Michaud frowned harder, looking at the jamming device on the table, and then pulled out his phone, looking at both. He turned, opening his mouth to ask another question, but the door was already shutting, the Informant gone. Michaud set his phone down on the table. He took a sip of his water and opened up his takeout to eat. He ate, but the feeling he had reminded him of when he was a kid and his parents were arguing over unpaid bills at the dinner table. Hungry, eating, not enjoying it at all. He didn't look forward to combing over his apartment, his office, and his car trying to ferret out listening devices.

Chapter Thirteen

Michaud, Simons and Karen stepped out of a police cruiser, all wearing protective vests. Michaud knew the area called the Annex well. It was located at the northern edge of what could be called the broader downtown of Toronto. Residential homes backed off of a main retail strip along Bloor Street, the main east-west subway line in the city.

The area mainly consisted of assorted small shops, the occasional chain store, peppered liberally with bars that catered to the largely twenty-something crowd coming from the nearby University of Toronto. Busking street musicians played up and down the blocks late into the evening during the summer, while shouting and hollering in the area could be heard long after bars closed on weekends regardless of the time of year. Michaud had spent more than one night of his university years stumbling through these streets. It was an ideal place for a cult member to hide in plain sight.

An Emergency Task Force van pulled up in the early morning sunshine and stopped as standard police cruisers cordoned off the portion of Bloor Street on both ends of the block. Officers set up barricades. A courier, a scruffy homeless man, and a handful of people carrying bags of groceries rushed away from the scene.

The back of the Emergency Task Force van opened and the grey and black-clad team fully outfitted with helmets, masks, goggles and automatic weapons burst out, moving for the front door of the address. No chances were being taken this time. The potential danger had been well-established at their last cult encounter, and they were a heavily armed and armored team that could deal with it. Even if their suspect turned out to be a nobody, or a "soft supporter"—someone who sent money, went to the occasional meeting, without any intent of violent action—it was better to be prepared for any eventuality, given what Michaud's team had faced at their last raid.

Michaud looked up at building in front of him. It was a

nondescript brick retail structure with apartments above, and two shops facing onto the street, a bookstore and a health food shop, the employees of which were being ushered out by uniformed officers and herded to a safe distance. The beige door to the right of the health food shop was streaked with graffiti and grime, and led to the upper apartments.

The trash-filled alley to the right of the building had a set of officers filing into it to cover all exterior windows, filthy as they were. A pair of inebriated homeless people ran, probably terrified of being taken in, and hopped over a nearby fence.

Michaud watched an officer escort an elderly woman to the door. Her hands shook as she raised a set of keys. The landlady was a wizened harridan who looked as though someone had pulled the loose skin of her face down, revealing deep red gaps under her eyes and a mouthful of foul brown teeth. She unlocked the door and backed away from it. The uniformed officer quickly hustled her back across the street.

The Emergency Task Force officers lined up, one covering the front door, while team leader Weltner crouched, holding the doorknob. He yanked it open and they filed in one after the other, submachine guns at the ready, stocks tucked into their shoulders.

Michaud, Simons and Karen trailed behind.

* * * *

Weltner's team filed up the musty stairs. It was clear that the landlady and owners of the building were direly neglectful of the premises. Assorted bits of flotsam and shreds of trash were sprinkled over the ratty and stained grey carpet up the stairs and through the hallway leading left. Cracked chunks of ceiling tiles and speckles of plaster dust from above had gathered in corners of the apparently never-cleaned floors. The tacky fake wood paneling along the walls was riddled with breaks and spotted with stains. One of the fluorescent lights stuttered on and off overhead, its casing badly cracked and broken. The few other lights in the hallway that worked were dim and provided a doleful tease of illumination.

The grey-clad team activated the flashlights and laser sights of their weapons, sweeping the darkened hall. The lights scanned back and forth becoming solid beams in the thickly dusty air. One member of the team stood watch at the top of the stairs, with Michaud, Simons and Karen behind him. The others focused the beams of their weapon-mounted flashlights on the door numbers. Weltner found what he was looking for: the door previously marked number two, which the layers of paint betrayed despite the door number being replaced with a newer brass number nine. He stepped back, covering the door from the opposite side of the hall. One of the others, Perry, gripped his shoulder mic with his left hand and muttered into it as the other members of the team lined up next to the door, covering it and preparing to enter.

Weltner turned as another grey-clad officer, Chow, rushed up the stairs holding his entry tool, the handheld metal battering ram specifically for breaking down doors. Chow took position behind Weltner, who was listening intently at the door for any signs of activity. His eyes darted, trying to discern any sound. He took a step back and pounded loudly on the door with the side of his fist.

"Police! We have a warrant to search the premises!" Weltner backed away.

"Chow!" he whispered harshly. "You're up!"

Chow stepped forward, bracing his feet against the floor and squaring himself up like a baseball player stepping into the batter's box. He took a deep breath, making a light practice swing, swaying the entry tool back and forth with both hands on the upper handles, before aiming carefully directly below the doorknob and smashing it forward. The door didn't budge, only making a muffled thudding sound with the impact of the blunt metal.

Chow gathered himself and took a bigger swing. This time instead of forcing the door open, the ram punched a round hole through it. With a baffled expression the human bulldozer yanked the ram out, tiny splinters of wood dropping to the floor. Weltner frowned, turning to the rest of his team. They were looking at each other, waiting for instruction.

"Hit it again," Weltner ordered.

Chow took another step back and swung hard, smashing directly above the doorknob this time. The door notched inward slightly, and Chow handed the ram off to Perry, then used his shoulder to lean his weight against the door.

"Must be barricaded," Chow grumbled.

The door had barely moved. Weltner joined in, using both hands to push. The other ETF officers maintained their watch, weapons at the ready. Finally, the door began moving inward with greater ease.

It became apparent to Weltner and his team why it was so difficult to get the door open. A revolting mass of sinuous organic material had been formed across the door from the inside, like a tangled web of black glue. As the men pushed, the material stretched, strained and the fibers finally broke, allowing them to force their way in and enter.

Chow and Weltner, followed by the rest of the team, stopped and stood aghast, unable to speak. Years of training fell away, leaving them utterly unprepared.

* * * *

Michaud rushed to the doorway. His curiosity had over-taken him and he couldn't stay back any longer. The room was completely covered in the chitinous black mass of organic material, not unlike the hive of a wasp or bee. All the furniture was overlaid. What looked like a lamp and television set left on underneath, created a dull bluish glow, giving the aspect of blankets thrown over everything. The window had twisted strings of the material running across it and the green curtains, but exterior illumination filtered through, creating sharp shafts of emerald light that highlighted the crevices and contortions of the repulsive webbing ensnaring the space. The air was heavy, humid, smelling of fouled meat.

Spellbound by the sight before him, one of the ETF team, McRae, turned to his right and came face-to-face with a par-tially skeletonized corpse, cocooned up into the wall, its arms and legs splayed out and restrained with encrusted black webbing.

"Ahh!" McRae exclaimed, shocked and surprised, his head jolting back.

The others all turned to see what he was looking at. Simons joined Michaud at the open door with weapon drawn. Michaud drew his own. Karen, the unarmed civilian, lingered behind them further down the hall.

As Michaud and Simons looked on, they saw what the rest of Weltner's team had raised their flashlights and weapon sights to—two other victims also entrapped up near the first corpse. One was a skeleton completely denuded of flesh wear-ing the tattered remains of a business suit. The other, a male body in a delivery uniform with only a few puncture wounds around its face and neck, looked only a few hours dead, if that. Weltner stepped forward and moved the face of the man back and forth, opened its eyelids and checked for a pulse. He turned back to the others and shook his head solemnly, sighing.

Michaud was disgusted, but not particularly surprised after the other recent events he had witnessed. Karen stepped to the door and peered in.

Michaud turned to her. "You said you hoped today wouldn't be any weirder."

Karen, awed by the room's bizarre state, answered as her eyes wandered up to the walls and bodies. "Yeah..."

"I think today is a *lot* weirder," Michaud said.

Behind Weltner, something stirred. Unnoticed by the assembled officers, Michaud spotted a moving shape. A familiar knot in his stomach began to form, and he dreaded what he knew would come next.

Karen, standing behind the others at the door, still monitoring the scene, turned at the movement, seeing the hulking shadowy figure creeping toward the group.

"Behind you!" she blurted.

Emerging from the black webbing in the kitchen to the left of where they stood was a vaguely humanoid form, its carapace blending perfectly into the walls. As it moved through the shadows, its outline became more apparent, like that of a tremendous insect, misshapen and asymmetrical, with one pincer-like foreclaw larger than the other. Its face was dotted with haphazardly placed round black eyes that glinted in the green light leaking in from the outside.

In the darkness it was difficult to discern and was little more than a horrifying, multi-limbed nightmare. As the light hit it, stepping silently across the wall, its shape approached recognition, something partway between a crab and a beetle, melded onto a humanoid form. Indeed, scraps of shredded garments hung from its limbs, as though it were once a man—or woman—and it metamorphosed so quickly as to destroy the clothing it was wearing from the inside.

The team members began to turn, but it was too late. With a sound like a barking hiss, the immense beetle-creature had leapt forward onto Weltner, latching onto his back and sending him stumbling forward. The other officers stood immobile, momentarily stunned for a millisecond as the insectoid gripped Weltner's neck with its mandibles. Chow stepped forward and tried to grab hold of the creature, but Weltner was flailing wildly, yelling.

"Help! What the fuck is this thing! Holy shit!"

The creature immediately injected something into Weltner's neck. His body shook with a seizure and his movements became jerky, spasmodic. He yanked his balaclava down with a shaking hand and vomited. He fell forward onto his stomach, his body stiffly paralyzed, a sickening orange foam running from his mouth.

Chow moved to kick the insectoid off and get a clear shot without hitting his commander, but the creature spun its head and sprayed orange venom. Chow was hit in the face and jolted back, swatting at his goggles. Michaud was ready with his pistol and fired on the beetle-creature, hitting one of its claws. It shrieked and leapt back, dashing into the webbing behind what looked like it had been the entertainment unit.

Chow wiped the orange muck from his goggles with the back of his glove and raised his submachine gun to fire, but suddenly let out a scream of pain. "Agghh!"

Behind him was another of the juvenile crustacean-creatures, identical to the ones seen earlier at the Dressed to the Nines Club. It had bitten into Chow's right leg through his tactical pants and latched on with its legs, but McRae turned and fired a burst from his weapon, causing the creature to fly apart in an explosion of yellow fluid.

Michaud, momentarily distracted by this, turned back to where the beetle-creature had moved. It emerged hissing, creeping up over the television, and acted as if about to spray venom, but Michaud was too quick and squeezed off two rounds from his sidearm, directly into the creature's head, ripping it apart. Simons had stepped forward as well as a grey-clad officer, Hadley, and they both fired into it. It tumbled off the television stand and fell to the ground, limp and headless.

Something behind Chow chittered—from the shadows and out of the room's webbing scuttled another crustacean-creature. In the semi-darkness, all that was visible was the movement of spindly insectoid legs.

"There's another one here..." Chow said, ominously, and he backed away, giving the others a clear shot. McRae and another team member, Perry, aimed, putting tiny red laser dots on the creature's head, and fired short bursts from their submachine guns just as it leapt in the air at them, spraying mustard-yellow slime across the room as it exploded.

A moment of silence fell upon the room, viscous yellow and orange ooze dripping from the walls and ceiling. Michaud looked around, then at Chow, who wobbled back and forth.

"I think...I think that thing injected me with something... my leg..." Chow said woozily. He gripped his calf and stumbled over. He fell to one knee, pulling off his helmet and mask, gasping for air. McRae went to his aid, trying to see what was wrong. Hadley was already speaking calmly and clearly into his shoulder mic. "We have two men down, require immediate medical assistance. Copy?" A garbled reply followed.

Simons crouched to check Weltner, who still had orange residue around his mouth, the pool of foam seeping into the floor's black webbing. Simons slipped on a latex glove, turned Weltner over, and wiped the orange foam away from his face, followed by a basic first aid check. "Weltner! Can you hear me?" He leaned in to listen for breathing. "I can't tell if he's still breathing. I can't get a pulse," he said, feeling the neck and wrists.

Hadley spoke up. "Shit, we need to get him out of here, now."

Simons turned to him. "I'm not sure what this substance is, it could be..."

"There's not time to argue, he's not gonna make it unless we get him to a hospital!" Hadley yelled. He turned to another one of his team members and pointed at him. "You! Take his legs, I'll take his shoulders, we have to get him in an ambulance!"

Michaud tried to take command of the situation, stepping in their way. "You can't move him out of here, we have no idea..."

Hadley refused to look Michaud in the eyes, and simply shouldered past him and into the hall. "Try and stop me! I'm not arguing with you right now!" He and the other officer carried Weltner down the hall, down the stairs, and out the front door.

Michaud looked out and yelled after them. "We have no idea what he was injected with!" Michaud felt his own face, and looked at the back of his hand, realizing he had the yellow and orange fluids splattered over him, as did everyone there, save Karen, who had stayed outside the room. "Karen," he said deliberately, "step back. Are you clean?"

Karen stood up from where she had taken cover in the hall from the gunfire. "Uh..." she looked herself up and down, scanning over her arms, hands, legs. "I think so. Yeah, nothing touched me."

Michaud held his anxiety in check and spoke in a very calm and measure tone so as to avoid agitation. "Now listen to me very carefully. Get on the radio right now. Seal this building off. No one in or out, including you, do you understand?" he said, looking her directly in the eyes. "Whatever ambulance those guys get in, they need to know it has to be isolated, including the Emergency Task Force officers and the paramedics that attend to Weltner."

Karen understood the situation very clearly. "I'm on it," she said, turning away from the room, pulling her walkie-talkie from where it was latched on her belt. The door farthest down the hall had opened slightly, a frightened unshaven young man with long hair peeking out. "Police, sir. Stay inside your unit. It's dangerous." The man nodded and shut the door, followed by the sound of the locks bolting in place.

Karen spoke into the radio as authoritatively as possible. "This is Wendleton with Michaud and the tactical unit in the Annex. We have a possible serious biological hazard. I need a Hazmat team in here immediately. Get on the horn to the Centre for Infectious Disease Control (CIDC), do it now. Do you copy?"

Inside Room nine, Michaud turned back to where Chow was lying dazed on the floor, his breathing labored and shallow. McRae and Perry kneeled around him. Sweat ran down Chow's face and he stared blankly up at the ceiling. Karen turned back into the door frame, keeping her distance from the scene. "Done, Boss. They're on their way. Building's being isolated. They've got a unit trailing the ambulance Hadley got in with Weltner."

Michaud looked back at her. "Who else was at the last raid?"

Karen thought a moment. "Montrose. He was exposed. That thing..."

"Make sure he's isolated as well. Everyone else who came needs to be checked, too." He looked down, asking himself how he could have been so stupid.

"Fuck..."

Behind him, Simons was doing chest compressions on Chow with the assistance of Perry. Karen looked on, worried.

* * * *

Hadley braced himself against the side of the ambulance, half-standing, half-squatting, his arms holding out against the side and back doors. The vehicle containing Weltner and him roared along the street, siren wailing insistently as it weaved through traffic. The windshield wipers swept back and forth periodically, clearing away the light rain that had started misting down. Weltner lay on the small padded shelf that served as a bed in the confined space. The red-headed female paramedic squatted over him, her hair knotted up in a bun, running her stethoscope over his pale chest. Weltner's stomach bulged as if engorged with liquid. A breathing mask covered the paramedic's mouth, and the one driving wore the same. Hadley read her name tag, Derocher.

She shouted to her partner behind the wheel. "Patch ahead to the hospital! Tell them we're coming in hot with an adult male that's been injected with an unknown substance. Severely distended abdomen. He's Glasgow Coma Scale three, respiration's ten, shallow and crackly, room air sat ninety-two percent, ninety-eight percent on oxygen, heart rate forty, blood pressure seventy over forty, blood sugar...high, pupils constricted." She mumbled to herself, "Looks good. Perfect."

"What? What did you say?" Hadley sputtered.

"Nothing," she said flatly.

"Can't this damn shopping cart go any faster?" Hadley yelled.

"You need to stay calm, please. He needs a hospital. Now can you tell us what happened?" The paramedic asked, her face a controlled mask of placidity, staying focused on her patient.

Hadley shook his head, took a deep breath and tried to hold himself steady. "We were attacked. He was injected with something. Like a toxin or...I don't know."

"Was it a syringe? A drug?"

"No, no. It was an animal. Like a snakebite. A venom. A big bug or something."

Weltner began twitching, then violently convulsing, his

eyes popping open. Orange foam started to exude from his slack lips. The paramedic reached for syringes, her gloved hands sorting carefully through the articles.

"What the fuck?! What the fuck is wrong with him?" Hadley screamed.

Weltner's spasms abruptly stopped and his body went limp, his eyes glassy and blank. The male paramedic driving the ambulance listened at the radio. A metallic radio voice commanded them to head directly to the CIDC for containment.

The paramedic in the back piped up. "What was that?"

Her partner turned over his shoulder "We're getting orders to go straight to Disease Control." The vehicle turned off the original route.

Derocher continued working on Weltner, running her stethoscope over his chest.

"Damn it!" Hadley shouted. He was ready to explode with frustration and smashed his fist back into the side wall of the ambulance.

* * * *

Derocher reached into her bag and worked on something keeping it out of the officer's sight. She turned and said, "Don't worry. We're not going to Disease Control." She raised a small injection device, clearly not standard medical issue, to his neck and fired a single burst with a dull *thunk*.

He looked at her, his eyes wide, and clutched his neck. "What the fuck do you think you're doing?" He spat out, suddenly bobbing drunkenly backing and forth on his feet.

"Just need you to calm down," she said, holding him up. "That's it..." she said, watching his eyes and his lids began to droop. "Just let it happen."

Hadley's eyes rolled back in his head and he dropped to the floor of the ambulance like a rag doll, his legs collapsing under him into a pile of limbs. Derocher looked down at him, her face blank. "For the Ninth Darkness," she stated icily. The paramedic driving looked over his shoulder calmly, then turned his attention back to the road.

"We lose them?" she said over the sound of the sirens.

"They have no idea where we are," he said, his eyes on the road.

"General Hospital," she said, sounding like a monotone

news announcer. Her partner drove on, sirens blaring. She carefully straightened Hadley's limp form into a lying position on his back. Working according to a well-rehearsed plan, she took the injector and moved it to Weltner, still unmoving, and pressed it against the inside of his elbow. She flicked a switch on the back of it and pressed the trigger, drawing blood into the injector, then moving it back over to Hadley. She flicked the switch again and pressed the nozzle back to Hadley's neck. She pressed the trigger, injecting the blood into him. Despite her outward calm, she was excited. The plan was proceeding perfectly.

The male paramedic driving turned his head over his shoulder. "That's really not very sanitary. You ought to use cotton swabs and alcohol."

She looked back at him, smirking, before taking the injector and slipping it back into her bag. She zipped it up then returned to Hadley, pulling his vest and uniform off. The sweat all over his body made it cling to him, but she proceeded with relative ease, placing his uniform neatly into a duffel bag. She stood and looked over her work. The two officers both lay motionless on the floor, Hadley now in his underwear.

The ambulance pulled into the drop-off area of the emergency ward for Toronto General Hospital. The paramedic driving threw a large empty duffel bag over his shoulder before he exited the vehicle. Derocher hopped out the back and they pulled out Weltner's body on a stretcher, acting as though he were in need of desperate medical attention. The paramedics hustled him through the waiting area, ignoring the nurses and attendants. They moved through several sets of doors before dropping the act and taking the gurney into a large elevator, then down three floors to the hospital morgue. Derocher looked at her partner, small beads of sweat forming on her forehead. He daubed at them with a piece of gauze. They both smiled.

They waited outside the morgue calmly for a few minutes. The attending pathologist shut the lights off and walked out, pulling his gloves and protective glasses off, heading out to his break. Derocher and her partner watched the man go, then nonchalantly rolled their gurney in.

The lime-green tiled room was empty and they switched the lights on, working quickly. They both unstrapped and pulled off Weltner's clothes, placing everything neatly on the floor in order. Their precision, appropriate for the venue, was surgical. Derocher noticed her hands were shaking, and reminded herself that no one knew they were there, or what they were doing. She took a deep breath before going back to work.

Derocher drew out a long clear plastic body bag with a light whoosh, which they slipped up and over the body. Her partner headed to the clipboard hanging on the wall by the door giving the log-in and examination schedule. Scanning for the next male John Doe on the list, he found the drawer number. "Drawer seven," he said to her.

She opened the latch and pulled the drawer and its accompanying body out. The male paramedic had moved another gurney over beside the drawer, which they rolled the body from drawer seven onto. Derocher's partner pulled off the toetag from the drawer seven body and placed it on Weltner's toe, then the matching label for the bodybag, which they zipped shut.

They moved Weltner's body into the drawer and shut it. The John Doe body from drawer seven they hurriedly dressed in Weltner's uniform—several sizes too big—and pushed him out on their gurney. *Few signs of trauma. Relatively undamaged. Perfect. By the time anyone notices the switch we'll be long gone and well underway in our transcendence.*

The male paramedic pulled a sheet up and over their "patient", then shut off the lights as they exited, rolling John Doe from drawer number seven out with them. Derocher led the way back to their vehicle, still containing the lifeless body of Hadley. She was barely able to conceal her smile as they returned to the ambulance. *The Ninth Darkness is coming, and we will be a part of it.* They sped out, sirens on.

They drove unimpeded to a desolate industrial street near Cherry Beach, approaching the Port Lands. The area had just begun its revitalization into a new residential area, but the street they turned down, further into the desolate emptiness of former industrial land in transition, was only populated by phantom warehouses that held nothing but pigeons and the occasional squatter. Derocher thought the ambulance might be spotted, but didn't care. No one would think anything of them. The lack of human inhabitants around them made it still more unlikely.

They drove up and over the curb as they reached a patch

of flat ground that looked like the remnant of a recently razed structure, and drove across, heading toward the water. They stopped as they neared the edge, and the driver carefully backed the ambulance into position until the back doors faced the lake. He put the vehicle into park and moved into the back, helping Derocher move Hadley as she kicked open the back doors. The overcast sky hung bloated like sagging concrete over their heads and matched the drab, broken grayness all around them. They rolled Hadley up into a sitting position, looked at each other, then gave a solid push, causing him to flop with a splash into the water.

The woman squatted and looked down, watching Hadley bubble and sink. "*Bon voyage*, Sailor," she said quietly. He was an unwilling sacrifice, not like Derocher and her partner would be. Their transformations would come late, and they would only see the new world through new eyes. She almost envied the dead man as she watched his form sink into the murky harbor waters. He would feel no anxiety, no excitement. Only the placid emptiness of eternity.

Her partner returned to the driver's seat as she closed the back doors. They drove out, back onto the road, and into to an area with a few decrepit brick structures, some boarded up, the rest with broken windows, none with functioning businesses. Derocher opened another large duffel bag and withdrew a jerry can, unscrewing the cap and spilling gasoline all over the interior of the vehicle, heavily dousing John Doe's body and the duffel bag full of Hadley's clothes.

Her partner, his hands gloved, stepped out of the driver's side door and came around to the back holding a road flare. They both unbuttoned and pulled off their uniforms, stripping down to shorts and T-shirts, before tossing the paramedic uniforms into the ambulance. They both moved several meters away from the open back door as he lit the flare and lobbed it inside, causing a whoosh of fire and heat as the ambulance immediately went up in flames.

They turned, and headed to a nondescript blue compact car parked nearby. As they walked, Derocher swung an arm around her partner's waist.

Joy. Joy for the new world we are building. For Olog'lahai'kuhul.

She pulled out a set of keys, entered and started it up, her partner sitting beside her in the passenger seat. They drove away as the ambulance burned, a column of black smoke rising from it.

Chapter Fourteen

Michaud stood chatting quietly with Simons, discussing their situation. Perry sat against the far wall with his hands resting limply on his knees, a look of bored resignation on his face, blankly watching the air filtration system work. Michaud, Simons, Perry and McRae had all been sealed in a small Plexiglas-enclosed quarantine room inside the CIDC complex, deep within multiple levels of security. There were three layers of windows all around them, and a triple-redundant decontamination airlock for access and egress that included showers and ultraviolet light banks, in what they had been told was a Containment Level Four isolation unit. McRae paced in frustration, obviously antsy to get out. All four of them had, upon admittance, had their clothes removed, then were subject to decontamination showers and multiple tests. Hours later, Michaud was still unable to get the smell of industrial soap and cleaner out of his nostrils.

They had been provided plain blue coveralls. Michaud found the outfit slightly more dignified than a hospital gown. Around the glass, large signs reading "Biohazard" were posted, and it didn't help his state of mind knowing that the interior of the room was fireproof due to the jets along the wall being capable of incinerating everything inside. Other members of the ETF team had been sent to another unit, further down the same hall. Michaud took minor comfort in knowing that Karen had immediately been declared safe and was able to stay outside the quarantine.

A young woman in a white lab coat walked by the windows with a clipboard tucked under her arm. McRae approached the interior layer of Plexiglas and knocked on it. "Hey! How much longer are we going to be in here?"

The young lab technician stopped. Of course, not a word McRae said was audible outside the isolation unit, but she knew what he was asking. She shrugged her shoulders and walked on with a look on her face that communicated "sorry, I have no idea."

McRae sighed loudly and turned away. As he did so, someone else came into view—this time it was Karen, wearing a visitor badge on her breast pocket, accompanied by a Centre official, also wearing a lab coat. The official was a Southeast Asian man in his late 30's, with a name tag reading "Ladrillo" and no title indicated. He was still very boyish-looking, his age betrayed by the speckling of grey throughout his very recently trimmed hair. His blank expression gave nothing away, he might be the bearer of news that was either direly negative or pleasantly surprising. Michaud and Simons stood and approached the windows, McRae turning to see what was happening. Perry looked up, expecting the worst from his dour expression.

Karen pressed her hand against an intercom device on the outer wall. "You're being released from quarantine. The final blood work is done, looks like you're all clean."

McRae, obviously relieved, sighed and threw his head back, while Perry slowly stood. Michaud and Simons smiled. Karen waited until they were through the airlock and handed Simons and Michaud "visitor" badges like hers, while McRae and Perry turned away with the Centre official. Karen held up a bag full of Michaud's clothes for him to change into, and led them down the hall opposite.

"I guess this means we're not getting our clothes back," Michaud grunted, annoyed.

Ladrillo, the Centre official, stopped and spoke up, his voicing carrying a slight Filipino accent. "No, I'm sorry detective. Everything was autoclaved, analyzed and destroyed as a precaution. You're all very lucky, the microorganisms involved appear to have a Class three or four level of pathogenicity," he said gravely.

Michaud looked at him frowning. "I'm sorry, I'm not a virologist, or a biologist..."

"Very, very dangerous," Ladrillo said with the hint of an amused smirk, before continuing away with McRae and Perry.

Michaud sighed, watching them go. "I really liked that tie. Gift from my uncle. Glad I left my jacket at the office."

Karen handed Michaud the bag of clothes. "Hope these'll do."

"None for me?" Simons asked.

"Couldn't get into your house...I don't even know where you live, actually. This was all I had time for."

Simons smiled and shook his head as if to say, "forget it."
Michaud looked through the bag and spoke without looking
up. "How are the other officers?"

Karen ran down the list. "One of the other reasons I came.
We can't get a hold of Montrose. Another Hazmat team is on
its way to his house. We've got teams analyzing the clubhouse
on Saint Clair as well as the apartment in the Annex. It's a real
mess right now."

The three walked down the stark hallways that Michaud
found sterile both literally, and figuratively in the sense of
their bland design. Form clearly followed function here, as
the flat white overhead fluorescents attested. Signs along the
walls warned of hazards and admonished staff to take all pre-
cautions, wear masks, gloves and consistently wash hands.
The smell of industrial cleaner was even more inescap-
able, amplified further by the one still lingering in his nose.
Michaud cleared his throat.

"What about Weltner and Chow from tactical?" he asked.

Karen met their eyes, but seemed to be searching for words.
"You're not going to believe this. Weltner...he...it doesn't look
like he made it. The ambulance that had him disappeared. No
radio communication. And the paramedics that attended to
Weltner...they're gone."

"Gone? How gone?"

"Like, not answering phones, no one at their homes, gone.
The ambulance though...turned up on a side street in the
Port Lands, on fire. And...Weltner was inside. We think he
was anyways, body was pretty badly burned, still working on
identification. No sign of Hadley either."

"You mean the paramedics..."

"We're not sure. Could be unrelated, but seems pretty likely they were involved."

"Shit," Michaud sighed in frustration. "Chow?"

"That's where we're going now. He's still in quarantine."
She parted a set of double doors, leading them into another
area of the Disease Control complex—just in time to see two
men in lab coats and gas masks carrying out of another quarantine unit the prone form of Chow on a gurney, covered with
a portable plastic isolation shield. Life support tubes fed into
it, connected to oxygen and fluid-dispensing tanks. At least
they knew he was still alive.

Accompanying the two men in lab coats were two others,

security guards by the looks of it, but dressed in full urban camouflage, tactical vests, gas masks, and both armed with assault rifles. Michaud and Karen noticed something familiar worn by all of them. The logo of Perpendex Pharmaceuticals.

"What the hell?" Karen asked out loud.

Michaud frowned, pursed his lips and roared. "Excuse me! Under whose authority are you here?" The Perpendex guards positioned themselves silently in front of Michaud, Karen and Simons, blocking them off from Chow and the two lab coats. The Perpendex lab techs continued out, ignoring Michaud's query. The double-doors behind them parted and the Centre official, Ladrillo, who had accompanied Perry and McRae out approached the tense scene. Michaud turned to him.

"What's going on? Who are these people?" he asked, indicating the arrogant Perpendex crew with a broad sweep of his arm.

"They have been authorized to do this." His eyes went back and forth between Michaud, Simons and Karen. He seemed to be restraining himself, clearly uncomfortable with the situation, but most likely ordered to simply deal with it as best he was able.

Simons' eyes widened as he spoke, his voice rising to a near yell. "That's one of our officers! Where are you taking him?"

Ladrillo's restraint was evident, concern showing in his eyes despite his cool tone. "Your officer is a serious biological hazard at the moment. He's been infected with something and the only facility capable of containing and dealing with it effectively is theirs."

"You can't do this!" Karen shouted, both to the Centre official and to the departing Perpendex employees.

Ladrillo stepped slightly in her direction. "I'm afraid it's necessary. Unless you want a highly virulent and deadly contagion spreading through a major metropolitan area tonight." The Perpendex crew had turned and exited with Chow, their security detail following. The hallway was left empty save Michaud, Simons, Karen and Ladrillo.

"You had us isolated in a unit that you said was capable of containing this," Michaud protested.

"I'm sorry," Ladrillo replied.

"This is crazy," Simons said.

Ladrillo gestured with his arm toward the double-doors, back the way they came. "If you don't mind?" The officers reluctantly moved ahead and pushed through the doors. Michaud cast a frown at Ladrillo, who returned a sympathetic look. "I'm sorry," he repeated. "It's out of my hands."

* * * *

Night had fallen on the city. The Beaches neighborhood was quiet, even for an early Thursday evening. Detective Montrose had been sleeping, or attempting to sleep, his rest interrupted by horrifying nightmares. Lying in bed, the only noises were a distant dog barking and the streetcar rumbling by along the main avenue. A light wind brought a cool breeze to an otherwise warm early autumn night, rustling the trees lining the street. Interminable itching all over his body and the pain in his stomach intruded on his sleep.

He had bought his house on this small row of homes almost on impulse and paid his way into a mortgage after his promotion to detective. He knew that others would see a downtown condo as his style, especially with his avowed bachelor status, but deep down he really wanted to marry a nice girl and start a family. Subconsciously perhaps, this was his way of jump-starting that plan. Over the last year he had put considerable work into renovating and modernizing the home, bringing it up to standard, but maintaining the general look of the building without ruining the design.

He closed his eyes only to awake again with beads of sweat across his forehead, and the blankets of his bed clung matted with moisture to his chest. He peeled them back and swung his legs out and onto the floor, forcing himself up. He shuffled to his bedroom window, looking out over the rest of the quiet neighborhood. He saw windows glowing blue with television and computer monitor light, while others exuded the warmer glow of reading lights or dining tables. Many were dark, their residents sleeping soundly. *Why am I sick? Something I ate?*

Upon his return home, he had disrobed and showered, but he still felt grimy. His boxer shorts, fresh from his dresser, were now soaked in sweat. In the dim moonlight, his vision was poor, but he remembered simply by routine how to navigate himself to the bathroom down the hall. He paused, holding his hand to his head, and swayed back and forth. He felt dizzy, far more so than he should have from simply being recently awoken. He moved through a patch of moonlight cast down through his study and he dragged his hand along the wall. It left a long smear of greasy custard-like ooze.

From outside came the sound of vehicles. Screeching tires, footsteps. A fist hammering at the door. Yelling voices. Muffled, indistinct. Montrose heard sounds, but couldn't understand any words, like someone yelling underwater.

Who the fuck is at my door at this hour? Don't they know I have to work in the morning? Assholes.

Montrose moved blindly down his hallway, trying to feel his way along, but his equilibrium was upset and his attempt to go by memory was not working as it should have. He shuffled forth, shaking his head, and accidentally pushed into a chest-high bookshelf and knocked over a small blue ceramic lamp, smashing it on the floor. Montrose ignored it, thankful that he was at the bathroom and pulled himself inside, switching on the light.

As he lifted his head to look at himself, he yelped at the sight of his own face. He was covered in huge pustules that pulsated and bulged with a loathsome yellow fluid. He leaned in, staring into his own face, trying to look into one of the sacs. In it was a tiny shape, like a fish or worm...it twitched, kicking its tail.

Montrose pushed away from the mirror, his eyes wide, his jaw hanging open. He noticed that several of the growths on his forehead were leaking, and he looked down at his hands, turning them over. Pustules covered his hands and arms.

"Uhhh! Uhhh!" He let out primal, terrified groans, like an overgrown infant trapped in a nightmare. The vigorous pounding on the front door continued, the thuds sounding like muffled drumbeats to him in his horrified state. He tore open his medicine cabinet, his shaking hands guided toward the hydrogen peroxide.

As Montrose shut the cabinet door, something behind him moved. The shower curtain seemed to pull back of its own accord. Montrose shuddered, then spun, looking at the movement. A gas-masked man stood in the clawfoot tub, pulling the curtain completely open.

Montrose's mouth turned down in a frightened grimace, his eyes wide with surprise and confusion. He was barely able to take in the outline of the hat, the overcoat, and the strange lantern in the man's hand. Before he could say anything, the intruder raised his lantern-device and activated it, enveloping

Montrose in a flash of green light.

* * * *

The Hazmat team and uniformed officers at the front door paused, hearing Montrose's frantic dying screams. The stocky male police officer who had been peering through the front windows with his hands cupped around his eyes turned to them. "Step back!" He pushed them aside. He took a run at the door and kicked it beneath the doorknob, forcing it open and splintering wood chips across the floor. He jumped back and let the CIDC team members access.

The two Hazmat-suited men in the front switched on large flashlights and swept the beams across the darkened rooms. They moved quickly, trying to find Montrose, assuming he would be passed out or squirming on the floor in agony. One looked up the stairs and could see that a light had been turned on, or left on, around the corner and presumably down a hallway. He turned to the other team members and gestured for them to follow. One near the front drew a hand taser, on the off chance that Montrose was violent and would need to be immediately subdued. From behind them, a female police officer yelled into the house, "Detective Montrose! Please make yourself known to the containment team! We need you to come into custody. It's for your own safety!"

At the top of the stairs, the lead Hazmat team member swung his flashlight back toward the lit room. A cloud of smoke was wafting out, and he moved quickly toward it, followed by the others. As he entered the bathroom, his flashlight beam quickly found the source of the smoke. The charred, crumbling skeleton of Montrose was lying in the tub.

"My God..." a Hazmat team member mumbled from beneath his suit.

* * * *

Outside, the Cleaner walked calmly away from the open back door of Montrose' house, off the back patio and through the yard. Members of the Hazmat team could be seen within the house, looking around with their flashlights, but the Cleaner did not hesitate. He pushed himself over the fence and into the neighbor's back yard, removing his mask and replacing his hat. He spoke into his wrist radio as he continued walking, through the small alley between the neighbors' houses.

"We're heading to the next assignment," he said in his metallic voice as he emerged from between the buildings and moved through the neighbor's front yard.

A black van sat idling in the street. The Cleaner moved to the back and the doors were opened for him. He stepped up inside, and the van smoothly pulled away at low speed with barely an engine rumble.

* * * *

Michaud sat in the back of Simons' car, utterly spent. Karen was in the front on the passenger side while Simons sat in the drivers' seat inserting his keys. The day was long and tiring, but thankfully, finally over. They sat a moment, silent.

"Who the hell are these people? Perpendex? What's going on?" Simons said out loud, not turning to the others.

"The guy who hit Michaud in the head yesterday is probably one of them. It looks like they're hunting down our cult suspects and anyone who comes into direct contact with them," Karen replied.

Simons turned the keys in the ignition and drove out of the vast parking lot, finding the highway. At this late hour, there were few other drivers on the road. "How can they do this?"

Karen's phone buzzed in her pocket. She withdrew it and answered, "Wendleton. Where?...They found him? Oh...I'll let them know." She turned to Michaud and Simons, looking mortified. "That was one of the officers with the Hazmat team from Disease Control. They thought you might still be in quarantine."

"And?" Simons demanded.

"They found Montrose. He's dead. Incinerated and left in his bathtub, like the others."

"Jesus Christ..." Simons mumbled.

Michaud spoke up, depressed. "He beat us to it again."

Simons spoke aloud in a slightly hushed, wearily frightened voice "What is happening?"

Michaud yawned, tired and frustrated, wiping a hand over his eyes. "I don't care right now. I just want to get home and have a hot shower."

The car pulled up to the curb in front of Michaud's building and he stepped out.

Karen rolled her window down and Michaud stopped, resting his hands on the door, leaning in. His eyes drooped, feeling the weight of the day's events. "I'm going to get some sleep. I suggest you guys do likewise. There's not a whole lot we can do right now other than wait and see how this all plays out." Karen and Simons looked worried, but nodded their assent.

"Good night guys," Michaud finished, turning to head to his apartment.

He turned back around, walking backwards, and watched as the car pulled away. He turned again and stepped slowly and deliberately up the front steps, fishing in his pocket for his keys, then fumbled and dropped them. He bent to pick them up... Michaud only had a fleeting glimpse of a gun-shaped device injecting him in the shoulder with a jolting hiss. Something thrown over his head. Darkness, then unconsciousness. Michaud immediately fell limp.

* * * *

Like stalking panthers they had him, a pair of men dressed head to toe in black tactical gear, balaclavas, gloves and boots. They had sprung up from behind him and wasted no time in securing Michaud's wrists with zap-straps behind his back. They pulled the draw-string of the bag on his head snug, before carrying him quickly to the driveway beside the building and into the back of the black van waiting there.

They carefully placed him on the floor, making sure not to injure him. He was a fragile package. His safety was important, and part of their overall plan; the two operatives of the *Ordo Sanctus* had been given strict orders not to harm the detective. They shut the back door of the van as it pulled away. The driver looked back. His face was obscured in shadow, but the outline of his hat was unmistakable, the Cleaner.

* * * *

Norman Cooper, the medical examiner, pushed through the double doors of the hospital morgue, nonchalantly eating a ham sandwich he held in one hand. In some alternate life the drab, curly-haired man in his mid-forties might have made an excellent bank robber because his average height, average build and utterly unmemorable average looks would have made him impossible to describe to a police sketch artist.

He stopped momentarily to finish the last bite of his sandwich, before checking the schedule for the next item. He scanned down until he found it, John Doe, drawer seven. Cooper licked off his fingers, and walked to the nearby sink to thoroughly scrub his hands. He carefully pulled an apron on over his scrubs, secured his surgical mask, and lastly the gloves, because he hated how sweaty they made his palms.

Cooper walked to the drawers, pulled number seven open and huffed loudly. He brought out the body, lowered it onto the waiting gurney, then wheeled it over to the examining table, finally stopping to look at his watch impatiently. His assistant Shawna should have been here fifteen minutes earlier, but she was frustratingly absent. Cooper grunted in annoyance and went to work.

He turned away from the examining table, pulled down a ceiling-mounted microphone, and spoke languidly, "Medical examiner Norman Cooper for uh, John Doe, time of death unknown, cause of death unknown. Time now is..." He looked up at the mounted wall clock. "Twenty-two-thirty..."

A light shuffling noise from behind him startled him, and he bumped into the hanging scale used to weigh organs. He shifted, looking over his shoulder, frowning. He turned completely around, but nothing was in the room other than the plastic-wrapped corpse of the John Doe, which lay motionless. Cooper looked around for the air vent. *Thought they fixed that damn air leak. Shouldn't be a draft in here anymore.* The weighing scale swung back and forth from his accidental nudge, then slowed gradually to a stop. Cooper turned back to the microphone and opened his mouth to speak, and again he heard the shuffling sound. He turned, this time more wary.

Cooper approached the corpse on the table, slowly. He stood, looking over it. He could see motion. The stomach area of the body was undulating perceptibly, as though something underneath the skin were pulsating. *What the hell is that?*

Suddenly, underneath the clear plastic covering, a seething custard-like liquid spouted up out of the chest and poured over the body, slowly enveloping it. Cooper stumbled back, gasping for breath, his hands shaking. Every nightmare he had ever suppressed through years of desensitization to corpses had exploded like a bomb in his subconscious. He raced to the nearby wall and grabbed the receiver of the emergency phone, fumbling it before getting a grip. "This is the medical examiner...I've got a situation here. Get someone down here now! C-call the police!"

He dropped the receiver, and it bounced off the floor, yo-yoing up and down on its cord. He could only stare helplessly at the repulsive substance, its bubbling growing louder as it crept over Weltner's body...

* * * *

Michaud was bound, his hands and ankles strapped securely to the arms and footpads of a chair, but he felt movement. Still in darkness, the bag forcing him to breathe stifled air, he guessed he was seated in a wheelchair.

A deep, powerful voice called out from the darkness. "Remove the bag."

Michaud felt a tug as a string was loosened. The bag pulled off, and light flooded his vision. He squinted as his eyes adjusted. As his view cleared, he saw two men in tactical gear through a fuzzy haze, both in balaclavas. The same type of strange rifles that Michaud glimpsed on the bodies of those found at the Dressed to the Nines Club hung from the black-clad operatives. *Ordo Sanctus? Where am I?* A spotlight shone down on him, the rest of the room deep in shadow.

Michaud was none the worse for wear, despite his grogginess from the injection that was just wearing off. He looked up, seeing partial silhouettes, men in suits, sitting in a row along their high seats of judgment and command.

The voice addressed him again. "We have summoned you before us, Detective, for a very good reason."

Michaud searched for the owner of the voice, trying to regain his senses. His throat was parched, and his voice came like a loud whisper. "Who...who are you?"

He tried to make out details, mentally record the men he could barely see. His head swam, his eyes unable to focus properly.

"You should know by now. We represent the *Ordo Sanctus*. We are an ancient order of Christian knights, and we have been at war with the Children of *Olog'lahai'kuhul* for over eight hundred years.

"It was in 1233 that the Templar Knight Henri de Vareilles, involved in the Albigensian Crusade, formed our order. The Church was engaged in an attempt to crush the heathen Cathars. The knight Henri tracked what he thought was a small sect of them into a mountain cave, but what he found was something else...something horrible. They had conjured, summoned something from beyond our world, a force of terrifying evil and destruction. Witnessing their ritual, he was driven mad. He strove forth, drawing his sword, then slew them all, disrupting their ritual, and burned their bodies. He had sent the foul beast they had summoned back into its stygian abysses. But he knew it would return, something he could never allow."

Michaud tried to focus, but the man's voice was almost hypnotic. He felt immersed in the history being given. The shadows seemed to part, visions of blood and fire replacing them.

"Going through the scrolls and texts in the cave he discovered they were the descendants of a tiny band of Druids that had fled Roman Britain hundreds of years earlier. They had fallen to the worship of the entity *Olog'lahai'kuhul*, a monstrosity from another world, from a plane of existence parallel to our own. The cultists came to live like beasts, degenerate and feral, succumbing to their animalistic tendencies without regard for the world of man. Rather than turn to the Church for guidance, they had cast aside morality in favor of their blasphemous depravity, becoming the Children of *Olog'lahai'kuhul*."

Michaud could almost see the form of the knight in front of him, seated in a cave, ringed with torches. *What did they inject me with?*

"In his madness, Henri took the scrolls and all their writings, and transcribed them into the book of forbidden knowledge—the *Encyclopedia Nefastus*. He destroyed the original manuscripts, heaping them into a great pyre with the bodies of the disgusting cult members, and with only one copy of the ritual remaining, he formed a new order.

"The Holy Order of the Soldiers of Christendom was to guard its secrets forever and keep them from the hands of lesser men, using its knowledge as a defense against the Ninth Darkness. Over the centuries, many have attempted to wrest the book from our hands. Sometimes by traitorous knights driven mad by its revelations, but other times by interlopers who sought to deceive us. Copies were made, stolen, re-made, but only one true copy still exists, the one that has been carefully guarded, re-transcribed and preserved any time the original was damaged. Henri's copy has long since crumbled into dust, but the one perfectly copied from it in the seventeenth century still stands."

Michaud's vision began to clear, the pages of the *Encyclopedia Nefastus* crumbling away into the darkness. He looked back up at the owner of the voice. Michaud could nearly see the face...

"So you see detective...it is our burden to carry, and no one else's. The book was stolen from us by one who worked his way into our ranks, as one of our security forces. We thought we had him well investigated, but apparently not. You will remember one of his coconspirators as the man you encountered in Rachel Atwater's house, in the basement. Our Cleaner took care of him. You will find more bodies, and then the cult murders will come to an end, and you will conclude that the cult members took their own lives in a suicide pact. We still need the book, and the thief, and that is our problem to deal with. For that you must stand aside."

Keep him talking. Just a few more seconds. Michaud spoke up. "You...you're getting in the way of my investigation. Burning evidence." Lucidity had become less evasive, and as clarity approached, Michaud scanned the other members of the Council above him. One of them seemed familiar, and he managed to stifle an expression of recognition when he realized that next to the speaker was the Informant he had met in High Park. The mysterious man who had snuck into his apartment to warn him of listening devices. *Who is with you? Who is that voice? Silver hair...mid-fifties...*

"No, Detective. We've been keeping you alive," the speaker continued. "Our Cleaner was somewhat overzealous with you in the alley, but we need to make sure not to draw undue attention to our organization, and as such you have been kept safe, for the time being."

"What do you want from me?" Michaud asked. He could make out more detail now, and the man's face was almost clear.

"Nothing. We want you to stay out of our way."

"I can't do that." *Who are you? I know that face. The news?*

"You must. Our Cleaner will take care of this problem. Stay out of his way or you risk serious consequences to yourself... and to your friends and family."

The speaker finished his sentence. Michaud had little time to digest this barely veiled threat before one of the two operatives stepped forward and jabbed the injector into Michaud's arm. Its hiss sent him again into a deep pit of unconsciousness.

Chapter Fifteen

Michaud awoke as the blinds in his bedroom opened, pulled by an unseen hand. Startled and confused, he blinked his eyes and shielded himself from the sunlight that was still too bright. As his eyes adjusted, he could see who was in his room. Karen.

"It's late. You didn't drink before bed, did you?" she asked. She stood with one hand on her hip. She had on work clothes, and ones that were more office-oriented than her usual bicycle-commute tank top. Clearly she hadn't ridden over. "What, you fall off the wagon? You look rough, pal."

"Well, you know what happens when I drink," he mumbled, implying their after-work revelry of a year previous. "Besides, I haven't had a drop in weeks," he said, putting a hand to his sore head. The bump he had received from the Cleaner felt sore again, as if his evening had re-aggravated the injury.

"Could've fooled me. You look like a hangover hit you pretty hard."

"The only thing that's hit me hard lately is that jerk in the alley," Michaud said, moving his hand around to cover his eyes. He looked up at her, still squinting.

"How'd you even get in here?"

"You left a copy of your keys at the office for emergencies. I picked them up yesterday when you were in quarantine."

"Right," he said, covering his eyes again.

"You can't just be exhausted. You didn't stay up even later last night, did you?"

He turned and looked to her. "Something happened after you dropped me off...I don't really remember."

"It wasn't the guy with the mask again was it?"

"I...I don't think so."

Karen looked at him with a wry smile. "You slept in your clothes again, eh? Maybe time for a change?"

Michaud looked down at himself. Either he had collapsed into bed of his own accord, too tired to take off the clothes Karen had brought him after he got out of quarantine, or someone put him in bed without bothering to do so. The fog in his head started to clear and the latter somehow seemed more accurate. "Yeah...yeah. I'm going to have a shower," he said, sliding off the bed.

* * * *

He stumbled toward the bathroom as Karen watched, with a slightly bemused expression on her face. "How is it that your apartment looks like something out of a catalogue advertisement, but your office looks like you hid steaks under everything and set loose a pack of wild dogs in it?" she asked.

The shower faucet started, and the sprinkling of water was audible. "What was that?" Michaud asked, voice raised over the sound of the shower.

"Oh, I just said you have a hot body and I'd love to jump in there with you right now," Karen said in a normal speaking voice.

"I can't hear you, you'll have to speak up!"

"I said they found another body!" Her smile faded as she realized what she had said. She shouted through the door, "We have to get to the hospital. They found Weltner."

"Is he all right?" Michaud called out from behind the door.

"It doesn't look that way," Karen said with a sigh.

* * * *

Karen led Michaud down a long hallway in the hospital toward the morgue. He had thrown on a pair of jeans and a short-sleeved collared shirt. It was more casual for him than usual, and moist rings of perspiration darkened his back and under his arms. The heat and humidity in the city had spiked and become borderline unbearable that day, and sweat beaded his brow. The cool, dry air of the hospital was a welcome relief. As they reached the large double-doors of the morgue, Karen stopped and turned to him with a look of trepidation on her face. "I didn't want to tell you about this before we got here. Figured it'd be best if you just saw it yourself."

Michaud, confused and concerned, let Karen open the door. He followed her in, but what he saw stopped him in his tracks.

The entire room was filled with large electronic units and

sensor equipment. Computers had been set up on tables displaying readouts and data, and a huge set of plastic curtains halved the room, cutting Michaud and Karen off from the rest of it.

Men in hazmat suits walked around with clipboards or small handheld electronic devices taking readings from off the gurney that held Weltner, still in the middle of the room, sealed off behind further plastic curtains and wrapped in the same plastic covering. Beneath the covering, Michaud could vaguely make out the pulsating form of a custard-yellow mass of tissue, what was once Weltner, now some kind of cocoon. He took his eyes off the disturbing spectacle and noticed the logos on the hazmat suits the men in the room wore: Perpendex Pharmaceuticals.

He turned to Karen, incensed. "Who let these assholes in here?"

The Medical Examiner, Cooper, approached. His complexion was ruddy, and beads of sweat were obvious on his forehead, despite the air conditioning. "I did."

"And you are?" Michaud asked.

Karen intervened, introducing the two men to each other. "Medical Examiner Norman Cooper, Detective Benoit Michaud, I'm sorry, I..."

Michaud interrupted her, holding his hand up, addressing Cooper. "Why'd you let them take over?"

Cooper stuttered and spit his words, "I have no idea how to deal with it. The Centre for Infectious Disease Control told me to let them, these...people I mean, take care of it, and they seem to be handling it well enough. I can't really do anything about it. They say they can't move him...it...right now."

"That's our man? That's Weltner under there?" Michaud asked, pointing.

"I picked him out from photos. I saw him last night before that stuff erupted out of his chest."

"Any idea who dropped him off? Was it the paramedics who picked him up yesterday?"

"I was just told he was a John Doe."

Karen piped up, "Was there any record of a sign-in? An activity log?"

Cooper became impatient. "No, nothing, I'm sorry. He was in the drawer we had listed as a John Doe. Someone probably switched bodies. I had no idea he was even a police officer until I was told. I've told the other detective all this already."

"Simons?" Michaud asked.

"Yes, I think that was his name."

"Where did he go?" Michaud's fists were clenched.

Again, Karen intervened, this time physically moving between the two of them. Her eyebrows were raised, suggesting to Michaud his conduct was unnecessary. "Simons was here earlier with me. Now maybe we should let the man get back to his business?"

Michaud took a deep breath, then sighed in frustration and nodded apologetically to Cooper. *This guy has no control over what's happening. He doesn't know what I want, and he's not the problem.* Michaud turned back to Karen. "I'm guessing someone already asked them for security camera recordings."

Karen nodded. "Simons took them. I'd lay solid odds on them showing the two paramedics who were with Hadley and Weltner as being the ones dropping Weltner's body off here and taking the other body. Once we identify the bodies from the ambulance fire I don't doubt it'll match the preliminary X-rays they took of their John Doe."

Michaud raised his voice. "The question is, why? Why drop Weltner off here?" Michaud asked, his arms up in exasperation. He knew Karen couldn't know the answer, but felt the need to vent.

Karen could only shrug her shoulders. The side of her mouth twisted and her brow furrowed into a look of apology.

"Any word on Chow from these clowns?" Michaud asked.

"Sorry boss, it's like they've blindfolded us, tied our hands behind our backs, stuffed cotton in our ears and we've got to get out of the building before it collapses."

"The apartment in the Annex? Anything new there?" he asked.

"Still waiting for some exam results. Found the identification of that guy on the list, so probably nothing that'll shock you."

"I don't think much else could shock me after this week."

Chapter Sixteen

Nathan Raponi, a young forensics officer, supervised the small research team that worked in the Annex apartment that had come to be known as "Room Nine," the site of the bizarre insect-like hive discovered just a day earlier. His forensics unit had scoured the space for evidence relating to the deaths of the people who were encased in the webbing-material along the walls, but the causes of their deaths seemed obvious.

Underneath the tough chitinous mass, they had found identification cards, a Dressed to the Nines Club badge, and photocopies of cult literature, ostensibly belonging to the tenant. Analysis of the webbing-like substance revealed it to be a mixture of an orally secreted, primarily protein salivary material, masticated and mixed with items from around his apartment. Shreds of clothing, wood fibers from furniture and shelving, chunks of the walls, and partially digested portions of the victims within. Once the black ooze was built up onto the walls, it hardened to nearly cement-like toughness, was waterproof and extremely resistant to damage.

Raponi, his curiosity unsatisfied, has read the autopsy of the massive beetle-creature as well. It had revealed the remains of a rapidly atrophying human skeleton, and dental records of it conclusively proved that it had been, or still was, Aaron Dennis, the final name on the Club Membership list. He had indeed grown a monstrous outer shell after shedding his previous skin and, at the time of his death at least, had both an endoskeleton and an exoskeleton. Raponi realized the implications for biology and genetics would be staggering. Even stranger was the fact that despite being male, the transformation had rendered Dennis the ability to lay eggs asexually...

The entire hallway and most of the building had been sealed off behind layers of plastic with air filtration units attached to exterior ventilation. Yellow police tape outside had cordoned off the doors, and the other residents of the buildings had been temporarily put up in hotels.

Raponi had sent a pair of uniformed officers to order the businesses below to shut their doors for two to three days while the teams upstairs worked. They needed first to catalogue and remove the odd organic samples, then sterilize the area of possible further contamination.

Four other people in hazmat suits identical to Raponi's worked as a team in Room Nine, two men from the Centre for Infectious Disease Control, and a man and a woman from the university biology department. Inside Raponi's hazmat suit, his sweat was building up—it was still hot outside, but the building was sweltering. He felt like he was seated in a steam room, breathing into a plastic bag. *Just a few more hours. The decontamination shower will never feel so welcome as it will after this.*

Bright mid-morning sunlight filtered through the spaces between the foul black encrustations webbed across the windows, highlighting the intricate honeycomb patterns covering the walls. Raponi could see remnants of the recent battle in the form of dried yellow and orange liquids on the walls and floor. Bullet holes were omnipresent, crisscrossing the room, while shell casings had been collected and removed after careful examination of the area by Raponi and his fellow forensics officers.

Raponi heard something, a noise above. The suit afforded no neck movement, so he tried to pivot and bend back. Something stirred, but he couldn't make it out through the film of condensation inside his face shield. He grumbled, annoyed, and managed to rub his forehead against the inside of the plastic and clear the view. In the black contours of the far corner of the ceiling, several sac-like masses pulsed and bulged outward, one of them splitting. They were directly over the head of one of the university researchers. As Raponi looked on in stunned silence, a drop of a viscous fluid dropped and hit the man's mask, running down the front.

Raponi heard his muffled voice through the hazmat suit, "What the…"

A grotesquely bloated white grub-like creature the size of a man's arm dropped from the split sac and plummeted toward the researcher. It latched onto the head portion of his suit and he screamed in terror, desperately trying to pull it off.

"Help! Help me!" he yelled, flailing his arms madly, trying to reach for it. Raponi rushed to his aid, swatting at the enormous squirming larva. The other members of the team in the room turned at the sound and collectively jolted back at the sight. The female member of the research team looked up and screamed. Raponi cast his gaze upward. The corner of the ceiling appeared to be rippling with an abhorrent undulation of life as the other sacs split and burst, releasing gouts of fluid down onto them as more of the enormous larvae hatched and emerged.

Raponi watched the others back toward the door, terrified, leaving him and the university researcher, who still screamed and thrashed about the room. Someone stepped into the doorframe behind them. He turned at the shadow cast upon them but did not recognize the silhouette, a man clad in bowler hat and overcoat. He pushed aside the thick plastic curtain separating the room from the hallway and stepped toward them, activating a lantern-shaped mechanism. Raponi let out a futile scream as the beam of energy swept across the room onto him.

* * * *

Karen followed Michaud, down the hall of the research building. Myriad pipes ran overhead and along the walls, and a low hum of electrical equipment and churning mechanisms filled the air. "Are you going to tell me how you know this guy?"

"School," was Michaud's only response. He carried a locked black case, one heavy enough to weigh him over.

She rolled her eyes. "Obviously. He just never left, right?"

Michaud raised one eyebrow. "Sort of." He seemed to be looking for the right direction as he stopped. "He's been doing weapons research since we were friends in school. It might not be the most ethical work, but Andy's a good guy and someone you want to know for investigations." Michaud stopped midsentence as they reached the open lab door.

Karen peered at a room lined with analytical devices, electronic equipment and multiple computer panels. She guessed Doctor Andrew Campbell preferred sunlight to artificial light like Michaud because the overhead lights were off and the room was cast in a warm afternoon glow from the windows.

Across the room, a man sat at a console with his eyes fixed on the lens of a microscope. He looked up, a smile spreading across his darkly bearded face.

He wasn't at all what Karen had expected. Instead of a

portly, fuzzy-headed lummox with bad skin and ill-fitting clothes, this man was surprisingly fit, well-kempt and handsome, if a bit pale. She wasn't surprised however that he was wearing a lab coat over a flannel shirt, jeans and had a pair of runners on instead of a suit.

"Ben..." Campbell said, frowning and pouting as he pushed his chair back.

He put his hands on his hips and frowned exaggeratedly. "You never call anymore unless you want something."

Michaud put the black case down on the floor and swung out his right hand, slapping hard into Campbell's who returned the vigorous handshake, before grabbing the locked hands with his left. Campbell looked him up and down, then hugged him, causing Michaud to laugh with surprise.

Karen looked on, smiling.

"Been what, two years?" Campbell asked as they separated.

"Yeah, about that," Michaud replied, nervously rubbing the back of his neck. "I think I came by about that bizarro explosive the fire-cult arsonists were using—"

"Right! Those nuts who set dumpsters on fire and blew up those cars around the city and tried to make a pattern on a map...Man that was weird."

"You read my email about this thing, right?" Michaud's eyes moved to the case.

Campbell frowned and bobbed his head side to side. "I certainly did, sir," he replied, pretending to be insulted. "Also, all the pieces of the reports detailing what happened to people hit by it too, very interesting. So, who may I ask is your friend here?"

"Yeah...oh, sorry, this is Karen Wendleton, my..."

"New partner?" he volunteered, looking at her.

"Assistant, I was going to say," Michaud finished.

"Well, pleased to meet you Miss Wendleton." Campbell smiled again as he shook her hand.

"And I you," she said, trying her best to conceal her fascination with the man. She found herself staring into his eyes as they shook hands a little too long.

Michaud coughed and cleared his throat. "If I may..."

Campbell broke the handshake with Karen. "Of course! I'm more than just a pretty face, you know. Let's see this new toy you've brought me!" he said with a childlike enthusiasm. He grinned and giggled, rubbed his hands together in mock deviousness and reached for the black case, hauling it over to the nearest examination table with a grunt as he lifted it. "Heavy sucker, ain't he?" Campbell muttered.

As he turned his back to the two, Michaud shot Karen a wry smile, shaking his head and raising an eyebrow. She shrugged and mouthed the word, "What?" acting incensed.

Campbell flicked the latches on the case and opened it, staring in awe at the rifle. "May I?" he asked, turning to Michaud, who responded with a simple shrug and gesture of his hand toward the weapon as if to say, "be my guest." Campbell ran a hand over it, feeling the contours of the piping along the barrel. He frowned, turning to Michaud, "Is this ornamental, or is it... I guess we'll find out," he said, turning back to pull the rifle out of the case. He held it up, cradling it with care as he looked it over, before holding it against his shoulder and looking down the sights. "Was the other one just like this?"

"Uh, looked the same to me, but I couldn't tell you exactly," Michaud replied. "We're actually more curious about the power source, and how the thing works. What it fires."

"Of course, well we'll see if anything I have here can tell us what you want to know!" Campbell said, his eyes lit with mischievous glee. "You're okay with me taking this thing apart, right?"

An hour later Karen half-sat, half-leaned against the counter top where Campbell was staring, glassy-eyed, down into the disassembled pieces of the rifle, spread out across it. He had strapped on over his head a magnifying glass that flipped down over his eyes with an attached light to illuminate what he was working on. Michaud, his fists supporting his chin, stood hunched over the table, watching his friend work.

Bored, Karen sipped her coffee and tried to break the silence. "So how did you two meet anyways? Study group or something?"

Campbell laughed without looking up from the circuitry he was examining. "No, not even close. Soccer. We played soccer together."

"There was a school team?" Karen asked, her interest piqued.

Michaud chuckled. "No, it was like a club. An extra-curricular thing."

"We just did it to meet girls," Campbell said, smirking.

"Did it work?"

Michaud, somewhat embarrassed, sighed and spoke at the same time, trying hard not to smile. "Yeah...yeah it did..."

Campbell looked up from the rifle. "Remember...remember the time we took those girls out after we won that semifinal match, what were their names? You got really drunk and climbed the statue in the commons, that weird art sculpture thing, and you passed out when you came down off it?"

"Laura and Stephanie," Michaud said. "And we were all pretty drunk."

Campbell turned to Karen. "When he woke up he had puke all over his shirt, and none of us would tell him if it was his own or one of ours."

Karen nearly spit out her coffee. "That's terrible," she said, holding a hand up to keep liquid from dribbling down her chin.

"But it was this shirt he got after seeing some band, what were they called?"

"I don't...I don't remember," Michaud said, shaking his head and smiling.

"Anyways, he didn't want to throw this shirt out that was completely covered in vomit, and I mean chunky salsa-lookin' barf that was from an hour of pub food, so the guy just shakes it out and rolls it up and carries it home with him, this gross ball of puke-soaked shirt, and rinses it out in the sink. The girls were so grossed out neither of them wanted to..."

"I think she gets the idea," Michaud said, interrupting him. "And it was my favorite shirt!"

"Well, I can tell you now it was Stephanie. She puked all over you when she bent down to try and help you up after you passed out," Campbell said, proudly.

"God, I dated her for nearly a year and she never told me that..."

Karen chuckled. "Wow."

"He never tell you this story?"

"Oh, of course not. He has to maintain his air of professional credibility," she said, still smiling.

"A year? Wow. How did I not know that?" Campbell said.

Michaud wrinkled the side of his mouth. "I never got close to her."

Campbell looked at Karen, his thumb pointing at Michaud. "Never get close, the guy always said. Like it was his slogan or something.

Michaud rolled his eyes. "Anyways, can we step back into *Beakman's World* for a moment and get back to what we came here for?"

"Right, sorry," Campbell said, straightening himself up. "It looks like what you have here is actually, kind of...a laser gun."

"What?" Michaud said, blinking rapidly, his head cocked to one side.

"Well, sort of. I mean, it uses a laser, but not the way you think. It's not like in the movies, it doesn't go *'pew pew'* when you shoot it or make cool red or green beams that spray sparks all over when they hit stuff. It's actually a lot like the Pulsed Energy Projectile weapons that were developed a few years back."

A look of recognition crossed Michaud's face. "Yeah, we use them as riot control sometimes, but mounted on the backs of trucks. Those things are the size and weight of a refrigerator, and they certainly don't kill people. You're telling me this..."

"Yup. Like a more advanced, compact version of it. And this rifle will definitely be lethal. You could also set it to 'stun' people though, it would knock a man on his back and probably out cold, but this thing is powerful enough to burn a hole right through someone."

"That's pretty crazy," Karen said. "So, what does it run on? That huge cylinder?"

"It's like a battery, sort of. Thing is, it's actually really fragile. I have to assume this is in some kind of developmental or prototype stage, or maybe not, I don't know."

"Why's that?" she asked.

"Well, if this thing got broken open, the expanding heat and plasma discharge would cause an explosion. If you had a bunch of guys using them in a group, one might blow, causing the others to blow, and then you have a chain reaction, kablooie, good-bye army of guys with cool laser guns," Campbell said.

"That's not good at all," Michaud said, in a deadpan.

"Yeah, it definitely poses serious practical problems, but they're sort of balanced by the huge advantages of this weapon."

"Such as?" Karen asked.

"For one thing, I'm guessing it's almost completely silent. It might make a sort of hum, a kind of popping thud when it hits someone. And there'd be no real beam of energy you could see, unless you were looking straight down the barrel, which means you'd be dead anyways...maybe a flash of light from these slots along the side," he pointed to the rifle. "From the heat discharge, of the laser it uses. Unless of course you were in a lot of smoke, or fog, any particulate matter, like dust. Then you'd see a bright beam, like from a flashlight, but that would partially dissipate the energy too, making it slightly less effective.

Campbell's eyes narrowed. "The beam would hit a target at near the speed of light, so there's no dodging it anyways, you could strafe a target by keeping the trigger depressed, and wind, gravity, all sorts of things would have negligible effect on it. Whoever managed to make this thing this small has really done a lot of work. Their research department must be pretty crazy." He shrugged, "Ingenious, really. The compact energy source is highly advanced. I'd love to get inside a radiation suit and pry the battery right open, see exactly how it works."

"But you said it would blow up and..." Karen said.

"Yeah, exactly. I mean, in some hypothetical situation, I guess. And that's the other thing, looks like this baby would give off quite a bit of radiation when fired, so whoever was using it would probably have to wear a heavy lead jacket or something."

"That sounds a lot like what we've seen," Michaud said, looking at Karen.

Karen knew he was thinking about the heavily shielded coats worn by Wellburn and his companion when they found the bodies. She took a step back, grimacing.

Campbell raised his hands, palms up, "Oh, it's perfectly safe. Right now you'd get more radiation from sunlight. Like I said, has to be fired. The battery itself is well shielded."

Karen folded her arms, unconvinced.

"Kind of silly, really. It does have advantages, but it's pretty dangerous. Real trade-off, you know? It's like they'd be using this for ideological instead of practical purposes. Like they felt as though they *had* to use it for some reason," Campbell said.

"Do you think it's what burned up all the bodies from the first case file information I sent you?" Michaud asked.

"Well...not exactly. It's definitely similar technology, but this is...less advanced? It's really hard to say without looking at the actual weapons involved."

"Could there be a targeting system that specifically hit only organic tissue and ignored anything in the surrounding environment?"

"It's...possible, I guess. Would have to be really advanced though. That level of specialization, I don't know, on a molecular level...it wouldn't really have to, though. It's as if this thing was designed with organic matter in mind. Like the designers specifically wanted to target living or dead tissue, rather than, say, metal objects. So it would be kind of useless against a tank...well, not completely useless. I guess if you had it on a high enough setting you might be able to knock a tank over with the—"

"Guy in body armor? Knock him down, yeah?" Karen interjected.

"For sure," Campbell continued. "The pressure wave from the exploding plasma on the 'stun' setting would send him right back. Like I was saying, any large enough object on a high enough setting. But I think the true purpose of it is to destroy organic matter. Like a super-cooker or something." Campbell chuckled. "You could vaporize a full-grown man in seconds... he'd be a pile of ash, literally. Totally sterilized."

"I think that's definitely what it was designed for," Michaud said.

"It's...almost like something out of biblical retribution," Campbell mused.

Karen and Michaud passed a simultaneous knowing glance at each other. "Indeed," Michaud said.

* * * *

The man Michaud came to know as his Informant was seated in the dim council chamber. Men in suits shuffled back and forth to their assigned seats along the towering U-shaped table. The level of activity and murmuring offset the normally sepulchral atmosphere of the chamber. Looks of anxiety and confusion were on the faces of many, and even as Horatio took his place in the middle. He, too, looked less than entirely authoritative. The informant wore a light frown on his face as he looked back and forth at the others. He didn't know the purpose of this last-minute summoning any more than the others, and such meetings outside their standard schedule were extremely unusual. As the others took their seats, Horatio remained standing.

"I'm sorry to have called you all here with so little notice. But this is an emergency situation. It appears that the Ninth Darkness cult has attacked, simultaneously, six of our facilities, four in North America, one in Japan and one in Russia. All others have been put on high alert."

Another council member, a bald and thickly white-bearded man in his sixties, spoke up with a quake in his voice. "Which facilities? Have they made any offensive moves against us here?" He looked back and forth at the other council members.

Horatio spoke in a flat tone, projecting calmness, "They detonated explosive devices within our military base in North Carolina and the training facility in Eastern Washington State. The others, we're not entirely certain, other than that there has been extensive damage. Communication lines have been severed or ruined.

"As of yet these filth appear to still be focused on their summoning ritual, and in my opinion these are diversionary actions. Attempting to expose us by bringing too much attention to our operations. Hoping to cause us to scramble in a frenzy of confusion, leaving us in disarray. But we will not succumb. Our focus must remain."

Another council member piped up, clearly on the verge of panic, "Our organization is nowhere near as numerous as they are. We are few, they are legion!"

"And we have endured just as long as they have, through crises worse than this," Horatio responded.

"What should we do? Should we increase our defenses here?" the bearded council member asked.

"I believe we should bide our time," Horatio answered. "We must be vigilant, and it is likely that this will move our timetable up, marginally, but as I said, these attacks are nothing but a distraction. They know we have them at our mercy. Their desperation may make them dangerous, but it only affirms our final plan." He paused, looking around. "Be ready gentlemen. Prepare your families. The end is approaching. Soon our time will come."

Chapter Seventeen

Michaud awoke with a start at his desk as Karen burst in, the door slamming against the inside wall of his office. He blinked rapidly, forgetting for a second where he was. A photocopy of the *nonagon* diagram from one of the books he'd been poring through the night before was stuck to his face with drool.

Karen stepped to the desk, tossing her jacket onto the chair opposite. "You're not going to believe this." She stopped. "No, you will. It's just more shitty news." She reached out and pulled the paper off Michaud's face.

"What is it this time? Is the city on fire?" he said, wiping his mouth.

"The room in the Annex, Room Nine. It's burned up, all of it. The research team too. That guy again, it looks like."

"Fuck! What the fuck?!" Michaud said, slamming his fist against the desk. He immediately regretted it as sharp pain swelled across the side of his hand. He shook his hand out and alternately flexed and clenched it, trying to rid it of feeling. "Damn it..."

Stupid rookie shit again, Michaud. You're supposed to be cooler than that.

"I know, just when it feels like we're getting somewhere..."

"Nothing left?"

"Sorry Boss."

"We need to make sure to post officers on guard detail on any more of these we find."

"Do you want me to..."

"Wait...the samples!" Michaud blurted, interrupting her.

"What?" Karen said, confused.

"The...stuff! The dead bodies of those things from the Dressed to the Nines Club. They were all taken out in isolation pods, remember?"

"Yeah, but..."

Michaud was already tapping buttons on his desk phone. Karen watched him, listening to his side of the conversation.

"Detective Michaud. Looking for the samples that were taken from the Dressed to the Nines Club...what? ...the Centre for Infectious... All right, thank you...No, good-bye."

He pressed two fingers of his free hand to the switch hook, ending the call. Karen opened her mouth to speak, but Michaud was frowning at the phone, and held his hand up to her, cutting her off as he punched out another number.

"Yes...this is Detective Benoit Michaud...yes, that one. I'm fine, thank you...I'm sorry, I didn't call for reassurance. This is...yes. Two days ago we raided a private club called the Dressed to the Nines. I've been informed that you were the ones who took possession of numerous biological samples from the scene and...excuse me? They're what?" He held his free hand over the phone receiver, looking around, clearly frustrated. He brought it back to his ear. "Thank you. That'll be all." He slammed the phone down. "This is ridiculous."

Karen looked at him, her mouth slightly ajar in confused silence.

"Damn it! If we don't have everything snatched up by Disease Control just to have them turn it over to whoever, probably the *Ordo Sanctus*, then this Cleaner asshole destroys all our evidence and these *Ordo Sanctus* fuckers bring me in and threaten me and tell me..."

"Wait, what?" Karen interrupted him. "They brought you in? And what did you call him, a Cleaner?"

"He's called a Cleaner. Listen, I started to remember what happened after you dropped me off the other night. They grabbed me, knocked me out, took me to some chamber, I had no idea where I was, told me their history and to stay out of their way because this was their problem."

Karen frowned, mouth open in shock. "You...you're a police officer. They can't do that. You can charge them, bring them..."

Michaud shook his head, eyes downcast. "Said that there'd be 'consequences' for my friends and family if I kept interfering."

"What are they, the mafia?"

"Might as well be. But I know they can do it. Look what the Cleaner's been capable of."

"So, what is he, a professional hit man or something?"

"I don't know, this guy I met told me about what he was doing..."

"Guy? What guy? Is this a different guy than whoever abducted you in the middle of the night?" Karen's face flushed.

"He started calling me, acting like some stalker or something, showed up at my house. But he seems legitimate. I think he's in with their organization, or something. Keeps tipping me off about things, intel and what not."

"Thanks for telling me."

"I didn't want to leave you out, but these people are dangerous."

Karen raised her arms, eyes wide. Her voice waivered. "More dangerous than the Children cult? Why wouldn't you—" Karen threw her arm out and knocked over Michaud's desk lamp onto the floor. "Damn it, I'm sorry."

Michaud moved around his desk to pick up the lamp. "Yes, actually, by the sound of it they are more dangerous, judging by all the burned bodies turning up. The Informant I met even told me that my place was..." Michaud stopped, looking down at the overturned green-shaded lamp. A sickening twinge of nervousness rippled in his stomach as he looked at it. A tiny, thumbtack-sized piece of hardware was attached to the bottom. *But I checked there. I went over this whole room the morning after he came to my apartment.* An itch grew down his back as sweat formed. He rubbed the side of his neck. *Didn't even have time to think. We were so busy, running from place to place. They must have been in here again.* He looked around, trying to find a pen and piece of scrap paper to write on. He settled on the photocopy that had stuck to his face overnight, and he flipped it over and began writing.

"What is it?" Karen asked.

Michaud held up the piece of paper. He had hastily written, "Go for your break. They are listening." Michaud found Karen's eyes and looked directly into them. "I really think this case is too much for me. I should probably just take a vacation. Head down to Cuba for a week." Michaud pointed at the listening device stuck to the bottom of his lamp.

Karen frowned, "Okay, uh...you're right. I feel kind of out of it myself. Might just go for a ride out to Leslie Spit today. That's all right?" She looked at him sideways, nodding her comprehension.

She backed out of the room, her brow furrowed in concern for Michaud. *Sorry Karen. My fault.*

He sighed, and looked around the room, thinking. Michaud recalled the words of the Informant, that any bug detector he might get probably wouldn't work on whatever the *Ordo Sanctus* used.

Great. I just love this spy game bullshit. Here we go again.

He went methodically, pulling open and emptying his drawers, turning them over, looking underneath his desk and chairs. He unscrewed power and network wall sockets, light switches, flipped through books, pulled off the light fixtures. He pulled open his computer case, went through his filing cabinet and files, and went about turning the room inside out.

* * * *

Karen stood in the lunchroom, sipping a steaming cup of coffee. She held under her arm a manila envelope she had picked up from Michaud's mailbox, fretting the whole time. She looked up at one of the several monitors around the café, mounted high on the walls displaying the city news. The sound was muted, but the titles crawling along the bottom of the screen caught her eye as the image of the reporter was replaced by aerial shots of buildings engulfed in flames.

"Simultaneous Terror Bombings At Private Military Facilities...Watershed Corporation...Ownership Tie To Locally-Based Perpendex..."

Karen stared, taking in the information. She took a quick sip from her coffee before tossing it in a trash bin on her way out the door, then broke into a trot to the elevator.

* * * *

Concluding his search, Michaud had found six tiny listening devices the size of thumbtack heads. Each one he crushed under a book, hoping to disable them. The phone he had simply pulled out and placed in the hallway. He'd have to requisition a new one, again. As he stepped back inside, Karen rushed in, the manila envelope tucked under her arm.

"Are you done yet?" she asked.

Michaud nodded, then rubbed his dry eyes.

Karen, oblivious to the messy state of the room, went to the tiny television and switched it on, then adjusted the cable for a clear signal from the local news. Michaud walked over, swishing papers underfoot as he walked through the scattered contents of his office, and they both watched.

The female reporter's face was grave as she spoke, a video window next to her head displaying destruction and fire, shot from a helicopter above a burning group of buildings. "The facility was apparently one of several private military training facilities for the Watershed Corporation, an organization that has handled many outsourced contracts for the US military and has a standing army of nearly 70,000 troops ready to be deployed for special operations missions around the world at a moment's notice. This is one of several linked bases around the world, six of which have been hit by bombings in the last twelve hours.

"It is unknown at this time who the perpetrators of the bombings were and how they were able to infiltrate the bases and plant explosives when facing highly trained military tacticians. Interestingly, the ownership group of Watershed includes the head of local company Perpendex Pharmaceuticals, Doctor Elgin Horatio. We attempted to reach Doctor Horatio for comment but were told that he was meeting with his fellow owners on the recent attacks and their increased need for security at their facilities." A photo of Doctor Horatio attending a gala function was displayed, and Michaud felt a pang of recognition. His face tightened up as he squinted, trying to reach back into his memory. *Silver-haired, mid-fifties...was that you I saw when they drugged me?*

"The Watershed Corporation has been tied through several reports in recent years to violent right-wing extremist religious and paramilitary organizations in North America and around the world who all share similar views on end-time prophecies and the encroaching final battle they believe will occur between their forces and the secular world of science and rationalism..."

Michaud turned to Karen. "This can't possibly be a good thing for what we're dealing with. Those attacks have to be by the Children."

She shook her head. "I imagine this will put them on the defensive, or escalate the conflict."

"And we're right in the middle of it," Michaud said, and sighed, before switching off the TV.

Karen looked around, taking in the piles of paper scattered over the floor, drawers upturned, even Michaud's chair upside-down. "So...success??"

Michaud held up the handful of disabled surveillance devices for her to look at. "I sure as hell hope so." Karen set down the folder on Michaud's desk and peered over them. She switched on the lamp and placed them under the light, frowning as she stared. Michaud took them from her and switched on his paper shredder, dropping them in.

"Whoa, wait!" Karen protested. Michaud stood watching them grind up with a satisfied smile on his face.

"Don't worry, I have ten more from my apartment. Now I'm worried though, I told you so much. They already know what we know."

"Great," she said. "Oh, this came for you." Karen picked up and handed him the manila envelope as if it were a second thought.

"What is it?" Michaud asked, opening the package.

"Uh, interdepartmental mail, but there's no sender written on it..."

Michaud, suspicious, carefully looked inside. The only thing it contained was a small white slip of paper, which he pulled out slowly. *Just a baseball game ticket.* "Weird," he mumbled. He looked over the time and date, today, and a get-away game, 12:37 p.m. He looked at his watch, still a couple hours until game time. "Looks like this might be a request for another meeting from our Informant. I guess I'll need to talk with him anyways." He stood up, pulling his jacket off the coat rack.

"You don't need me to come along?" Karen asked.

"If he saw you there, he'd leave right away. And I have to warn him now, too. What's the weather like out there now?"

"Uh...cooler than yesterday," she said.

Michaud stepped out without replying, closing the door behind him.

Karen looked around. "What am I, his maid?" she asked out loud.

The door opened. Michaud stuck his head in.

"Uh...I forgot to clean this place up, didn't I?" he asked.

"Yes, you did," she said, with one raised eyebrow.

Michaud stepped in and shut the door. "I'll clean up. I still have at least an hour before I need to leave."

Karen smiled. "Yeah, what's some papers and books? It's not like you've got puke all over your shirt, right Detective?"

"Hey, now that's not fair," he said, putting his jacket back on the coat rack. He began turning things right-side up, as Karen started putting the drawers back in the desk.

Chapter Eighteen

Michaud tried not to think of how many "sick" days were being taken amongst Toronto's workforce, but he really couldn't blame a city that had endured decades of poor sports teams. He had taken the subway from the station to the stadium, knowing it would be faster than driving and looking for parking. He walked the four blocks from Saint Andrew station rather than coming from Union station, trying to avoid crowds. He mostly succeeded, encountering only scattered groups of fans. The ticket he had was for the upper level, the "500s," and made his way through the northwest entrance, managing to avoid drawing attention to himself.

The last bastion of the Major Leagues in Canada. No more Expos, just these jokers. At least they finally put a real grass field down. The building formerly known as Skydome had often been derided as a "concrete toilet bowl," a monolithic mega-stadium with no soul or character. Michaud knew that despite its unsightliness, it at least had the benefit of a retractable roof—still an engineering marvel all these years later—that kept it from being as gloomy as places like the Metrodome had been in Minneapolis or the Kingdome in Seattle.

This was a getaway game, meaning the team would be flying out immediately afterward for a road trip. This close to the end of September there were no summer camp kids as there were during June and July, but rather regular school groups in attendance in high numbers, bussed in on field trips. The stadium was also busier than it would normally have been during a weekday game because the Blue Jays had been playing exceptionally well that year and were in the hunt for a playoff spot.

Smart. Out in public. He'll probably be in a jersey like everyone else. Big crowds. Hiding in plain sight.

As he maneuvered up the ramps past a few small groups of people clad mostly in blue, he thought about the appropriateness of the venue for this meeting. He had been investigating and trying to outwit two groups, one a violent cult, the other a secret society that was itself quite violent, both in perpetual conflict with each other. That he was coming to a sporting event, which was essentially a distillation of a similar, sanitized form of conflict, was not lost on him. The tribal underpinnings may not have been stated, but they were certainly implicit.

Michaud felt the warmth of the sunlight on his face as he stepped onto the upper deck. It was a welcome contrast to the dimly-lit upper concourse he had just exited. The walk up the ramps would have left him wheezing a few years earlier, but now he took a deep breath of hot-dog-scented air and removed his confining jacket. He blew out a long sigh and pulled his shirt in and out, fanning himself. The crowd was loud and raucous. The game was several innings in, now.

Michaud looked at his ticket and found his seat. From his spot on the end of a high row, he looked around, barely paying attention to the game, trying to see his contact, despite the futility. He knew trying to find any single individual in a crowd of 35,000 people was a fruitless endeavor.

From behind him, a voice spoke. "You a fan, Detective?"

Michaud turned around. The Informant was sitting directly behind him, sunglasses on, wearing a team jersey and hat, a bag of oily popcorn in hand. "No, I don't usually care for sports," Michaud replied.

"Not even hockey? Basketball?"

"Used to follow football a bit. Played some too," Michaud answered with an impatient sigh.

"Oh? Argos fan?"

"No, Euro football. Fifa. Soccer. World Cup."

"Ah, never could get into it. Not enough scoring, too much running around," the Informant said, stuffing a handful of popcorn into his mouth.

Michaud looked at him, waiting for an announcement of the purpose of this meeting.

"Thanks for coming on such short notice. I thought you might want to get out of the office," the Informant said.

"Were you waiting long?" Michaud asked.

"I watched batting practice. But the tickets were cheap, and I don't mind coming out. Been a good game so far."

Michaud stared back at him, waiting for more.

"You're a busy man, so let's take a walk," the Informant

said, and moved down the long set of stairs toward the exit to the concourse.

* * * *

The two men stood a level down from the 500s, having walked down the concrete ramp and away from the crowds. The ramp was empty, and security tended to turn a blind eye to fans who snuck out during innings to smoke, so they were assured of privacy here next to a large set of windows overlooking the lakeshore, with the Toronto Islands visible. Air traffic moved in and out of the Island Airport.

The Informant stood looking at the view before speaking. "You know there used to be a stadium over there? Babe Ruth hit his first professional home run in it. It was his only home run in the minors before he hit the big leagues. Man, I wish I could have seen that. Used to be a fantastic stadium at the bottom of Bathurst, too—"

Michaud interrupted. "Did you bring me here to talk baseball history? Or is there something actually important?"

The Informant pulled off his sunglasses. "The plan the *Ordo Sanctus* has, it's going to be put into play soon, because of what's happened south of the border. I should be getting details within a day or two. I'll need to meet you again, probably tomorrow. I couldn't chance even sending you a basic message electronically, it was too risky. They're getting more security-conscious because I think they know there's a leak."

"They don't know it's you, do they?"

"I doubt it, I've been very careful. They might know there's information getting out, but they won't know by whom."

Michaud looked around at the concrete walls and ceiling. "And this place. You're trying to tell me something?"

"The two groups that are fighting each other, they're not just playing a fun game, where the worst that happens is someone gets hit by a pitch, or fans yell insults at each other. These people are playing for keeps. They want the world and they don't care how many people die, including you and everyone you know. They'll wipe out entire populations."

"So what do I even do? They have people everywhere. I try to make a move and all I do is run into a brick wall."

"The Children cult is relatively easy to deal with, their numbers in the city have dwindled since the Cleaner was activated. The *Ordo Sanctus* is a tougher nut to crack."

"I know that. They've got people all through the police."

The cheering within the stadium was growing noticeably louder, echoing up and down the ramps. Michaud and the Informant had to lean in toward each other, raising their voices slightly.

"More than you think. And some of them will be the ones activating dispersion units across the city."

"Dispersion? Of what?"

"I'm not entirely sure yet. Most likely a viral agent, a biological weapon. I'm not privy to the full extent of the plan yet. I'm sorry. This...might give you an idea. I don't know." The Informant produced a tiny computer data storage card the size of a fingernail.

"What is it?"

"The information you wanted. On the samples taken from the Dressed to the Nines Club."

"Thanks," Michaud said, taking the card.

"It might give you a better idea of how the *Ordo Sanctus* is planning to counter them. The reports were suppressed, but I was able to retrieve them. It's the best I can do."

Michaud looked at him for a few seconds. "You know that two of the paramedics who were transporting a body were probably Children cult members? I'm beginning to wonder if anyone I work with is who they say they are." He looked around, hearing crowd noises echoing. They sounded expectant, furtive—chanting and cheers that seemed to be waiting for something. Michaud felt his stomach flutter. *The game must be almost over. If that crowd comes down here, I won't get a thing.*

"I'm sorry about that, letting them take your officer was an oversight on the part of our intelligence department," the Informant said.

Michaud's heart beat faster. He looked over his shoulder to see if anyone was coming their way, then turned back to the Informant. He shot his words out, rapid-fire. "Is there anything else you can give me?"

The Informant looked at Michaud carefully. "That's a nice jacket. Be a shame if it were to get damaged."

"What?" Michaud said, confused. *This is no time to change the subject!*

The Informant thought a moment, then turned to their

view of the airport. "Convenient airport, that. I've used it to fly to Montreal. Have you ever flown out of it?"

Michaud sputtered impatiently. He felt as though he was being teased. "The airport? What about it?"

"It's an interesting place, that's all I'm saying. Right where that stadium used to be. That Babe Ruth home run was an important date in sports history."

Michaud almost felt short of breath as he heard cheering rising, rising, until it exploded in wild and jubilant screaming. The distinctive foghorn sound which played when the team hit a home run or won a game blared all around them. *Not now damn it!* Michaud could hear the cheering and chanting coming closer. *They're all coming out now. Fifteen seconds, maximum.* With an anxious gulp, Michaud looked up the ramp, then back to the Informant.

"That's a walk-off win, Detective. Just like how Carter won the '93 World Series. Another important date for sports in this town. I'll be seeing you," the Informant said, as the crowd started surging down the ramp toward them. Smiles lined the faces of the blue-clad mass, and hands were raised above their heads as they chanted, "Let's Go Blue Jays!" and clapped in time together.

"Wait!" Michaud said, "I need to know if you're one of them! Can you get me inside?" he blurted out, his words enveloped by crowd noise. Michaud looked to the approaching crowd, then back to the Informant. The man raised a hand to wave goodbye as he walked away. Michaud tried to follow, but the crowd spilled along the ramp like a massive blue amoeba, swallowing up the Informant and making him one with it. Within moments, Michaud could no longer discern him from the other individuals, all wearing blue. All he could do was push his way down among them until he hit the exit. As he had realized when he first entered the stadium, it was futile looking for him.

* * * *

Karen stood leaning against her bicycle, waiting nervously in front of the equestrian statue of King Edward VII at the center of Queen's Park. The enormous black monument had been moved from India in the 1960's and now loomed over passers-by, a reminder of the British colonial past. The leaves of the trees were still a fervent green and had not yet begun to make the inevitable shift to more autumnal hues. Despite the warm sunshine, a cool wind blew through, rustling the trees. Karen shivered. She reached into her bag and withdrew a grey hooded sweatshirt, which she slipped on. As she zipped it up, another bicycle pulled up in front of her and stopped. The pedal made a distinctive click as the rider disengaged his shoe from it.

"Hey Wendleton," the man said with a broad smile. Mike Banatine was an old friend and occasional bed-partner of Karen's. She had known him from her university days working summers as a bicycle courier. He was tall, lean, almost gaunt, with a battered messenger bag wrapped around his plaid shirt. He pulled off his helmet revealing his perfectly trimmed hair done in a 1930's side-part style, something he had maintained consistently for fifteen years. He was surprisingly pale despite working outdoors year-round.

"Did it go okay? Did he have what I wanted?" Karen felt as though she was taking part in a drug deal.

"Nice to see you too," Mike said, snickering. "You still look good."

"Thanks, you too," she said, giving him a brief glance over. He was handsome, probably still good in the sack, though she didn't feel even the slightest urge to jump back into bed with him. Maybe it was the weather.

He reached into his bag and pulled out a brown paper bag-wrapped package. "What do you need this for? Pretty obscure stuff."

Karen looked to the side coyly, her eyes rolling. "Research project," she said. "And you shouldn't be looking at it anyways." She reached for the package and Mike pulled it back slightly. He held up his hand palm-up and open, widening his eyes as he looked at her. "Right," Karen said, and reached for her wallet. She pulled out three fifty-dollar bills and handed them to him.

"Great, now I can take you out to dinner," he said, smiling his enormous white-toothed grin.

She looked at him with raised eyebrows, the side of her mouth wrinkled up with a look that said, *"are you serious?"*

He laughed his infectious cackling laugh, one she hadn't heard in years, and Karen couldn't help chuckling at it. "Sorry Wendleton, you gotta give a guy credit for trying though."

She continued smiling. "What was the shop your man got this from?"

"I don't know, Phoenix, or Felix, or something. You're lucky I owe you a favor or this would cost you even more. I don't normally make pickups and deliveries on my own time. And why here? Why not at your office? Not like I love going there, but…"

"This might get you in trouble if anyone sees you come in with it," she said darkly.

Mike chuckled. "Really? You're joking."

"No, I'm not. My boss, partner, whatever you want to call him just tore his office apart for bugs. Listening devices, not insects."

"That's a little weird. He's a cop, right?"

"Exactly. I'm sure you've seen the news reports. Some weird and dangerous stuff happening in town lately."

Mike's cheerful demeanor dropped noticeably. "Hey, you better not be involving me in anything that'll get me in shit. I've still got a charge from that protest I was at last summer, if I get arrested again—"

"That's why I just got you to pick this up from a guy who got it from the book dealer. Three steps of separation. If anyone looks into this, they won't look at the middle links of the chain, they'll look at the ends. Don't worry about it. Besides, anything that would happen to you would probably be outside the law anyways."

"That makes me feel so much better, thanks," he said sarcastically.

She sighed. "It'll never come back to you. Trust me."

The side of Mike's mouth curled up as he smiled sideways. "Well, we're even now, okay Wendleton? If I need any more tickets wiped out I'll make sure to wait until all this weird shit blows over."

He shook his head and pushed off, riding east towards Yonge Street. Karen opened the paper bag and pulled the books out halfway, making sure they were the correct ones, which thankfully they were since Mike had made a hasty departure. She slipped them back in, put the package in her own bag and rode off.

* * * *

Michaud sat, fixated, almost rooted to the bench in David Pecaut Square, reading through the contents of the file he had been given by the Informant. Birds chirped in the trees nearby, some flitting along the ground as they picked up scraps of bread scattered by an elderly man sitting at another bench. A bell from a streetcar clanged as the red behemoth rattled by on nearby King Street. Michaud's legs were numb from sitting and his back was sore from the uncomfortable bench, but his absorption in the reports had made him oblivious to the discomfort and the sounds of the outside world.

The reports consisted of suppressed information collected by the Centre for Infectious Disease Control before the samples were seized by the *Ordo Sanctus* (or rather, Perpendex Pharmaceuticals, since Michaud reasoned they were nearly the same group of people). It was appended with further conclusions drawn by *Ordo* researchers.

It looked as though the transformations of humans—and potentially other life forms—were accomplished by a rapidly reproducing infection of colony organisms, not unlike a jellyfish, but far more insidious. The microscopic zooids would enter the host body and begin consuming cells, similar to the function of flesh-eating bacteria, but with a much stranger result.

The zooids would then restructure themselves to resemble the consumed cell, working in concert as they took over the host, effecting a change in the appearance and behavior of the greater body. Eventually, the original host organism would become radically altered in appearance, for all intents functioning as a different animal, but in reality something of a fusion between the previous form and the newly structured colony organism.

The very term "colony" organism seemed apt, and given the fact that it was a forced takeover of another body, "colonialist organism" might be even more appropriate. The researchers were perplexed as to whether the microorganisms involved should be classified as a Category A biological agent—immediately putting it in the same group as Anthrax, Ebola, and the like, or Category C—newly discovered emerging pathogens with disruptive potential. The transformation wasn't technically a fatality, although functionally it might as well have been.

Michaud looked up, blinking. *Who can I even go to about*

this? He pinched the bridge of his nose, scratching the corner of his eye, as the man who had been feeding pigeons wandered by. Michaud rubbed the other eye, and returned to reading.

What disturbed him most was the suggestion that these restructured lifeforms, hybridized colonies, or whatever they might be referred to as, were immediately able to reproduce asexually. In some cases they could start the reproductive process before the entire body was transformed. Budding of young could start shortly after infection, small egg-like sacs containing embryos growing directly on or in the host. The researchers who had put together the file Michaud held seemed to lack an actual example of this process to verify its accuracy, leaving him to wonder if the newly formed young would be colony organisms like the parent, or even more different, potentially restructured to have a standard cellular organization.

The cult members displayed characteristics of specific animal, vegetable and fungal forms, but was that accidental...or intentional? Given the nature of their ritual and its results, it was plausible that they either exerted some form of control over which zooids they became infected by, and thus chose the forms of their transformation, or the colonies of organisms themselves were possibly somehow intelligent on a base level and themselves directing the alterations. The fact that they were able to restructure themselves to resemble the cells and their functions within a host organism was further to this possibility.

Michaud rubbed the back of his neck. He almost wanted a cigarette.

Could they leave their host, potentially colonizing another organism, transforming it as well? It was unlikely, given that the zooids consumed those they encountered, rather than simply imitating them and coexisting side by side. *Like cloning by replication on a cellular level, using themselves as subjects on which the cloning was grafted onto, but mutating and changing the overall organism as they went?*

Not unlike the process of duplicating a painting going section by section, analyzing each square, using whichever colors they wanted instead of copying, but seemingly with an almost frightening pre-awareness of the end result. The image floated through Michaud's mind of the Informant on the ramp at the stadium, being engulfed and carried away by the blue-clad crowd of sports fans until he was no longer discernible from them—it almost felt like a macroscopic analogy for what he was reading about.

Michaud shuddered. *Were these zooids truly intelligent, or did they simply have the appearance of an intelligence due to millions of years of evolution, and the broader process only took on the facade of a plan due to human prejudicial observation?* If they were indeed intelligent, was this collective over arching will they exerted—was that *Olog'lahai'kuhul*?

Michaud's phone buzzed inside his pocket, breaking him out of his mental contortions. He drew it out and looked at the call display—his uncle's bookshop.

"Yes? What is it Uncle?" he asked as he activated the phone.

"Benoit, there's someone here at the shop you need to talk to. He says it's urgent. I think it is too."

"Who is it? Do I know him?"

There was a moment's hesitation. "He's a friend. You should speak with him. I can't talk about it." Felix hung up without saying goodbye.

Michaud was hesitant, knowing the strangeness he had recently encountered, but his uncle wouldn't call sounding like this unless it was truly important. He blinked away the dryness in his eyes. His mouth felt dusty with thirst. *Water? Or the other kind of drink...* He got up, walked to King Street, and raised his hand to hail a cab as he hit the curb.

After giving the cabbie the address for the bookshop his attention returned to the report.

Strikingly, many of the higher brain functions appeared partially unaffected by the changes upon infected individuals. Michaud wondered if this meant they were still conscious of their original human form, behaving the way they did voluntarily, or if they were submerged utterly into a non-human behavioral mold, their memories and consciousness trapped within the collective functioning of the zooids, acting like billions of cells while in reality being separate organisms working in concert. *Was the cult controlling these things, or were they controlling the cult? Who really was using whom?* The very idea of millions, or billions of these microscopic organisms functioning in tandem as one, was nearly overwhelming—but that was, in a way, very similar to the human brain. Brain cells worked together collectively to form a larger consciousness. *If these things were able to mimic the same action, but on a more spread out scale, across distances, breaking apart and recombining...*

Michaud was thrown forward as the cab driver slammed the brakes, blaring his horn and cursing simultaneously. Ahead of them, the King streetcar had stopped, its doors open to disgorge passengers into their lane. Michaud snickered at the cab driver's fury. "These damn new streetcars are even worse than the old ones!" he said, shaking a fist.

"I don't really think they're that bad," Michaud mumbled, turning back to his reading.

The ritual, the attempts to sacrifice outsiders—what purpose did that serve? It might have been purely ritualistic, as it appeared. Or...the cultists could actually have some kind of insight into communication and summoning these organisms from wherever they came from. If they had samples that they used, kept preserved somehow, that might explain where they were getting the organisms. It could be that there really was a conjuration, or what looked like one, but in fact being the calling to the organisms from wherever it was that they originated...

He was over-thinking again. Spinning his mind in circles over things like this was mortgaging his health, with a debt to be paid in insomnia and digestive upset. His stomach gave a warning rumble which he ignored. Michaud put a hand to his midsection and slowly rubbed in a circle. *Hunger? Anxiety? Haven't eaten since breakfast. What the hell time is it?*

Without further resources and a well-equipped biology laboratory, Michaud was unsure how this information would be useful to him in combating the process of infection. He could speculate for hours on the myriad possibilities of intention, intelligence and the nature of the *Olog'lahai'kuhul* zooids. He needed to focus on practical information and applying it to bringing this case to a conclusion; unless he was able to communicate with the organisms, or use their functioning as a determinant in the cult's moves, it didn't seem like much of this would help. Deranged as it was, the *Ordo Sanctus* plan became more understandable, despite its lethality. Kill them all and let...a different "God" sort them out—literally.

The cab slowed to a stop. Michaud looked up and saw he was in Kensington Market. He took a deep breath, rubbed a hand over his eyes, and paid the cab driver before leaving.

Michaud opened the door to the shop. He caught himself

as he did so, and reached up just in time to grab the bell and prevent it from ringing...He held a hand to his sidearm in the event that the call he received was some kind of coded summons in regards to Felix being taken hostage. He stepped in, head cocked to one side, trying to pick up sounds. *Voices?* Michaud slowly moved in, looking down the stacks of books toward the counter. He breathed out in relief as he saw his uncle standing in animated and serious conversation with an Asian man who appeared to be in his early forties. Michaud noticed that his uncle was holding his spectacles in his hand as he gesticulated and spoke. He never did that unless it was something he felt very strongly about. Felix looked up to Michaud, followed by the stranger.

"Uncle? Everything okay?" Michaud asked, somewhat warily.

"Fine, Benoit. Come." Felix gestured to him to approach, replacing his spectacles on his nose.

Michaud walked up, eyeing the strange man. He was dressed in a set of dark jeans, walking shoes, wearing a plaid short-sleeved collared shirt. His black hair was short, undistinguished, streaked with gray. "What's this about?" Michaud asked.

"Thank you for coming detective. My name is Vince Liu. I've...I'm a devotee of *Olog'lahai'kuhul.*"

Michaud frowned, dismayed. He stepped back and reached for his sidearm.

"Wait! Wait..." Liu said, raising his open hands. "You don't understand. I'm the one who took the *Encyclopedia Nefastus* from the *Ordo Sanctus* to begin with. I...I was working with some of the Children here in the city...it was a bad decision."

Michaud relaxed somewhat. "You don't say," he said, over-flowing sarcasm.

Felix spoke up. "I...have some books to sort. You two have things to talk about." He stepped away, gathering an armload of thick leather-bound volumes, carrying them out to the shelves. Michaud kept his eyes on Liu, still not trusting, as Felix walked by.

Liu swallowed nervously. "I'm on my way out of town. I wasn't going to stop but I had to talk to you."

"Do you still have the book?" Michaud asked, point-blank.

"No, no, you don't understand. I was working with a pair of the Children. They acted like they weren't what they really were. It seemed legitimate, and I thought I was doing something good..."

The hunger, exhaustion and tension pounced on Michaud. His stoic exterior crumbled and the angry rookie broke free. He grabbed the man by the front of his shirt, yanking him in threateningly, and growled his words through clenched teeth. "Listen to me you little shit! Officers, good officers are dead, do you hear me? I'm sick of you and your little war. So you better start making some goddamn sense fast, or you leave here with a big dental bill."

Felix leaned back from the bookshelf across the shop, his brow furrowed. He cleared his throat, letting Michaud know he was watching. Michaud relaxed his grip, letting Liu move away.

"I'm trying to explain," Liu said. "These people, these Children of the Ninth Darkness, they're not what it was all about in the beginning."

"You're not really selling me on this. Try harder."

Liu sighed deeply, seemingly searching for words. "They're...they're like the militant fringe group, but one that took over. *Olog'lahai'kuhul*, it's not a thing, it's not a giant creature that's coming down from the stars to wipe out humanity, it's...it's hard to explain. It's like a collective will amongst billions of lifeforms. I can't be any clearer than that."

"I thought something a lot like this reading over the reports of what the *Ritus Mutatio* was doing to people."

"It is, kind of, but what they're doing is some horrible, distorted version of it. Thousands of years ago, amongst Neolithic people, there was a sort of...very basic, very primitive understanding of it. They had no real grasp of it. There were sects, groups, that worshipped the idea of *Olog'lahai'kuhul*, but not as a god, more like...a force of nature. The *Ordo Sanctus*, the way they saw it...you know about them."

"Yeah. And I'm starting to wonder how *you* knew about *me.*"

"I've been keeping tabs on you. I told you, I was in with them. I managed to work my way in as a security contractor with Watershed, then with Perpendex, and finally the *Ordo Sanctus* itself. It took me years. My aim was to destroy the *Encyclopedia Nefastus*. The final copy."

Michaud was dumbfounded. "What?"

"It's not the real ideas of *Olog'lahai'kuhul*. Not at all. It's what the Templar knight who stumbled upon one of our rituals thought it was all about. He thought it was a monotheistic religion. But it's not! It wasn't supposed to be!"

"All right, but the people I've been running into..."

"They're wrong, all of them. Like I said, their version of the belief system is a corrupted one, made up by the Templar knight. The militants, they took those ideas, those ideas that were all about a big monster in the sky coming down and carrying the believers to some magic place and swatting away the unbelievers, and didn't even question them, because they didn't sound all that different from what they'd always heard from their parents or their feudal lords or whoever. The original ideas...they were all about the explosion of life that would occur, the process of change, and rebirth, and..."

"Yeah, I've seen the explosion of life, and the process of change, it isn't pretty."

Liu's brow wrinkled. "No, it's not like that. It was never supposed to be. They took the ideas that were transcribed by the Templar, and over the centuries have modified them, rewritten and reinterpreted them even more. That's where the 'Ninth Darkness' came from. It...you have to understand, these people got the wrong idea from the start, they twisted it into something worse, and it was warped even more by centuries of conflict with the *Ordo Sanctus*. They're like the members of any other religion who shoot doctors, or have armed camps in the woods, or fly planes into buildings. Now they're the majority, and me, a few others like me, we're the tiny minority who went back to the source to understand."

Michaud's jaw jutted to the side. He raised an eyebrow. "Uh huh. The original knowledge was destroyed, and you know all this how exactly?"

"The true knowledge, it doesn't come from a book, it's...it's an interface with the universe."

Is this guy on drugs? "You're not being very convincing. Give me more," Michaud said.

"I'm getting to that. The process of transformation, the *Ritus Mutatio*, that's not the way it's supposed to happen. What they are right now, they're...they're like selectively bred animals or plants for specific characteristics. In the true state of it, it's totally different." He took a deep breath, trying to slow himself down. "The way dog breeds are, created by human intervention...you get dogs like pugs for example, that have congenital disorders, breathing problems, all that, because humans want to have cute animals."

"These things do stuff that's a lot worse than humping your leg or pissing on the rug," Michaud said flatly.

"I know that. What I'm saying is, even in an urban environment, without being specifically bred, dogs will become mongrels and revert to their feral behaviors within a few generations. That's what the organisms are like right now—like specially bred tools. The organisms that enter a human body, they aren't supposed to infect or take over or consume the cells, they're supposed to be...like partners for a lifeform. Does that make sense? They can work alongside an organism's cells, help them, even enhance them. They guide and nurture evolution, they don't hijack it for their own ends..."

"You sound like you know a lot about this process already."

Liu sighed. "I am...I *was* a biologist. I had studied genetic engineering, recombinant DNA, molecular cloning, but this... this was like there was a natural way to do what we had been studying, so much easier and simpler. And faster! It was a revelation, if it could only be guided, controlled!" Liu caught himself, and realized Michaud was staring at him with concern, then continued. "Maybe you know of...I *know* you know of Rachel Atwater. She was one of my students."

Michaud perked up. "Now you're coming around to making-sense territory."

"We studied the functioning of the organisms. She knew as much as I did, but I made the mistake of showing her the *Encyclopedia Nefastus*. She was with someone...Patrick," he said.

"Garneau, I know," Michaud interrupted.

"They seemed so enthusiastic. But they already knew, they were just using me. They had bypassed everything I was trying to show them and went straight for the *Encyclopedia Nefastus*. They took it from me, I had no idea. They wanted... they *wanted* to become the Children of the Ninth Darkness. And there were others, scattered, and it wasn't difficult for them to assemble after they had the book, and the power and knowledge it gave them."

"What does the Nine mean? Why that number?"

Liu shook his head. "Nothing. It doesn't mean anything, not really. When the knight first stumbled upon the ritual, the true ritual, there were eighteen devotees participating. Nine times two is eighteen. One plus eight is nine. So he decided that it was meaningful. It's been thought of as a 'magic' number for centuries, and long before the *Ordo Sanctus* and the Children of the Ninth Darkness. So now they've built it into their symbols and rituals, and the cult needs nine 'lieutenants' for *Olog'lahai'kuhul* to spread and create their own children and converts."

"Converts...sounds like what I've been running into the past while."

"Exactly. It's the whole aim now, making 'converts'...if they can even be called that. Go forth and multiply."

"The ritual, the *Ritus Mutatio*..."

"That part is real. It's hard to explain." Liu scratched the side of his head. "The chanting, the symbols, all of that, it's sort of the mask for communicating with the universe."

"Sounds like magic gobbledygook."

"Anything sufficiently advanced will appear as..."

"Magic, I know the line. Sounds flaky though."

"No, it's not some new-agey hippy thing. It's real. Interfacing with the universe, like I said. Opening a conversation and asking for a passage to somewhere else."

"Somewhere else?"

"Where the zooid organisms originally came from. Maybe where we all came from. They come through, sometimes they're preserved, held by the cult, bred, re-engineered, like I said, it's..."

"Hard to explain, you said that. And this advanced technology that looks like magic, it comes from..."

Liu cocked his head to one side, shrugged, and raised a hand, pointing straight up to the sky. "You don't need to understand how something works in order to use it. And that's what's happened. The technology, whatever it is, has been appropriated by people who don't really understand it, but can still use it."

Michaud thought on this. "All right, say this is all true. What good does it do me? I still have to stop the crazy ones. They just went on the offensive against *Ordo Sanctus* facilities. This secret war isn't very secret any longer."

"I know. There aren't many of the Children left in the city. The *Ordo Sanctus*, or you and your men, have gotten most of them. Their legacy is left behind, but what Horatio and the *Ordo*..."

"What? Do you know their plan?"

Liu sighed. "No one does. I was nowhere near high up enough in the hierarchy to get near Horatio. But you need to stop them. They're even more dangerous…"

"I already know that. I've tried to convince my superiors in the department to let me go after them, but—"

"I wouldn't trust them," Liu said, cutting him off.

"You're not the only one to tell me that. Can you give me a name?"

"I never saw specific names. I know there were a lot of people within the police, ones who were either part of the *Ordo Sanctus*, or paid off by them. It's not surprising that you're not getting anywhere going after them."

"But you don't know who or how many?"

Liu shook his head 'no'. "I can't…"

"You're not all that good to me then, are you? This is already the weirdest case I've ever worked, and you're just making it weirder. Unless you have some serious intel for me that I can use to break these shitbags…any of them, you should probably hit the road and get back on your way out of town."

"I thought…I thought maybe knowing this would help you devise a strategy, some way of fighting them…the book, the *Encyclopedia Nefastus*. Did you seize it from the Ninth Darkness cult, in any of your raids? It still needs to be destroyed."

"I can't destroy it, it's evidence."

"It's very important. It's, it's…"

"It's literature."

"I guess…that's one way to see it, but it's very dangerous, so destructive that…"

"No. We haven't seen it at all," Michaud interrupted. "It might have been burned up by that Cleaner guy…"

"No. No, he would have taken it back to the *Ordo Sanctus*. They want to maintain possession of it. The knowledge in it, it still has tremendous power."

"And you don't know if they took it back or not?"

"I don't. I wish I knew where it was. I'd feel less guilty about leaving town, knowing there's a loose end I'd rather tie up."

"I've got more than my share of loose ends right now. But the organisms, the zooids, you know about them. You must know a way to stop them, to arrest their growth?"

Liu shook his head. "Everything I know, that I've tested

or examined, suggests they can't simply be poisoned or specifically targeted, not without extremely sophisticated techniques. They're just like any other cell, they'll succumb to extreme heat, lack of nourishment, high level radiation, anything that would of course just kill the host body they're in. But without some kind of genetically targeted inoculation—a biological weapon, maybe—that's all you'll do, kill the host as well.

"Which is exactly what the *Ordo Sanctus* has been doing." Michaud sighed, frustrated.

Liu nodded. "If you'll excuse me, detective, I should be going. I don't want to stay here any longer than I should. I'm sure the Cleaner, or others are after me. The remaining members of the Children, maybe."

"Is that the real reason you came here? You're running out of time?"

"You needed to know the truth." He stepped away, turned and walked for the door. He stopped before he exited. "And we're all running out of time." The bell above the door rang softly as he left.

Felix approached Michaud, slowly sauntering over, a broom now in his hands. "Did he tell you anything interesting?"

"It just makes things more complicated, Uncle," Michaud said. He gave Felix a strong hug, patted his back and turned to leave.

"Wait!" Felix called after him. Michaud turned. Felix reached for a sheet of paper on his counter. "New stock came in earlier. One of the books, I didn't even have time to see it. I was putting some up on the shelf and one of my customers, he was looking through all of them, he just left money on the counter and ran out."

"What was the book?"

"It...I think it was about the *Ordo Sanctus*." He showed Michaud the order sheet.

Michaud frowned. "Damn it."

Chapter Nineteen

Michaud entered his apartment with the sun dipping out of sight. The dusky light that made it through the blinds only emphasized the emptiness of the space and how little he used it. Even after going through his place several days earlier for listening devices it didn't look unkempt. Finding the bugs was quick and simple—the lack of clutter helped him considerably, and tidying was just as easy. Now it looked as it had before, like an unused show suite.

He pulled off his jacket. He hadn't bathed for days and it was starting to become noticeable. He sniffed an armpit and turned away in disgust. He sighed, frustrated, at himself, at the bizarre situation, and at the world in general. He shuffled to the bathroom, disrobing (and for once, lazily) tossing his clothes onto the floor as he went.

The hot water of the shower was relaxing, but Michaud couldn't stop his mind from racing through all the head-spinning new information he had, on the cult, what the results of the transformations were, what Liu had said it was supposed to be. Michaud couldn't shake the revelation that the *Ordo Sanctus* had the *Encyclopedia Nefastus*, and based on the leaked reports knew about the functioning of the cult's transformations. With the Informant now letting him know there was the potential for use of a biological weapon, Michaud wondered if it was related to the zooids, or a use of them, reprogrammed or bred somehow for even more destructive purposes. Such a bizarre scheme couldn't be put past them, and they wouldn't be the first group in history to have used their enemy's own weapon against them.

"Stop over-thinking," he mumbled out loud. *Hot shower, time to relax. Trying to force it all to make sense would only make it worse.*

He tensed up. Relaxation wasn't happening. It was if he could feel all the information in his brain straining at a point where it was about to tip over a weigh scale into the "realization" zone, and he had to write it all down, or else he might forget something and the scale would tip back into the "confusion" area. Something he had always feared was having a great idea, some new angle on a case, and would forget unless he jotted it down. Keeping a note pad beside his bed was paradoxically something that helped him sleep, yet also kept him awake when he knew he could write more thoughts out.

He shut off the water. Stepping out of the shower, he grabbed a towel on his way out the door and into his living room. Behind him was a trail of watery footprints as he walked around his apartment looking for something to write on and with. He grabbed a pen and note pad sitting on his coffee table and began scribbling notes down based on what the Informant had said. Water dripped off him onto the paper, causing the ink to run.

He thought for a moment. *What the hell did it all mean? Sports trivia, dates, more numbers...this was as bad as the Ninth Darkness cult's numerology.* He stared at the soggy, water-blotted page, frustrated, and tossed it back down on the table. His head throbbed with fatigue. His tired state of mind and heavy eyelids made clear thinking unlikely.

Bed.

He could sleep on it, or more likely, think of something just as he was dozing off...

Michaud lay back in his bed, trying not to think of anything related to the case, instead hoping to visualize sitting on a beach in Cuba watching the sun set. Of course, trying not to think of the case only pushed it to the forefront of his mind, and he could neither relax nor lie still. *The numbers... the dates he had been told...what were they?* The ride home had him wracking his brain over his Informant's cryptic statements, and why he had made them. It seemed like more than the usual inane small-talk. *What was it he had said? Important dates...*

Michaud's eyes widened, and he looked around rapidly. "Son of a bitch!" he blurted, then tossed the covers aside, swinging his legs over so he came up to a sitting position. He switched on the light beside his bed and grabbed the note pad he always kept there, immediately scribbling more notes, mumbling to himself. He stood, nothing but boxer shorts on, and walked back out of his bedroom. His desktop computer, rarely used, would come in handy. He moved to it, which was sitting forlornly on a tiny white desk in a corner of the room, and flicked it on. Michaud sat, tapping his feet impatiently as the computer booted up.

He punched up a search engine and began his quick re-search. Sports trivia was not an area he had any background in, but he found the information he needed quickly enough: the dates of the two home runs the Informant had mentioned. September 5th, 1914, and October 23rd, 1993.

But what was the significance? The numbers, they had to mean something. *A code?* Seventy-nine years between them. Halfway between September 5th and October 23rd of this year would be ...the 28th of September?

That was tomorrow. It couldn't be a coincidence, Michaud thought to himself.

He took his pen and paper and began scribbling on it again. International dating notation, 05-09-1914, 23-10-1993. American style, 09-05-1914, 10-23-1993.

Was one of these a time? 5-09 could be 5:09 a.m., 1914 could be 7:14 p.m., 23-10 could be 11:10 p.m., 09-05, 9:05 a.m., 10-23, 10:23 a.m. *It could be any of these.* The use of the date code based on sports history was probably intentional, a mild joke on the use of numerology by cults that Michaud de-cried. Sports fans, after all, were somewhat cult-like in their devotion, and the obsession with player statistics, along with superstitious attitudes over jersey numbers and any number of things on and off the field of play was certainly appropriate. Michaud shook his head, smirking. *At least the guy seemed to have a sense of humor.* What else had the Informant said? The airport, he kept mentioning it. *My jacket. What did he say about that?*

He stood up, looking around. It was on the floor where he had dropped it. He stepped away from the desk and reached for the jacket. He picked it up, holding the fabric out widely with both arms, then feeling it all over, rifling through the pockets, feeling for anything. No strange lumps, no bulges...

Michaud held it under the light of his desk lamp, staring in closely at the buttons. They seemed fine...until he looked in at the third one down. It was off somehow. The thread was dif-ferent, almost imperceptibly so. The brown was lighter, more tan, not as weathered. He reached into his desk for a pair of scissors, quickly snipping off the button—hoping this wasn't simply paranoia, because re-sewing this button would be a real pain, then dropped the scissors with a light clatter back into the drawer.

He held the button up between two fingers, looking at it under the light. For all appearances, an ordinary button. Flat, round, light brown, holes for sewing.

Michaud turned around, and moved to the kitchen counter, opening the drawer underneath his stove. He found what he was looking for, a small frying pan, and pulled it out before placing the button carefully on the island in the middle of his kitchen under an overhead light. He looked in, raised the frying pan over the button a few centimeters, then brought it down with a crunch.

Michaud pulled the pan away and placed it aside. He leaned in, looking at the crushed button. He poked a finger at it, sifting through the broken pieces. Tiny pieces of microcircuitry. A transmitter, or tracking device, or both. He looked around his apartment again. *No wonder the other devices had seemed so easy to find.* They already had one on him nearly every day he was at work and out on a case. The others around the apartment might as well have been decoys, ones they wanted him to find and thus give him back a false sense of security. Michaud wondered just how long this fake button on his jacket had been there. They could have easily replaced it when they abducted him and took him to their council chamber...or even earlier, when he had left his jacket behind in the office while he and the task force went to raid Room Nine in the Annex. He took the crumbled pieces of button tracker to his bathroom, dropped them in the toilet and flushed it.

The Informant knew, or guessed, that they were being monitored in the stadium. He was even more cryptic than usual, but he had been trying to communicate something to Michaud. The other thing he mentioned—an old stadium at the foot of Bathurst street. *Of course, the park next to the island airport.* If it was another meeting, he'd have to be there for each of the possible times, and 5:00 a.m. wasn't far off.

* * * *

The Informant tried to maintain his detached demeanor in the face of the gruesome experiment. He watched Officer Chow lying restrained on a table inside a thick plastic isolation pod. Outside the compound, it was early morning, but within, it would be impossible to tell. The huge room he and Horatio stood in was lit with a handful of fluorescent beams that barely cut through the darkness. The sole bright light was focused down on Chow's containment bubble. The officer was unconscious, with a multitude of tubes attached to his arms and feeding into his mouth.

Massive sensor units several meters tall and electronic panels lined the walls, some displaying readings on monitors, others of a function indiscernible to an outsider. Horatio peered into the containment unit, unaffected, possibly taking some obscure enjoyment in the situation.

Horatio had insisted on Chow being stripped to his undershirt and underwear rather than completely nude. The Informant had known Horatio for years. He knew that Chow had been given a sliver of dignity in his condition, but only inadvertently by Horatio because of his hatred for human nudity. Horatio automatically associated sexual activity with it, which he found particularly abominable. The Informant knew he might tolerate female nudity, but a nude male subject was unthinkable to him.

The Informant and Doctor Horatio wore protective masks, smocks and gloves, watching the proceedings as a Perpendex technician in a lab coat and mask worked adjusting the machinery hooked up to Chow.

Chow's features had already begun to alter perceptibly. The injection by the crustacean creature was having its effect, causing Chow's skin to peel away, revealing a black and green chitinous layer beneath. Horatio leaned in, his hands clasped behind his back, staring at the peeling skin across Chow's face. The Informant forced himself to look, to feign interest as he rubbed his chin.

Chow began to stir, his eyes opening. At first groggy, he rapidly assumed a look of panic, trying to move his arms and legs, but only able to twitch them helplessly within the restraints. His eyes searched the room, settling on Horatio, the closest face, and the only one seeming to show any discernible emotion. Chow tried to speak, but the tubes down his throat turned every sound into a meaningless gargling gibberish. The Informant watched Horatio turn up a slight smile—one he recognized as not of malice, but of a disturbing kind of sympathy.

"Your sacrifice is appreciated. You can't understand the importance. But rest assured, it is," Horatio said. He patted the isolation chamber. "I'm sorry, Son."

The Perpendex technician flicked a switch, ensuring the device he stood at was functioning properly and its recording cycle had initiated. He then looked to Horatio and nodded silently. The three of them turned to leave the room, depositing their smocks and gloves in a disposal chute as they exited. As Horatio left, he withdrew a bottle of hand sanitizer from his pocket, depositing some on his hands and rubbing it in judiciously. They ascended a set of steps and out of view.

The trio reached the shielded booth that overlooked Chow through a large rectangular window. The Informant stepped to the window as the technician activated various sensors and the microphone inside Chow's pod. His stifled breathing was relayed to them through overhead speakers. The Informant took a deep breath, looking for something else to focus on. Chow, unable to speak or move, looked around frantically, making pitiful noises of helplessness unable to muster anything further. Machinery around the lab hummed with activity, the sounds growing louder. Most prominent among the devices was the panel that the Informant noted had stamped on it a large radiation symbol.

Within the observation room, the lab technician adjusted controls on the panel before him. He turned to the others. "You can remove your masks, it's safe. But please put on safety goggles." They did as he asked, pulling on darkened goggles before turning back to the room below. The technician turned to them. "Are we ready sir?"

Horatio nodded, and the technician slowly turned a large dial until it was rotated completely clockwise. The three of them leaned in to the window slightly, watching Chow. The Informant turned his eyes to the side, but was drawn back. He wanted to help the man, do something. *He's infected, and already mutating. Maybe this is the only way to help him.*

Chow twitched at first, looking not unlike an electric shock was running through his body. He no longer focused his sight on the observation booth, and his eyes slowly rolled back in his head. A bright white glow began to emanate from his mouth, nose and eyes. Despite their goggles, the Informant and the lab technician both shielded their eyes with their arms. The Informant turned to Horatio, seeing the look of astonishment parting his lips. He then clenched his jaw, the reflection of the glow casting broadly across both his goggles and his perfectly white teeth.

"It's working..." Horatio whispered.

The overpowering white light engulfed Chow's body and his back arched. The echo of a scream managed to escape from his mouth despite the tubing. In an intense flash, he exploded in a cloud of grey ash, trapped within the containment bubble. The Informant turned his head away, then back. The ash was settling slowly back to the table. The ends of the tubes that had been attached to Chow's body were singed and melted, nothing more than tiny stubs just sticking into the thick plastic shield.

The Perpendex lab technician removed his goggles and let them hang around his neck as he smiled. He turned to Doctor Horatio and extended his hand, hoping for a congratulatory shake, but Horatio's smile disappeared as he glared back at it. He slowly pulled his goggles down and looked disapprovingly at his employee.

"Uh, sorry sir. I forgot," the technician said, withdrawing his hand. "Oh, another thing. We have another test case we can engage for a second trial. The other officer's body, in the hospital morgue." He reached for his clipboard, sitting propped on the control panel, and then flipped a page up. "Weltner is his name."

"Excellent. The technicians there can administer the agent today upon delivery," Horatio replied.

The lab tech nodded and headed down into the laboratory. Horatio resumed his smile, watching the man go. The Informant pulled his goggles down, concern wrinkling his brow. "Do you really think such an extreme step is necessary?" he asked. Horatio faced his colleague. "The body politic is infected. Unfortunately, to cleanse it we must take such measures to preserve what little morality remains in this...degenerate world. To avoid the *bellum omnium contra omnes*."

"I think the Cleaner is doing a fine job of eliminating the problems, with a minimum of exposure."

Horatio turned back to watch the Perpendex technician at work in the lab below. "The conflict is coming, whether we want it to or not. We can either wait for it to happen, or take the offensive and come out victorious."

The Informant considered these words before he spoke, "I'll inform the Cleaner of his new directive." He sighed, bowing his head.

"He will not be deployed with the new device."

Horatio's words caught The Informant off guard. His head jerked back up in surprise.

"Once the sleepers have been activated, send The Cleaner to eliminate anyone connected with the detective who might jeopardize what we are doing. The detective must be taken care of last, and last only. We risk discovery and the unraveling of everything we've worked to initiate if someone so high-profile is targeted too soon."

The sleepers? Already? The death toll...I need to pull all the plans, get this to Michaud. If the Cleaner doesn't get there first. He forced his concern deep down, clearing his throat. "I understand," the Informant replied. He exited through a set of automatic metal doors and out into a hallway.

* * * *

Horatio watched him leave. As the doors shut behind his fellow council member, Horatio raised his wrist radio to contact the Cleaner himself. Having a private line of communication was advantageous, especially at times such as these.

Chapter Twenty

Karen sat at Michaud's desk going over her research material on the *Ordo Sanctus*. The soft early morning light filled the room with warmth, but she was still laboring under the desk lamp she had turned on seven hours earlier after coming in to work with only a light nap at home. It was appropriate that she had just had a reunion with an old friend from her university years, because pulling an all-nighter reminded her of her former studying habits—good for her grades, bad for her health.

In front of her was spread out a huge map of the Greater Toronto Area, over which she used a red felt-tip pen to try and trace out a pattern. She had spread open her newly acquired books. These were the only two that she could locate with substantive information on the group, their symbology, and beliefs in end-time prophecies.

Across the map were photographs and photocopies, stuck on at specific spots over the map based on series of numerical codes detailed in the books Karen had found. One was the *Codex Sanctus*, or rather a reprinted volume based on a badly burned copy retrieved from a dead *Ordo Sanctus* operative some seventy-five years earlier, stolen and transcribed, then republished occasionally by fringe publishing houses specializing in conspiracy theories and secret societies.

The information Karen was finding was invaluable, and she hoped, useful in understanding the plans this organization had.

Michaud's new desk phone started ringing. Karen yawned, stopped and looked at it a moment, unsure of whether or not to answer it.

The door flew open and Michaud rushed in. "Any messages?"

"Good morning to you too," Karen said.

Michaud ignored her, attracted by the ringing phone. "Michaud...yes...all right, go ahead," Michaud said, grabbing a pen and note pad to write on, jotting down scattered words as he listened. "Thank you," he said, and hung up. "Analysis of Montrose's body is in."

"What'd they find?"

"Looks like he was infected with something before he was killed yesterday. Lab barely found anything, but there was a substance smeared on his wall that corresponded to traces on his body, even though it was almost completely fried."

"From what attacked him at the club?" Karen asked.

Michaud was oblivious, closing the note pad. He exhaled loudly.

Karen tried to draw his attention to her map and the photos across it. "Hey, I think I found something here..."

"I've got to go to a meeting, can you—"

"Boss..."

"Hold down the fort, I'll be—"

"Boss..."

"Back in an hour..."

"Benoit!"

He looked at her. "What is it?"

"Look at the book I found," she said, holding up the *Codex Sanctus*.

"Is this about—"

"Yup, *Ordo Sanctus*," she interrupted. "Loaded with their prophecies, codes, symbolism."

"Where'd you find this?" he asked, turning it over and flipping through it.

"I know a guy..." she said, one eyebrow raised, her mouth turned downward in exaggerated smugness.

Michaud frowned, his head cocked to one side "Yeah, I know a guy, too. I think both our guys might be the same one."

"My guy is just a courier, knows someone who knows a shop that sells this kind of thing, he brought it over for me an hour ago."

"Was the shop, by chance, called Felix's?"

"I think so, yeah, how'd you know?" Karen asked, pulling her chin in.

Michaud shook his head and rolled his eyes. "I need to talk to my uncle..."

"What?"

"Nothing. I'm going for my meeting. Had a few today already and there could be a few more. I'm taking the subway, so watch my car." He tossed her the keys, which she caught in midair. He sped out the door quickly before Karen could divert his attention back to the map.

"But I think you should see this..." she said as he shut the door behind him.

* * * *

Felix sat on a stool behind the counter of his shop, one foot propped up on the display case, as he read a newspaper. Despite his adamant directive that no one lean on or touch the glass case, he felt no compunction against breaking his own rules, especially since he knew precisely where he could lean his foot without putting any stress on the frame. He looked up at the entrance by a pair of Goth kids clad all in black and snickered to himself as they began looking through the shelves. Felix turned back to his newspaper, reading the headline: "Occult Murders Increase." It included a timeline of the recent spate of deaths, and the speculation that a serial killer was stalking the cult members, making for an even bloodier scenario.

Felix's gaze was drawn to a photo from the outside of the first crime scene. Far in the back of the crowd was a distinctive shape—the outline of the Cleaner's hat as he stood apart from the mass of people, observing. Felix filled with a deep and terrifying recognition of the man, one that sent him far back into his past, remembering something.

He took his spectacles off, placing them in his breast pocket, then looked up to the two kids in his shop. "I'm sorry. I have to close early today."

* * * *

The Informant stood at the southern edge of Coronation Park, watching boats sailing on the lake in the cool afternoon wind. He took a drag off his Good Catch brand therapeutic cigarette. Nearby, the Island Airport hummed with air traffic, coming in and out with regularity and splitting the otherwise calm day with the buzz of jet engines and propellers. Behind him, an amateur softball game was in progress, the distinctive echoing clink of aluminum bats hitting balls in the air.

"I've been here twice already this morning," Michaud said

as he walked up beside him. "I even took the subway because I was worried there's something tracking my movements in my car."

The Informant continued looking out toward the lake, refusing to turn his head. "You were right to do so," he responded, puffing on his cigarette. He squinted slightly, looking at the water. "They say the lake shrinks a little bit every year, you know that?" He took a final drag from his cigarette before dropping it to the ground and crushing it underfoot.

"I met with one of them yesterday. One of the Ninth Darkness cult members," Michaud said.

The Informant turned, surprised. His face just as quickly returned to its usual placidity, like a pond's waters after a stone thrown in. "What did he say?"

"He didn't believe in the Ninth Darkness. Said he represented the true way, that the cult we know is just a corruption brought on by the interpretation given it by the Templar knight who wrote the *Encyclopedia Nefastus* in the first place."

"Not surprised, I've heard of them before. Every belief system has its moderates and its extremists."

"Pretty sure the extremists are carrying the day with this one."

"An unfortunate inevitability."

Michaud folded his arms. "Anyways, I figured out your weird little trivia code, so tell me what this parlay is about," he said, looking for the Informant's eyes.

"I'm sorry about that, but I thought they might be monitoring, and if they had, the scrambler I used the first time would be useless a second time. Which meant I could only give you a few possible meeting times, in the event I had new information. I wanted to let you know without saying so directly that I should know what was happening by now, and I do. It's become imperative that I meet you because of what's happening. What's going to happen."

* * * *

Karen stood gathering some of her notes, with a piece of paper clenched in her teeth, as the phone rang twice in rapid succession. The signal of an interdepartmental page. She grabbed the note out of her mouth and answered.

"Michaud's office," she said.

"This is the front desk, is Detective Michaud in? There's a fellow here says he's his uncle."

Karen thought a moment. "I'll come down and see him," she said, then hung up the receiver.

She put her notes down, leaving the map spread out over the desk as she exited.

* * * *

Felix stood wearing his antiquated three-piece suit with his hat in his hands. Karen approached, recognizing Felix from Michaud's photos. He was looking up and around at the natural light and open space of the indoor courtyard, with its multitude of plants and a huge skylight providing illumination. It had an open air feel while still clearly designed to be a modern police station. When Karen first reported for work she was intimidated—probably the intent of the design.

She offered her hand with a smile.

"Are you...do you work with Benoit?" he asked, shaking her hand. He had large gnarled hands, dry from years of work, and she respected how tough they felt.

"I do. I'm Karen, I'm a researcher who works with him. Not really his partner, but we do work together all the time."

"Is Benoit here?" he asked, pushing his spectacles up his nose.

"No, he's gone out to a meeting. Did you try calling him?"

"He's turned off his phone. I'm sorry, my name is Felix, I don't think I introduced myself. I'm his uncle."

"I know, I recognize you from his photos in the office," she said, looking up to her floor.

"He came to see me in my shop this week. I need to show him something, something I think he'll want to see."

"If it's related to the case, you can show me," Karen offered.

Felix looked at her a moment, opening his mouth to speak, but hesitating. He looked back and forth, out of thought rather than suspicion. "We need somewhere safer," he said.

"A police station is a pretty safe place," she said, smiling.

Felix's head angled to the side a notch. "Maybe not for this."

Karen thought briefly. "I have a good idea of somewhere we can go where we won't be bothered by anyone."

She led the way out, and Felix followed.

* * * *

The Informant pointed out toward the control tower, where some planes sat idle, while one taxied along a runway. "What does this look like to you?"

Michaud looked back and forth, unsure if this was part of the usual pointless banter. "It's the airport. What about it?"

The Informant paused, as if weighing the information he was about to impart. He sighed. "Ever since it was built there's been a secret underground facility. A lab."

"Why here? Why not somewhere more prominent?"

"For exactly that reason. Anywhere else could draw too much attention. But this city is taken for granted, ignored by many. It still has all the capabilities and personnel that were required though."

"Perpendex?" Michaud asked.

The Informant nodded. "They've been conducting research into both genetically engineered viruses and nanotechnology for years. I wasn't sure what the exact focal point of the plan was until today. It's a cybernetic bio-weapon."

"What?" Michaud said, astonished. He tried to envision such a bizarre creation as he weighed the Informant's words.

"It combines molecule sized machines with a virus. It's one of multiple projects that have been under development, but this is the one that's being pushed into action. I wasn't sure what was going to be used, but the schedule's been set. The plan is being enacted. The ultimate solution, the one we never meant to implement unless absolutely necessary..."

"You *are* one of them, the heads of this group. I knew it was you I saw that night. What the hell did they inject me with?"

The Informant shook his head apologetically. He sighed. "I was going to tell you. But you understand why I had to avoid full disclosure. There's a reason you still don't know my name, and will never know."

"What were you planning?" Michaud asked, ignoring his words.

The Informant met his eyes. "The weapon will be dispersed by people who don't even know they're working for the organization. Sleeper agents. It's a continuation of the

Canadian branch of Mk-Ultra conducted at McGill in the sixties. They're programmed to respond to a signal. I don't even know what. When they do they'll pick up the dispersion units across the city."

Michaud searched the Informant's eyes. "What...is it?" he asked, gritting his teeth.

"It spreads easily by touch, mucus or saliva particles expelled in a cough or sneeze. After a time the viruses self-destruct using a controlled reaction. The host is destroyed. Everything is wiped clean, sterilized. Within hours of the successful launch of this first wave, sleeper agents in other cities around the world will receive their signals as well. It's meant to happen in a fashion with no centralized command structure, and once they've sent out the weapon, it will cause death on an unimaginable scale. Not millions detective, *billions* of people.

"It's why the Watershed Corporation has been raising a private army for years, for this very moment, so that when there's the one final push, they're ready to move in and fill the power vacuum. They create their own crisis, wipe out everyone they have the slightest disagreement with, hollow out all existing authority structures, and take over in the ensuing chaos."

Michaud could only look at him trying to discern if this was truth, or just deranged fiction. "That's completely crazy. The agents who are used to disperse the weapon will be killed. They can't want innocent people to die like this, they..."

"We're not dealing with a reasonable organization headed by reasonable men. The sleepers are expendable, like shell casings. They're shot off and forgotten on the field of war. Nothing can be traced back to the *Ordo Sanctus* or Perpendex either. The people who die...that's all part of the plan."

"You could just go public, tell the news."

"I'd be dead before anything made it out in the open, and I'd be dooming however many reporters, news anchors and website programmers to death too. They have people everywhere. All forms of communication will be severed and cut off as soon as they put their manufactured crisis into effect."

Michaud was barely able to speak with the weight of the information pressing down on him.

The Informant continued, "But if you stop it here, they'll take that as meaning that the plan is a failure and give you more time to breathe before there's a reorganizing, and any other attacks occur. You have to get inside that facility. The samples need to be destroyed before they're distributed."

Michaud was unable to accept the information and could only shake his head in disbelief.

"The Cleaner's been sent for your associates. You're last. You won't be hit until after the sleepers are activated," the Informant said gravely.

Michaud thought, taking all the information in. A tremble went up his back, his stomach somersaulted into a knot. Realization—terror—crept over his face as his entire body tensed up. He looked north, toward the police station. "Karen..." he mumbled.

* * * *

Felix sat down in the passenger side of Michaud's car, sitting in the police underground parking garage, as Karen got in the driver's side. Felix's concern was evident, but he seemed reluctant to speak.

Karen searched out his eyes. "Okay, what's this about?"

Felix seemed nervous. He started to speak, stopped, then took a deep breath. With a trembling hand he pulled out a neatly folded newspaper clipping from the breast pocket of his suit jacket. He unfolded it carefully and held it out to Karen. It was the photo from the newspaper in which the Cleaner's silhouetted hat could be seen.

"This man," he said, "I've seen him before." His voice seemed to shrink as he said the words.

Karen's concern was piqued as she studied the photo. "How?" she asked.

"My family have been believers in Vodou for generations. It is harmless, we..." He paused. "We escaped from Haiti because of the dictatorship. But we were harassed by this group, this *Ordo Sanctus*. They have people, soldiers, men who work like...like assassins. This man, the man with the hat and the bag, and the mask, or a man just like him...he killed my parents when I was a boy. Years ago. I was the only survivor, I hid, and he didn't find me. He came with soldiers." He shook his head, squeezing his eyes shut. Karen could see it was a painful memory to relive.

"The *Ordo Sanctus*, they tried to wipe out other religions, but they had too much exposure and were too...noticed. They needed to go back into the shadows. They had to stop, until their true enemies revealed themselves." He pointed at the newspaper clipping with a shaking finger, aiming for the photo of the Cleaner's silhouette. "And now I think Benoit is in danger from him." He almost sounded on the verge of tears.

Karen raised one eyebrow. "We've been in danger from this man for some time now. I hate to ask you this, but do you know anything..."

Her phone buzzed in her pocket, interrupting her. She pulled it out and looked at it, and saw that it was Michaud's number. "It's Benoit," she said to Felix, then flipped the phone open. "Hey, I've got your uncle here..."

"Where are you?" he asked, almost yelling the words. Michaud's voice was crackling with static, cutting in and out.

"I'm in the parking garage under the station..." she said, "but I can barely hear you, the reception isn't that good down here."

"Karen! Listen to me! Take Felix and go upstairs, go where there are lots of people, do you hear me?"

The crackling over the phone was stronger and Karen strained to hear him, pushing her hand over her other ear. "I can't...what do you mean? I'm sorry, you're all staticky..."

As Karen spoke into the phone, she had her head down, squinting as she held the phone tightly to her ear. Something threw open the door and grabbed Felix by the collar.

In one brutal motion Felix was hauled out of the car with inhuman speed and tossed onto the ground, sending him out and away from the car.

Karen turned and she felt time seem to slow. She could barely move as she watched the man from the photograph, the man she had shot with Michaud's gun—the Cleaner draw out his lantern-device. He aimed it at Felix as he activated it. The beam shot out and Felix screamed, his face burning, as he threw his arms up to shield himself.

Do something, Wendleton! You shot this guy, you can do this! Do it now!

The Cleaner didn't seem to hear Karen switch the vehicle on. She shoved the gearshift into reverse and slammed her foot into the gas pedal, sending the car back and smashing into the Cleaner with the passenger side door. He fell and rolled, dragged by the car before he went under the door and was left lying on the ground. Karen slammed on the brakes, causing a loud echoing squeal of car tires before the passenger side door swung shut with inertia.

Michaud's voice yelled out, barely audible from the phone. "Karen? Karen!"

Karen stared, mouth open, gasping for breath. The throbbing in her ears made it seem like she could hear her own heartbeat. Out the front window she could see Felix, moaning in pain, trying to crawl along the smooth cement floor. The Cleaner lay motionless. Karen reached to open the door, intending to run to Felix and call for help, but movement caught her attention. The Cleaner used one hand to push his shoulders up, and then lurched into an upright pose, wobbling noticeably.

Oh, come the fuck on! What does it take with this guy? Karen's heart pounded harder. Within the insulated confines of the automobile, the only thing audible to her was the thudding in her chest, real or imagined. The Cleaner pulled away his mask and dropped it aside, but his hat, seemingly attached to his downcast head, still obscured his face under the brim. He began to raise his lantern device, aiming it toward the car, but Karen was ready. She shoved the gearshift into drive and thrust her foot against the gas pedal, sending the car shooting forward toward the Cleaner.

The toxic green-yellow glow of the lantern surprised Karen as the Cleaner raised it, and she threw one hand over her eyes. Before the energy beam could be unleashed, the car pummeled through him, sending him flopping up and over the hood, then tumbling over and over behind the car. Karen slammed on the brakes, bringing the car to another screaming stop.

She turned and looked through the rear window. The Cleaner was a limp pile of clothes for all appearances. *Got you, you bastard!* Karen swallowed hard and opened the door.

She rushed to Felix, who lay on his side, but he had stopped moving. She crouched down slowly, looking over the burned clothes and skin that were still seeping wisps of smoke, unsure of whether or not to touch him, or how to offer assistance.

"Oh, God...Felix? Felix?" she said, forcing the words out in a tiny meek voice. She reached out a hand, touching Felix's shoulder. There was no response. She rolled him slowly onto his back, gently, afraid of making things worse. The life was gone from his body. She held her hands to her mouth, unable to speak, staring at the charred remains of a man she had been speaking to only minutes earlier.

Karen went to the Cleaner. She pulled out her phone, intending to call upstairs for help, but her hand hung at her side as she stared helplessly at the bizarre figure lying prone on the ground before her. From beneath the body was the familiar green glow of the lantern. Blue fluid leaked from around his head. Bringing a frown to Karen's brow was the far stranger sight of the Cleaner's face, laying to the side of the body and broken into three large pieces, like a ceramic mask—an emulation of a human face as though from a mannequin. A pair of artificial eyes lay on the ground, disconnected from the Cleaner's head, peering up at her.

She nudged the body with her foot, then kicked him over. The face wasn't human. Grey and stony, it looked more like a statue, featureless, blank, as though it were worn down through slow erosion, but by design rather than age. The mouth was like a tiny grate on a vent.

Her eyes were quickly drawn to the glowing lantern shaped device the Cleaner's body had been concealing. To her horror, she could see that the casing was cracked, revealing the brightly glowing core, humming softly and seeming to grow in intensity with each passing moment.

The glow grew, expanding, and in a split-second Karen realized what was happening. She turned and bolted for the entrance ramp to the parking garage. She sprinted, but the green-yellow glow expanded and intensified too quickly. She felt the wave of heat blast at her from behind, followed by a tremendous thump, like a fist punching the earth. With a bright flare of energy, Karen felt herself jettisoned up and out the ramp.

She landed rolling on the street. A car swerved to avoid her. The splash of debris and the growing cloud of smoke caused traffic to grind to a halt as vehicles slammed on brakes, bumped into each other, and spun onto the sidewalks. The explosion was small, but the building shook with the force of it.

* * * *

Inside, the police station the lights flickered, the floors shook noticeably, and the distant rumble caught officers off their guard. A fire alarm sent out intermittent electronic tones. Simons, working at his desk, looked up to officer Kehoe, walking by with an armload of papers. Kehoe stumbled and spilled his papers across the floor.

"What's going on? Is it an earthquake?" he asked, steadying himself on Simons' desk.

"Don't know! We have to get out of here! Alarm's sounding." Simons stood, pulling his jacket off the back of his chair. They filed out with the other officers, and the loud murmuring of hundreds of voices in collective confusion filled the station.

* * * *

Michaud's cab stopped across the street, and he stepped out, looking up at the building. His stomach went into a screaming knot inside him. Officers were spreading out and away from the station, as multiple wailing fire trucks and ambulances drove up, sirens blaring. A large cloud of smoke billowed from the western side, coming from the parking garage. He paid the driver, and the cab sped off and away from the scene, leaving Michaud standing. His heart pounded. The weather was cool but his jacket felt stifling, and he pulled it off to carry in one hand. He trotted toward the crowd of officers, terrified at what he might discover.

* * * *

The morgue still held the makeshift Perpendex containment area, staffed by two technicians in full-body hazmat suits. Cooper, the medical examiner, stood outside the plastic barriers, pacing back and forth as he waited for the men to clear out.

"How much longer are you going to be? You guys said you'd be gone by now," he said toward the barriers. "I know you can hear me!" The Perpendex men ignored him as they went about their work. One of them held a large metal tube which Cooper recalled had recently been delivered to them. *What the hell is that thing? And when are you assholes going to get out of my morgue?*

The technician holding the cylinder began attaching it to one of the tubes feeding into the plastic containment bubble in which the enormous cocoon that had once been Weltner sat. Cooper saw movement in the containment pod, but neither of the Perpendex men seemed to. One was turned away, while the other worked at a computer panel. *They can't see a damn thing in those stupid suits!* The rippled surface of the cocoon started splitting open, a repulsive green-black slime oozing out and dripping onto the floor.

Cooper, outside the barrier, saw the shuddering movement of the organic mass within the containment vessel. He felt the heat of fear spread over his back and chest as sweat formed. At first stunned into silence, he forced himself to move. He began smacking his hands against the plastic wall. "Hey! Hey! On the table!" he yelled.

The Perpendex technicians ignored him, but it made no difference. The cocoon split open, and what emerged was a seething mass of wriggling tentacles, some the size of a man's arm, others small and worm-like.

It was not unlike an immense purple octopus out of water, spotted with dark mottling, devoid of a skeleton, yet moving fluidly around the inside of the containment vessel, seeming to feel the interior surface. The tentacles found grips and pulled, straining against the hard plastic surface, then pulled it apart barely a centimeter and pushed itself through the tiny opening, over the table and onto the floor.

As it slopped toward the technicians, the spread of its tentacles could be discerned—at least the length of an adult man. Cooper continued his screaming and thumping on the plastic to no avail. The foul mass reached out and entangled the leg of the technician working the metal cylinder onto the tube. He looked down and screamed. Cooper watched the disgusting spectacle, his mouth hanging slack. The other tech turned, hearing the muffled noise as his colleague was dragged down to the floor.

The still standing tech backed away, and spoke into a wrist communicator, terrified. "We have a containment breach! Containment breach!"

The seething pile of undulating tentacles crawled off the other technician, his suit torn apart, leaving behind a denuded skeleton, drenched in slime. The technician who was still standing whimpered, and then rushed for the exit. He pushed up against the plastic barriers.

Cooper, facing him across the divide, was frozen in terror, unable to do anything but watch as the writhing abomination wrapped itself up and onto the technician, dragging him down screaming.

Minutes ticked by with Cooper paralyzed as the thing finished off the second tech. The mass of tentacles then pulled open the small drainage grate on the floor. The grate should have been far too small to admit such an apparently large form, but it managed to squeeze maddeningly through, escaping into the sewage system...

Cooper wiped sweat and tears from his eyes. He stepped back, tripping, before turning and fleeing away from the morgue, yanking down a fire alarm along the way. The bell clanged loudly and an intercom voice urged the denizens of the hospital to remain calm. Cooper was anything but as he tore up the stairs, gibbering to himself.

* * * *

In the *Ordo Sanctus* council chamber, Horatio and the other council members watched a projected video image of the last moments of their technician's transmission, his face screaming hoarsely into the tiny wrist communicator, cut off at "containment breach. "

The council seemed to shudder as the members turned to each other, some shaking, others stammering their words. Horatio's cheek twitched microscopically as he clenched his jaw. *I hold them all together. God grant me strength. I am a calm island among violent seas. I am the eye of the storm.* He stood, his voice overpowering the others.

"We have tried long enough to keep the sick patient alive. But the cancer has penetrated too far. Fellow council members, the time has come to enact the plan. Send out the Final Transmission...awaken the sleepers!"

The slight, grey-haired council member to his left took a deep breath and turned to a computer panel in front of him, tapping keys slowly and deliberately.

* * * *

Michaud pushed through a confused crowd in front of the police station. The frenetic scene mirrored his racing brain, his heightened adrenaline. He shot looks back and forth, trying to find Karen, Simons, any familiar face. Bewildered and curious passers-by had begun to gather, held back by a hastily organized group of firefighters and uniformed officers. Smoke and noise filled the air. Paramedics rushed across Michaud's path, a uniformed officer helped the Deputy Chief to safety, and firefighters pushed into the grey and black plumes escaping from the parking garage.

Across the road, television vans, sides painted gaudily with station logos, their roofs adorned with broadcasting equipment, arrived, like predatory birds descending on a wounded animal. Cameramen spilled out, setting up their gear while accompanying reporters tried to make sure their hair was straight before going on air with a live broadcast.

Michaud spotted Simons amongst the crowd, his tie pulled out and his top collar button undone, talking over the noise with a paramedic. Michaud rushed over and took Simons by the shoulder.

"What the hell's happening? I just got here!" he yelled.

"Bomb! Think it was terrorists! Happened in the garage!" Simons shouted in response.

Michaud leaned in closer to Simons, his face contorted into a look of frenzied concern. "Where's Wendleton?" he demanded. Sweat ran freely down his back, soaking into his shirt.

Michaud heard Simons' phone faintly ring as he reached into his pocket to answer it. "Don't know! Haven't seen her!" Simons said to Michaud, shaking his head. "Hello!" he yelled into the phone.

Michaud leaned in closer to Simons. Out of the phone Michaud could make out a short burst of electronic pulses, like a string of arrhythmic notes beamed into Simons' ear. Michaud stared, watching Simons' features change, as though all the emotion had suddenly drained out of him. Simons' eyes became filled with a stark mechanical automation.

As Michaud watched, Simons dropped the phone to the ground and walked, his face blank of expression, through the crowd and away from the chaotic scene.

"Simons! Simons! Where the hell are you going?" he yelled after him.

Michaud looked around, confused. He turned to the police station to head inside.

* * * *

Through a blurred haze of smoke and noise, Karen's eye cracked open. Men running. Yelling. Sirens. *Felix? Where...* She felt as though she were floating, and tried to look up. A pair of paramedics carried her on a stretcher, moving away from the chaos. Every step as they moved felt like a jolt of agony through her. Her body was nothing but a mass of pain. She strained her vision, seeing someone, a man carrying his jacket as he ran into the building. *Michaud.* A pair of firefighters blocked her view of him. She tried to reach to him, to say something. "Boss..." she squeaked, the sound muffled by the oxygen mask that obscured her bruised and battered face. The paramedics were saying something as they reached the ambulance. She only heard a distant dull murmur as she lost consciousness.

* * * *

Pushing his way through the scattered emergency personnel in the station lobby, Michaud ignored or avoided anyone trying to impede or question him. He headed for the stairs, racing up them two at a time until he came to his floor.

Red emergency lights in the hallway cast a scarlet glow into his office, offset by the bright sunlight from the exterior windows. Michaud threw the door open, looking back and forth.

"Karen!" he yelled, but the room was clearly empty. He looked around gasping for breath, his eyes wild. His heart felt as though it were at the top of his chest. He stopped as he saw Karen's map on the desk. He grabbed it, looking at it in a beam of sunlight, and scanned over the areas Karen had circled. He remembered what the Informant had told him. Sleeper agents, people who didn't even know they had been programmed, would release a toxic substance at key locations around the city as a first run of their attack. His stomach seemed to be punching him from the inside.

Michaud looked over the books on the table, still open to pages Karen had marked. He realized what she was trying to tell him, what he had only just missed. She had calculated the most likely locations for attacks, based not just on their ability to disperse the weapon to large numbers of people, but on the prophecies and ideas presented by the *Ordo Sanctus'* literature.

The sick feeling grew in Michaud's stomach. His mouth went dry. *Simons.* Michaud remembered the way he had answered his phone, and suddenly it was if a switch had been flipped. "Men in your own department," the Informant had said.

Grief, anxiety, frustration, and anger at himself swirled in a self-destructive tempest around him. He shook his head. *All emotional luxuries I can't afford and a waste of valuable time.* He rubbed the back of his neck, hard, squeezing the base of his head. He clenched his fists and pressed them to his forehead, taking deep breaths. He knew the lives of thousands of people rested on the rapid dissemination of Karen's information to his fellow officers and that they needed to move quickly. He rushed from his office, his purpose clear in his mind.

* * * *

As forensics officers carefully photographed the interior of the parking garage, a dark-haired man in his mid-fifties, wearing a jacket marked "Coroner" across the back in large yellow letters, was helped by an assistant with the badly burned body on a stretcher they carried away from the scene. The mutilated form was covered in a sheet and strapped down, seemingly lifeless and beyond any hope. The two men grunted with the effort of lifting the stretcher into the back of their van.

"Why isn't the regular coroner here?" the assistant asked. "Why'd they call us in from Hamilton?"

"Wasn't responding to calls. Heard he was hospitalized for something."

"Fuckin' guy's heavy..." the assistant complained.

Just before they shut the door, the arm of the Cleaner fell limply to the side of the gurney, outside of the straps on either side. The burned grey surface of his body was partially visible through the badly shredded fabric of his coat, and his wrist radio was broken and blackened on his arm. The assistant sighed, and groaned his frustration. He carefully placed the arm back under the sheet and closed the van door.

* * * *

Michaud rushed into Friesen's office. The Inspector was standing at his desk, his sleeves rolled up, going over reports from a uniformed officer and two plainclothes. Other officers ran up and down the hallways. The station was a chaotic flurry of activity following the explosion. Friesen looked up from his desk and straightened up as he saw Michaud.

"Detective. Have you got something for me about this nonsense? Does this have anything to do with the people you were investigating?"

"I'm not sure, sir. It might."

"The only thing I'm concerned about right now is figuring out what the hell happened to us. If it's not about this shit, I don't want to hear it."

"I think this might have something to do with the other group. The one who controls the guy who was burning the bodies. Killing the cultists, you remember?"

"What other group? Did we talk about this?"

"Only a little sir. But I think...if I'm right, this could just be the opening salvo of a series of attacks, and the next ones will be much worse. I have a source who's told me that they have agents, possibly dozens of them, around the city ready to release a potent toxic substance, highly contagious, into multiple locations, and very soon."

"Michaud, unless this has anything to do with what you were assigned to, you have no business—"

Michaud cut him off, locking eyes with him. "*Ordo Sanctus.* Those words mean anything to you?"

Friesen kept his eyes on Michaud as he spoke to the other officers in the room. "You three—out. I need some time with Detective Michaud here."

The other officers gathered their papers and filed out, closing the door behind them.

Michaud broke the silence. "Are you going to let me take my task force after these people?"

Friesen stared, simmering, at him. "What people? This mythic group you keep talking about? Do you have any evidence they even exist?"

"They're preparing an attack. I don't need to penetrate their organization. I just need to keep them from killing a lot of innocent people."

"I'm sorry detective, unless you can..."

Michaud's patience had worn through. "You've been trying

to keep me away from these people since the start of my investigation. I've been told by multiple sources they have operatives inside the police. I can't imagine that's a coincidence."

Friesen was acting calm, but his skin was growing redder by the second. "You're getting dangerously close to insubordination, Michaud. So unless you want to find yourself standing in front of a parking garage ushering cars into traffic I suggest you do yourself a favor and—"

"I knew that 'Cleaner' couldn't have gotten inside and to the holding cells with only Wellburn's help. There weren't too many people who knew exactly when I'd be talking to Rachel. Karen, you..."

Friesen stared at him in silence. He spoke flatly, quietly. "You haven't got a single molecule of evidence. So you're going to turn around right now and walk out that door, do you hear me?"

"And I'll bring you up on formal charges of impeding an investigation. Not to mention aiding and abetting terrorism, being an accessory to murder, withholding evidence, criminal negligence..."

Friesen drew himself up fully and sniffed arrogantly. "You do what you think is right, Detective. But in a week, it won't matter. I don't answer to you, or your man-made laws. I answer to a higher power. If I've withheld anything, aided anyone, it's because I had to. When the trash is cleansed off this world, myself, my family, my associates, we're the ones who will inherit it back. The *Ordo Sanctus* isn't going anywhere because of your little task force, which last time I checked is a couple members short."

Michaud refused to be goaded. "Well, we're sure as hell going to try."

Friesen's voice rose. "What do you think you're going to do? Stop all our sleeper agents? Do you think you can even locate them? You make me laugh!" He forced out false laughter, the kind faked by bullies when they try to crush someone's spirit.

Michaud smiled. He turned to walk out.

"That's right Detective. Go back to your condo. You're done here."

Michaud stopped. He drew his digital recorder out of his pocket, holding it shoulder high so Friesen could see. "No, you're done here. And you can tell it to the news. Once we stop your little treehouse gang of dickhead zealots I'm sure there's a nice tidy cell waiting for you. I hear they love fat old ex-cops on the inside." Friesen's eyes widened, his jaw slack. As Michaud closed the door behind him, his Inspector was slowly sitting back down into the chair, deflated.

Chapter Twenty-One

Michaud sat alone in his office, phone in hand, radio in the other. A laptop was opened in front of him and he stared fixated at a map of the Greater Toronto Area Karen had marked. His breathing was labored, his frustration simmering as he bit his lip and rubbed the back of his neck. He leaned back in his chair, casting a look up to the ceiling. He blinked away the cold dryness the computer screen had given him.

Why am I in here? I'm not a desk jockey. I should be out there, with them, catching these guys before they can kill anyone. I'm not a damn coordinator.

He had sent uniformed and plainclothes officers out across the city to Karen's marked locations. Michaud was wary of the Informant's claim that there were *Ordo Sanctus* operatives and members amongst the police force, but if there were, they weren't making any effort to stop Michaud.

He had hoped that they did not yet have their canisters of the dispersal agent, which might give the police a short window of time in which to fan out across town. In that he was right.

Ideally upon capture they might be "awakened" back to their normal selves, or at least interrogated so that their orders could be fully understood. More importantly, who delivered the weapon. None of that had played out...

We've got six in custody. Three shot dead. Six committed suicide on discovery.

I gave the officers all the information they needed to do their jobs. They had to use discretion, in case the sleeper agents released their payload early upon discovery. Detection should be easy. They'd look like Simons, blank, mechanical.

Damn it, kid. Why'd it have to be you?

Michaud pressed a fist to his mouth, and breathed out deeply.

When was the last time I had anything to eat? You're losing it, Michaud.

Those margaritas and pina coladas are going to taste

so good on that beach at Varadero. Hell, one right now. Michaud's mouth felt dry again, thirst nagging him. *How about a bottle of scotch? They can come in tomorrow morning and find me passed out with an empty bottle in my hand. Might as well go full burnt-out detective stereotype. Smoke a few packs too.* He frowned and rubbed a temple, dispelling the fantasy.

No time for that. The locations Michaud went over on the list were major hubs, Pearson Airport, The Eaton Centre mall, Bloor-Yonge subway station, and, oddly, an inconspicuous diner to the west of Christie Pits Park. *The sleeper agents haven't succeeded in doing their job at all. We've got them whipped.*

But no Simons.

Unfortunately, prying information from these sleeper agents proved more difficult in practice. Their programming made them entirely unwilling to impart anything, and further, they had to be restrained in order to prevent suicide attempts. All that could be done was holding them in detention until a way could be found to either de-program them, or ideally give them the metaphorical splash of water in the face to wake them from their stupor.

A twitch at the back of Michaud's mind, the one thing that he couldn't let go of. *Simons is still out there. And here you are, all by yourself. Sitting in your damn office.*

Michaud kicked his desk. He stood, then kicked it again, twice. He looked around for his jacket, threw it on and strode to the door.

I can't just sit here. There's one location left with no contact. He must be headed there. I have to take him in. We're going to stop him, but I can't let him kill himself.

* * * *

The automated voice on the subway train spoke in a flat monotone, devoid of emotion. "The next station is Union... Union station..."

Its robotic voice mirrored Simons' mental state. He rode, blankly staring, face forward as he sat bathed in the bright grey fluorescent light, looking entirely indistinguishable from any other subway commuter. Not a trace of nervousness was evident, and he felt no anxiety over the cold metal canister he held in his hands, wrapped in a cloth bag. His simplicity of purpose provided a clarity others lacked and prevented doubts that might cause anyone else to have clammy hands or second thoughts.

* * * *

Inside the enormous main hall of Union station, plainclothes officers sat on benches pretending to read newspapers, stood talking on payphones, or reading the terminal schedule for out of town trains. Others stood against columns on the lower concourse near the area in which intercity "Go trains" arrived and departed, next to the entrance to the subway system. Michaud stood casually lounging, or appearing to do so, against the counter of a newsstand. He turned slightly, looking over his shoulder, his eyes scanning back and forth across the crowd. Hundreds of people were moving in and out, the endless din of murmuring and shuffling footsteps echoing back in upon itself across the permanently stained floor.

Michaud held his finger to his earpiece, listening for reports from the other officers.

"Station one upper level. No sign of him."

"Station two payphone. Nothing here."

From Officer Kehoe working the far end of the lower floor came a static-filled reply. "Station three, lower level. Haven't seen...wait."

Michaud turned fully around. He looked to where Kehoe stood on the far end of the floor, newspaper in his hand. Kehoe made eye contact with Michaud, then touched his finger to his ear, speaking into his wrist mic, "Target sighted. Moving to the upper level on west stairway."

Michaud turned. Simons was heading away from them. He had slipped right by Michaud. He must have averted his eyes for just a second as Simons walked behind a column. Frustrating, to be sure, but they had a job to do, and at least they had the advantage of knowing, very clearly, what their suspect looked like.

Michaud quickly moved to follow Simons, with Kehoe was right behind. They had to keep their attention focused on the back of Simons' head, watching him weave through the crowd. A group of tall college students in basketball jerseys moved by in the opposite direction, obscuring Michaud's view of Simons just long enough to lose his view of the young detective.

Michaud turned to Kehoe. They looked at each other, then continued up the stairs to the main concourse.

"Upper stations, do you have the target?"

Michaud heard nothing for several painful seconds until a voice spoke out, "Station two, ground floor restrooms."

Michaud, Kehoe and the officer from station one rapidly converged on the men's restroom, drawing their sidearms. Security staff ushered concerned travelers away and tried to keep anyone as far back as possible without causing an immediate panic. The three officers headed inside, scanning the room, ducking down to see underneath the toilet stalls. Only one pair of feet was in evidence, on the farthest stall, which they moved to, aiming their weapons.

Michaud signaled to the others with his hands, positioning himself and Kehoe to cover the stall while the third stood in the middle. Michaud nodded, and the third officer stepped forward and kicked hard, slamming the door wide open, revealing a chubby, bald businessman reading a magazine, who shrieked and curled back on the toilet in fright.

Michaud, unfazed, simply shut the stall door. He turned to the other officers. "Women's restroom."

They moved to exit. A muffled gunshot rang out from nearby, and Michaud spoke into his wrist mic as he rushed out with the others. He felt a wave of adrenaline-fuelled heat pass over him. "Station three, this is Michaud. Station three, do you copy?"

As they entered the women's restroom, weapons drawn, the first thing Michaud saw was the other officer from station three, lying on the ground in a spreading pool of blood, a gunshot wound in his upper chest, just above the collar area of the protective vest he wore. Standing over him was Simons, a Glock 9 mm in one hand, and the metallic cylinder in the other, his thumb positioned over the release valve button. Michaud's senses seemed to become muffled, isolating everything but a tunnel-vision of Simons in front of him.

Michaud spoke in a calm, clear voice, "Don't move, Simons. You don't want to do anything stupid. You're a good cop. You have to remember who you are, and this isn't it. Just put them both down and—"

Simons interrupted Michaud's attempt at diplomacy by

raising both the pistol and the injection device toward the assembled officers. Michaud's reaction was immediate—a single shot fired.

* * * *

The back door of the coroner's van opened, and a figure stepped out, stumbling before righting himself, buttoning his Coroner's jacket with latex gloved hands. He turned around the van and walked further down the dank alley and away from the street. It was a vile and trash-filled area, permanently smeared with a thin layer of oily scum. The web of power lines overhead, strung between rotten decades-old wooden poles and backlit by the bright moon overhead, turned the area into a surreal urban tableau, like some kind of charnel grease trap. It provided an ideal cover for what the man had been working on.

The man walked down the alley limping noticeably. He turned back, looking to make sure he wasn't followed. Inside the van lay two bodies, one of which was stripped of both clothing and epidermis, leaving a skinned corpse in a pool of spreading blood.

He looked in the van's rear-view mirror. His face was not his own. The skin of the coroner was stretched over his blank grey features. On his wrist was the burned communicator device, which he tapped, trying to activate it. The Cleaner had taken over an hour to strip this coroner of facial skin and apply it to his own, and while it may have been crude, it would be effective enough for him to accomplish his next objective.

* * * *

Michaud walked into the familiar lab of his old friend carrying another locked case. While his previous visit carried more levity, this one was considerably less upbeat. The need to move quickly, reassemble the task force and mobilize almost the entirety of the police over a sizeable urban area to counter the terror threat had turned him into something of an automaton. Focused solely on the job, he had to keep the city from being burned up by the fanatical organizations he was up against. He hadn't heard from Karen after the explosion at the police department. While he was glad that at least currently the toxic weapons being used by the *Ordo Sanctus* had been seized, a deep sense of foreboding hung over him.

Campbell spun around in his chair, speaking aloud before seeing his old friend. "Twice in one week Mister Michaud, if I didn't know better I'd think you have a crush on me..." As he saw the flat expression on Michaud's face, Campbell's smile drooped. "That bad, eh?"

Michaud nodded. "Sorry, Pal. This one's pretty serious. I need results, and I need them fast."

"On the call, you said..."

"Yeah, here it is." Michaud carefully lifted the case up onto the counter and opened it. Inside, nestled in foam and wrapped in plastic, was the cylinder taken from the hand of Simons after he had been shot.

Campbell rolled his chair over and stood up, leaning in to look at the package. "Doesn't look like all that much, does it?"

"It doesn't, but what it does is."

"Have you seen the effects?"

"Only had them described to me. I was hoping you could test it, put it in isolation. It's still pretty dangerous."

Campbell frowned nervously. "So...isn't this a biological weapon? Shouldn't the Infectious Disease guys be..."

Michaud shook his head. "No, they're under the thumb of the people who spread this thing. I need someone independent to look at it. And that, my friend, is you."

"Oh...joy. Lucky me!" Campbell said, mugging and rolling his eyes. "Don't get me wrong Ben, I do love when you bring me new toys, but this...I'd prefer that they not have a mind of their own."

* * * *

While Campbell frowned, looking over the reams of data scrolling across his monitor, molecular diagrams flashing light on his face, Michaud sat hunched over in a chair nearby, eyelids drooping, barely resisting nodding off. He had been waiting for hours and fatigue had finally caught up with him, and one of the few things keeping him awake was Campbell turning around every ten minutes to apologize for the delay. Michaud rubbed the back of his sore neck and groaned a yawn. *A cigarette would make this so much easier.*

It was not lost on Michaud that the cult had been attempting to transmit a dangerous biological agent, while the *Ordo Sanctus* and Perpendex were combating them with the transmission of a highly advanced piece of nanotechnology combined with a virus. Not to mention that the orders for the sleeper agents were a transmission of another kind, a simple radio signal meant to trigger an immediate, programmed response. It was as if this war they were fighting was taking place on multiple levels, each one like some kind of fractal extrapolation of the level below it, expanded into a manufactured analogy of mutual destruction on the biological and molecular levels.

Given the time, Michaud was sure he could fill volumes with metaphors on tribalism, this ridiculous microscopic arms race. He realized that he, too, was in a tribe, one with its own colors, symbols, rituals. *What were the police if not the forward army of the ruling tribe?* One, it seemed, that was frustratingly either unaware or indifferent to the hidden conflict happening right in front of it. He pulled out his badge, rubbing a thumb over its embossed surface.

Does this really mean anything anymore?

The police attitude would probably change very soon, of course. The processes had been set in motion; something was going to happen, sweeping changes, either rapid and destructive, or slow and incremental, but they were inevitable and would be impossible to ignore. Such was the nature of the world. He hoped whatever they were heading toward could avoid any great loss of life. There must be a way to use these forces, shape them once wrested from the control of these two groups. His hands felt cold in the air conditioned lab. He held them up in fists, blowing into them.

Michaud wondered what might the zooids have been like in their natural state. *Something like what Liu had told him about? And the nanotechnology, surely it had other applications that weren't destructive. The potential must have been awe-inspiring. If only the tools were in other hands...*

He looked at them, his own hands, turning them over. An awful thought struck Michaud—*what if I'm infected?* The zooids seemed to have some kind of rudimentary intelligence, perhaps even a frighteningly powerful collective intelligence—what if they were waiting for something? He put two fingers to his neck for his pulse, then felt his forehead.

Not that it matters now. Could they have fooled the CIDC tests somehow, using him to spread themselves? If they were intelligent, surely they were capable of subterfuge, waiting for their moment to strike, guiding his actions, making him their unwitting accomplice. For all he knew, everything he had done was part of some grander plan, one not visible from his perspective, only making sense at a distance. He felt more aware now, his heart quickening.

*And Karen...*her passing the tests for infection at the CIDC might be meaningless. She could just as easily still be infected too...or was this just paranoia? He had no idea where she was or why she wasn't answering calls. He needed to warn her... Michaud shook his head, trying to stay awake.

No, that was crazy. They would have done that with the others, like Montrose...wouldn't they?

Transmissions...that's really what this was all about. His pulse slowed, his eyes fluttered. Information, be it biological, genetic, or simple communication, the transfer of language, or disease, or radiation. Michaud was losing the battle with his fatigue, and his thoughts contorted in his mind.

The zooids, what were they really doing? Weren't they just reproducing, transmitting their genetic information along, borrowing from others, to continue what all other lifeforms do? Clearly, in a terribly perverted form for the purposes of some scheme, but reproduction nonetheless. And the cybernetic-virus, wasn't that just an attempt to render sterile biological organisms, render their species unable to reproduce itself by wiping them out?

Michaud's eyes flitted closed...*human frailties and failings, particles moving back and forth, atoms dancing with each other, conversing, communicating, destroying, creating, the universe talking to itself...*

Michaud awoke instantly with an upward snap of his head, his eyes opening as he heard Campbell clap loudly. He had an arm cocked backwards, as though about to pump a fist. Campbell was about to speak, but the computer chimed merrily, its analysis finished, interrupting him. He turned back to the monitor, and Michaud drew himself up, immediately curious.

"Hmm," was the only sound from Michaud's friend.

"Hmm? What 'hmm'?"

"Well, the canister is just like any other, nothing special

about it, just an air pressure release. Not really that different from the ones used to conduct dispersal of biological agents in the years before they were banned for use in warfare. You could use it to spray plants with water if you wanted, so no surprise there."

"The contents..."

"I'm getting to that. Um..." He turned to Michaud. "You know I know a lot more about nanotechnology than biotechnology, right?"

Michaud nodded. His foot tapped on the ground as his impatience grew. He put his hand to the back of his neck. "Okay, well, based on what little I know, and mind you half of this is guesswork, but this isn't really a biological weapon. Not entirely. What your Informant told you was pretty much accurate. It's..." Campbell paused, his eyes seeming to scan the ceiling. "It's basically a virus that's been artificially bred—very sophisticated stuff—and fused with pieces of nanotechnology that are working in concert with it to get into a host and do what it has to do."

"I know all that. How does it work? Can you tell me that?"

"Well, the computer simulation I've run, and this is just a simulation, so you know. It looks like what it does is get inside a living cell and use it to manufacture copies of itself, just like a regular virus. But here's the kicker, the nanotech segment, which replicates itself along with the virus inside the cells, gives the signal to cease replication. And once these cyber-viruses have been confirmed to move on to another host, they detonate."

"Detonate? You mean..."

"Destroy the host. They just use it to make enough copies to send to another host, then blow themselves up. And by that time, there are enough of them to turn the host into a dust pile."

"Sounds like something these people would come up with."

"Oh, it gets better. The replication is so fast, that you're looking at a gestation time of maybe...an hour. Before the host goes. But the programming is such that they won't just keep spreading and replicating, they stop after maybe...three, four generations of hosts. They're miniature suicide bombers in a way. After they detonate, there's nothing left, maybe tiny traces, but if you didn't know what to look for, there wouldn't be anything to find. Absolute genius."

"Enough to spread out and cause total panic and chaos, but not enough to kill everyone on the planet. That fits."

"Still, definitely wouldn't want to be anywhere near a release of this stuff. Enough in this canister to infect...maybe 500 to 1000 people in a densely populated space, like a bus station. Each of those people infects ten, each of those infects ten..."

"The cities would be empty within days."

"Yup. The crazy thing is, you could probably program the nanotech segment to do whatever you wanted. Go after certain kinds of cells, certain kinds of organisms."

"That's very likely the intention."

"Devious, but really brilliant. Frustrating, too. They could probably be programmed to enter and repair cells, and in turn program other cells to do the same...wish I knew more about biotech. Just seems like such a waste of a really innovative piece of technology. You could use these to, say, reprogram cancer cells to die off, or instruct, uh, the optic nerves to re-grow in someone who was blind. Such a waste."

"Hmm...more transmitting of information after they transmit themselves and their offspring..."

"What?" Campbell said.

"Oh, nothing. Just something I was tossing around in my mind earlier."

"Where'd you say this thing came from?"

"I didn't," Michaud replied, an eyebrow rose.

"Because..." Campbell assumed a pensive look, his eyes drifting. "The Japanese developed a huge biological weapons program in World War II, used a lot of them on Chinese cities, too. After the war they were given immunity from prosecution by the American military in exchange for their research and expertise."

"Yeah, I know, they did the same thing with Nazi rocket scientists."

"Well, it was alleged that the US used biological weapons in the Korean War, never proven, and the official military program was shut down by Nixon in the 70's. And all the major governments agreed to ban the use of biological weapons. Pretty sure Canada did the same. Viruses, bacteria, they're not controllable, and they have this nasty habit of breaking through your security protocols and infecting your own people. It's why there was no strenuous objection to the ban. So...

who developed this thing? Terrorists?"

Michaud studied his friend, then spoke carefully. "The treaties only covered governmental bodies. Not private organizations, and not medicinal uses of biotechnology."

"So...someone hires out a firm to do medical research. They then develop their own untraceable, fast-acting lethal super-weapon that's totally controllable thanks to a nice little nanotech leash and collar, unlike standard biological weapons."

"You feel like switching jobs? I get the idea yours is less stressful than mine," Michaud said.

"Exactly. I like my lab juuuust fine, thank you," Campbell said, smiling.

"So, how do we kill it? Can we?"

"Wouldn't be that difficult, I don't think. Probably a high enough dose of radiation. Might cause cancer in the person infected, eventually, but it'd shut down the nanotech for sure, and the virus would be essentially just a...common cold after that. Without the programming, it wouldn't do all that much."

"So, that weapon I showed you a few days ago..."

"That'd do it, yeah. I mean, on a canister or something. If you wanted to wipe out lots of them, you'd have to blow up one of those power cells, like I told you about. Of course, you'd kill everyone you were trying to save, so it's sort of pointless. And all this is my speculation anyways, if you really want to talk to someone who knows this stuff inside and out, you should go see Elgin Horatio, he's in the biology department and into viral research."

Michaud's eyebrow rose. "No, that is someone I definitely do not want to take this canister to. But I will be talking with him...eventually."

"Suit yourself," Campbell said, turning back to the monitor.

Michaud's phone buzzed, and he took it out to answer. "Michaud. Yes, that's right. Oh...oh my God. I'll be right down." He shut the phone and put it in his pocket, standing and throwing his jacket on, a look of disbelief on his face. His eyes were distant, unfocused.

"What is it?" Campbell asked, concerned.

Michaud swallowed. "Karen. The woman I work with. She's in the hospital," he said while heading out.

Chapter Twenty-Two

Karen lay unconscious in her hospital bed, an intravenous drip attached to her arm. Her face was bruised, swollen purple-black on one side, and bandages crisscrossed her body. Light burns were visible peeking out from underneath the white gauze, not as severe as they might have been had she not been thrown from the garage.

Her family had visited earlier, shared somber discussion with Michaud, then shuffled out into the hall to give him some time alone with her. He had met them earlier in the year at a city function. They seemed so happy then, so vibrant, seeing their daughter succeeding. He had laughed with them, enjoying their stories of life in Canada, being himself an immigrant as a young boy. Karen's father had a strong English accent, and looked so lean and fit for a man in his 50's. Karen's mother was, Michaud thought, surprisingly tall, her hair jet-black with only a hint of grey, her eyes sparkling as she smiled. Not a hint of a Japanese accent either, and Michaud recalled she was born and raised in Canada. He remembered how Karen looked that night in her evening gown, her hair done up, so unusual for her. She was at once striking, statuesque, even gorgeous.

She had been unconscious and unresponsive since being admitted, bringing to their minds the terrible possibility that she might slip into a coma, or worse. Now he shared the blandly green hospital room with her in relative silence, the only sound being the repeating chirp of the Electrocardiogram monitor beside the bed.

He sat beside her, hunched over in his chair, depressed, cold moonlight filtering through the blinds and spilling onto his back like the guilt he was drenched in. The barest hint of a craving for a cigarette crept into his thoughts, but dwelling on it for more than a second started to make his stomach turn. His mind filled with the nightmarish events of the day, of the past week, all rushing back up on him at once. He had shut it all out, kept pushing forward, but it tore into him now.

Deaths of fellow officers, Karen lying broken in hospital, and his being forced to shoot Simons. *Just a kid.* A good kid that got his mind stolen and didn't deserve what happened. But shooting him...he had to. He shot another officer, was about to do something worse than any terrorist bombing.

The danger was immediate, reacting was crucial. *That was the job.* It could have been a lot worse. People would have died, a lot of them. He sighed, the weight of the dead bearing down on his spirit.

He held Karen's limp hand gently, and he spoke aloud, not directly to her, his eyes downcast, as though feeling too ashamed to speak to her face, "I'm sorry I wasn't there for you. You've always been there for me when I needed you, and when you needed me I wasn't there." His voice cracked slightly, tinged with emotion. "Maybe I acted like I was made of stone sometimes, like I didn't even see you. But I always noticed everything you did. Don't ever think I didn't notice." He sighed again, a rickety, bouncing sigh, then coughed, keeping his emotions held deeply inside, his guilt washing over him like a wave of self-destructive pain.

Michaud's phone buzzed, and he stood, moving away from the bed to answer it. The familiar voice of the Informant came through a layer of static.

"Detective. You need to get out of the city..."

Michaud interrupted him. Michaud walked further from the hospital bed, standing almost in the corner of the room where the windows met the far wall. He tried to avoid disturbing Karen and limited himself to a harsh whisper into the phone. "I'd appreciate it if you wouldn't contact me any longer," he said, trying to keep his voice down.

* * * *

The Informant, his suit disheveled, walked quickly along the darkened laneway behind his house. His car would be invariably tracked. He had bought a used suit of clothes from a vintage shop, trying to look inconspicuous, and knew he would have to strike out on foot, then take a cab to the airport. The cab should be arriving soon, as he had instructed it to wait two blocks south of his house—out front would be far too obvious. In one hand he carried a briefcase hastily stuffed with papers, in the other his cell phone held to his ear.

"You don't understand," he said. "You'll be their next target. The plan isn't finished, they—"

"Listen pal." His voice crackled from the Informant's phone. "You've brought me nothing but grief. You helped me, sure, and thanks for that, but—"

"I'm leaving town. They're preparing another outbreak. They're coming for you. Just do what I tell you!" The Informant said, haste in his voice.

As he spat out his last words, a sinister shape appeared in front of him in the laneway, stepping out from an intersecting alley. It was the Cleaner, still wearing the uniform and skin from the dead coroner. His hand jabbed out, enclosing around the Informant's neck, hoisting him up and squeezing. The Informant's cell phone clattered to the ground, his briefcase following as it landed flat on its side.

Michaud's voice came from the phone, "Hello?"

As his consciousness swam into a deep blackness, his pulse droning in his ears, thoughts shot through his mind. *Parents...high school sweetheart...no children...divorce... military... Watershed Corporation...house...wealth...alone. No joy, only employers. Repentance. Whistleblower.*

A silhouette under the nearby streetlights, the Cleaner brought his other hand to the neck he held, and tore the Informant's head from his body with a snap and a swift twisting motion. The head hit the ground with a wet thud, a dull, flat roll along the ground before it stopped, face down.

As the oxygen faded from the Informant's brain, life draining away, his vision blurred. For one tiny moment he became completely aware of his own mortality, that this was the end, and held in his heart nothing but regret for the life he had lived.

* * * *

Michaud listened on the phone, but could only hear the sounds of movement, the rhythmic beat of footsteps against the concrete, but nothing else. He shut the phone, mildly upset and confused by the strange call he had just received. A tiny voice whispered behind him.

"Hey Boss..."

Michaud turned, seeing Karen looking toward him. He moved back to his chair at her bedside and sat, taking her hand. She barely moved, only turning her head slightly toward him, the rest of her broken body motionless in the bed.

"How are you feeling?" he asked quietly.

Karen managed a weak smile, which quickly became an expression of grief and shame. "He was there...the man with the hat...the Cleaner guy...it was him."

Michaud frowned, taken aback. "What?"

"Benoit, he...he killed your uncle."

Michaud was stunned, unable to process or believe what he had heard.

"Are...are you sure? Did you see him...I mean..." The words rattled around in his mouth, a jumble of emotional chaos. He looked into her sorrowful eyes and knew she spoke the truth. Devastation flooded him.

"I'm sorry...I'm so sorry...I couldn't stop him..."

Michaud looked at her. He wanted to comfort her, but the swirling tempest of emotions within him left him unable to cope with the gravity of his uncle's death and Karen's situation at the same time. Karen made another feeble attempt at a smile as she tried to buoy her colleague's spirits.

"I got him though...I got him for you..." Karen's smile quaked as tears formed in her eyes and ran down her cheeks, soaking into gauze. "I did what I thought you'd do." Her smiled faded, and her eyes seemed to go blank, her expression slackening as Michaud gripped her hand. She squeezed it back, and let out a pained sigh of breath.

Michaud searched her face. Panic ran through him. It was happening too fast, there was still so much he needed to say to her!

"Karen? ...Karen?"

He looked at her, not believing his friend, comrade and colleague could possibly be dying in front of him. She was still so young, so full of potential, so much left to do. Her electrocardiogram flatlined, a dull monotone quietly sounding through the room.

"No...not yet. Not yet, I..." He stood and rushed to the door. "Nurse! Nurse!"

His yelling abruptly awoke Karen's parents, who had slumped onto each other in slumber on a pair of chairs across the hall. A nurse and doctor came rushing down the hall toward them.

Michaud looked at Karen's mother and father, his eyes

wide as he breathed heavily, unable to force out a word. They looked back at him and knew immediately. Karen's father rushed into the room. Her mother lingered a moment, holding her hands up clasped together at her mouth as she looked at Michaud. She brushed past him, choking back sobs. The nurse and doctor were trying to revive Karen, but Michaud, grief-stricken, refused to turn and look. The sound of Karen's mother wailing took on a screaming quality, which was rapidly muffled into her husband's chest as they held each other.

Michaud shuffled over and planted himself with his back to the wall outside the door of Karen's hospital room. He was wide-eyed, frozen in a moment of uncertainty, staring at the floor in front of his feet, feeling nothing but disbelief. *Never get close. You didn't, and you won't, ever.* Thirst hit him. Now he wanted a drink, badly. It would be so easy to dull the pain, swim away into a dark ocean of blurry forgetfulness.

Officer Kehoe approached, walking down the hall still in uniform, a hopeful smile on his face, and a bouquet of flowers in his hand. The smile disappeared as he heard the crying of Karen's mother. "Detective Michaud, how is…"

"She's gone," he replied bluntly.

"Oh." He stopped, swallowed. "I'm sorry…"

"Save it."

Michaud's lower lip quivered and he bit down on it, frowning. He wanted to keep up appearances, stay strong. He shut his eyes tightly but a pair of tears escaped, streaking down his cheeks.

Kehoe looked at his feet. He turned to leave. Michaud coughed and cleared his throat, took a deep breath through his nose, then stopped Kehoe with a question, "The evidence we collected from the cult house, the place in the Junction… is it still in storage?"

"Mmm, should be. Nothing was damaged in the explosion."

Michaud nodded, thinking. Kehoe walked down the hall, turning a corner and going out of sight.

Michaud put his hand over his face for a moment, choking back a tiny sob. He refused to cry over his fallen comrade. A drink right now wouldn't help, it would just make the feelings worse. He looked up at the ceiling, blinking away the wateriness. He wanted to tell Karen how much he appreciated, even loved, her. But time had caught up with him, and he missed his chance. His pain boiled over into anger, anger at the cult, the *Ordo Sanctus*, the world, the universe for allowing this to happen. He gritted his teeth in frustration and limply hit the side of his fist against the wall behind him.

His brain churned. He felt a plan formulating. He wiped the back of his hand across his eyes, his grief turning to vengeance. *Not the angry rookie. Angry now, here, today.* His face hardened into a mask of glacial determination.

* * * *

The noise of the door unlocking and opening broke the emptiness as Michaud entered the evidence room in the sub-basement of the police station. Like a miniature warehouse, it was immense, dark and quiet. The dense concrete walls insulated it from outside noise and the densely packed space absorbed so much sound that it made for an aurally dead room, silent in an unnerving way. Silhouetted against the bright hallway behind him, Michaud carried only a small empty sports bag in one hand. He flicked on the bright overhead light, looking around the ceiling-high metal shelves as he pulled a slip of paper from his pocket on which he had noted the catalogue number of his evidence from the cult's Junction house.

He knew weapons were kept in a specially reinforced cabinet with a caged door. Moving past the rolling ladders latched onto the high shelves and their myriad contraband items, Michaud went directly to the back of the room. He fished a set of keys from his pocket and looked back over his shoulder, more out of his mild anxiety than worry that someone might find him. What could they think? Nothing, really. He was a police officer going over his own evidence from a case he was working, evidence that he himself had found and catalogued with his colleagues.

Matt Simons and Karen Wendleton. He stopped, holding the keys, steadying himself with his other hand on the top of the cabinet. Memories welled up, but he shook them off. It was too easy to fool himself into thinking they'd be coming along, but they wouldn't. They were the reason he was doing this.

His Uncle Felix. Michaud had called Felix's phone repeatedly, gone by his shop, his apartment, in the vain hope that Karen had been mistaken, that maybe she was just delirious in her last moments. But she was right, Felix was gone too.

They always leave. Or they're taken away. Like mama and papa. Like everyone. Michaud took a deep breath and blew it out forcefully, then slipped the key in the lock and turned the latch.

Within the cabinet were automatic weapons lined up on a rack with handguns and submachine guns on shelves beside them. He looked through the shelves until he located what he had come for—the grenades seized at the Junction house. He pulled off their small paper tags, then unzipped the sports bag and placed all of them inside. There were only seven, but he hoped this would be more than enough.

He looked at the handguns, and on impulse picked up one that had a silencer. The gun clanked against the metal of the shelf as he lifted it. It had a trigger lock, as did all the firearms, but it wouldn't be difficult to remove. He looked it over—a Ruger .22, smaller caliber than his Glock 9 mm, but he knew from experience that the .22 would still be entirely useful. He held it, weighed it in his hand, and held it at arm's length, looking down the sights. In movies, guns with suppressors tended to make the sound of a shot into a tiny blip, which Michaud knew was artistic license. In reality the sound was still loud, just not ear-piercingly so. This silenced .22 however was the real deal. He knew from experience that this one would release no more noise than the sound of the shell being ejected. Probably about as loud as a stapler, he thought. He'd have to try it out to make sure, but still...

Michaud pulled the paper tag off the handgun and placed it in his now much heavier sports bag, then zipped it up. He shut the cabinet and locked it. As he turned around, he looked up and saw the security camera in the corner of the ceiling staring down at him. He smiled up at it, reminding himself that there was nothing wrong with what he was doing, at least not in the eyes of any casual observer.

He thought a moment, remembering the other thing he might need, then turned around and headed back between the shelves. He rolled a ladder over two sections before climbing it until he was nearly at the ceiling. Huge clear plastic bags filled with bundles of banded cash twenties, fifties and hundreds, seized in drug busts. He pulled out a small box cutter and sliced the bag open with a zip, then put the knife back in his pocket. A single bundle would be all he'd need.

He unzipped his sports bag, tossed the twenties in, and

closed it up again, before climbing back down to the floor. He switched off the lights and shut the door behind him as he left.

Chapter Twenty-Three

Crowds of drunken baseball fans had clogged the streets near the waterfront after the latest night game, but were mercifully dispersing, leaving Michaud's path clear for travel. He stepped out of the cab on Queen's Quay, wearing a black jacket shorter than his usual three-quarter length coat, over a black turtleneck, along with dark jeans and a pair of sneakers.

He pulled out his sports bag and handed cash to the driver, then walked a short distance down to the docks along the water. Taking the direct route via the island airport ferry would be too obvious, and surely *Ordo Sanctus* men in plainclothes would be watching for him, even if he were able to run out across the tarmac toward the area pointed out by the Informant.

He'd have to hit the far edge of the airport, fenced off from Hanlan's Point, where ferries to the other parts of the island would dock. The city-run ferry service to the island had stopped running an hour earlier, but he was looking for a water taxi. Spying the orange roof of one, he walked down the dock, the lone figure at the lake's edge in the semi-darkness. The water taxi's operator, a stout, balding man, pale and clad in a light blue jacket and company captain's hat, was tying the boat to the dock as Michaud approached.

"Got time for one more run?" Michaud asked.

"Nah, sorry pal, closing up shop for the night. Come back tomorrow. First trip's at eight," he said without looking up.

"Does this change your mind at all?" Michaud asked, displaying his police badge.

The operator looked at the badge, then eyed Michaud. He returned to his knot tying. "Gotta do better than that I'm afraid. Besides, don't you guys have your own marine patrol boats?"

The banded wad of cash flopped down on the dock beside the operator. He stared at it, then picked the cash up, flipping through it. He studied Michaud before undoing the knot.

"Guess I've got time for one more ride."

* * * *

Michaud strode through the grass, the city's skyline high-lighting the night behind him. A light wind rustled the trees around him and far off in the city an ambulance siren wailed, echoing between the concrete and glass towers. The dock at Hanlan's Point, lit by humming streetlights behind him, fad-ed away behind the trees as he walked. The only other sounds around him were crickets chirping, and the water softly pat-ting at the concrete edge of the island dock.

He stopped at the towering fence before him, leading onto the tarmac of the island airport. He could see a small building just inside the gates—that would be his target. A pair of bored guards stood at the building's entrance, chatting aimlessly with each other. They were attired identically to Wellburn and his companion as they were found dead at the Dressed to the Nines Club, in long heavy coats, wearing helmets, gas masks, and huge rifles of odd design.

At his distance, Michaud couldn't make out what they were saying, but their tone, muffled as it was by their masks, seemed bland, amicable, harmless. He regretted what he had to do for a moment, but the memory of Karen's last breath burned and hardened his mood. He noted the position of the security camera over their heads, aimed out into the spread of the floodlight and away from the entrance. He hoped it would barely, if at all, pick up the space flat against the doors.

The gate in the fence was chained shut, but luckily the chain wasn't tight enough to keep Michaud from squeezing himself through. He kept his eyes on the building and moved along the fence, deeper into the dark and away from any ar-tificial lights, until the front of the small building was away from him. He stayed low, creeping through the grass and up to the edge of the building. It looked for all outside appear-ances to be the same as any airport building on the edge of the field, aluminum siding walls, utterly nondescript, but Michaud suspected it held more. He moved slowly along the side of it until he was near the front, and could see the shadow of the guard closest to him shifting back and forth under the light over the building's entrance.

He thought a moment about how he would approach the situation, thinking over multiple possibilities. He hadn't fore-seen that guards might be wearing those thick, lead-lined coats. He worried that the .22 he carried, deadened as it was by the silencer, might not effectively penetrate them. He had hoped, or at least thought, that they would be the same type of urban camouflage-clad security officers who had carried Chow out of the Centre for Infectious Disease Control.

At night though he supposed the *Ordo Sanctus* soldiers might be on guard duty, since they would be far less visible. It would have been only too convenient to take the damaged uniform off the body of Wellburn or the other contractor from the Dressed to the Nines Club. Unfortunately they had both been taken by Disease Control who carted off all the dead life forms and weapon pods that day, then had everything seized by Perpendex. For all he knew, those bodies might be stored inside this very building.

Michaud picked up a few small stones from the ground, and moved back toward the corner of the building, away from the entrance. He looked at the corner, then threw a handful of stones at the aluminum wall, making a loud spattering of clanks, stone on metal. He watched the shadow of the guard begin to move over, then Michaud dashed quickly around the small building to the other side, peering around to where the entrance was. One guard still stood at the far corner facing away, but the other seemed to have gone further into the shadows to investigate the sound, just as Michaud had hoped.

He swallowed nervously, then ran out. His feet made tiny speckling noises along the gravel near the doors, as he rushed toward the still-visible guard. The guard began to turn at the sound just as Michaud was on him, but Michaud wrapped his arms around from behind and grabbed the rifle. The other guard, an indefinite shape in the darkness turned and rushed back. Michaud fired the rifle as he struggled with the guard he held. The light from the beam revealed for a split second their forms in the darkness. The one hit by the strafing energy was jolted back up and off his feet with a yelp muffled by his mask. Michaud only heard a heavy thud as he hit the ground.

Michaud was still scuffling with the guard he had his arms around. Keeping his hands on the rifle, Michaud slipped his arms over the guard. Yanking the weapon away, he then jabbed as hard as he could back into the guard's midsection. The guard doubled over. Michaud raised the rifle high over his head and brought it crashing down onto the guard's helmet. The man slumped to the ground on his stomach. *Out cold?* Michaud prodded him with the rifle to be certain, then pushed him over onto his back.

Sorry guys, you or me...or the entire city.

Michaud looked over at the front doors to the building. Naturally there was a security scanner in place, a card reader and a larger pad next to it, he guessed for a handprint. Michaud fished through the pockets of the guard's coat, then stopped himself, thinking.

He cracked a smile, before pulling off the coat, helmet and mask, then donning them himself. A little tight across the shoulders, but a convincingly good fit, he thought. He slung the rifle over his shoulder, the sports bag held in his other hand, and almost wished he had a mirror to check over his appearance, hoping he might be convincing. The disguise wouldn't get him very far, but it wouldn't have to, only needing to be so from a distance, or with his back to anyone inside.

He went back into the pocket and found what he was looking for, the plain white security card, a tiny gold chip embedded in it. Picking up one arm of the unconscious guard, he pulled him over to the scanner, and placed his hand on it. The pad lit up, and Michaud slipped the card into the reader next to it. The muffled sound of the door unlocking followed. Even across the water, he could hear that the sirens in the city behind him seemed to have multiplied considerably—must be a big fire. He adjusted the mask on his face, then turned the door handle, opened it, and stepped in.

The hall was lit from above by overhead spotlights, creating dim pools of light. Michaud moved along trying his best to act casual without betraying his desire to remain inconspicuous. Thankfully staff was barely in evidence amongst the drab grey-green interior. "Barely in evidence" was an exaggeration. The building seemed deserted. He paused at a corner. He had hardly an inkling of where he might be headed.

Time. How much time? Michaud pulled out his cell phone to check the clock. He had missed a call while on the water taxi to the island. *The hospital? Why would they be calling? It couldn't be Karen. I rushed out so fast...*

No. Stop thinking like that. She's gone. You know what you're here to do.

He drew a handheld Geiger counter from his sports bag. Switching it on he looked at the readings as it clicked slowly. He aimed it in different directions, before settling on a metal-grated door near the end of the hall.

He looked at the door for a moment before realizing it was

a freight elevator. Unsurprising, given what the Informant had told him. This was a large facility with labs. All he had seen so far was a rather average looking set of offices. It made sense that their true nature would be hidden out of sight. He switched off the Geiger counter, slipping it in his pocket.

Gripping the handhold on the door, he pulled it open to a deep and heavy gear-grinding sound. It was a monstrous piece of machinery, a relic of decades gone by, but clearly still functional. It was from an era when things were made to last, instead of having planned obsolescence built into them. He stepped inside onto the roughly grated floor and looked at the panel that would display which floor he was on, but it only indicated up and down. He assumed this was the only way in or out of their subterranean level from this building, so pulled the metal door shut, and simply pushed the "down" button.

The elevator shuddered to life. The cable squeaked as it lowered the metal box containing Michaud, until it finally stopped with a jolt.

But the call, what if it was about Karen? What if the doctor had gotten to her in time? I can't make a call in here. Find out later. If there is a later.

He craved a cigarette to allay his nervousness, then realized that even if he had one, he wouldn't bother. Not because he had quit long ago, but because he felt very little nervousness. He was in fact feeling a blank numbness. He knew why he was here and had set his path before him in his mind. Michaud steadied himself, then pulled the door open.

There was a short hallway, lit only by a caged spotlight, and at the end of the short hall was a set of double doors with a long, thin vertical window in each of them. Next to the doors was another card reader, one he hoped would be activated by the stolen keycard. Michaud stepped out of the elevator, walking lightly and attempting to carry his weight to avoid making unnecessarily loud footfalls. An absurd precaution, since if the *Ordo Sanctus* guards were loud in their boots, so should he be, and he would more likely be caught for any number of other reasons.

He looked through the doors' windows, back and forth trying to see what was on the other side of them, and could discern that it was another hallway, but one apparently much longer than that upstairs. This one stretched much farther to the right, in the direction that would have been the end of the building above ground. A pair of guards, identically attired to the ones upstairs, and as he now was, rounded a nearby corner as Michaud watched. He ducked back instinctively as they passed. As he watched them go by, he saw what they were accompanying. A gurney was being pushed by a lab coated Perpendex technician or doctor, who was wearing a gas mask and long heavy gloves.

On the gurney lay a badly burned human corpse. Apparently in the early stages of the mutations induced by the cult rituals, its limbs were curled up into an awful death pose of obvious agony. The horrific condition of the body made Michaud wonder if the burns were the result of the cybernetic nanotech-virus creation he had been told of by the Informant, or some other variation with similarly lethal results.

He waited for the gruesome trio to pass by, then pressed his keycard to the reader pad beside the doors. Once opened, he slipped through. The group had rounded a corner, and Michaud saw clearly the hallway stretched on for what looked like the length of the island. He wondered if it in fact extended below the water and underneath the waterfront of the city itself. It was unlikely, given their almost obsessive level of secrecy and desire to stay isolated. Certainly their fanaticism forbade them from allowing any experiments gone wrong to be unleashed onto an urban area before they intended.

This location was ideally situated for them. Surely no one would suspect an advanced experimental and militarily equipped facility, owned by a private organization, could exist right on the waterfront of the country's largest city. It had its own air strip just above ground it could use for its own purposes. Likely with planes disguised as those from a legitimate airline which could when necessary, deploy probably hundreds of troops into the city almost instantly, with thousands more flown in from outside locations within hours. A short walk from a major tourist destination, beyond a thoroughly ordinary looking fence, where it looked like nothing unusual, attracting no attention—hidden in plain sight. Even the freight elevator. No one would question it if they made their way inside, it looked so ordinary, and surely it wouldn't lead to anything of value, or so the reasoning might go.

Michaud looked back toward the direction the guards and technician had gone with their gurney, then walked the opposite direction, to the right, down the long hall. Many of the doors on either side of the hall had small windows, and he examined each, trying to find something that looked like what he had come for. A particularly bright window caught his attention, and he peered inside. It was clearly an operating room, the floor and walls tiled in a stark, bleached white, with a central table around which several technicians in lab coats and gas masks were gathered under the sickly blue fluorescent lights. Michaud guessed this, or a room like it, might have been where the trio he saw earlier had come from. On either side of the room were guards, *Ordo Sanctus* soldiers, dressed similarly to the others he had seen, their weapons at the ready...for what, he couldn't see.

The technicians around the central table stepped back and parted slightly, and Michaud could make out what it was they were working on. Underneath a repulsively smeared containment pod lay a mutated specimen—whether a member of the *Olog'lahai'kuhul* cult, or some unwilling victim, it was impossible to tell. He—or she, again, impossible to discern—must have transformed into an immense lamprey-like organism, legs and arms atrophied into stubby flippers, skin a mottled and slippery grayish-green, an enormous toothy mouth covering half the head with barely visible eyes and no nose in evidence.

It was apparently sedated, but sadistically cut open and held so with large metal forceps, revealing internal organs that pulsed and moved while its exterior features were motionless. The technicians had been manipulating the body with huge gloves they were able to reach into, attached to the inside of the pod. The ghastly sight was a nightmarish distillation of everything awful Michaud had seen over the past week. He felt nauseated. He backed away and turned his attention back to the Geiger counter after making sure there was no one else in the hallway.

How large was this facility? What else did it contain? The Informant spoke of "multiple projects" the *Ordo Sanctus* and Perpendex were working on, and Michaud was morbidly curious as to what they might be. Obviously their cybernetic nano-virus was tailored to destroy both normal human and mutated tissue that had been transformed by the *Ritus Mutatio.*

The report Michaud had read made it clear they understood the nature of the colony organisms and how best to destroy them. It wasn't implausible they had studied and manipulated the zooids to their own end, possibly for bio-mimetic applications in weaponry and pharmaceuticals, among other things. The weapons as well—*just what were they working on?*

Michaud took a brief look in the small windows of each door he passed, most revealing little of interest. They were either dark and of unknown purpose, or labs that were empty and apparently devoid of recent activity. He stopped at one, dimly lit, and spied what appeared to be a long room with a barrier at one end near the door and multiple stalls along it, opposite the far end of the room backed by huge pads and concrete blocks. Clearly a firing range.

Set up in front of the concrete blocks were mannequins, some badly burned, strafed with fire, or smashed apart by projectiles. He was almost tempted to take the strange energy rifle he carried inside and test it, since he had only fired one in the scuffle above ground by the front entrance, and it was hardly a fair assessment of the weapon's capabilities for him. The descriptions of what it could do given by his friend Doctor Campbell were tantalizing...from a purely professional perspective, of course.

Michaud stepped across the hall and looked in the opposite room. This was a lab not unlike the one he had seen containing the vivisecting operation. The stark sterility and whiteness of the room was almost blinding, even in the power-saving half-lit mode the lights were in. In locked compartments along the far wall, separated from the rest of the room by a second clear Plexiglas wall, were organic weapon pods, corpses of dog-sized crustacean creatures, pieces of the tentacled anemone-like life form—all from the Dressed to the Nines Club. Nothing moved. Everything looked dead. Each compartment appeared to be isolated and encased, arranged like the wall of drawers for bodies at the hospital morgue, but with considerably upgraded technology. Each case had a transparent, lit window, revealing its contents, and judging by the keypad next to each, its own electronic locking mechanism.

So this is where they had been taken. Chow—what had happened to him? He might still be in this place somewhere. Michaud reminded himself to stay alert and watch for him... if he were even still recognizable. The compound already seemed mazelike. It might have started out as a simple bunker, one they built onto, increasing in size over time, like an ant hill, growing and spreading, riddling the earth beneath the islands with tunnels and catacombs...

Something inside the room caught his eye, something that looked oddly familiar, laying on the counter in the center of the room, surrounded by instruments...he touched his keycard to the pad beside the door, hoping it would unlock. With a click, the door opened, and Michaud proceeded inside, slowly. He moved to the table and looked closer. Something about it...and then he recognized it.

The mask worn by the Cleaner, or one just like it.

They must have been testing it out, for some reason, probably related to the samples in the drawers. He picked it up, turning it over, looking at it. He looked into it, held it to his face, then looked through the eyepieces. It immediately lit up and activated, startling him slightly. It wasn't a gas mask after all. Sophisticated electronic readouts dotted his field of vision when he looked around from inside the mask. He recognized displays giving chemical and biological analyses, options for enhancement of the field of view, and magnification, among others.

Michaud pulled the mask away and laid it back down on the counter among the instruments. *Fascinating, but there's no time for this.* He looked up at the drawers containing the dead organisms, and headed back to the door. He checked back and forth through the small window, then stepped back into the hallway.

Were they only studying these things, or wiping them out? Michaud was curious about the potential for competing factions within the *Ordo Sanctus*, as the Informant's existence had demonstrated must exist. If Perpendex Pharmaceuticals was responsible for the research efforts, he wondered how much pull they had within the *Ordo Sanctus*, since they were for outward appearances at least, a stand-alone business entity. The *Ordo Sanctus* was seemingly composed of ideologues and fanatics who followed dictates that ignored practicality—the Cleaner was proof of this principle. Certainly there were members of Perpendex who held disdain for their *Ordo Sanctus* overseers, while the *Ordo Sanctus* ruling hierarchy might only tolerate Perpendex's research operations as an unfortunate necessity.

Give your head a shake, Detective. You've got a job to do. Overthinking was what he had always done, what had kept him up at night, what had made him good at what he did. He tried, inside, to turn away from the awful things he had already witnessed, and succeeded. This time he wanted to distract himself.

Stay on target. Stay focused.

He wished the Informant, or Liu, had been able to furnish him with a blueprint or floor plan, as he found himself meandering, his only direction coming from the increasing intensity of the Geiger counter's clicking. He looked up from the readings and found himself beside several sets of double doors, oddly, not a flat metallic like the others, but rather painted deeply crimson. He ignored doors marked "Chapel" and "Prayer Room" and continued on to ones with a small sign reading "Waiting Room."

Somehow, the red of the doors seemed familiar, as if from a half-forgotten dream. Curious, he pressed his keycard to the pad beside the doors, pushed one open and peeked inside. A lushly furnished lounge was filled with large leather recliners, shelves full of books, antique standing floor lamps, thick red carpeting...and a set of carved wooden steps leading a short way up to an intricately sculpted, copper-plated door. Michaud switched off the Geiger counter. He looked over his shoulder, up and down the hall, then stepped into the strange room.

It felt surreal to him, moving from the bleak sparseness of the concrete hallways into this invitingly warm lounge. The padded softness of his footsteps on the carpet felt somehow suspect, as if in a bizarre hallucination. He stopped for a moment in the middle of the room, looking around. On the end table beside one of the fat recliners was a copy of a newspaper, folded over to the business section, accompanied by a crystal ashtray in which sat a pair of stubbed out cigars. *Someone checking his stocks. Won't have those for much longer if your plan works out, will you?* He looked up the carved wooden staircase, only a few steps high, leading to the ornate door that appeared to be the focus of the room.

* * * *

The door opened a crack, and Michaud's head slowly moved out from behind it, looking into the empty darkness. He moved slowly into the space, and the dim lights around made the outlines of where he was partially visible. A space of at least the size of a school gymnasium, was presided over by a row of seats behind a high barrier. Something felt deeply unsettling about being here, and he recalled why. It was here that he had been taken while drugged. Brought in while strapped to a wheelchair. The *Ordo Sanctus* council had lorded over him. *By wheelchair.* If that was the case there had to be another entrance. One that was accessible by a ramp rather than stairs, and hopefully one that would connect to the area behind that row of seats—that was of particular interest.

Michaud felt along the wall, groping in the darkness what seemed like alternating wood paneling and thick velvet curtains. A light switch might be nice, but that could draw attention from someone outside, and even in his stolen outfit he would easily be caught as an outsider. His hands brushed along the outline of a doorframe, and he felt along until he came to the door handles. Cautiously, he turned one and pulled, peeking into the next room.

What he saw was another hallway, but unlike the sparse concrete of the area he had come from, this was a continuation of the lavish furnishing and design of the waiting room and council chamber. Michaud reasoned that where he had entered was the "back door," most probably the laboratories and testing facilities only. There would surely be a separate area solely for the benefit of the organization's leaders and higher tiers in their hierarchy, and one equipped in the style and comfort they were accustomed to. He stepped through and closed the door behind him.

On either side of him in this hallway were more doors. Checking the left, he found they led to a set of ascending stairs, which he walked up, thinking it would be the easiest access to the higher platform in the council chamber. Reaching the top, he found that his assumption had been correct. There was a row of comfortable chairs facing down into the chamber. Each seat faced a computer panel on the back of the barrier that separated the long table they sat behind from the chamber's level below. Unfortunately, nothing of obvious value was in evidence, and surely the computer system would be password-protected.

Michaud realized he didn't really need anything further from these people and this was all essentially a distraction. They would never be criminally convicted, no matter how much evidence or information could be gathered and brought to light. Their infiltration—or rather, insinuation into—the government and economic power structures was no doubt so complete that an *Ordo Sanctus* operative could probably kill someone on the street in broad daylight and get away with it. *Or more likely given up as a sacrifice for the greater good of the organization, branded as a lone maniac with no ties to them.* But they weren't about to kill just one person, it was, as the Informant had told him, millions, potentially many more.

What worried Michaud was that even if this maniacal plan was revealed to the public, if they knew what the Ninth Darkness cult had hoped to cause—mass mutation in their creation of an "army" of followers—the public might actually support the *Ordo Sanctus* plan of blanket slaughter and sterilization, foolishly believing they would somehow be spared the carnage.

Michaud stepped lightly back down the stairs and looked back and forth along the hallway. It was more than a little unnerving how empty the facility was. The labs were clearly still active or very recently so, but this portion of the compound was seemingly devoid of personnel. It might be that the council heads were absent because they had fled to areas outside the city, private shelters with their own guards, in anticipation of the impending release of their weapon on the populace.

Were the lab techs staying behind because they had no such places to go, and this was safer than anywhere else for them?

He moved across the hall to the opposite door and opened it, finding another set of stairs. Instead of leading to a platform above the council chamber, at the top of the stairs was a metal door. This was leading back in the direction of the laboratory section of the complex as he opened it.

Inside was what looked like a control room, with computer panels and huge windows looking out over a larger space—*a testing area of some kind*, he thought. This could be more of the same but it seemed less likely that if what he was looking for were in the facility, it wouldn't be in the more extravagant area of the compound meant for the ruling elite.

He flicked on the Geiger counter, still in his pocket, and drew it out halfway, its clicking much stronger and more regular now. He moved across the room and looked down into the large space. The lights were on already, and...movement.

He ducked back from the windows, shut off the Geiger counter, and then slowly peered back. It was a technician in a lab coat, working on a large console, his back to the windows and Michaud. He appeared to be checking things off, going back and forth from the console and his clipboard, absorbed in his work, and clearly hadn't heard or seen the detective.

Michaud hazarded a look around the large room, which was probably a testing area. In the middle of the space was a table with straps, more than likely for holding down a human, animal...or other subject. The area Michaud stood in was clearly the observation booth, probably shielded and equipped for control of some of the equipment below. The comical thought crossed Michaud's mind that if he were to start punching buttons on the panels he faced, he might somehow vaporize the technician below. The lab tech shut off the console at which he stood and moved for the far door. Seeing this, Michaud craned his neck watching the technician head out. He decided to discretely follow, and took the door exiting the booth that led down into the testing area.

Michaud walked across the floor of the large room. The smell was acrid, unpleasant, like burnt hair and corroded metal...It reminded him of something—the stench left behind after the Cleaner had sterilized Rachel's cell, the basement, the Junction house.

Had the Cleaner been here?

This could simply be a similar process or experiment carried out on someone, or something, with the same result as the Cleaner's weapon. *But Karen, she said she "got him."*

The dryness in his mouth again, the soreness in his neck. His heart raced. The Cleaner might still be alive, or worse, there might be more than one of him. Of course, that made sense. He could be unique, or there could be a team. Had they been chasing more than one of these Cleaners the whole time?

The Informant had said nothing of it. Michaud realized it might have been better to wait a day until he could reassemble his task force, the tactical unit, and whoever else he could muster, and assault this compound in greater numbers. On the other hand, stealth seemed to be working reasonably well.

Michaud reached the door on the other side of the room, he waited, listening before he approached too closely. In this door was another long vertical window, and he approached slowly. He held the rifle and hung the sports bag over his shoulder. The room was deathly silent. Michaud was half-afraid he would start to imagine sounds from lack of stimuli. He looked through the window, the massive rifle ready, but saw nothing. The technician seemed to have departed, at least from the small field of view afforded by the glass. *If I make it out of here alive, that beach in Cuba is going to be so great. And if Karen made it, I'm taking her, departmental rules be damned.* Michaud hesitated a moment, then pushed the door open.

The hall was empty. As he suspected, it looked much like the lab area he had come from into the council chamber. He heard a clicking, as a lock being reengaged, far to his left. Looking down the hall, he saw movement—the door at the end vibrating slightly, having closed seconds before, and he could hear footsteps faintly receding at a distance.

He kept his eye on the door, pulling out the Geiger counter and switching it back on. As he progressed down the hall, it increased in intensity, finally bringing him to a set of doors that terminated the hallway, not the ones the lab tech had entered. Michaud switched the Geiger counter off and put it back in his pocket, his eyes fixed on the doors. As he reached them, he swiped the keycard against the pad beside them, and they twitched with a click as they unlocked.

He entered an immense room, the size of a warehouse. *How far underground am I? Under the lake?* The size of the space appeared grander through the semi-darkness, as spotlights shone down from overhead, disappearing into the distance among the inventory, nearly roof-high stacks of plastic crates. Along the far wall to his left was a staircase climbing nearly the height of the room, he guessed leading to somewhere under or near the terminal of the airport—some other part of the facility that might be its "front door."

Dwarfed by the enormity of his find, Michaud was stunned with awe. The stacks of unlabeled crates looked sealed shut. *Very recently moved inside. No dust.* He walked to one sitting alone on the floor in front of a towering pile, putting his rifle down as he did so. He felt along the edges of the lid, looking for a release. There were clasps on each side and he pulled them open, then pried the lid off. He wasn't sure if it was the room, or the effect of being in close proximity to the crates, or his nerves finally getting the better of him, but the warmth under his jacket felt prickly with heat, and he could feel sweat beginning to run down his back.

Pulling the lid back, he cast his eyes on the contents: five rows of five metal cylinders, carefully packed in solid foam, each identical to the cylinder he had taken from the hand of Simons after shooting him. Michaud carefully lifted the foam tray, peeking underneath, and discovered (as he expected) another tray of vials. He looked at the crate, sizing it up. There had to be at least ten trays, which meant two hundred and fifty cylinders per crate, and the crates were in the hundreds. He stared, wide-eyed at the end-of-the-world sitting before him, and he tried to take in the breadth of the silent horror he was witnessing.

Perpendex really had come up with a miracle-cure for their imagined disease, the disease of potentially all human life, and this was the clearinghouse for their manufactured apocalypse.

The sheer lunacy of a group of people trying to create their own end-times in order to combat another group that was also trying to bring about the end of the world struck him as some kind of cosmic joke. He knew people believed what they want to believe, they saw what they wanted to see. And if they thought the world was going to end, they wouldn't just sit and wait for it, they'd make sure it happened. If only one vial had the effect the Informant had told him about...Michaud picked the rifle slowly up off the floor, weighed the bag of grenades he had over his shoulder in his other hand, then put it on the ground. *So much for that beach in Varadero.* He held the rifle up, trying to figure out if it were possible to do the kind of damage he was hoping for...

"That won't accomplish anything, Detective," a voice called out across the room.

Michaud turned to see who was addressing him. Doctor Horatio stood atop the side staircase. He descended the stairs, apparently unarmed, looking entirely unconcerned in his business suit. His hands, clad in black leather gloves, made tiny squeaking sounds amplified by the huge room as they brushed along the stair railing. Michaud pulled off the helmet and mask he wore and dropped them to the ground with an echoing clunk. His charade was over. He turned the rifle to the stairs, vaguely recognizing the man.

"Doesn't mean I shouldn't do it," he offered back.

"I don't think you understand. You can fire that weapon in here if you like. But if you did, you might manage to destroy, oh, about ten percent of our inventory before security took you down."

Security, of course. Michaud looked around, trying to ascertain where outside the room they might be positioned. The situation was oddly amusing. As if Horatio were now the lone negotiator attempting to calm a dangerous terrorist with a force of armed men at the ready just outside. Michaud suppressed a snicker. He unzipped the sports bag and drew out a grenade, holding it up for Horatio to see. "No, you're the one who doesn't understand. I'm going to blow this place back to hell where it belongs."

Doctor Horatio paused for a step before continuing, but seemed unfazed by Michaud's gesture, appearing as over-confident as ever. "And let's say you detonated that in here. You'd kill yourself, maybe injure me, and you'd probably blow up a few crates. Leaving hundreds untouched, of course." He shook his head, chuckling. "You really haven't thought this through very well, have you?"

"I've thought plenty through," Michaud grumbled. His eyes inadvertently glanced back to the sports bag, the weight of the grenades reminding him of how many he had. He slipped the one in his hand into the pocket of the *Ordo Sanctus* overcoat he had on.

"What was that?" Horatio asked, sarcastically holding a gloved hand up to his ear. He had reached the bottom of the stairs and walked closer, but slowed to a stop, making sure he was still far across the room from Michaud. Horatio shook his head again. "I really had thought it wouldn't be so easy with you, Detective. You were such a thorn in our side this past little while, being a good investigator, finding all the angles, with some help from one of our people of course."

Michaud frowned at this while Horatio continued, "Yes, yes, we knew about him, have for a couple of days now. He's dead, by the way."

Michaud sighed. "I thought so," he replied, squeezing the rifle.

"Did he ever tell you his name?" He stood, looking Michaud in the face for a few seconds. "He didn't, did he? Bernard. His name was Bernard. To his friends, that is. I was his friend in years past. Shame. Was an excellent soldier, once. He was very good at covering his tracks, making himself hard to listen in on, but we managed it eventually. The Cleaner...very good at what he does."

"Where is everyone? Where's the rest of the Council?"

"I'm sure you know. They've left the city, headed to other places they feel safer in. Me? I've stayed here because I know that this is exactly where I want to be when everything finally goes into motion. This facility, everything under my dominion is graced by our protector."

Michaud wanted to hate this man, the man who had indirectly been responsible for the deaths of his uncle Felix, Karen, and countless others. He wanted to be able to raise his handgun and put a bullet into this despot-in-waiting, a man deluded and fanatical. But he could only feel sorry for him, and Michaud looked on him with pity furrowing his brow. He raised the rifle, aiming at Horatio. "The colony organisms, from the cult, you used them, didn't you?"

"Of course we did," Horatio said, almost laughing. "How else could we craft their defeat? In order to destroy your enemy you must understand it."

"But it was more than that, wasn't it? You modeled your virus on it. The way it acts, the way it functions," Michaud said, one hand gesturing to the stacks of crates. "What was your plan for all this? Where was it going?" he asked, his voice a flat monotone now.

"Detective, you can't be serious. This is our *backup* supply. The containers have already shipped. You're too late. Surely you realize you couldn't have intercepted all our sleeper agents. And I waited for you to come, delivering yourself straight into my hands, so we didn't have to send the Cleaner out after you. Because, as we both know, his job is to clean up messes, not make bigger ones."

Michaud studied Horatio's face. He lowered the rifle a notch, smiled, then lowered it all the way.

"Doctor Horatio, right?" he asked.

Horatio nodded.

"Doctor Horatio. You know that I'm a detective. You know that I'm a *good* detective. And I've taken pride in something in over the years. One of the things that has allowed me to *become* a good detective, and get even better at, is spotting a liar.

"And you? You are not a good liar. You're not even an

average liar." Michaud shook his head, again almost amused. "This isn't your backup supply."

Horatio's face betrayed him, despite his attitude. His lips sneered further, his facade of arrogance stretching too far past believability. "Detective, do you realize we've made so much of our weapon that we hardly even know what to do with it all? Why do you defend them?" He spat out. "You're right, you are a good detective...*too* good. We brought you into our council chamber and warned you. All you had to do was get rid of the cult members. Publicly, on the stage and under the lights of the media.

"Your Inspector was supposed to guide you as we wanted you, but you just couldn't leave us well enough alone." Anger spilled from him now, the mask of calm entirely gone. "Of course those organisms were an inspiration, they were destructive, and efficient...Most great technological innovations of humanity were inspired by natural phenomenon, if you can even consider those *things* as 'natural'. We took the weapon of the darkness and used it against them! But it was us cleaning up our own mess. We failed the world, we failed our God, and this was our solution."

"You're insane," Michaud said. "You can't believe this scorched earth plan will actually work."

He sighed. "I am sorry, Detective, but you had to know this was coming."

Michaud frowned, momentarily confused. Suddenly he felt a hammering thrust from behind into his back as if he had been hit with a battering ram. The sports bag dropped from his shoulder. His head snapped back and his legs and arms trailed out behind him as he flew forward and landed on his stomach. Skidding across the floor, he stopped a few meters in front of Horatio. Grenades spilled from his sports bag and rolled away, wobbling as they bumped against crates, while the rifle slung over his shoulder was underneath him. Horatio stepped back toward the stairs as Michaud blinked rapidly, trying to regain his senses. He rolled over onto his back to see what he had been hit by.

Striding rapidly toward him was the Cleaner, wearing an overcoat and hat. Gone was any pretense that he was human, as his skin-like covering was entirely absent, revealing fully to Michaud his strange, stone-like appearance.

Michaud's mouth dropped in shock at what the Cleaner

truly looked like. Before his brain could work out any possibilities of what he was looking at, he instinctively raised the rifle and fired, holding the trigger down. With a bright flash and a sizzling blast, the Cleaner was sent back and off his feet, a smoking black wound in his chest. Michaud watched only long enough for the Cleaner to sit upright, the fist-sized mark in full view, burned through the overcoat.

Horatio had moved back up onto the stairs. He watched the melee unfold, smiling. Michaud staggered to his feet, and the Cleaner stood up and ran directly at him. Michaud, overtaken by the Cleaner's speed, was only able to raise the rifle partway up. The Cleaner plowed into him, the rifle sideways between them.

Horatio spoke loudly from the stairs, his voice echoing through the room. "You can't keep a filthy, degenerate world like this alive, Detective. It needs to be cleansed."

Michaud struggled against the superhuman strength of the Cleaner, who had thrown him up against a short stack of crates, pushing against the rifle in an attempt to crush it into Michaud's chest. His feet kicked helplessly as the Cleaner hoisted him further from the ground. Michaud feebly used one hand to push against the face of his attacker, but he might as well have been trying to push away a marble statue that was bolted to the floor.

Horatio spoke again. "It's a shame you have to be cleansed away, too."

Michaud grimaced, sweat dripping down his forehead as he groaned through his bared teeth. With one hand he reached into his jacket, barely able to reach the pistol he still had holstered under his arm. Drawing it out, he could only move his forearm, the rest of it pinned against his body by the Cleaner's pushing against the rifle. With a flick of his wrist, Michaud turned the pistol to the Cleaner's face, and squeezed the trigger repeatedly. The suppressed .22 caliber shots sounded like a hammer slapping against a boulder as the slugs fired into their target. Startled, the Cleaner stumbled back a step, dropping Michaud to the ground.

Michaud used one hand to take the strap of the rifle and throw it over the head of the Cleaner, the other hand fishing in his pocket to pull out the grenade he had dropped there. He held it up and popped the pin out, raising it to head level.

"Let's see you clean this mess up, you son of a bitch."

Michaud jammed the grenade into the Cleaner's immobile grey mouth, slamming his hand up against the inhuman
face and pushing the grenade through the metal grill. Doctor
Horatio, still on the stairs, saw this and his expression of calm
was broken, replaced by one of helpless fear.

The Cleaner fumbled to get the grenade from his mouth,
the energy rifle hanging from around his neck. Michaud
smiled and gave a solid push against the Cleaner's chest with
both his hands. Michaud then leapt back onto the ground,
shielding his face.

Horatio went flat, hugging the stairs.

An ear-splitting crack tore the air with smoke and a flash
of light, as the grenade exploded, knocking the Cleaner back
and along the ground, his face smoking from the explosion,
his body motionless.

Michaud gasped, then coughed, blowing dust away from
under his face as he tried to push himself up. His head swam,
his vision blurred and he flopped over to his side as he tried to
regain his bearings.

Michaud turned, seeing a blurry Horatio push himself up
as the dust cloud dispersed and drifted to the ground. The
Cleaner was still, smoke wafting up from him

Horatio coughed, bringing himself to a crouching position
as he brushed dust and bits of debris off himself. Michaud
blinked away the blurriness, seeing the door behind Horatio
open and security personnel file in. The door at floor level
from which Michaud had entered also opened, revealing further *Ordo Sanctus* security contractors, moving in with rifles
ready. Their boots rumbled along the concrete until they encircled Michaud. Two on the stairs moved to Horatio, helping him up. Another security officer stepped closer to the
Cleaner's body, squatting down and looking over him.

Blinking rapidly, Michaud tried to push himself up, to
be greeted with multiple rifle barrels pointed at his face.
Someone was saying something to him, loudly he thought,
barking an order of some kind, but it sounded muffled, indistinct as an awful ringing filled his ears. He touched a hand to
one and realized they were bleeding, and whatever the men
were yelling, he didn't think he was in any condition to oblige
them.

At the periphery of his vision he saw a bright glow, and
for a moment thought it was an injury-induced hallucination,

until he rolled his head over to look. Behind the circle of feet around him he could see the energy rifle that he had thrown onto the Cleaner before the grenade was detonated. It glowed brightly now, a green haze growing around it. Michaud looked away and up to Horatio on the stairs, who was looking down at it as well. He had no more snide remarks, no more plans to save himself, his hubris completely shattered. All that remained was craven terror.

Michaud smiled. For just a moment, he could feel beach sand under his back, the sun beating down on his face. He could see Karen lying beside him, smiling back at him.

The *Ordo Sanctus* men turned as the ball of expanding plasma grew, engulfing them with blinding brightness before it exploded.

* * * *

Outside the doors of the building, the guard who had been knocked unconscious was stirring. As he pushed himself up, the ground rumbled, then tore open, spilling outwards in a tremendous explosion.

The guard was sent sailing through the air, and he bounced off the security fence and onto the ground. He looked up. The island airport tarmac was rent open, an enormous chasm spread outward. The remains of the underground facility were a smoking ruin, twisted metal and crumbling earth. Water began seeping in, and the island airport would likely soon be gone.

The guard stumbled to his feet, and momentarily lost his balance before righting himself. His rifle hung slack at his side from the bandolier it was attached to, and he pulled it up, holding it ready. He stood for a moment, staring into the remains of the *Ordo Sanctus* compound, but as silence descended on the airport, his attention was drawn to the city skyline—now lit brightly in flashes of orange as plumes of smoke rose from fires raging throughout the downtown core.

* * * *

Easily audible was the repeating "*whup-whup*" and buzzing of helicopters as they flew about through the clouds of smoke, leaving vortexes of black and grey vapor in their wake.

Helicopters weren't the only things moving through the air between and over the buildings—things unidentifiable on outstretched membranous wings screeched and wailed as they flew, some carrying prey in their talons.

Up the sides of buildings, multi-limbed creatures, some like insects, others like sea-dwelling arthropods crawling on dry land, moved about. Many wore the tattered shreds of their former garments hanging from their new forms.

In the streets below, people ran terrified as many among them collapsed. They clutched their bodies or stared at their hands as the heat they felt within themselves overwhelmed them and they detonated, bursting outward with flame and ash, causing everything around them to burn.

* * * *

The guard, standing stunned on the island, could see the light of the fires illuminating the undersides of the black clouds billowing up. While the echoing sounds of sirens carried across the water to him, the screaming did not.

Epilogue

Thomas Atwater, the now orphaned son of Rachel Atwater, sat on the bed in his pajamas, watching the scenes on the television intently with innocent fascination. The noise depicted was far off. The outside of his building was quiet. Crickets chirped, and the occasional automobile could be heard several blocks away.

The television set in the government-run care home filled the small room with a blue-white glow, contrasting with the naturally cool moonlight filtering through the venetian blinds. The sound was down low, but not so loud that it couldn't be heard. A harried reporter tried to speak above the clamor behind her—screams, sirens, crashes and explosions, with a continuous rumble of fires—as she reported from a third floor balcony overlooking a street engulfed in chaos, smoke billowing up and police lights blaring back and forth.

"Police, fire, and emergency crews are desperately trying to keep the situation under control in the Greater Toronto Area tonight as fires burn unchecked throughout all districts.

"Unidentified wild animals are on the loose, attacking people at random, and several incidents of individuals actually going up in flames spontaneously have been not only reported by citizens, but also recorded and verified by authorities.

"The city is like a war zone, with the mayor nowhere to be found and the city council convening an emergency session in an attempt to maintain order in the face of these bizarre, unexplained events. Provincial and federal aid is on its way, but reports have filtered in of similar incidents in other cities, here in Canada and throughout North America.

"Unconfirmed reports link the chaos to the recent terrorist bombing of the downtown police headquarters as well as the attempted use of biological weapons by a cult or terrorist cell. With the recent rash of murders and strange, violent phenomena increasing unabated, police are asking everyone to stay indoors until civil authority has been reasserted..."

Under one arm Thomas had tucked his stuffed dinosaur.

In the other hand he held one end of the bag of books he had been allowed to bring that morning. The bag, the one he brought from the basement where he last saw his mother, had spilled open while Thomas fixated on the television broadcast.

The books had not been examined or screened by his social workers. They were all his books now, mostly children's books. He looked down at them in the moonlight, light from the television flashing across his curious face. One large leather-bound tome stood out among the colorful picture books. Its title was embossed in centuries-old metallic letters affixed to the cover, the *Encyclopedia Nefastus*.

About the Author:

Brian F.H. Clement was born in Kelowna, British Columbia, Canada and comes from a multicultural family with both Japanese and English heritage. He lived in Japan for a year after high school and returned to Canada in 1997. He then took up independent film, writing and directing 7 features, which were distributed by small labels around the world during the DVD boom of the early 2000s, and received screenings at film fests from Germany to Brazil, Australia to Argentina, as well as all over North America.

One of these films, *Dark Paradox*, serves as inspiration and background for *The Final Transmission*. Brian is the recipient of several film-related awards and decided to rewrite his screenplay for *The Final Transmission* into a book more fully able to explore the scope of the ideas within.

Visit him online at:
http://www.brianclement.com

Also from Damnation Books:

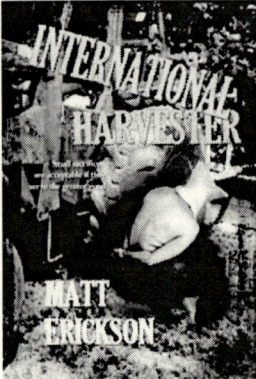

International Harvester
by Matt Erickson

eBook ISBN: 9781615727568
Print ISBN: 9781615727575

Horror Thriller
Novel of 135,597 words

What is the life of one when compared to the salvation of many, Phillip Gant asks, visualizing himself as a savior, a giver of life, a god. The decorated pilot roams New York stalking and abducting his prey. He harvests his victims and flies their organs to Canada. Upon returning home he sinks the deceased in watery graves, but first he claims his prize. Handsome and charismatic, Gant adds another disciple to his congregation of adoring worshippers. Who can stop the International Harvester?

Also from Damnation Books:

Vengeful Pursuit
by Dave Bullock

eBook ISBN: 9781615726868
Print ISBN: 9781615726875

Thriller
Novel of 85,191 words

When the prey turns out to be as dangerous as the hunter.

The most vicious cartel in Mexico has done as it pleases for years, but when one of its leaders sets up a new drug lab in western Montana, things don't go as planned. A sixteen-year-old boy discovers they've murdered his father and sets out to prevent the killers from escaping, but things don't go as he planned either. Now, the boy's only hope for survival rests with a special 'gift' he was born with and an estranged uncle with demons of his own. Somehow, the two must forge a relationship and a plan, quickly, because the fiercest predator either has ever faced, is coming.

Visit Damnation Books online at:

Our Blog—
http://www.damnationbooks.com/blog/

DB Reader's Yahoogroup—
http://groups.yahoo.com/group/DamnationBooks/

Twitter—
http://twitter.com/DamnationBooks

Google+—
https://plus.google.com/u/0/115524941844122973800

Facebook—
https://www.facebook.com/pages/
Damnation-Books/80339241586

Goodreads—
http://www.goodreads.com/DamnationBooks

Shelfari—
http://www.shelfari.com/damnationbooks

Library Thing—
http://www.librarything.com/DamnationBooks

HorrorWorld Forums—
http://horrorworld.org/phpBB3/viewforum.php?f=134

CPSIA information can be obtained at www.ICGtesting.com
Printed in the USA
LVOW06s2221170214

374043LV00001B/2/P

9 781629 291109